I0742295

THE RED WRAITH

Nick Wisseman

EDGE SCIENCE FICTION AND FANTASY PUBLISHING
An Imprint of HADES PUBLICATIONS, INC.
CALGARY

The Red Wraith

Copyright © 2016 by Nick Wisseman

This is a work of fiction. Names, characters, places, and incidents are the products of the author's imagination or are used fictitiously and are not to be construed as real. Any resemblance to actual events, locales, organizations, or persons, living or dead, is entirely coincidental.

EDGE SCIENCE FICTION AND FANTASY PUBLISHING
An Imprint of HADES PUBLICATIONS, INC.
P.O. Box 1714, Calgary, Alberta, T2P 2L7, Canada

The EDGE Team:
Producer: Brian Hades
Editor: Ella Beaumont
Cover Artist: Andrey Kiselev
Book Design: Mark Steele
Publicist: Janice Shoults

ISBN: 978-1-77053-132-1

EDGE Science Fiction and Fantasy Publishing and Hades Publications, Inc. acknowledges the ongoing support of the Alberta Foundation for the Arts and the Canada Council for the Arts for our publishing programme.

Library and Archives Canada Cataloguing in Publication
CIP Data on file with the National Library of Canada
ISBN: 978-1-77053-132-1
(e-Book ISBN: 978-1-77053-095-9)

FIRST EDITION
(20161105)
Printed in USA
www.edgewebsite.com

For Fable

Tribe Names

Original Peoples' Names for Themselves	Europan Names for Original Peoples
Dine	Apachi
Dzune	Puebo
Hellani	Illineye
Hodensee	Irqouis
Kiksha	Chicksaw
Lepane	Delware
Lnu	MikMak
Metica	Aztek
Matowak	Montauk
Pekout	Peqwat
Tsalgi	Cherkee

Preface

For thousands of years, the peoples of the world lived on two sets of continents, ignorant of each other's existence except for half-remembered folklore that told of an ancient separation via temporary land bridges and small, tenuous vessels. Contact was abruptly renewed, however, when seafaring explorers from the "old" continents "discovered" the "new."

It was not a happy reunion.

But as conflict and disease surged, something else grew stronger too. Something ancient, and primal, and powerful.

Something magical.

And history was never the same.

Prologue

The midday sun festered like a corrupted wound, and Naysin still didn't know how to save his people.

He shook his head, sending his hair — smoky gray, despite his mere twenty-one winters — sweeping across his ankles; he was sitting cross-legged on the earthen pyramid's broad summit, staring at a patch of crabgrass as he waited for the many-hued ascenders. Naysin couldn't actually see them: they'd yet to master the mound's steep sides, and he'd positioned himself at the plateau's center. But he could picture the climbers perfectly. In appearance, they were unchanged from the second morning of the last moon, when Tay had helped him plant the beacon.

"Naysin?" she lisped.

He didn't look up; he could visualize Tay as clearly as the ascenders. After hours of pacing, she'd finally sat next to him, double-bladed rainstick balanced on her thighs and deceptively milky eyes scanning the plateau's perimeter. His earth-toned breechcloth contrasted sharply with her brilliant tunic and feathered leggings.

"You had a question?" she asked gently.

Spirits and lakes — how long had he kept her waiting? "Forgive me…" His focus had warbled like a blue jay since Tay spotted Quecxl, the first ascender to arrive. The fellow original man had been little more than grit on the horizon, but through some vestige of the beacon, Naysin had envisioned him fully: muscular build, middling height, and badly pocked skin shaded somewhere between Tay's dusky brown and his own muted red. Quecxl wore a loincloth and a sleeveless poncho, and with each step he chanted a different word, to which the gull perched on his shoulder bobbed its grimy head.

Had the pair seen who waited for them on the pyramid? Naysin doubted it. Few creatures' eyes were as sharp as Tay's, and Quecxl and the bird's had likely been fixed on the monument itself. It had clearly known better days; weeds obscured the north side's crumbling steps, and the mound's once-smooth slopes had been sullied by erosion and burrowing animals. But the peak remained the highest point in the flatlands, and the dirt edifice still emanated authority.

Naysin and Tay had moved back from the summit's edge once the other ascenders came into view. He'd blinded them to each other's presence, but they'd still chosen to climb separate sides of the pyramid, as if claiming them for their respective races. Quecxl churned up the north slope, eschewing the treacherous stairs. Conquering the east side was Amadi, a tall night skin whose ill-fitting breeches were as ragged as his salt-and-pepper beard. His chest gleamed with tattoos of glyphs and beasts, and he walked with a limp as he carried on a whispered conversation with himself.

That aside, Amadi seemed relatively calm. So did Quecxl. Maybe they hadn't heard what Naysin had wrought since their last meeting. But on the south slope…

"What of the burned man?" asked Tay, intuiting where Naysin's thoughts had turned.

He considered the pale man for another breath as the stout Anglo used an exposed root to steady himself. His ropy blond hair only partially concealed the fire scar protruding from his collar, and the equally red imprint of an open palm on his forehead had grown no less horrific since their clash at Fort Kaska. In his free hand, he clutched a dragonhead blunderbuss as if his life depended on pulling its trigger. Perhaps it did. "He's sweating," Naysin said eventually. Ironically, the burned man appeared to be feeling the heat more than anyone else.

"Pleasant. And Isaura?"

The Espan had chosen the west side, her creamy skin every bit as beautiful as Naysin remembered. Both ankles clinked with bracelets, and somehow she was managing the climb without tripping over her flowing dress. But although festive braids corded her auburn hair, filling it with blue flowers and intricate knots, her eyes betrayed less joyous emotions; she at least must have learned what he'd done at Edgeland… Had her lover survived? Had she found him? "She doesn't want to be here."

Tay nodded.

"Why do you think they've come?"

"Because they must." Lifting one end of her rainstick to the height of her ribs, she let it fall back against her thighs, setting off a storm of tiny rattles. Then she glanced at him. "Was that your question? If you want me to play at reading fates again…"

"I know — yes or no only." Naysin uprooted a blade of crab grass and twisted it to the point of breaking and back. "Do any of them want to be here?"

"Do you?" Tay said softly. Without waiting for an answer, she closed her eyes, took a slow breath, and tapped the ground twice. "That means no."

It was his turn to nod.

"Naysin…" Tay reached her left hand toward his right before pulling back. "How much longer? I know they're to arrive at the same time, but…" She anticipated his answer by rising and brandishing her rainstick, setting it rattling like a slash of hail.

He dropped the crab grass. "It's now," he said unnecessarily as, in eerie unison, the ascenders crested the summit.

While the specters from his past had converged, he'd shamaned two flows around them: one to hide them from the others, and one to speed or slow their steps as required. Now Naysin lifted the collective veil, and the ascenders saw each other for the first time. Eyes flickered back and forth as Quecxl sneered at the burned man, who glared at Amadi, who smiled and beckoned.

But no one acted faster than Isaura: as Tay screamed a warning, the Espan drew a pistol from beneath her dress and shot Naysin through the stomach.

Head still down, he twitched… and then laughed while everyone else exploded into motion. Tay took a step toward Isaura before doubling back to Naysin; Isaura lowered her pistol and shrieked, her face a mixture of triumph and grief; Amadi yelled a battle cry and charged the burned man; the burned man brought his blunderbuss to bear on Amadi, squeezed the trigger, and let loose a column of fire; Quecxl sprinted toward Naysin.

But just before flesh and flame came into contact, Naysin whipped his arms around in a circle. Everyone else froze, paralyzed in mid-stride — except for Tay, who'd dropped her rainstick to press her hands against his side.

"Why didn't you stop her?" Tay's voice was steady, but her lisp had grown thicker.

"I was watching the burned man." He paused as the pain set in. "It wasn't in the vision."

Blood oozed between Tay's fingers, and she pressed harder. "Can you heal it?"

Naysin finally raised his head, revealing a swirling brand pulsing around his left eye. With each beat his veins shone darker, as if his skin were being stretched thin over a sable spider web. "No. I'd just worsen it." A vortex of wind encircled the pyramid while he contemplated the stasis he'd created. "And balancing this is… taking a lot out of me. It hurts more than the bullet." He laughed again, this time more with sorrow than surprise, and blood trickled up from his mouth, carried aloft by the increasingly violent air.

"Then let me reduce the burden."

"What?"

"Let me reduce the burden for you!" Shouting to make herself heard above the wind, Tay pulled Naysin's hands over his wound and picked up her rainstick. "Starting with her!" She jabbed the clattering weapon toward Isaura, whose brilliant tresses snapped about her head, each flailing braid trailing blue petals behind it.

Naysin didn't raise his voice. "No, Tay."

She turned her unsettling eyes back on him.

"That wasn't in your vision either."

Tay stared at him a moment longer before jamming her rainstick in the ground and sprinting to her pack, where she began shredding her spare tunic into bandages, cursing as the wind tried to snatch each new strip away. "Your cougar-

Chapter One

Cougars

"They're here," Alsoomee whispered, shivering slightly.

Naysin followed her eyes: the tribe's Master of Ceremonies and his assistants from the Wolf, Turtle, and Turkey totems had entered the Longest House through the far door, and now they were lighting the pure fires.

The time had come.

"See Matunga there?" Naysin whispered back, mostly to calm himself. "He looks like the manitouk in the corner."

Alsoomee and two other children of twelve winters stifled nervous laughs, and then she rapped his ankle. "Hush. You'll get us in trouble."

But he was right. The windowless temple featured a soaring ceiling supported in the middle by a massive wood column, and every major structural feature was carved with a face: two adorned the center post, six marked the long walls' vertical supports, and one watched over each door. None of the visages were human — their eyes were too big, their noses too pointy, their hair too wild. They were also red on one side and black on the other. But from the right angle, Matunga, the youngest (and ugliest) Turtle priest, bore a passing resemblance to the face in the northwest corner. It was the cleft chin that did it. And the bushy eyebrows.

Naysin swallowed another giggle. Then it was his turn to shiver, setting his charcoal hair swaying in front of his chestnut eyes. In a few heartbeats, the culmination of the Harvest Ceremony would begin. And all the children of twelve winters — newly adults — would have to disclose the outcomes of their guardian-spirit quests. The prospect filled Naysin with equal parts dread and pride. He'd had a successful encounter, but something about it had seemed ... different. And he kept reliving it at inopportune moments.

At least he wouldn't have to hold it in much longer; silence swept over the congregation as the Master of Ceremonies approached the center post and clasped his hands. After waiting for his assistants to shut the doors, he began to speak, the now-roaring fires highlighting his face's protrusions and shadowing its recesses.

"When we Lepane come into this house of ours, we rejoice and give thanks for everything Gilmekon has provided for us." The Master of Ceremonies nodded toward the faces on the center post — they represented the Creator's constructive and destructive aspects, the pillars that supported the world.

"We are thankful for the East," the Master of Ceremonies continued with a nod to the faces on the eastern wall and door, "because everyone feels alive in the morning when they wake and see the bright light rising.

"And when the Sun goes down in the West," he said as he turned in that direction, "we are grateful we have seen the passage of another day.

"So too," he went on, rotating again, "are we thankful for the North, because when the cold winds come, we are happy to have lived to see the leaves fall again.

"And we thank the Thunderers," he said with a pivot to the South, "for they are the manitouk that bring the rain, which the Creator has given them power to rule over."

Finally, he knelt and touched his head to the dirt floor. "But most of all, we thank the Earth, whom we claim as mother because she carries us and everything we need."

The Master of Ceremonies stood and swept his arms around in a circle. "This floor is the Earth, this ceiling the Sky, and these walls the Horizon, where the Ten Great Spirits sit around Gilmekon, their Creator. And ours. Join me in sending prayers to your guardian spirits, so that they may take them to the Ten, who will in turn carry them to Gilmekon. And in his compassion, let him renew our world, bless the harvest we have gathered, and avert catastrophe for another winter."

The last words were powerfully spoken, but Naysin barely heard them; he was too busy staving off another vision of his guardian spirit day. Later in the night, when it came his turn to share, the vivid remembrance would have been appropriate. But not before the elders had taken their turns, and certainly not before the ceremony had even *begun*.

Except resisting was like trying to keep water from soaking into sand. With a sigh, Naysin relented and let the memory flow through him...

— « o » —

...He was so hungry that he wasn't. Naysin's stomach, after howling in pain for the better part of two days, had finally stopped moaning. Likely because it had started eating itself.

Yet he hadn't had a vision. He'd daydreamed — there was little else to do in the unfamiliar forest clearing — but he hadn't seen anything out of the ordinary. No premonitions, no ghostly animal sounds. Nothing to suggest a guardian spirit had adopted him, despite how pathetic he looked; most of the mud his mother had smeared onto his skin and into his hair was still there, still marking him as a human wretch in need of protection.

Of course, if his guardian waited much longer, Naysin might eat the spirit when it appeared. He chuckled at the idea, then groaned as his hunger pangs returned.

But as much as he wanted to appease them with the elderberries lining the clearing's borders, he knew he couldn't. Not without dishonoring his mother and the memory of his father. Fasting, as everyone had hammered into him before he left, was the only way to receive a vision.

And giving in now would be soft. Some of the other boys went more than a half-moon before they saw their guardian spirit. If he was going to return to his mother a man, he had to find a way to bear the hunger.

A drink would help. Naysin's mouth grew dry at the thought. Food was prohibited, but water was allowed in modest amounts. And a third drink this morning wouldn't be excessive, would it? Surely not. Not if it kept him from defiling the ritual and giving in to his hunger.

Naysin launched himself upright by pushing against the ground with his mud-stained hands. The stream his mother pointed out to him before she left was only a short walk. Shorter if he ran, which he often did; his fondest ambition was to be the best distance runner his far-striding tribe had ever seen.

For now, though, running just got him to the water faster.

He stopped himself after the third handful, forcing himself to pause and look around before taking a fourth and final sip: the banks of the stream were mild, gently rounded by erosion's patient caress; the hickory trees overhanging the water were majestically large, their branches shadowing the stream's minor eddies; and...

That wasn't a shadow.

That, there at the bottom of the stream, was a cougar, swimming toward him and rapidly growing larger as it approached the surface.

Naysin blinked, but this was no trick of the light; the tawny cougar was still there, still racing to reach him. In his haste to back away, he nearly lost his balance. But he kept his eye on the cougar, compelled to watch as the cat swam furiously to the surface and...

Stopped. As if it had run into a sheet of ice.

Snarling soundlessly, the cougar pawed in frustration at the invisible barrier and began to pace, somehow finding enough purchase in the water to stalk along the edges of Naysin's reflection.

Awed, he watched the magnificent beast make several circuits before he realized this was what he'd been waiting for...

— « o » —

...Several in the congregation — dressed in their best clothes, the ones they wore only for ceremonies and festivals — stirred and stood, moved to boldness by the sanctity of the moment. Taking the tortoise rattles offered by the Master of Ceremonies' assistants, they lined up around the center post. Then, without any audible cue, they began dancing around the post and the two pure fires, shuffling along in a shadowy figure-eight.

After the first circuit, the leader of the line began to chant from deep within his throat, recalling what was never spoken about except during the Harvest Ceremony: how he'd first seen his guardian spirit. For him, it was a badger that appeared on the eighth day of his childhood fast. Once he'd finished telling the tale, he asked the badger to bless the tribe's harvest and his sick son. Next, a woman took up the chant and spoke of how a falcon came to her on the fourth day of her fast.

The pattern continued until everyone in the shambling line had shared their visions and prayers. As they sat down, a new set of dancers stood up, accepted the tortoise rattles, and renewed the cycle. This pattern continued for what seemed like days, until all the mature adults had contributed.

Now — finally — it was the children of twelve winters' turn. The time had come to take up the rattles and share what had been revealed to them at some point during the last cycle of seasons.

As he stood, Naysin looked back to his mother for reassurance and took heart from her gentle smile…

— « o » —

…Sensing more was required of him, Naysin rapidly weighed his options. He could back up and give the cougar more space (tempting), he could swim down to the cat (not at all tempting), or he could try to break the invisible barrier. For some reason, this seemed like the appropriate course of action.

Until the cougar stopped pacing and stared at him expectantly, as if it knew what he planned to do. Its tail began twitching in anticipation, and he could see the cat shrinking into its haunches, coiling for a powerful spring.

Still … Naysin didn't know what else to do. The experience felt incomplete, and he didn't dare go home unfulfilled. So without even taking a deep breath — pausing any longer would cripple him with doubt — he bent over and jabbed the index finger of his right hand into his reflection…

— « o » —

…Naysin's knees grew weak as Alsoomee neared the end of her story about how she was given seven berries by a black sparrow on her ninth day of fasting. He wasn't ready to share his own experience, but there was no turning back, nothing to do but shuffle along behind her, shake his tortoise rattle, and give voice to the words welling up inside him...

— « o » —

...He recoiled from the water as ripples grew from the point of contact and distorted his reflection. Backpedaling, Naysin tripped and fell, but he didn't get up. He was too focused on the cougar, which was focused on the water, waiting for the invisible barrier to be disrupted enough to...

Spring.

He screamed, wrapping his arms around his head, wishing with all his might that he hadn't broken the water's surface.

An eternity later, he summoned the nerve to lower his arms, amazed he wasn't in the cougar's stomach, but half expecting the beast to be standing in front him. Instead, he found the cat still underwater, pacing furiously and growling soundlessly. And the water — the water was unnaturally calm, perfectly smooth. Smooth to the point that it looked like someone had taken the flat end of a rake and softened every eddy and ripple out of existence.

His temples ached as he contemplated this latest oddity, but otherwise he was fine. Except for being completely bewildered about what he was supposed to be doing. Maybe—

Without warning, the cougar charged the water's surface. Naysin flinched, but this time he kept his eyes open long enough to witness the cat slam against the invisible barrier. Maddened, it roared.

And then it divided.

Splitting into two cougars, one black and one white. Two cougars who shared the same tawny hindquarters, but had their own torso, front legs, and snarling heads...

— « o » —

...heads with mouths that sprayed spittle and gleamed with teeth.

Talking about the memory made it even more vivid; as Naysin danced and sang, he began to *see* the cougars again. Not just in his mind's eye, but shimmering in the flames of the pure fires, coalescing into life-like renderings that pulsed to the rhythm of his tortoise rattle and the growing pain in his temples — he hadn't known sharing his guardian spirit story would be so intense.

But he kept going, relating how the combined fury of the cougars...

— « o » —

...was enough to fracture the barrier that so infuriated them. The light cat broke through first, smashing its head free and roaring in triumph. Then the dark cougar forced its front paws out of Naysin's reflection. He scrabbled backward, crab-walking furiously until his head slammed against a tree. It hurt, but he kept watching the portion of the bank from which the cougars...

Weren't launching out of the water.

They should have been loose already, bounding forward to rip him in half between their eager maws. But even after ten ten-counts of white-knuckle waiting, the clearing was still quiet, the bank still empty, and the water he could see still perfectly calm.

The water he could see ... which no longer included the point the cougars had all but escaped from. The portion of the river over which he'd cast his reflection, the reflection the cougars had been using as their ... doorway?

Naysin stood carefully, making sure that increasing his height didn't cast his image back on the water. Gingerly, he put a hand to the back of his head and felt for damage: a little blood and an acorn-sized lump, but nothing significant.

Nothing like what the cougars would have done to him. He was sure of that now, sure that this wasn't a normal guardian spirit vision. And that he wouldn't be looking into that river again. Ever.

It was time to go home.

But...

— « o » —

..."Where did the cougars come from?" Naysin wondered once more, shaking his tortoise rattle as he gazed into the eastern fire, his dance slowing to a walk. "And why did it seem like they were *inside* me? As if they were trying to get out?"

Aware of his surroundings again, he looked around and found that *everyone* — the other first-time dancers, the Master of Ceremonies, the adults sitting against the log walls, his aunt and uncle, and his absolutely horrified mother — was staring at the fires, where the picture of the now empty riverbank was still visible, still wavering with each flicker of flame and gust of air.

They could see it too.

Feeling small — embarrassed and guilty without fully knowing why — Naysin hung his head and hurriedly tried to make things right. "Please, cougars of mine, tell Gilmekon to bless this harvest, and our tribe, and my mother." He looked up to ask her forgiveness ... and felt his headache quadruple in intensity, as his question, *"Where did the cougars come from?"* echoed around the Longest House again, this time in a voice that sounded both guttural and reedy ... as if it were being snarled through water.

In response, the eastern and western fires flared brilliantly, projecting their unnatural imagery onto the ceiling as the scenes began to change, morphing from a riverbank he recognized to one he didn't. But he knew the figure approaching the water: his mother. Younger, with less care-lines and a slimmer waist. Same long black hair, though. And the way she was drumming on her thighs...

— « o » —

...as she walked to the river's edge was something Kanti had done as long as anyone could remember. But the rhythm she was tapping wasn't a happy one: it was listless, out of sync and off-kilter. And her gait was just as unsteady. She didn't look down, but from the way she kept pawing at the middle of her dress, it was clear the growing blood stain there had something to do with her unevenness.

The section of river she was approaching flowed through the remains of a stone building, gray in hue but shot through with lines of black and white. No doubt it had been an imposing monument to human achievement in its day. But time had caused much of the structure's walls to crumble, forming a jagged, tenuous line that looked like the crest of a dying wave. As Kanti drew near, a hunk of rock detached from the tallest point and splashed into the water.

She stopped to watch the aftermath, following the ripples with dry eyes but wet cheeks. Then she nodded and began walking purposefully into the water ... as if she wouldn't stop. As if she would keep going until she vanished like the rock.

Movement deep within the river brought her up short. But she didn't look scared. And she didn't step back when the motion coalesced into a figure: the figure of a man. A naked, gray-skinned man swimming toward her.

He came to rest just beneath the water's surface, seemingly uninterested in the air mere fingerbreadths above. He was handsome, in an otherworldly way: distinct lines and taut muscles, with smoky hair streaked by the same black and white bolts that crisscrossed the broken building. Kanti regarded him blankly — even a little defiantly — as if she were more concerned about the steps he'd prevented her from taking than his sudden, impossible appearance.

Smiling, the gray man gestured with his hands and somehow caused Kanti's reflection to begin moving independently. She reacted to this theft with her first real display of emotion, shocked into yelling an unintelligible question. But she stayed where she was, watching as her representation moved nearer the gray man, accepted his embrace, and began to kiss him, caressing his back with one hand while the other took off her dress...

Kanti cried out, this time in anger, as she raised her arm to splash the water in front of her and ruin the fierce, false coupling. But she stopped when the gray man raised his own hand, gestured, and replaced the passionate version of her reflection with a new one, in which she had a large and growing belly...

The gray man gestured again, her pregnant reflection vanished, and her original, natural reflection returned. Then the pale man cocked his head invitingly.

Kanti's hand pushed through the water to the bloodstain on her dress, where her fingers lingered, and she nodded her assent.

They began by following the steps rehearsed moments earlier: holding hands, embracing, kissing, sliding off her clothing... But they didn't stop there, and they didn't finish for a long time. When they did, it was with a powerful climax, one that left Kanti's eyes shut tight and the gray man grimacing in satisfaction so intense his face divided.

Splitting into two faces, one dark and one light. Faces that shared the same legs, but had their own torso, arms, and smiling mouth…

— « o » —

…Naysin screamed, and the eastern and western fires sputtered down to coals. Silence prevailed as all eyes turned to Kanti, whose sobs were interspersed with half-hearted denials.

Then the Master of Ceremonies pointed a shaking finger at the weeping mother, another at her son, and shrilled, "You have defiled the Harvest Ceremony!"

The Longest House erupted into pandemonium.

Chapter Two

Defiled

Naysin couldn't look at his mother.

Not even the next day when the Master of Ceremonies commanded him to. "Your mother coupled with *water spirits*, Naysin," the old man repeated for the tenth time, pacing around the middle hearth during the Elder Council's meeting in the community's central longhouse. "Naysin, look at her. Look. At. Her. Do you know what that means? Do you know what that makes *you?*"

Eventually, Hausis, the council's oldest and most respected woman, ordered the Master of Ceremonies to restrain himself. But after the session finished, and Naysin and his mother were led out of the longhouse under armed guard, he still couldn't meet her eyes.

"Naysin … Please, you need to listen to me." She pleaded when they were left alone together for the first time. As she crouched next to him, her black hair fell to the floor of the poorly lit menstruation hut, their temporary prison.

"I'm not proud of what I did." She traced a pattern in the dirt floor with her left hand. "But your father — Machk," she corrected herself, "had just been taken by the plague the same day I lost…" Her voice broke, and it was some moments before she was able to go on. "You have to understand, I thought I would never have a child. And I'd wanted to give Machk one so badly. I didn't ask for what happened in the river, but when it did, it seemed like Gilmekon was … giving a little back.

"Please, Naysin, believe that I love you more than anything. I'm not at all sorry about what I had to do to have you."

She started to stroke his hair, but his head still hurt and he pulled away, scooting along the wall until he slammed into the southeast corner, his eyes on floor.

His mother tried to reach out to him again, but he still couldn't bring himself to look at her, much less respond to her desperate justifications. Because she'd filled his childhood with tales of Machk, the mighty hunter who would have been chief were he not struck down by a terrible disease twelve winters ago. Machk, the dutiful husband, the cunning warrior, the unbeatable runner...

All lies. His mother had made him spirit spawn. Part manitouk. An affront to the natural way of things. His very presence had spoiled the Harvest Ceremony. Now his tribe would suffer the bitterest winter it had ever experienced, filled with poor hunting and dying fires. Because of him.

Because his mother had let water spirits into her body and her womb. Into him. And they could make him do things. Unnatural things, like causing images to appear in the fires. Naysin's mind skirted around this thought as it formed. It wasn't something he was ready to comprehend. For now all he could manage was anger.

The following evening, when the council passed its judgment, his anger turned to loathing.

In contrast to the private meeting of the previous day, this session was open to the entire tribe. And everyone was in attendance: every man, woman, and child, with fear in their eyes, to watch him and his mother be sentenced to a fate one deserved and one didn't. Even his aunt and uncle looked on in a tumult of dread and worry, the conflict clear on their faces.

The council had anticipated such a turnout: the partitions separating each family's section of the longhouse had been removed so that the middle hearth was visible from every angle; the beds along the walls had been arranged into cushioned benches; and spare skins had been draped over the floor to create additional seating.

Tonight's meeting, Naysin realized as he was led in through the eastern door, was meant to be a spectacle.

Once he and his mother were positioned in front of the hearth — which was guarded by two warriors carrying enough water skins to extinguish the fire in case anything other than flames came out of it — Hausis began to speak.

"Everyone knows why we're here," she said, staring into the winding smoke. "What happened two nights ago, and why this pair stands before us now." The other council members nodded, their hands clasped behind their backs. Most of the Elders' faces were screwed into unreadable masks, but the Master of Ceremonies' expression looked triumphant.

"And everyone *expects* a certain sentence," Hausis continued, turning her old eyes toward Naysin and his mother. "Which, unfortunately, we have little choice but to deliver."

His mother hung her head, using her long hair to curtain her tears.

"Before that sentence is given, however, consider this." Hausis changed the target of her gaze once more, passing it over the entire congregation before letting it come to rest on the Master of Ceremonies. "Kanti made a terrible, dangerous decision. A decision that brought ill fortune on herself and her tribe. But..." Hausis lowered her voice for emphasis. "She made that decision as a young woman who'd just lost her husband and any hope of having his child, a young woman who was two steps short of *drowning* herself. In circumstances like those, who's to say the rest of us would have resisted the charms of a manitouk?"

Naysin's aunt nodded slightly as his mother began sobbing audibly. He still refused to look at her, but for the first time in the last few days he felt his resolve wavering; the words *"in circumstances like those"* echoed within his skull, breaking down his anger and dissolving it into pity and love.

Until Hausis spoke his name. "And remember that the boy, Naysin, had no choice in who his fathers were. He is what he is through no fault of his own."

"Through no fault of his own... Through no fault of his own..." This new echo was even more powerful, overwhelming his sympathy and reverting his emotions to hot, virulent fury.

"Still." Hausis returned her eyes to the fire, looking even older than her three twenty-counts of winters as she gathered herself for what everyone sensed would be the final pronouncement. "Decisions have consequences. And for entering into impure union with a water spirit and defiling a Harvest Ceremony, the council has determined that the consequences are branding and exile.

"The exile begins after this session is complete.

"The branding begins now."

The old woman allowed her words to permeate the silence before gesturing to either end of the longhouse. Two men — the tribe's most accomplished tattoo artists — approached the middle hearth. Each carried a gourd of ink, a dabbing cloth ... and a razor sharp, deer-bone needle.

Naysin swore he wouldn't scream, but when his uncle looked away from him, he couldn't control his voice.

— « o » —

Living off the land was more difficult than Naysin had imagined.

He and his mother had been on their own for a moon now, but it seemed like twenty. They'd stayed in the northern forest, careful not to stray too close to their former tribe's hunting grounds. Knowing the general area had helped, but finding food still wasn't easy. Naysin couldn't fully draw the bow the Elder Council had allowed him to take, and his mother had never learned to aim one.

Thankfully, a wealth of wild plants were in season. The cattail's flowers and seeds were ripe, as were the stick roots of the yellow pond lily. And his mother could do many things with leeks.

But foraging only went so far. Their diet was sparse and more monotonous than it had been when they were part of a larger community, and they had to work hard to keep their bellies even partially full. The amount of labor involved was a shock for Naysin; in the tribe, he wouldn't have been expected to be a fulltime contributor for another winter.

At least they'd been lucky with shelter. Four days into their exile, a word Naysin still hadn't come to terms with, his mother had found one of their tribe's old winter shelters.

It was traditional for their people to cluster around the crops for spring, summer, and fall, and then split off into smaller, more easily sustainable groups for winter. This shelter had waned in popularity, meaning he and his mother could use it without fear of being evicted.

The cave wasn't much to look at. It was small, only big enough for two to three families. And it was dirty. The last inhabitants must have known they wouldn't be coming back. But nothing larger than a few rats had taken up residence in the interim, and the crack at the far end of the cavern provided natural light and a readymade smoke-hole.

"Naysin?" his mother asked cautiously, interrupting his reverie as she pulled more leeks from the ground in preparation for that day's incarnation of wild stew.

He avoided her gaze. They each now bore a swirling black-and-white brand over their dominant eyes: his left and his mother's right. Looking at her was a graphic reminder of how long the excruciating tattooing had lasted. How the Master of Ceremonies had chanted the words of binding over and over, invocations that were supposed to draw on Gilmekon's power and seal in their sins: the impurity of his mother's actions, and the resulting impurity of Naysin's nature.

"Do you mind if ... if I ask you about that night?" she continued. "About the images in the fire?"

He jumped a little, surprised she'd brought up the moment that had ruined their lives. Until now, any references to the subject, aside from the initial tear-filled apologies, had been avoided.

She glanced at him. "I don't want to talk about what was in them, just..."

"What?" Naysin finally replied.

"Did they hurt? I mean, did calling them cause you pain? I saw you squinting near the end."

He decided there was no harm in telling the truth. "They hurt."

"Oh, Naysin, I'm so sorry." His mother looked down at the pile of leeks she'd amassed in the folds of her skirt. "Can you tell me where it hurt?"

"My head. It still does."

"My poor child." She raised her head and returned his gaze, the brand over her right eye mirroring the mark above his left. Her hand reached for his forehead, but he shied away. "Naysin… Did anything else hurt?"

He studied her face, guessing there was something more than just motherly concern to this line of questioning. "No," he said. "Just my head. Why?"

His mother licked her lips before responding. "For an instant, just before the coug — before the first vision ended, I glanced over at you, and I saw…" She paused and looked down again. "You looked like you were in pain, and I wished you weren't," she finished, but the words were limp.

"…Oh."

Naysin turned his attention back to the leeks, and he and his mother spent the rest of the morning in silence.

— « o » —

Naysin…

He jumped in surprise and whirled to look for the speaker. But he turned a full circle without finding anyone. Or anything, for that matter — the little clearing had suddenly become eerily quiet. Even the pine trees looked somber.

He'd heard a voice, though. Of that he was sure. A voice that somehow conjured both the rush of water and the flicker of fire…

Naysin.

This time he dropped to the ground and pressed himself flat against its moist dirt. The second voice was filled with the stability of stone and the strength of wood. And it was just as disembodied.

Panicking now, Naysin slithered back toward the cave. His mother couldn't have gone far — she'd said not to stray more than a few twenty-counts of paces in search of beechnuts, and she'd never been one to break her own rules. For an instant, his anger evaporated in a surge of need…

I'm sure Kanti will be happy to see us.

Naysin froze, as confused as he was terrified.

I would not be so sure about that.

It seemed like the thing to say.

Naysin still couldn't see anyone — or anything — but he *felt* something's gaze on him.

Naysin.

He flinched at the use of his name again.

You need not be afraid. We are here to help.

He's right. You're among family now.

Slowly, Naysin raised himself to a crouch, setting his right leg behind him in case he had to start running. Then he forced a question from his shaking lips: "Who... where are you?"

I think you know, Naysin.

We are your fathers.

We are inside you.

Rage and denial bubbled up from Naysin's heart. "Machk was my father. He was a brave man who killed many moose, and—"

He died of disease before you were born.

Well before you were born.

Even more furious, Naysin stood to his full height, forgetting his earlier impulse to stay low and seek cover. "What does it matter?"

So maybe you should put more stock in the words of your "Guardian Spirits."

Unbidden, the hurtful visions from the Longest House re-flooded his sight. Two cougars, one black and one white, merged into one man ... who seduced and coupled with his mother in a dark river ... and *divided* into two men: one dark and one light. Every few moments, their bodies flickered, and the cougars flashed in and out, the black cat replacing the dark man and the white cat replacing the light man.

But this time the images continued past Naysin's birth. Unseen but ever-present, the cougar-men hovered *inside* him from the instant he was born, and as he grew, their hybrid bodies became increasingly defined.

They were there for his first fight.

They were there when he learned to throw a spear.

They were there for his first kiss.

And they were there when, thinking himself alone, he went into the woods to find his guardian spirit.

As I said, you need not be afraid, my son.

Our son. As hard as we know that is for you to believe.

They were right on the last count; with all his heart, Naysin wanted to reject everything he'd seen and heard during the previous moon. "You're lying," he growled, ignoring the hot tears rolling down his cheeks.

Your mother's already said otherwise.

This left Naysin mute. His mother hadn't broached the subject since they'd been forced to leave the tribe, and he hadn't asked. But he still thought about the vision of his mother in the water, and he'd sensed that she did too.

At some point you must come to terms with it, Naysin. We are a part of you, and you are a part of us.

Which isn't a bad thing. Quite the opposite, in fact. We can make you stronger than you ever believed possible.

Naysin stamped the ground as hard as he could. "You're lying!" he yelled. "You ruined my life!" Then he ran back to the cave, not at the long-distance speed he was working so hard to perfect, but at an all-out-sprint, causing a rabbit and several birds to scramble out of his way.

He didn't get the last word, though.

Take all the time you need, Naysin.

There's no hurry. We're not going anywhere.

— « o » —

"Mother?"

She almost dropped the reed mat she was weaving. But not in surprise — she was clearly delighted that her son was initiating a conversation and looking directly at her. "Yes, Naysin?" Then she frowned. "Are you all right?"

Naysin didn't respond until he'd caught his breath and worked through what he wanted to ask her. "What did you see?" he eventually blurted out.

"What did I see when?" she replied with a puzzled look.

"When the cougars were in the Longest House. You said you looked over at me and saw something, but you wouldn't say what."

She cast her gaze down at her mat and continued working. "I just saw how hurt you looked. I told you that."

"Mother!" Naysin stamped the ground like he had in the forest.

It had more of an effect here; startled, his mother glanced up at him with an anguished expression. But her face quickly softened. "When I looked over at you in the Longest House, I saw every vein shining black through your skin. It was just for an instant, and I don't think anyone else noticed — most people were focused on the images in the fires — but ... it was like your blood *died*."

Naysin took a step back and slumped into a sitting position. "Why did you do this to me?" he moaned as the first tears escaped his eyes. "My head always hurts now!"

His mother winced. "Naysin, I've only ever acted out of love—"

"What am I supposed to do?" he hissed.

It took her several breaths to say anything, and by then Naysin knew she didn't have an answer.

— « o » —

Feigning sleep was harder than Naysin had thought it would be.

Of course, he'd never actually tried before. Back home, playing all day had usually left him exhausted. And here in the cave, sleep was a respite from everything that had happened. But there was always a first time. His uncle used to say that: there was always a first time, or at least there was once, and we repeat that first time when we circle back to it...

His uncle used to say that. Not his father.

As subtly as he could, Naysin moved his right leg to keep it from falling asleep. It didn't sound like his mother was still awake — her breathing had always been heavy at night — but it didn't hurt to be careful.

Not if he really meant to go through with this.

He couldn't stay, though. His mother had betrayed him. She'd betrayed their people and the memory of his father by coupling with angry spirits and...

Getting with child.

Naysin started shaking his head before he caught himself and checked the motion. No. No, those awful voices were right. He had to come to terms with this. He was part manitouk, and his father wasn't — had never been — Machk the mighty hunter. Denying the truth was a waste of time.

So was staying here.

We are with you, Naysin.

We'll always be there for you.

The sudden intrusion caused his stomach to tighten. "I'd leave you too if I could!" he whispered furiously.

His mother stirred, and Naysin froze. But after a few anxious moments, her soft snoring resumed, and the tension in his muscles subsided.

Drawing on a reservoir of resolve he'd never tapped before, he worked his way out from under the blanket he shared with his mother and slithered into the cave's cold night air. When he was finally free, he crept outside, guided by the stars' meager light. He only looked back once. His mother was still asleep. She seemed … peaceful. Comforting.

Lovely.

With a horrendous effort, Naysin tore himself away and slipped into the night.

Chapter Three

Alone

His village was a completely different place in the winter. Everything was white, buried in so much snow the long-houses' roofs groaned in protest. And with the smells of human occupation buried until spring, the air was wonderfully crisp.

His former home was also empty.

Devoid of everyone he'd known, everyone he'd called friend or family. Which was how it had to be — Naysin knew that. He'd accepted that on his way here. He'd even *prayed* he wouldn't find anyone, that they'd all scattered for cozier winter shelters.

But part of him had still hoped he wouldn't be alone.

Huddled in borrowed furs next to the fire he'd managed to keep going for almost a moon now, Naysin shook his head gingerly, careful not to agitate his ever-present headache. He thought about his return too often. But it was hard not to. When he'd first approached the village and found it unoccupied, the pang of loss had been worse than anything he'd felt since leaving his mother.

He hadn't known where else to go, though. His mother hadn't mentioned any other abandoned winter quarters before he'd run off — literally *run* off. After creeping out of earshot of the cave they'd sought refuge in, he'd settled into the long-distance stride he was so proud of, pushing himself to keep moving, to keep putting one starlit foot in front of the other despite the lingering pain in his temples. But he hadn't found another viable shelter, during that first mad dash or any of those that followed.

For a time, he'd thought a cache of canoes along the bank of the Rapanoak might serve. When overturned, the boats' bark-covered hulls looked like fallen trees; he hadn't seen through the disguise until he'd stubbed his toe on a carelessly-placed oar. The pain had brought tears to his eyes … until he'd remembered that the more prudent members of his tribe often prepared for their next journey by leaving behind packets of smoked meat.

Most of the elm-hewn vessels were too heavy for him to shift, but one of the lightest had been set on uneven ground. It had taken him forever to turn the stupid thing over; three times he thought he'd rocked it hard enough, only to slip and lose momentum. But he'd managed it on the fourth try, and shouted in triumph when he saw that Gilmekon had guided him to the right canoe; not one but *two* packets of hickory-fired whitetail deer had been tucked inside. So for three whole days, he'd had meat to eat, water to drink, and the bed of a canoe to sleep in. It made him feel like he might actually be able to do this on his own.

When he'd run out of jerky, however, the other canoes had been too stable to turn right-side up, and too dense for his flint knife to puncture — he'd had no choice but to move on.

The next several moons had merged into a horrific blur.

He'd run at first.

Then walked.

Then crawled, eating whatever he'd been able to find: dried-out berries, strange mushrooms, fetid carrion…

Naysin shuddered at the memory of a raccoon he'd eaten a moon into his time alone. The creature's coat had been matted and fly-ridden, and he hadn't even blinked. He'd just eaten slowly enough to keep that day's unexpected "bounty" down.

There had been worse meals too. And a few better ones. Nothing to match that first find of smoked whitetail, though. Not until he'd found himself back within shouting distance of his village.

He hadn't meant to end up here. After the canoes, he'd stayed close to the river, remembering how his mother had insisted on keeping water nearby. It hadn't taken long to lose all sense of direction; the river curved seemingly at random, and for most of his journey he'd been too focused on food to pay much attention to his heading.

But the patch of forest he'd stumbled upon the day of the first snowfall — he'd known that area. The old elm in the center had been his favorite climbing tree, its upper limbs an excellent perch for playing, hiding, and pretending. And the well-worn trail was one he'd taken more times than he could count; it led back to the village, through the longhouses, and up to the central fire.

It had taken him a long time to work up the courage to walk the path again.

When he'd found the village empty — fulfilling one hope and dashing another — Naysin had taken a slow walk around the perimeter to soak in the details of the home he'd come back to…. But only for one season, until his tribe reconvened for spring planting and he had to leave again, fleeing from his friends, his aunt, and his uncle.

This wasn't home anymore.

After two of these reflective circuits, Naysin's stomach had brought him back to the present. It had been three days since his last meal — if you could call a half-rotten fish a meal. His tribe must have left something behind. A few heavy gourds in the root cellars, or, if today was truly meant to be a turning point, maybe some smoked meat in the chophouse.

Fortunately — despite what had happened that night in the Longest House — it had been a fruitful harvest. Naysin had found so much food that he'd been able to gorge himself *and* leave piles of supplies for the cold moons to come. He'd also gathered a mountain of furs for his bed. Old clothes were in abundance too, water was just down the path, and he had the pick of several longhouses.

Not his own, though. He'd only entered it once, to check for food and furs. And that had been more than enough. He avoided the central longhouse too. The memory of his final night there was still strong enough to spark phantom pains around his eye, where the tattoo seemed to be growing larger as his face grew thinner.

No, those were two houses it was best to stay out of.

There were plenty of others to choose from. The east and west longhouses were both comfortable enough, and some of the smaller buildings, like the medicine house and the sweat hut, were well insulated. But in the end, he went with the southern longhouse, the coziest of the large buildings. It also had the softest bed in the whole village (which he'd determined after extensive testing). And its central hearth was the easiest to section off with partitions.

Then there'd just been the small matter of starting a fire.

Wood wasn't a problem; there were already stacks of small logs along the walls. Kindling was easy as well. That at least, he could fetch on his own.

But creating the first spark ... that had taken some doing.

He'd never really *used* any of the techniques he'd been taught. Mostly he'd just watched someone else do it and marveled at how obvious they made it look. Smashing two stones together, twirling one stick into the base of another ... none of it had worked for him. Not on his first try. Not on his fifth. Not on his twentieth.

By his sixth day in the village, Naysin had known he was in trouble. To that point, the nights had been bearable as long as he'd buried himself beneath his furs. But winter had been settling in fast, and without a way to generate heat, death had seemed inevitable. So on his eighth day in the village, he'd had to appeal to the part of himself he hated.

The temperature had dropped overnight, and the sky had seemed ripe for another snowfall. After a few moments of sparkless work, Naysin had thrown away his starter stick in disgust. He must have been doing something wrong. Something obvious. It couldn't be that difficult; his uncle and everyone else he'd watched always ignited their kindling within the first few tries. Yes, they were used to doing it, but it had never seemed hard.

Maybe he hadn't been approaching this right. He'd been too focused on the end result, and not enough on the process. His aunt used to tell him that: "Concentrate on the doing, not the getting." Well ... maybe he hadn't been picturing this clearly enough. Maybe he needed to stop thinking so much about how wonderful the fire would feel when it was lit, and worry more about how the fire would start from a tiny spark. A spark that would be born from the point of his starter stick, catch hold of a leaf or twig, spread to another piece of kindling, and erupt into full-blown flames. A sudden surge that—

Had begun on its own in the fire pit.

Naysin had blinked in disbelief, but the wood had still been burning when he'd reopened his eyes. Burning, and burning well; most of the larger logs had already caught. Had he cast a spark from that last effort without knowing it?

No. Even as the question had crossed his mind, Naysin had known the answer. Because his headache had lessened considerably, and he felt unnaturally *good*, in a wild, untamed way that was the exact opposite of the rigid *bad* he'd felt after stilling the waters above the cougars and conjuring their images in the Longest House's fires.

Opposite, and yet in the same vein.

Skittering away from this conclusion, Naysin's thoughts had turned frantically to the mundane needs of keeping his fire going. He'd grabbed more left-behind kindling, more logs, more of anything that would burn and heaped it on the hearth, adding so much fuel he'd almost smothered the flames.

And now, almost a full moon after he'd returned to his village, he felt like a *survivor*. The original cache of food he'd uncovered had held up surprisingly well, supplemented by the stray morsels he kept finding in the corners of otherwise empty root cellars. He couldn't cook very well yet, but he was learning, and even his worst attempts tasted better than the unspeakable meals he'd had on his way here. And while he was still too skinny, his strength was returning.

Life, for the first time since that night in the Longest House, was — if not good — at least bearable.

Well done, my boy.

Indeed. Very impressive.

The first voice flickered like the fire; the second was heavy like the hearth. Both originated inside him. "Leave me alone," he muttered.

The cougar-men laughed.

Oh, but we did. To let you grow, Naysin. To let you become strong on your own.

And you have. We are very proud.

"If it's so good for me, why can't you keep leaving me alone?"

Ah, but the returns on that strategy are rapidly diminishing.

You are ready for more now. Much more.

Naysin sunk as far as he could into his mound of furs. "I don't need your help."

Really? Do you think you could start a fire again if you had to?

"If I had to." He did his best to sound confident.

Can you prove it?

He felt the dare reverberating in his head … mocking his inadequacy and inexperience … laughing at everything he'd accomplished on his own so far … suggesting he was only alive because he'd stumbled on the food and shelter others had made, lucky finds he'd be long dead without. "No. I already have a fire going. I don't need another one."

Put out the one you have now.

Naysin paled. If the fire went out, and he couldn't start it again… "I could if I wanted to, but I don't want to."

You forget: we are here to help.

For starters, we can help you put out that fire without you having to raise a finger.

"I don't want your help," he said automatically, shaking his head as if to convince himself.

It is not hard.

Not at all. Just think of the wind that's howling outside and picture its energy, its power, its motion. See it beating against the door, rushing through cracks in the walls, demanding entrance into this house…

Despite himself, Naysin began visualizing what the reedy voice had described. The wind outside *was* moving quickly, with an enormous amount of energy. And it *was* knocking hard against the door, and slipping through weak points in the walls. Slipping through and battering at the fire like waves against a shore, crashing one after another, each stronger than the last. Knocking the flames more and more horizontal with each blow, until…

They were gone.

His mouth was too dry to cry out when he realized how easily the voices had manipulated him — and how *good* it felt to have used the wind like that.

Now you can restart the fire.

We'll let you take it from here, the reedy voice added cheerfully.

Trying to ignore the euphoria coursing through his arteries — the sense that the wind was moving *inside* him — Naysin flung off the top layer of furs and began a frantic search for his starter sticks. He could already feel the temperature dropping in his little section of the longhouse as cold seeped in like fog.

He had to start the fire again. Quickly. Much faster than he had the first time.

It took two laps around the now-silent hearth before he found his starter sticks. Then he spent several moments trying to create a spark before he realized he needed fresh kindling. There wasn't enough left in the room, so he had to open the western partition and let in even more cold air as he accessed his outdoor stores.

By the time everything was finally in place, Naysin's hands were starting to stiffen.

But he pressed on, telling himself he didn't have any other choice. Even though he knew he did. Even when, after it became all too apparent that he couldn't restart the fire naturally, he knew it was the only choice, the only option if he wanted to live.

Still, Naysin avoided the inevitable as long as he could by huddling under his mound of furs and thinking of times he'd been warm. Times like the summer afternoons he'd lain next to other boys along the banks of the river … the winters he'd spent in the low-set, half-buried wooden shelter his mother had kept cozy for moons on end … all the days before today when he'd had a fire. Soon enough, however, he sensed he was approaching a moment of no return. The decision would be made for him if he didn't choose now.

And there would be no one to bury him.

Naysin straightened in alarm, ignoring the protest of his chilled muscles. If he died, there would be no one to prepare him for the journey to the afterlife in the West or South — wherever game was most plentiful. No one to give him gifts of wampum, beads, tools, and food. No one to paint their face black and mourn him after he was buried in sacred ground.

He was alone. More so than he'd realized. And now he wanted nothing more than to start the fire again.

Closing his eyes, he pictured the whole process, from spark to tendrils to localized inferno. But this time he saw more of it; he could see the air itself moving around the fire pit. No ... not the air, but lines of ... *energy*, moving so fast they blurred together, wicking infinitesimal pieces of wood off his kindling. Enthralled, Naysin urged the lines to move even faster, amazed at how quickly they responded, how they started to pull tendrils of smoke from the wood, how imminent a spark seemed, and—

Pain suddenly flowed through his arteries, as if the blood in them was rushing out of control.

He opened his eyes with a yelp of terror and found the fire roaring to life.

Chapter Four

The Power of Gods

"Are you still there?"

Naysin regretted the question as soon as he'd blurted it out. But for a while the only answer was the drip of melting snow. His footfalls were noisy too, squishy thuds punctuated by heavy breathing; he wasn't in running shape. The cold air burned in his lungs, but in a good way. This probably wasn't the end of winter — he was pretty sure he still had another moon or so to go — but it was the first real lull, the first chance to get out and *move* without wading through snow up to his knees.

Running hadn't diminished his loneliness, however. He hadn't heard from the cougar-men since he'd restarted the fire and screamed, "Never come back!" over and over until his voice went hoarse. He didn't miss them, exactly, but it was nice to talk to someone other than himself. Even manitouk.

We never left.

We've just been respecting your wishes.

Naysin slowed down so abruptly he almost stumbled, unsure if he was angry or relieved. "I thought ... you ... said you ... wanted to help me," he panted.

Always. But you proved with the fire that you are more than capable of taking care of yourself.

Congratulations on that, by the way. We were both impressed.

"I'm sure." Naysin picked up speed again.

All we're trying to do is help you realize your full potential.

Naysin, we know you have questions. And if you are ready to hear answers, we are ready to give them.

This brought him to a complete halt, his slender, barely-adolescent frame heaving with exertion as he weighed the offer. "Are you … really manitouk?"

The first voice laughed. *The thought bothers you, doesn't it? Don't let it; we're men. Human as you are.*

Or at least we were, before we learned to harness our power. When we did, we became gods.

Just like you could be, if you let us teach you.

"Like Gilmekon?"

Not quite.

Nowhere near the responsibilities, thankfully.

But almost as powerful. More so than any man, woman, or child you have ever known, than anyone who draws breath, in fact.

And definitely more powerful than every member of the council that exiled you. Especially that charlatan Master of Ceremonies.

Naysin's breath was calmer now, but his mind was churning. He leaned against a tree to consider what he was hearing, ignoring the wet bark pressing against his back. "So you're not my guardian spirits?"

This time both voices laughed. *Well, I suppose we are after a fashion.*

But we would prefer if you called us Father.

Naysin crinkled his nose before responding with his own laugh. "There are two of you! How will you know which one I'm talking to?"

Call me Father Enki.

And me Father Enmul.

The names fit. "Enki" sounded light and quick and free; "Enmul" was heavy and stable and structured. But Naysin still wasn't sure he wanted to use anything other than "cougar-men" … and then his mind moved to the question that, when he let himself think about it, bothered him more than any other. "Why does it hurt sometimes, but not always? Sometimes it feels … really good. What's the difference?"

Ah, now that gets to the very heart of the knowledge we can share with you. You mean when you use your power?

"Yes."

Why don't you make your way back to the village? We'll tell you there — it's going to take time.

"All right." Naysin leaned against the tree awhile longer before he started moving. As he jogged back, he wondered if he hadn't made a serious mistake by talking to the cougar-men again.

— « o » —

"Just so you know, I'm not putting out the fire again." Naysin crossed his arms in what he hoped was a defiant pose, even though he wasn't sure the cougar-men could see it. But the stance helped him feel more in control as he stood tall in the section of the longhouse he'd made his own ... the section still riddled with cracks opened during his last "lesson." He'd applied fire-thawed mud to repair the wind damage, but he kept finding holes he'd missed.

You don't need to do anything more with fire.

But if you are willing to try something else, we have a different task in mind, one that will go a long way toward demonstrating what we would like to impart.

Realizing that his crossed arms had turned into a self-hug, Naysin thrust his hands behind him and clenched them together. "Like what?"

Naysin, to get anything out of this, you need to trust us.

Father Enki is right. We only have your best interests at heart. Now, can you do that? Can you trust us?

"Like what?" he repeated sullenly.

Have it your way.

It was several moments before Naysin realized the voices were gone. Really gone. Like they'd been for most of the time he'd been on his own. He couldn't sense their lingering presence in the back of his skull, or feel the tingling sensation before one of them spoke.

They'd just vanished.

"Wait!" he surprised himself by calling out. "I trust you now! I'll try what you want!"

Excellent.

Naysin felt ashamed at how relieved he was to hear Father Enmul's voice. But he didn't regret asking the cougarmen to come back.

All we've ever wanted is to help you Naysin.

And now you are ready to take the next step. Remember how Father Enki had you use the wind to put out the fire?

"Yes…"

Well, I would like you to do the opposite now. See that water in the old bowl by the door? The snow you melted by the fire?

"I see it."

Freeze it.

His doubts came surging back. "Why? I need that to drink."

Naysin … you can just melt it again. We've already established that you won't be putting out the fire this time, remember?

"Right." Naysin felt the blood rising to his cheeks, and now he hoped his fathers *couldn't* see him. "How?"

Start by focusing on the water. Ignore the bowl and everything else around it — just the water. See how even though it seems like the freest thing you can imagine, the most fluid substance in existence, it is still made of something. Little building blocks of structure. Structure that you can use. Pull together, link, connect … and harden.

"Spirits and lakes!" Naysin's hands let go of each other and grabbed his suddenly aching temples. "You said I could trust you!"

I am sorry, Naysin. But I could not be sure about the pain, and it is one of the things I am trying to explain.

"It really hurts," he murmured, trying to blink back tears.

Naysin, look at the water.

Something in Father Enki's tone made Naysin obey. When he did, he saw the water had frozen solid, cracking the bowl's worn ceramic surface in several places.

Don't worry about the bowl. We can show you how to mend that.

The important thing is that you just did something men around the world would gladly suffer a thousand headaches to be able to do themselves.

Because you exercised the powers of a god.

Naysin sat down abruptly, his legs folding under him as the weight of the voices' words sank in.

What you want to do with this power is for another time. For now, we will keep it simple.

So tell us: what was the difference between putting out the fire and freezing the water?

He shook his head slowly. "You mean besides how much the freezing hurt?"

Yes. Again, I am sorry about that.

Naysin slowly breathed in and out. Slightly calmer, he raised his head and leaned against the nearest partition. "Using the wind was like … speeding things up. Freezing the water was like slowing things down."

Well put.

We always knew you were a quick boy.

Naysin couldn't help smiling.

Really, though. That's a great way of describing it. Speeding things up versus slowing them down.

Motion versus stillness.

Freedom versus structure.

Chaos versus order.

Mir versus…

…Kug.

Naysin squinted in confusion. "What?"

Those are the true names of the two essential powers in the world. Mir, the energy that suffuses the air you breathe and moves the blood through your veins…

…And Kug, the structure that binds your bones and muscles together and gives your air and blood something to move through.

They're as opposite as two things can be.

But together, they create and destroy everything that is, was, or will be.

And only you, of all the people in this world—

Including your fathers.

—can control both.

Naysin sat still as a stone for several breaths before wiping the last tears from his eyes. "That's.... Can I get something to eat? I'm really hungry. From running."

Of course.

We'll be here when you're ready.

"I know," Naysin said as he stood with equal parts wonder and regret.

— « o » —

"So why ... does it ... hurt ... sometimes?" he asked, picking up the conversation as if there hadn't been a two-day break. Naysin was running again, down a different, longer path. He'd thought a lot about what the cougar-men had said, but he hadn't asked anything more until now. Somehow, running made it easier.

It hurts, Father Enki responded immediately, *because you're drawing Mir and* **Kug** *from within yourself.*

And just as there must be balance in the world between the two, so must there be balance inside you.

Naysin accelerated into a short sprint before slowing down to an easy trot. "You ... lost me again."

It's as simple as this: throwing off your internal balance hurts; restoring it feels good.

For example, take our last two lessons. By starting the fire with *Mir*, you brought yourself back into balance after using all that Kug in the Longest House. So you felt good. But then I asked you to freeze the water. By doing so, you drew more Kug out and upset your balance again, because now there was more *Mir* inside. So you hurt.

It also means that if you were to channel a roughly equal amount of Mir now...

"I'd feel ... good."

Exactly.

"That's stupid."

Father Enki laughed in lilting tones that trilled wildly from one breath to the next.

Father Enmul didn't. **It is unique Naysin, not stupid. As we said before, no one else can do this. A little discomfort is a small price to pay for the incredible**

flexibility you have. And a little pleasure is not a bad thing.

Naysin slowed to a walk, trying to get his breathing back to an easy rhythm. "I suppose not."

Not at all.

"But…"

But what, Naysin?

He pressed his hands together, palm to palm with fingers facing down. "Why am I so special? Is it because you're my fathers? Or because you're inside me?"

It took the voices a moment to respond.

Both.

The whole of it is a longer story than you want to hear, but suffice it to say that we once held most of the world's loose energy within ourselves. Immense quantities of it: Kug in me, and *Mir* in Father Enki.

For the greater good.

No one else could be trusted with it.

But even overflowing with all that power, we weren't immune to treachery. Someone jealous of our capabilities tricked us, locked us in a river temple, and threw away the key. We were trapped for thousands of years. Thousands, Naysin.

Until the seal finally weakened enough that we could meet your mother.

And through her, we were at last able to escape our dungeon and re-enter the world.

Into you.

*Bequeathing an inheritance of not just our abilities, but our reservoirs of **Kug** and Mir.*

Which, as we keep trying to convince you to accept, makes you nothing short of a god.

Naysin blinked in bewilderment as follow-up questions cascaded through his head until the most ridiculous query won out: "So I should really be calling you Grandfather Enki and Enmul? Or great grandfathers? Great-great-great-great-great-great grandfathers?"

If you'd like, but if you really want to say an accurate number of "greats" every time you address us, we'll never get anything done. Father Enki laughed again.

Jests aside, Naysin, we are your fathers, as hard to believe as we know that is.

Naysin stopped moving altogether, except for his arms, which he crossed unconsciously. "No, I believe you ... now. I didn't want to, but..." He shrugged his shoulders.

But it's the truth.

And the fact that you are willing to accept it speaks to your maturity, Naysin.

Speaks highly.

He felt his face flush. "Thank you." Looking down at his fraying moccasins, he suddenly had another thought. "Who tricked you?" he asked, looking back up even though there wasn't an actual face to direct the question to.

Our mother.

— « o » —

Two more days passed, but this time Naysin didn't spend them in silence. He talked with his fathers constantly, peppering them with questions and accepting small lessons. His favorites had been when Father Enmul taught him how to repair his moccasins by forcing the deer hide to renew itself, and when Father Enki showed him how to shaman enough fire to melt a cup's worth of snow into drinking water. The pain hadn't been bad; Father Enmul said it was because they were keeping the uses of his power small, so that even when he created an imbalance, it wasn't a *big* imbalance.

He also learned more about what his fathers wanted from him: freedom. His body was still a prison for them. *A much more enjoyable prison than that dank river temple*, Father Enki had reassured him, but a prison nonetheless. They still couldn't act, except for speaking to him and each other.

Once you are strong enough, however, Father Enmul had told him solemnly, **you can let us out.**

The one topic they shied away from was mothers. Naysin had clammed up as soon as Father Enki had said it was the cougar-men's mother — his grandmother? — who tricked and trapped them. Naysin hadn't asked anything more about it, and his fathers hadn't elaborated. But even without details, the revelation had dispelled a lot of his lingering distrust.

It felt like it gave them more in common: a shared sense of being ripped from the world.

On the third day of near-constant communication, Father Enki told him he was ready to fly.

It's a big step, but I know you're ready for it, Naysin. You've been remarkably quick to learn, and you're already so strong.

Outside the longhouse, Naysin could hear water trickling from every rock and tree as the sun assaulted the snow. It still didn't seem quite soon enough for spring, but he knew he couldn't linger here. His people would be back soon, and he needed to be gone when they returned. Or at least, that had been the plan before he'd accepted who he was and what he could do.

"What if ... what if I stayed here?" he asked aloud, ignoring Father Enki's suggestion for a moment.

Naysin, my son, you know you cannot.

The sober part of him did. The part that acknowledged the futility of confronting his people with his newfound abilities and daring them to turn him away again. The part that knew his fantasies of forcing the Elder Council to bow to him were just that: fantasies, daydreams that would only lead to more abandonment and rejection.

But the rest of him didn't want to believe it. "My mother's not here anymore — it's just me. And everyone said I didn't do anything wrong!"

Still, they will not forgive you.

People will always be jealous of you. Which is why you need to grow stronger.

Father Enki is right. You must choose: do you want to slink away from this village with an old woman's outstretched finger at your back again, or do you want to fly off in triumph, moving in a way no one else can.

He pressed his palms together, twining his fingers as he pointed them down. "All right. Teach me."

Wonderful. The first part you already know how to do: climb the biggest, tallest tree you can find.

Naysin took a step back. "Why can't I learn from the ground?"

Necessity is the mother of invention, Naysin. It took your fear of freezing to light the fire. It's going to take your fear of falling to make you fly.

If you trust us, you can do this.

Reluctantly, he opened the longhouse's door and contemplated the old elm he used to love climbing. "Would that tree be all right?"

Yes. I knew you could do it.

A slippery, harrowing ascent later, he was as far up the elm as he could reach. And very sick to his stomach.

The worst is behind you.

Now for the fun part: start picturing yourself losing weight.

"What?"

Concentrate.

You can do this. Pound by pound. You're not physically losing anything, but try to feel yourself becoming less heavy … losing density … shedding mass. The branch beneath you is bending less and less, slowly rising as the burden of your body becomes easier to bear. And the air around you is growing thicker, buoying you up as it becomes unnecessary for your feet to support you…

"I can't feel it!" said Naysin with rising alarm, clutching the trunk of the tree for reassurance.

Yes you can. I have faith in you.

Feel it, Naysin. Believe it — that's the only way. You have to want to soar through the air, lighter than a leaf, faster than a falcon. You have to need it. And it starts with a step.

He sobbed as the ground beneath him seemed to hurtle away, stretching to an unimaginably far distance. "No, I don't want to!"

Yes you do, Naysin. You can do this.

Close your eyes. Focus on believing, on having faith that you can soar like no bird has ever soared before. Rising and diving and rolling through the air… You can do it all if you just take the first step.

Take your hands off the tree and step, Naysin. Just step.

He was completely panicked now. "It's too hard!" he screamed as tears and snot streamed down his face.

Naysin, you trust us, yes? If you trust us, take a step. It'll be fine if you just step.

Trust us, son. You have to trust us.

Two more sobs wracked his chest before he swallowed hard and squeezed his eyes shut. "I trust you," he whispered hoarsely. "I trust you."

In halting movements, Naysin eased his fingers off the trunk. Then his hands, and then his arms, until he was supported only by his feet, precariously balanced on a wet branch that seemed to sway violently with every breath he took.

Swallowing again, he murmured, "I trust you," once more, stepped...

And fell.

Chapter Five

The Pale Men

Naysin woke to cold water dripping on his face and pain worse than he'd ever experienced. The day he'd slipped and banged his head while trying to cross a river by leaping from rock to rock … the morning he'd brushed against a heating stone his mother had just pulled from the fire … the night he'd cast images in the longhouse… Even combined, they still hadn't hurt as badly.

This was so excruciating he couldn't even cry. He was paralyzed with pain, stilled by agony that only intensified as he became aware of his surroundings. He lay in a mix of slush and mud formed to his body as if the muck had birthed him. Melting snow cascaded from above, pelting the ground with the sound and fury of a hard rain.

And his leg… His right leg was twisted beneath him and radiating pain.

The rest of his body was mostly just scraped and bruised, battered and aching but nowhere near as ruined as his shin. Which, Naysin realized as the pain became less diffuse, was what was broken. He remembered turning at the end, trying to use his arm to absorb the worst of the impact. But he hadn't twisted fast enough, and his right leg had taken the worst of the blow.

After he'd fallen. Not flown.

"Liars," he hissed as the tears finally came. "Manitouk liars." Naysin also remembered wondering, just before he hit, why his fathers — the cougar-men — hadn't mentioned

Kug or *Mir* when they'd asked him to visualize what was going to happen, hadn't asked him to see any type of motion, or focus on any sort of structure. They'd just told him to believe, to trust them … and step.

Somewhere behind Naysin, a man yelled. Then the woods were filled with the sound of a tree creaking, groaning, and smashing to the forest floor.

After the impact, everything went quiet … until another man started talking. His unfamiliar accent hurt to listen to. "Do we really have to do this when it's so bloody cold?" the man asked. "Why couldn't the Penn's wait until spring, when my arse would only be wet instead of freezing?"

The first man laughed derisively before answering. "Didn't you ask that five minutes ago? And didn't I answer it?"

"Aye. You said 'The Penn's, in their infinite, lily-white wisdom, decided to measure off the Walking Purchase in the winter, so that their grasping settlers can carve up the land in the spring.' And you also said to shut my 'bleedin' hole, because this is good paying work, frozen as it may be.'"

"And?" the first man asked.

"And I don't disagree with you. Or even the damned Penns. But we've run out of things to fucking say, so I reiterated the fact that my aged arse prefers to be warm."

Two more men guffawed at this, and one of them added, "Hear! Hear!" After a moment, the first man laughed as well, and the conversation meandered on.

Naysin still couldn't place their accent, but he didn't care. His leg was throbbing too much for him to worry about which tribe the men came from. Even if they turned out to be Hodensee.

"Help," he squeaked. "I need help — I'm hurt."

"Did you hear that?"

"Sounded like gibberish."

Naysin repeated himself, trying his best to speak slowly and clearly so that the men could understand what he was saying. Doing so gave him a slight headache, but it seemed to work.

"See there? By that old elm."

Footsteps thudded toward him as he gave a prayer of thanks. Then a face appeared above his.

A *pale* face. With bushy red hair — on the man's head *and* face — and a great big wrinkly wart on his left cheek.

"While I'll be damned. It's a little red devil. A broken little red devil."

Three more men crowded into Naysin's vision. Three more *pale* men, one with black hair, one with brown, and one with yellow. Their clothes were hideous, and their bodies stank. They didn't look like the cougar-men, but they definitely weren't Lepane, or Hodensee, or any other people he'd seen or heard of. "Who are you?" Naysin asked in amazement, forgetting his pain.

"Fuck all," Red Hair said, with a similar note of wonder in his voice.

Brown Hair, the smallest of the four men, raised one of his bushy eyebrows in surprise. "Where did you learn to speak Anglo, little devil?"

Naysin looked from one face to the next in bewilderment. "What's Ang—" And then the agony roared back, consuming him like fire engulfing a dry forest. "Please ... help me. My leg... Please fix my leg..." he managed to get out before dissolving into whimpers.

"Looks to have taken a tumble," Yellow Hair observed.

Black Hair wasn't moved. "What's it matter? He's a red devil. We can't take him with us — you know how fast we have to move."

Red Hair shrugged. "He's just a lad."

"There must be other devils nearby. I'm sure they'll find him."

Brown Hair shook his head. "He speaks Anglo..." Standing up, he pulled the rest of the men back. "Do you realize how rare that is? My cousin would snap him up in a second."

"We can't take him with us," Black Hair repeated. "Too much deadweight."

"No," Brown Hair eventually agreed. "But we're meeting Conrad's boys tonight to resupply. I know one of the riders. I bet—" he cut himself off, as if he didn't want to say more.

"Give me your extra shirt," he said instead to Yellow Hair. "And your walking stick. Snap it in half first."

Yellow Hair stared mulishly at him before turning to walk toward the fallen tree. "You better cut me in," he tossed over his shoulder.

"You'll all get your shares." Brown Hair turned to Red Hair and Black Hair. "I need a blanket, a spare bowl, and a bit of jerky... Now!" he shouted when the other two pale men didn't react immediately. "We're losing time."

Once they were in motion, Brown Hair bent over Naysin, who — through his pain — had only registered half of what had been said. "What's your name, little devil?" the pale man asked with a disarming smile.

Wincing, Naysin somehow managed to smile back. "Naysin. And I'm not a devil. I'm Lepane. You're the ones who look like devils."

Brown Hair laughed. "That attitude may get you in the sauce later, but for now it'll keep you alive. So I won't begrudge it." The other pale men returned with the supplies he'd asked them to fetch. "All right," he said, holding up the bowl and dumping water into it from the skin at his belt. "Drink this." He put it down next to Naysin. "Eat this," Brown Hair continued, holding up the strip of dried meat before setting it next to the bowl. "Use this to keep you warm," he said, patting the tattered blanket.

Naysin gave him a look of weak thanks. "What do I do with those?" he asked, nodding toward the sticks and the strange-looking shirt.

Brown Hair smiled again, but this time it had a hard edge. "Those are going to hurt." He turned to the other men. "Give him a shot from the flask and hold him up." Looking back at Naysin, he offered another dour smile. "I'm going to set your leg, and we'll be on our way. But if none of your kind comes to get you before tomorrow morning, one of ours will."

Panic crept back through Naysin's haze of hurt. "You're leaving me? I don't want to stay here. Please—"

Yellow Hair cut Naysin off with a brusque yank that brought him to a sitting position. Rivers of pain flowed through his leg, but before he could cry out, Red Hair filled his mouth with a dollop of burning liquid from a flask.

Then Brown Hair grabbed Naysin's leg, and the sky went black.

— « o » —

When Naysin regained consciousness, he was bouncing several arm-lengths above the ground.

At first he thought he was on the shoulders of an extremely hairy man. But the neck in front of him — the neck *supporting* him — was far too long. And the ears were too active, ceaselessly twitching and turning. They also came to a point.

He was on top of a giant beast.

Naysin started to struggle, but he was constricted by two arms. Two *human* arms — there was a man behind him. A pale man who held a cord connected to the mouth of the beast, which was angling to get a look at Naysin as he squirmed. Its eyes were big and wild, and its teeth were large and square.

"Ho, Ragger, ho… You mind the trail, and I'll mind the boy." As the man spoke, he used one arm to restrain Naysin while the other tugged the beast's head forward. "I'd stop that if I were you, little devil, unless you want to fall and break your other leg."

His leg. The pain hadn't registered when Naysin woke, but now it blazed like a grease fire, even though his ruined limb was all-but immobilized, wound tight with Yellow Hair's sticks and shirt. "It hurts," he hissed through gritted teeth.

The man behind him — whose face Naysin still couldn't see — let out a low whistle. "So you do talk like us. I'll be damned. Here: drink some of this." The man leaned over to grab a water skin and pressed it to Naysin's lips. "Drink."

Naysin wrinkled his nose. The sack *looked* like a water skin, but it smelled like it was full of the same stuff the other pale men had given him before they bound his leg. He didn't need that burning sensation running down his throat again … but every step the beast took jolted his leg horribly. So he swallowed.

And gagged. This stuff tasted even worse.

It helped, though. Not right away, but eventually the beast's strides became bearable as Naysin's pain dulled and blurred, and his thoughts turned back into questions. "Is Ragger some kind of deer?" he asked, tentatively patting the hairy, too-long neck in front of him.

"I'll be damned," the faceless man behind him repeated. "Talks like us, I'll be damned."

And that was all. The man didn't comment on anything other than the fact that Naysin could talk. It made him scared without knowing why. And it didn't help that he couldn't see the man's face. Maybe it wasn't even a man at all...

Clamming up, Naysin kept the rest of his questions to himself, no longer sure he wanted to hear their answers. Instead of talking, he watched the beast's front legs, focusing on how their massive hooves looked like enlarged versions of boar's feet, except without the cleft in the middle. He also studied the trail they were following — the newly cleared trail.

This, he realized after some reflection, must have been what the first four pale men had been working on. The name they'd mentioned — the "Penns" — didn't mean anything to him, but the people it represented must be powerful indeed if they could make four men blaze a trail during winter.

Even stranger, the pale men had blazed a *straight* trail. They'd made no effort to wind around intervening terrain; they'd gone through it, be it tree, hill, or, in the case of one stream they'd bridged over, water. What a waste. The pale men were fighting the forest rather than working with it, as if maintaining the path's regularity was more important than creating the thing efficiently.

It didn't make sense.

In between wondering about this unusual method, marveling at the beast that was carrying him, and managing his pain, Naysin kept coming back to the biggest questions on his mind: where was he being taken, and what did the pale men want with him? He had vague memories of rousing in the woods ... finding a blanket wrapped around him and sticks tied to his leg ... sipping a little water ... chewing a bit of rock-hard meat ... and drifting back into unconsciousness.

But none of these scattered images explained why the pale men had saved him.

The camp the mysterious man brought him to that night only raised more questions.

At first glance, it looked temporary: a large, oddly-covered wigwam flanked by several smaller ones. But as the man behind him directed his beast toward a herd of its furry kin, Naysin realized there was a permanent shelter here as well, built into the side of the hill that overlooked the wigwams.

It was the type of structure his tribe often used as a winter sanctuary.

Then he noticed people who looked like himself huddled under the larger wigwam, and pale men walking in and out of the hill-house. The sight sobered him so much that he barely reacted when his escort finally revealed himself. "Brace yourself, little devil," the dark-haired man said as he grabbed Naysin by the armpits and dragged him over Ragger's side, with no regard for how his leg bounced against the hairy hide. His sharp intake of breath made the man laugh dispassionately.

"I suppose I could have done that from the left, eh?"

Trying not to cry, Naysin let himself be carried to the large wigwam, whipping his neck back and forth to take in everything he could. Men, women, children: at least two families. Maybe three. They weren't Lepane, but they easily could have been from one of the tribes Naysin's people traded with.

And they were all bound by a shiny rope.

It looked like a two-reed braid, but the thick cord *glinted* in the firelight as it entangled every available ankle. It was as if a giant snake had planned ahead and snared its meals for the next moon. The image struck Naysin so forcefully that he started looking for the serpent's head, half expecting to see it at any moment, mouth open and dripping venom.

Instead, as the pale man set him down and walked away, Naysin registered one more presence: his mother's.

Kanti was staring at the wigwam's smoke hole as she drummed absently on her thighs.

Chapter Six

Captive

They were parted at the sea.

The Anglos led Naysin's mother, along with most of the women and children, to the larger vessel, and he and most of the men to the smaller.

Both "ships" were magnificent.

He'd heard the word spoken by one of the pale captors. Even confused and scared as he was, Naysin couldn't stop marveling at the strange canoes' size. Many times longer than the leanest dugout, and many times wider than the broadest round-boat, the ships' hulls were enormous, and immense posts sprang from their depths to support giant sheets of cloth — the current they had to negotiate must be mighty indeed.

It made sense when he looked at the sea. This, at least, he'd heard stories about. But it was still a shock to see so much water stretching into the horizon. Especially when he realized he was going to pass *over* it, in a craft that no longer seemed quite so large.

Another journey. The march to the port had already taken many moons ... as well as a young girl and an old man who'd had a bad cough since the beginning. They'd almost lost several others as well, mostly from beatings administered by the increasingly impatient pale men. Naysin had never been at serious risk, however. He hadn't even had to walk until the last few days; until his broken leg was strong enough to bear weight, he'd been borne by Ragger and his rider Jonas.

Naysin had felt slightly guilty about sitting atop a "horse" when everyone else had to walk with a shiny "chain" around their ankles. But he'd been in no hurry to get down.

He'd been more conflicted about deceiving his mother.

The deception had started right from the beginning. When he'd noticed her in the wigwam set aside for the captives, he'd wished she wouldn't see him, that when she looked at the new boy in camp, she'd see someone else in his place. A Lnu, or a Pekout, or even a Hodensee. Just not her son.

His wish had come true; when she'd finally glanced at him, there hadn't been any recognition in her face. And for the first time, Naysin had been glad to feel the tell-tale ache of shamaning. From things his mother had said over the course of the next several days, he'd gathered she was seeing a young boy similar in appearance to him. He'd also noticed her staring at him with a forlorn look on her face, a heart-rending expression that had almost been enough to make him remove the veil from her eyes.

Almost.

Instead, it was the pain that finally broke him. Maintaining the disguise with what he thought was **Kug** had led to larger and larger headaches. He'd gotten some relief when he slept; he couldn't manipulate the stiff energy when he wasn't awake, so he'd just crossed his arms in front of his face and been thankful for the forced respite.

But by the fourth day, the strain had become too much. He'd had to start picking and choosing his spots, erecting the disguise when his mother was near and dropping it as soon as she looked away. It had been easy when he rode in front of the party, because Jonas blocked his mother's view. When they'd ridden in the rear, however, Naysin had kept a constant eye on his mother to make sure she didn't look back unexpectedly. She hadn't done it much; walking fast enough to appease the pale men while connected to the moving chain had taken most of her attention. But Naysin had felt like he always had to be on his guard.

And on the fifth day, he'd slipped. The sunlight had made him drowsy as he'd swayed to the rhythm of the horse's plodding strides. He'd dozed off ... only to wake abruptly when the beast pulled up short. When Naysin's eyes shot open, he'd found his mother had stopped the line to stare at him in disbelief.

Hastily, he'd donned his disguise and watched her expression change to doubt. Then a pale man had hit her for causing the delay, and Naysin had looked away.

That night, as Naysin had relived the scene while staring at the pale men's fire, he'd realized there was an easy way to make the pain go away and reduce the chances of slipping again; he needed to start using equal amounts of *Mir*. Part of him had shied away from the thought, suspicious of any course of action that required more shamaning. But the cougar-men had already helped him prove that balance removed the hurt.

He'd begun with the first trick he'd learned while on his own: manipulating flames. The pale men's fire had started to burn low, but at least a few of them would keep it going into the early morning as they gambled and bragged. Naysin had waited until one of them dropped several more logs on the fire, after which he'd focused on enhancing its motion, speeding up its already fast-moving lines and the specks of energy that comprised them. The resulting burst of flame had forced the pale man to stumble backward and lose his balance. After a moment of shocked silence, the other pale men had roared with laughter as their embarrassed comrade scrambled to his feet.

And the pain in Naysin's temples had ebbed.

From that night on, he'd actually begun to enjoy shamaning in small doses. It was difficult to do anything the cougar-men hadn't shown him — without their descriptions, he had trouble figuring out what he was supposed to *see* — but he knew enough to cause satisfying bits of havoc: gusts of wind that knocked off hats; skins of water that became hot just before they were drunk; knots that loosened as soon as they were tied... Each of these *Mir* counterweights had felt good, the more so because they disturbed his captors. After a half moon of this, they'd become visibly unsettled, muttering about witchcraft and hexes.

His pranks had also given his fellow captives a measure of hope. Naysin had seen it in their eyes before they started talking about it, and a few days later he'd overheard murmurings about "friendly spirits." The indirect praise had made his tricks feel important; he wasn't just doing them for simple relief anymore. He was *fighting back*. And for the first time in his life, he'd felt like he had a purpose.

Until the afternoon his mother heard some other murmurs.

It had been several moons into the journey, on a rainy day that had churned the path into grasping mud. Naysin hadn't minded; on the horse, he'd been well above the muck, and he'd always loved the rain. As soon as the first drops fell, he'd turned his face to the sky, causing Jonas to grumble about "damn fool red devils."

Naysin had kept staring at the clouds even when the party stopped for a rest. So he hadn't noticed his mother's approach until her face overran his vision.

She'd looked ... hopeful, as she'd stared at his left eye and unconsciously traced the tattoo encircling her right. Then she'd looked annoyed, glaring at one of the women she occasionally talked to. And finally she'd looked blank — like she usually did — as she'd turned away, the chain trailing behind her.

It had taken Naysin several wet moments to puzzle out what had happened, but eventually he'd realized someone had finally asked his mother about their similar tattoos. He'd heard a few of the women talking about it before, but he'd thought his mother had simply ignored the chatter when she couldn't see his.

From that moment on, the image of her expression changing from hope to hurt had stuck in his mind. He kept seeing that transformation, even when he closed his eyes. It had been most vivid when he thought of playing another trick on the pale men; within two days of the encounter, he'd stopped the pranks. Instead, he'd started blowing off bursts of *Mir* in ways no one would notice.

But he'd never dropped the disguise.

He'd maintained it through the final steps of the long march, past a village teeming with pale men and toward the water's edge, where he and his fellow captives had been herded into a round pen like animals, pressed body-to-body for most of a day — so close he could feel at least five different people breathing on his neck — and finally divided into groups by a short, wrinkled old man who looked stiff and cruel.

Now, though... Now they were taking separate ramps to separate ships. Naysin's leg still hurt every time it hit the ground, so his ascent was more hop than walk. But he kept glancing at the other ship. And when he made it to the top of the ramp, he wished the veil away from his mother's eyes and prayed for her to look at him. It had suddenly become all important she know he was alive, that he was sorry for running away. He opened his mouth to yell that to her ... but the call died in his throat as she cast a look his way, passed over him as if he wasn't there, and disappeared into the other ship.

Had she not seen him? Seen only what she expected to see?

Or seen and not cared?

Naysin wasn't sure what to think as Jonas led him into the depths of the smaller ship, down a shaky ladder and into a dark hold that stank of human waste. More captives followed, and soon he was once more packed against people he still didn't know that well — he'd mostly kept to himself on the march, and it hadn't helped that he was treated differently by the pale men, broken leg or not. None of the other captives had been hostile toward him, but no one had been overly friendly either.

The dim lighting and low ceiling only added to his sense of isolation, especially after the opening to the hold was sealed. In many ways, he was just as alone as he'd been in the woods, after he'd left his mother. Maybe more so.

"You'll have to be tougher than that to make it out of this hole, little Lepane."

Embarrassed, Naysin wiped the tears from his cheeks and looked for the voice's source. It was a man's, but not one he recognized; his eyes hadn't adjusted to the dark yet, and all he could see were silhouettes.

"That's better," the voice said.

This time Naysin was sure it came from behind him. Moving carefully so he could favor his leg, he edged toward the unfamiliar profile, squeezing between two captives he'd shared the march with. They were still attached to their group's chain — the women and children had been freed from it, but not the men — and they grumbled as he sloshed through an intervening puddle whose origin he didn't want to think about. Gritting his teeth, he kept moving until he was beside the stranger, and then followed his lead by leaning against the hull. There wasn't enough light to see what the man really looked like, but Naysin could tell the stranger had a lot of hair, and that it all seemed to come from the middle of his head. Was he a Hodensee?

"Good boy," the stranger said after a moment. "Your father's not with you, is he?"

Naysin's thoughts strayed to the cougar-men — he hadn't heard anything from them since they'd tricked him into falling and breaking his leg. He hoped that meant they were gone. "No," he answered, forcing himself to think about Machk. "The plague took him before I was born."

"I'm sorry," the stranger offered after another pause. "But we're all about to be a lot sorrier."

Naysin didn't want to ask, but he couldn't help himself. "Why's that?"

"Because less than half of us are going to make it out of this stinking hole."

Chapter Seven

Degan

The man's name was Degan, and he was right. Within a few days, captives started dying in droves.

At first, they tried to preserve a measure of hygiene by relieving themselves only in one corner of the hold. It helped with the solids, but the rolling of the boat caused the liquids to slosh back and forth before they leaked between the floorboards. And that constant swaying, greater by far than anything the captives had experienced in a canoe, made many of them sick too suddenly to reach the designated spot.

After a stretch of time that might have been a morning but felt like a moon, the pale men came down and fixed everyone to a new chain: a single length that bound the different groups of hostages to each other and the hull. It made maneuvering in the tight confines almost impossible. After a few futile attempts, no one bothered with the corner anymore.

Several days later, the first bout of plague struck. Pustules erupted on the skin of at least five captives; then their blood turned black; then they died. The pattern was just as deadly on the ship as on the mainland, and it kept repeating every few days. Naysin had never seen the disease up close, and he continued to be amazed that, aside from removing the dead each dawn and providing daily rations of food and water, the pale men seemed indifferent to their cargo's suffering.

Degan's included.

The pale men had chained them together for the simple reason that they'd been sitting near each other. Degan hadn't said much after his initial prediction. Naysin hadn't either, weighed down by apathy and claustrophobia (but thankfully, not the plague). Walking the few steps the chain allowed wasn't worth the effort; even if his leg hadn't hurt, he didn't like constantly ducking to avoid the hold's sharp angles and beams. And it wasn't as if there was anywhere to go. He especially hated the fact that he couldn't *run* — he hadn't run in more than a season, not since the day the cougar-men betrayed him and broke his leg.

But when Degan started shaking, Naysin snapped out of his lethargy. "Are you sick too?"

The older man shook his head smiled weakly. "No. Just … deprived."

"What does 'deprived' mean?"

Degan laughed darkly. "It means, little Lepane, that I grew too fond of the pale men's drink. Now my body's crying for it." Then he closed his eyes and bowed his head.

Naysin took the hint; he didn't ask any more questions until the pale men tossed the day's food into the hold … and Degan refused to eat. "You need your strength," Naysin said determinedly.

"No," Degan eventually replied. "But you do. Eat it for me. I'll be all right in a few days." He was sweating, though. Naysin felt it when the ship shifted unexpectedly and knocked him against the Hodensee man — Degan had confirmed his tribe on the second day, a blood-truth that would have terrified Naysin as recently as a few moons ago. But it didn't matter who you were down here in the dark. Lepane, Tsalgi, Hodensee: everyone was just a captive now.

"Please, you need to eat," Naysin tried again.

"Save your worries for the ones that are actually sick, little Lepane." Degan gestured tiredly toward the rest of the hold. "They're the ones who are going to die. I'm just going to wish I had." He bowed his head once more, and that was the end of it.

Until he passed into a wordless daze, making Naysin feel even more helpless.

He barely knew this man, but it didn't matter; he just wanted him to get better, wanted to know that someone could go through the worst of this and survive. He also didn't want the chain to be empty on *both* sides of him — the captive to his left had been carried out three mornings ago.

After another meal was dropped from above, Degan started talking again. But not in a good way. He wasn't talking *to* anyone, just himself. Raving in a stupor about things Naysin didn't understand: codes and spirits and purification. None of it made any sense. The only comfort was that the wild words seemed to strengthen the Hodensee — when the morning came, Degan wasn't among the bodies hauled out of the hold.

He woke shortly thereafter. "Still here," he observed.

Naysin wasn't sure if the comment was directed at him or not. He didn't care. "You're better."

Degan cracked his neck and rolled his shoulders. "I suppose I am." He clutched his stomach as it rumbled noisily. "And extraordinarily hungry. I don't suppose you saved any slop?"

Naysin shook his head in shame — he'd taken the Hodensee at his word when he'd said to eat both their shares.

"No matter." Degan rolled his shoulders forward and back again, and then looked hard at Naysin. Even in the near dark, he could see the Hodensee's eyes had a new light in them: zeal, rather than fever. "Tell me... Naysin, right?"

He nodded.

"Tell me, Naysin: how did a little Lepane such as yourself learn to speak Hodensee?"

As if on cue, Naysin's temples chose that moment to ache guiltily; the **Kug** he'd been expending to follow the hold's diverse dialects was catching up with him again. Later — when Degan wasn't watching — he'd have to shoot off a little *Mir* to compensate, maybe by blowing another fresh breeze through their stinking prison. Everyone had seemed to like that the first time. "I don't know. I just ... do."

"Is that right?" Degan leaned back and crossed his arms. "Well, you'll have to keep talking to me, because no one else in here can."

Naysin didn't like everything he heard in Degan's voice, but he was also tired of sitting silently in the dark.

So they talked.

Or at least Degan did. Some days almost without stopping, others only for a short session or two. Naysin occasionally interjected a question or answered one asked of him, but for the most part he just listened.

At first, Degan didn't speak of their situation; he focused on legends, like the story of how a Lepane chieftain was tossed over Taughanna Falls by Hodensee warriors. Naysin hadn't enjoyed that one very much. Degan told his tales well, however, and for the most part, they were a welcome distraction — the dank hold was nowhere near as full as it had been, and it reeked of filth and death.

Gradually, Degan's monologues turned to the captives' circumstances. He spoke of how their imprisonment was in fact a chance for redemption, that when they escaped, they could start fresh. Begin anew, become whoever they wanted, and redeem the world in the process. Naysin didn't understand everything the Hodensee said about the subject, but he liked the emphasis on atonement.

And he wanted to know more. So during a particularly wandering story, Naysin interrupted to ask about their captors. "Where did the pale men come from?"

"Now there's a question." Degan laughed softly and cracked his knuckles. "I don't know how they came to be on this earth. You'd have to ask them that ... since you can understand them as well?"

Naysin thought quickly of the times he'd listened to the pale men when they'd opened the hold. Degan must have noticed him following their conversations — there wasn't much point in lying. "Yes."

"I thought as much." The Hodensee nodded to himself. "But as to how they came to our lands ... they crossed the ocean. In great canoes like this one." He tapped a nearby beam. "The first arrived around the time you were born. With new plants, new animals, and new weapons — you haven't seen them use one of their fire sticks, have you?"

"What's a fire stick?"

"Those long, shiny spears they carry. The pale men don't even have to throw them; they just point, and out bursts smoke and fire and a little rock that can kill at great distance."

Naysin's eyes grew wide as he thought of the cougar-men. "Is it magic?"

Degan snorted. "No. Even the dumbest among them can do it. It's just … they're a different people, from a different place, with different ideas. And it's those ideas, little Lepane, it's those ideas that are the most dangerous thing about them. More so even than the way they claim our lands without recompense, or capture our people without accepting them into their tribes. Their ideas — their temptations — are making us weak. They make us desire things we never knew we wanted, like their fire sticks, and the hornless moose they call 'horses' … and their drink."

He fell silent for a long moment before shaking his head and continuing. "And yet, on some things we think alike. Their priests speak of a man with great powers who will return when he's needed, much like the Hodensee believe."

Naysin's breath caught.

"They name him Jesua; we name him Hiawatha. Perhaps they are one and the same. But I doubt it, little Lepane. I doubt it very much." Degan craned his neck to look hard at Naysin. "Because I don't think one savior can help two peoples. I think he can only help one."

Naysin was glad Degan couldn't see him swallow. "I guess so."

The conversation stayed with him for days — he repeated the words to himself when he had trouble sleeping (which was often). But the more he wondered about the Hodensee's meaning, the less able he found himself to ask about it. So the topic lingered in his mind, a coal that refused to grow cold … until it was displaced by another of Degan's stories.

"Have I told you how the world began, little Lepane?"

"No," Naysin answered warily.

"It's time you heard: Long ago, Whena, the wife of the celestial chief, grew pregnant unexpectedly. Jealous beyond words, the chief tore a hole in the canopy of Heaven and hurled her down to the place below. But Whena lived and bore a daughter, Onato, who was in turn made pregnant by a man who never touched her. To this daughter were born twin boys, so different they couldn't even agree how to leave the womb. The good brother, Oterong, wanted to be birthed the normal way. The bad brother, Tawiskaron, wanted to come out the side. Neither would compromise, so when the time came, Oterong glided down and entered life safely, while Tawiskaron emerged from his mother's armpit and killed her.

"Of the two, Oterong looked more like a man; he was strong and handsome and moved with the grace of a deer. Tawiskaron was made of flint, with a stony mohawk that announced his presence long before the rest of him could be seen. And when Whena asked the twins how Onato died, it was the strangely-beautiful Tawiskaron she believed. He convinced her to exile Oterong, just as she had been cast out herself. Then she turned her beloved daughter's body into the sun, and her head into the moon. But she kept the heavenly orbs confined to her hut, wanting to keep their light for Tawiskaron and herself.

"Undismayed, Oterong paid tribute to his dead mother in his own way by creating the world's places, plants, and animals. When he learned of his grandmother's selfishness, he stole into her hut and threw the sun and the moon up into the sky so everyone could bask in Onato's brilliance. Later he created man in his image and woman in hers.

"Envious of his abilities, Tawiskaron and Whena trapped many of Oterong's animals in a cave; those we see today are the ones who escaped. Tawiskaron also tried to imitate Oterong's greatest creation by producing feeble, gangling copies of humanity.

"At last, a confrontation could no longer be avoided, and Oterong slew Tawiskaron. His flinty body became the mountains, and Whena fled beyond the horizon. When his work was finished, Oterong ascended to Heaven, and the world has looked the same since."

Naysin didn't believe the Hodensee's story — his own people knew a giant named Maushop had come from the sea to free the first men and women from the trees that encased them — but one part had caught his attention. "The good and the bad brother ... they didn't come back? No one's heard from them again?"

Degan gave him another hard look. "Not that I know of."

"Oh." Naysin winced as he said this, annoyed at how invested he sounded in the topic. "That's too bad. About the good brother, I mean. I guess it's better the bad brother stays dead. He's probably more useful as a mountain."

Degan folded his arms behind his head and leaned back. "No doubt he is."

Feeling awkward and transparent, Naysin clamped his mouth shut. Neither of the cougar-men had seemed particularly good ... but Degan's story still made him wonder.

He didn't have long to consider it; the next day, the ship stopped moving.

Shouts from above rang out as pale men raced overhead and something splashed down on either side. But everything went quiet in the hold — the usual murmur of conversation vanished, as did the rustling of bodies and clinking of chain links.

"We've arrived," Degan said into the silence. Only Naysin understood him, but his words set off a new burst of talk and movement. Everyone realized something was about to change, but the exact nature of that something was fiercely debated.

"Listen well, Naysin — to me, not them."

With an effort, he focused on Degan, trying not to be distracted by the ambient unease.

"You recall when I was sick? When you thought I would die like the half of us that aren't here anymore?"

Naysin nodded.

Degan grabbed him by the arm and pulled him closer. The Hodensee's eyes were feverishly bright again, their energy visible even in the hold's perpetual twilight. "During the darkest moments of my sickness, when I was finally starting to sweat the pale men's poison from my veins, I had a vision. A true vision — not a dream, not a hallucination. A vision. I saw the coming of the pale men, and how they brought death and disease to more peoples than anyone knew existed. Even worse, I saw how tribes likes ours *allowed* this to happen by forsaking their old beliefs and whoring themselves to the pale men's needs. Then I saw what giving into these desires will do to us in the fullness of time: we will grow weak. And weaker. And weaker. Until there are no more than a handful left of our kind, and the pale men overrun this land like a herd of deer too long un-hunted."

Naysin swallowed painfully, his mouth so dry it felt like his throat was scraping against itself. This was intense even for Degan.

"But amidst all this despair, I saw hope. I saw that if we renew our faith in the old ways, if we purify our behavior and beliefs, we *can* avert this extinction. I also, little Lepane..." Degan's voice dropped solemnly as he loosened his grip on Naysin's arm. "I also saw Hiawatha, the savior I've spoken of. Mighty indeed, with powers even the greatest spirits were jealous of, abilities he could use to rally the many tribes and forge a coalition strong enough to turn back the pale flood.

"But it wasn't until I opened my eyes that I realized the savior looked like an older version of you."

Stunned, Naysin couldn't do anything but blink in response.

"I don't except you to believe this all at once. That's why I've been trying to tell you things slowly. But when we climb out of this hole, we'll be back in the world. And I need you to start thinking about whether you want me to help you grow into that savior. I can spread word of your coming, but only *you* can be that man."

Naysin looked away from Degan; the Hodensee's eyes were too hopeful, too *sure*.

Then the lid to the hold was removed, and a cold voice plunged down with the light: "Welcome to Bimshire, slaves."

Chapter Eight

Bimshire

"The Walking Purchase," Naysin — sixteen winters, lanky, and prematurely graying — said to the Matowak. "Have you heard of it?"

The other slave snorted in disgust. "Yes. I know what it was about too. Theft."

Naysin arched his eyebrows in surprise. He'd been asking the question for so long that he wasn't sure how to react now that someone on the plantation finally had an answer.

Fortunately, the Matowak didn't need any encouragement. "Outright theft," he repeated, his forehead furrowing in anger. "From the Black Hill in the north to the Red Mound in the south, and as far east from the Crooked Forest as a man can walk in a day and a half. As far as a man can *walk*. That was the agreement the pale Penns made with our chiefs. It seemed a fair trade: a small strip of land in exchange for peace and some of their fire sticks." The Matowak spat on the ground and massaged his shoulder — he'd just been beaten by an overseer.

Naysin finally recovered his voice. "The Penns were Anglos, right?" During his captivity, he'd learned a lot about pale men, including that they had tribes of their own.

"They were. Not that it matters much. The Francs or the Espans would have cheated just the same."

Foreboding knotted in Naysin's stomach. "How did they cheat?"

"By sticking to the words of the agreement, but not the spirit. They cleared their own trail through the Crooked Forest, straight and unnatural, and provisioned three men to pace it as quickly as possible, without stopping to sleep."

The knot stretched to Naysin's throat and became a noose. So *that's* why those first pale men had been creating such a labor-intensive path... Long ago, he'd realized his capture was just an afterthought. But he'd never suspected that the men's real purpose had been this devious.

"My cousin saw them measuring it off. Pumping their arms and swinging their legs like fools while their friends urged them on from the backs of those hornless elk. He said it was the funniest thing he'd ever seen — even better than when the pale men try to dance with their women." The Matowak spat again and looked away. "If only he'd realized they were laughing back at us. Maybe we could have done something. Instead, they used their falsehood to soothe their greedy consciences and take everything up to the Flint Peak, including my homeland." He shook his head. "As far as a man can *walk* in a day and a half..."

Numb, Naysin chewed his lip for a moment before signaling to the overseers. He was supposed to have been scolding the Matowak, translating how "fucking hard" the pale men would wield their whips the next time they caught the slave resting. But Naysin usually used these interludes to spread Degan's word. And, until now, to ask about the Walking Purchase.

It was exhausting work.

The physical labor, which his status as an interpreter didn't excuse him from, was tiring enough by itself. And then there was all the energy he spent being the mouthpiece for the two dominant forces on the plantation, a role that earned him equal parts special treatment and enmity.

But the Matowak didn't seem to care — he resumed working without complaint, mindful of the need to look busy. It was harvest time, when the race was on to cut as many sugar canes as possible. It was also the tensest period of the year; in the field, every slave had a cane knife in his hands, which made the overseers twitchier than usual. Degan liked to joke that the jumpiest pale men flinched every time a slave swung one of the blades at a cane's trunk. The notion was an exaggeration, of course. But there were days when it came close to the truth. The overseers definitely used their whips and fire sticks more during the harvest.

And an increase in confrontations meant an increase in calls for Naysin to translate reprimands, threats, and sarcastic apologies. Today was no different; he'd barely walked back to his position on the line before a different overseer called him over to deliver another "message" to another bleeding slave. Still overwhelmed by what he'd learned about the Walking Purchase, he went through the motions and said nothing about Degan.

But when Naysin finally returned to his post, the Hodensee's call to arms started to take on a new relevance. His exile had been unfair, an injustice he'd never forget, but that didn't mean his tribe deserved to be displaced by the pale men's trickery. The forest had been their home for longer than even the elders could remember.

And now it was probably overrun with pale men.

Pale men, women, and children who were hunting the game his people used to hunt, farming the fields his people used to farm, and playing on the courts where he and his friends used to play.

It was enough to make him swing his cane knife so hard he nearly lost his balance.

That night, when it was too dark to work and everyone was collapsing for a bit of badly-needed sleep, Naysin found Degan and finally said the words his mentor had been waiting to hear: "I'm ready."

— « O » —

Bimshire had been their prison for three years. A pretty prison; it was a picturesque, Anglo-controlled island in a sea the pale men called the "Carib." But it felt alien; the animals were small and strange, the vegetation was too bright, and the ocean was oppressively close.

Bimshire was also hot as fire.

Naysin and the rest of the slaves rarely had time to feel homesick, however. The pale men worked them to the bone, from sunup to sundown. During and after the harvest season came the boiling season, when they refined sugar out of the canes and into wooden barrels. After that came shipping season, then maintenance season, planting season, and harvest season again. It was a harsh, unforgiving cycle that left little strength for matters that didn't relate to survival.

But Degan was driven.

Despite — and maybe because of — the daily punishment, he found the energy to preach his message of redemption. Naysin had been his only audience in the beginning, but now the Hodensee tried to make a new convert every few nights. Sometimes they attempted to inspire two slaves at once, and occasionally they were bold enough to talk to three, but never more — the pale men were constantly on the alert for suspicious gatherings. And small groups were more efficient anyways. It just didn't make sense to have members of different tribes present, not when Naysin was the only slave who could speak to everyone without resorting to Anglo. Time was always short, and they didn't want to waste it translating words more than once.

Tonight, though, Degan and Naysin talked only to each other.

"Are you sure, little Lepane?" the Hodensee asked after a long pause. His black hair had grown out within a few moons of their arrival — he'd said he couldn't justify a mohawk while he was subservient to pale men — but Naysin could still see the original pattern's outlines. He wasn't comfortable with Degan's crooked nose either, or the way his tendons jumped off his hands like taut cords. In the dark of the ship's hold, Naysin had formed a different image of his mentor, and even three winters later, part of him refused to reconcile that projection with the reality sunlight had revealed.

"I said I was ready, didn't I?" His voice nearly cracked on the last word. He hated being called "little Lepane" now, and Degan knew it.

The Hodensee shook his head. "I'm sorry. It's just ... a sudden change of heart."

"I can suddenly change my heart back, if that would make you feel better."

Degan laughed solemnly. "No. No, I'm glad you're ready to do more than talking and listening."

Naysin shrugged impatiently. He found eavesdropping more enjoyable than interpreting — being able to understand anyone on the plantation meant he was rarely bored — but both roles seemed empty to him now. He was ready for action.

"All right," Degan continued, sensing his apprentice's mood. "Tomorrow, show me what you can do."

— « o » —

Tomorrow turned into the next day and the day after that before they found an opportunity for a private demonstration. The pale men didn't keep them chained like they'd been on the boat, but it wasn't easy to go unnoticed, even briefly. And not just because the overseers were ever-watchful; Degan had good reason to believe that, in return for petty favors, several of the slaves fed information to their captors.

While he watched for a chance to slip away, Naysin did his best to stick to his routine. His anger at learning the truth about the Walking Purchase had cooled, but the sense that he needed to be *doing* something remained. It wasn't enough to blend into the background anymore; for the first time in a long while, he wanted to be noticed.

But on the second day of waiting, a brief exchange between overseers temporarily interrupted Naysin's brooding.

"Collins found another devil with pustules on his forehead," said Danny, the smaller and more vicious of the two pale men. Collins was the plantation's version of a medicine man.

"You mean the pox is back?" Arthur, the other overseer, shuddered and spat. They'd summoned Naysin to translate a message for them, but they'd decided to make him wait while they ate their lunch. It was absurd how often they forgot he could understand gossip as easily as he could orders.

"Collins thinks so. Maybe black this time."

"Black pox. Bloody hell, Danny, this is the fourth time in three years. These devils have weaker constitutions than my daughters."

As the conversation lagged, Naysin thought about the friends he'd had on the plantation — all two of them. Last summer they'd both been struck down by the plague. And according to the steady stream of new arrivals, it continued to wreak similar devastation back across the water, even on tribes that had never seen Anglos or Espans. The pale men weren't immune — Naysin had seen several with the symptoms — but they seemed to catch it less and survive it more. Degan said it was because they'd carried it from their homeland, so they were less vulnerable to it.

"Did Collins start a quarantine?" Arthur eventually asked.

"Of a sort." Danny raised his eyebrows. "He dug a pit."

Arthur whistled. "But I can't say I disagree. If we lose half the devils before boiling season again…"

"Miller had a notion about that. He said the last time he went to the market, the cotton merchant was talking up these tar skins he bought in Afrii. Swears they don't get sick as easy, and that they're used to hellish heat like ours." Danny shrugged. "Not sure if I believe it, but if he's right, maybe we'll change out our stock with something a little hardier."

Arthur laughed. "It wouldn't take much."

Usually Naysin had no trouble suppressing his anger when his people were disparaged by a pale man — Degan had helped him sort out discretion and valor a long time ago. But today … it was hard not to say something.

So he forced himself to focus on the overseers' new words: "tar skins." From "Afrii," wherever that was. Another people in bondage to the pale men … a people the pale men might use to replace his own. Naysin couldn't decide if that was a good or bad thing. Degan would probably say bad, but Naysin wasn't sure he wanted to mention it. When he and the Hodensee finally had a chance to step out behind the slave quarters and slip into the undergrowth, though, Naysin couldn't think about anything but proving himself.

"Show me," Degan said softly once they'd reached a small clearing. They were still on the plantation, near the border but not close enough that they needed to worry about the guards who patrolled the perimeter.

Naysin took a deep breath and crinkled his nose. "How?" he whispered. Suddenly all the ways he blew off *Mir* — to compensate for the **Kug** he expended while translating — seemed like little nothings.

Degan laughed quietly. "Good question." Walking over to the nearest tree, he picked up a coconut, turned, and hurled it at Naysin. "Defend yourself."

The furry missile smashed into his chest and stole his wind. He felt dual flickers of anger and shame as the coconut ricocheted away, but just before it would have hit the ground, the fruit burst into a spray of juice and shards. Spattered but unharmed, Naysin wiped his face clean and smiled defiantly.

Degan swallowed his smile and nodded. "So you can destroy. That's good — you'll need to show strength." Clucking his tongue, he walked back to Naysin, bent down, and picked up one of the larger fragments. In one quick motion, the Hodensee used the shard to cut a thin line into his right forearm. "Heal me."

The longer Naysin looked at the oozing red streak, the sicker he felt. "I haven't done anything like that before."

Degan's response was simple: "Try."

Naysin chewed his lower lip for a moment before taking hold of his mentor's injured arm. Exhaling slowly, he stared at the wound, searching for something to manipulate: lines of energy ... beads of motion ... a hint of the underlying vitality...

But he couldn't see anything but skin and blood. "I don't know if I can do this."

"Try harder."

Naysin shook his head. Then a thought struck him: was he supposed to be using **Kug** or *Mir*? Out of habit, he'd been looking for ways to apply *Mir*, since he normally only tapped **Kug** for translating. But wouldn't healing involve injecting order? Strengthening weakened bonds and restructuring broken ones? It made sense. Armed with this new perspective, he searched again, doing his best not to focus on the way blood was pooling under Degan's arm hair, like a languid river flooding a dark forest.

After several breaths, Naysin finally began to *see* the sundered connections on either side of the wound, the severed fibers that were already creeping toward each other as the Hodensee's body started to heal itself. All he had to do was accelerate the process and get the fibers to knit themselves back together at a faster rate. He tried to visualize the ends of the wound doing just that ... but the task was more difficult than anything he'd attempted.

"Try harder," Degan hissed.

Redoubling his efforts, Naysin leaned in, coming so close to the wound he could have licked the blood away. With a horrendous effort, he summoned a huge quantity of **Kug** and hurled it at Degan's arm, half expecting the impact to knock the Hodensee down like a blow from a moose. Instead, the cut healed over.

"By Awhen's tears." The Hodensee sounded truly awed.

Naysin didn't care. He'd clenched his eyes shut as soon as he'd seen his mentor's skin restored — the pain in his head was suddenly immense, worse than any previous aftereffects; he'd never shamaned that much of one energy before.

Amidst the agony, he felt Degan's fingertips on his arm. "Your veins..."

Gritting his teeth, Naysin forced his eyes open and saw what the Hodensee was marveling at.

"Black. Every one of them."

His blood had turned to ash, just like that night in the Longest House.

"And your tattoo — the black is spilling into the white."

Then Naysin lost control, and a surge of *Mir* roared out of his core and detonated every coconut within sight.

Panting, he fell to the ground as sticky shards rained down around them. It hurt when some of the fragments punctured his skin, but a surge of wellbeing washed away the pain, a sense of equilibrium restored.

His relief faded when he noticed his hands, which he'd pressed against the dirt to cushion his fall, were crisscrossed by *two* colors now: a fading black in his veins, and a gleaming white in his arteries.

Chapter Nine

Rising

This is the one I've been speaking of." Degan glanced at Naysin, a subtler acknowledgment than pointing or resting a hand on his protégé's shoulder. "His smoky hair speaks of his transcendence, and his powers are as formidable as the Twins'."

Naysin tried not to squirm. He didn't like anyone talking about his graying hair, and he really didn't like Degan comparing him to Oterong and Tawiskaron, the brothers of Hodensee lore. He still wanted to *do* something, but every time Degan held him up as a savior, he remembered his hands riddled with lines of light and dark.

At least tonight's recruits were both Hodensee, so Degan didn't need him to translate. Repeating his praises had made the earlier versions of this presentation especially uncomfortable.

He wasn't allowed to remain idle for long, however.

"Degan, you know you have our respect," Oheo, the older of the two Hodensee, said after an incredulous pause, "but you'll pardon me if I need more than your word."

"I'd expect nothing less," Degan replied. "Naysin? Remember: this is for our eyes *only*."

He nodded. After the demonstration in the clearing, they'd talked about the need to prove himself in a way that was more circumspect. Degan had emphasized this point several times before they parted that night, but he'd left the details to Naysin.

He looked up and waited for the Hodensee to do the same. "You see the Hunter's Belt?" It was a cloudless night, and the constellation was clearly visible through the smoke hole in the shack's ceiling. Out of the corner of his vision, he saw Oheo nod, and heard Otetiani, the youngest Hodensee, murmur an expectant, "Yes."

"Watch closely." Naysin allowed his audience another moment to focus and then began shamaning three small streams of **Kug**. The first flow looped the middle star to the right; the second arced the right star to the left; and the third swung the left star to the center. It was a simple yet effective illusion that had drawn gasps every time he'd employed it.

As soon as it was over, Otetiani looked down at Naysin in disbelief. Oheo studied the new sequence for a few more beats before whispering, "We're with you."

Degan smiled wolfishly. "Tell only those you trust."

— « o » —

Acceptance didn't come over night. During the day, Naysin still had to fulfill his role as the pale men's voice, and for many skeptics, this was too much to put aside. But others appreciated the strategic advantage of having a "fox of many pelts" in a position of prominence.

And some just believed.

They were the hardest to deal with. Most of those who knew regarded him with simple respect, a welcome change from their previous indifference. The ones who outright worshipped him, however — whispering about a "young god in our midst" and casting their eyes down when he passed — made him feel like an impostor.

Even worse, part of him liked it. A large part; he daydreamed constantly about living up to this type of reaction. Degan would have approved. The Hodensee was always pressing him to be *more*, to do everything he could to turn back the "pale tide threatening to drown the original people."

The original people. A play on "Lepane," which Degan knew full well meant that very thing. The Hodensee had started using it to refer to all tribes — anyone who'd lived on the mainland before the pale men came. Naysin still wasn't sure how he felt about this appropriation. Or really, anything else right now.

Being a savior was confusing.

But while Naysin spent most of his free time bouncing between doubts and fantasies, Degan was inhumanly busy during the moon before the uprising: spreading his message, organizing the theft of weapons, fine-tuning his plan... The Hodensee was a cone cloud of impassioned action. It was exciting to be a part of, but it was also terrifying. And one night by the fire, three of the more devout Pekout drove home the true risk.

"Karakwa," the shortest one began solemnly, using Degan's new name for Naysin. (It meant "Sun," and he hated it). "We're glad you've come."

"Truly," the tallest agreed softly. "You give us hope."

"More than hope," the third added. "Certainty. For the first time, I *know* we'll escape this rock."

When they didn't say anything more, Naysin offered an awkward, "You're welcome," hoping it would be enough.

It wasn't. "And we are grateful," the short one started again. "But we've come to ask a favor."

"Degan says I shouldn't do anything to attract 'undue attention' until the time comes."

"No, you misunderstand... I ... I spoke badly," the short one stammered. "Nothing you have to do now. Just..."

"Make sure Uncas lives through it," the tall one said, putting his hand on the third Pekout's shoulder.

"One of the three of us," Uncas corrected angrily, looking back and forth between the other two.

"Just Uncas," the tall one reiterated.

"His wife," the short one explained, finding his fluency again, "our sister, is waiting for him. He must live."

Uncas balled his hands into fists. "That wasn't what we agreed to."

"Uncas ... it's been said, and it can't be unasked."

The three stared at each other in heated silence before turning back to look at Naysin.

Utterly bewildered now, he started to voice a question and then stopped, unsure where to begin. Eventually he just nodded.

This time, his response was enough. The three breathed their thanks — with varying degrees of sincerity — and left with slight bows of their heads. Naysin didn't figure anything more out by watching them leave, and he remained just as confused when he finally went to sleep early that morning.

The next day, as he labored next to Degan under the ever-brutal sun, he quietly asked the Hodensee how likely their attempt was to succeed.

"With you?" Degan paused to wipe sweat from his brow and glance at Naysin. "We won't fail, but there will be casualties."

"How can you be so sure?"

"Because I believe in you — although I'm still waiting for you to do the same — and because these things are always messy. Savior or not."

Naysin ignored the "savior" comment. "These things?"

Degan started wielding his cane knife again, punctuating his sentences with quick, powerful swings. "There have been at least two other major attempts on this plantation. The most recent was seven winters ago. And some of our brethren who've worked other fields in the area know stories about three or four more. One uprising ten and twenty winters ago reached almost every building on the island."

"Then we already know it's possible. Right?"

The Hodensee shook his head. "We know an 'attempt' is possible, but I could have told you that before I asked around. Succeeding is another matter. Of the five rebellions I know about, treachery undid the first, three were crushed within two days, and the last one — the biggest — only made it a half-moon before pale men from ships came to hang everyone involved."

"That's encouraging."

"But they didn't have you."

Naysin blew out a slow stream of air. "What if I'm not enough?"

Degan shook his head again, started to say something, stopped, and changed tacks. "Let's say everything I've been telling you is a lie. Fine. Forget it, and just think about the last three years. Now tell me you don't want to at least try."

“...I suppose.”

— « o » —

The pressure kept building: the significant looks, the weighty expectations, the ever-present tension in his body... Degan wouldn't name the day yet, but everything seemed to be falling into place. His agents had secured access to enough cane knives and clubs to arm everyone willing to fight, and the pale men were beginning to relax their guard now that harvesting season was nearly over. The time had almost come.

And it made Naysin sick to think about.

He wanted to be free — truly wanted to be free — but every morning he woke to a legion of doubts. There was so much riding on his "abilities," so many lives depending on something he couldn't fully control. He'd never felt more insecure.

Meeting Chogan didn't help matters.

The young Lepane was from a tribe Naysin's had often traded with. But the two boys hadn't met each other before the night Degan proselytized Chogan and his friends. After Naysin finished realigning the Hunter's Belt, his near-kin seemed even more impressed than the others. Quiet, but impressed. The next day, he approached Naysin at what passed for dinner and respectfully asked if he could share his (moldy) bread with the "Lepane shaman who goes by a Hodensee name."

Naysin wasn't sure whether to bristle or laugh, so he just shrugged and motioned with his head toward the ground.

"Thank you," Chogan said solemnly. Sitting quickly, he pursed his lips, as if he wanted to say something but couldn't figure out how to start.

Naysin spent the silence finishing his bread and comparing the other boy's chubby cheeks to a woodchuck's.

"That was real?" Chogan eventually blurted out.

"You mean last night?"

"Yes."

"It was."

"Spirits and lakes." Chogan looked suitably impressed again.

Naysin felt his head swelling despite himself.

"That's incredible. Is it ... do you think it's Gilmekon flowing through you?"

Pride turned to anger as Naysin stared at Chogan for several moments before pushing himself to his feet. "Who else would it be?" He started walking away.

"No! No, you mistake me, Karakwa." Chogan's voice sounded wretched as it came to Naysin over his shoulder. "I only meant ... I don't know what I meant. I'm sorry."

Naysin imagined his fellow Lepane hanging his head in shame. He didn't turn back, though — he was too afraid of what he might do.

The next night, Oheo made him wish he *had* done something. The old man was like a grandfather to him now, but the Hodensee gave too much credence to idle talk, and when he approached one evening, his eyes were even flintier than usual. "There's a new rumor about you," he whispered.

"When isn't there?" Naysin murmured tiredly, falling into line with the other slaves as the overseers herded them toward their meager quarters.

"This one's dangerous — not just some foolish claim about you being the pale men's lackey. This is from another Lepane boy who says he knew your tribe. Says he knows that mark over your eye too; supposedly his medicine man put the same symbol on an evil tree near their sweat house. He drew the mark to lock in a manitouk that entered the tree through its roots."

Naysin stared at the old Hodensee for a breath before stamping the ground and pointing at his toes. "Do these look like roots to you?"

"Peace, boy! I'm a messenger, not a believer." Oheo rubbed his work-stiffened fingers together. "You might want to address this one, though. I know Degan prefers not to acknowledge them, but I've heard grumbling."

Naysin nodded and headed for his section of the hut. Chogan's face flickered across his mind as he lay down; what a viper. Acting respectful the day before when all he really wanted was a better look at Naysin's brand. He'd never noticed the other Lepane speaking Anglo, but Chogan must have been fluent enough in the pale men's tongue if he could spread the lie this quickly.

Except that it wasn't really a lie.

Naysin raised his head off the dirt floor and then let it fall back, trying not to cry. The tattoo said everything to those who knew what to look for. Degan called it a mark of power when anyone asked, but that was the true lie. The tattoo was a brand, a symbol of his tribe's disdain, his mother's betrayal … and his real fathers' presence. *Fathers* plural. The tattoo was a signal fire for all of this, one that would burn brightly for the rest of his life.

Unless he took it off.

The thought tumbled through his head like a boulder pushed down a ridge. Everyone kept telling him he could do anything. So why not this? Why not remove the stain that made his life so miserable?

Surging with energy, he sprang up and looked around. He was alone; the rest of the slaves were at dinner. If he could do it quickly… But what would he tell them if he succeeded? How would he explain?

Naysin decided he didn't care. If he could do this, he'd gladly deal with the consequences.

He needed to be able to *see*, though. And nothing in the one-room hut was shiny enough to cast a reflection. He could walk to the water's edge … or he could warm up by creating his own reflective surface.

Swallowing, Naysin traced a circle in the dirt and pictured it melting, fusing together like he'd once seen happen to sand after an enormous bonfire on the beach. It took more *Mir* than he'd hoped, but after a moment's concentration, he had a black mirror.

Swallowing again, Naysin crouched in front of his creation … and realized he didn't have any idea how to go about removing the tattoo staring back at him. The brand was equal parts black and white again; the ratio of dark to light ink had rebalanced itself shortly after he'd destroyed the coconuts.

Deciding it was best to start small, he began with a little **Kug**, hoping to use it to heal the scar. The attempt failed, but it reduced the headache he'd developed while making the mirror.

Less certain now, he stared harder at the tattoo, zeroing in on its center ... on the crooked slash it made across his eyelid ... on the individual needle-pricks he could still feel when he recalled that night ... on the first dot, just below his lower eyelash — the first puncture...

He tried to erase it.

When his initial burst of *Mir* didn't do anything, he tried successively larger ones, until the pain in his head made him gasp. But the black and white dots were still there, still surrounding and crossing his eye.

Then he used fire.

Naysin cried out as a whisper of smoke rose from the central dot. The pain in his head tripled, and his skin began to ache. Even as he smelled his flesh burning, however, he knew the tattoo wasn't diminishing in the slightest. He could *feel* its stability, its unnatural resilience.

Sweating profusely now, Naysin lowered his head to within a finger's breadth of the dirt mirror, using its guidance to throw everything he had at the brand. **Kug** ... *Mir* ... the first combination of the two he'd ever attempted ... he tried it all.

None of it made a bit of difference.

Crushed, Naysin rolled onto his side. The pain in his head had subsided to a dull ache — that last surge must have righted his internal balance — but he was exhausted. He felt weak. Weak and ravenous, so hungry that flashes of those terrible first moons on his own started coming back. And the brand was still blighting his face. It had a weight to it now, a taunting heft that wasn't just his imagination. The council's tattoo artists must have etched him with truly powerful magic, something stronger than even he could break.

But his skin could still tear.

Turning back to his mirror, Naysin curled one hand into a fist and brought it down on the dark surface. It shattered like dirt shouldn't, breaking into shards of all different sizes, several of which lodged in his hand. Panting, he eased the largest fragment from his palm and raised the edge to his face, just below the tattoo. But as streams of blood ran down his arm and a single red drop slithered along the side of his nose, he hesitated.

The sound of footsteps broke through his indecisiveness, and he cast the shard away like a hot coal as Degan entered the hut.

The Hodensee drew up short when he saw the blood.

"I was trying something," Naysin said quickly. "It didn't work."

Degan gave him a hard look before shaking his head. "Well I hope you have more success tonight. Because we're moving."

It was Naysin's turn to widen his eyes in surprise. "Tonight?"

"Are you up to it?"

Naysin couldn't meet Degan's gaze any longer, so he turned his own on his injured hand, carefully spreading his fingers so he could extract the other dirt shards. He wasn't ready, but… "I'll try to be."

Chapter Ten

Release

The dog's head didn't look appetizing.

They were in the boiling house, the stone building where some of the slaves spent their lives distilling sugarcane juice down to raw sugar. Degan had gathered the rebellion's "vanguard" to distribute the weapons they'd managed to collect: mostly cane knifes and a few axes, all buried beneath the gigantic brick furnace, below the opening used to stoke the fire and pull out the ashes. He'd passed the weapons out one by one, each handoff illuminated by coals and moonlight.

But arming wasn't Degan's only purpose here. Upon arriving, he'd laid the spitted corpse of a freshly killed yellow dog — one of the overseers' — atop the smoldering furnace. The smell of cooking cur had filled the air as the Hodensee murmured instructions to each rebel.

And now that the last blade was in hand, Degan was climbing up the furnace scaffolding again. When he reached the top, he smiled at the dog and smacked his lips. Then he jumped back down, studied the other slaves, and turned to Naysin with four fingers held up.

Naysin froze. The plan had always been three, and even that was pushing it; he would have preferred two. But Degan wore the same expression he'd flashed earlier that night in the hut, and his fervor shamed Naysin into nodding.

Visibly pleased, the Hodensee turned back to the other slaves and rapidly pointed to four of them. Once they'd stepped forward, Degan streaked their left cheeks with a dab of bone char, the granular remains of burned animal skeletons. Normally the stuff was used to dye raw sugar from yellow to white, but tonight its application signified something else.

"These Four were chosen to be the fingers of Karakwa," Degan said softly, his own fingers pale with char. "They will lead the fight."

The four men stood proudly as Naysin translated, their eyes glittering in the dim light. The rest of the slaves gazed at them enviously until Degan raised his hand. "But first, we feast on our enemy."

With a fierce smile on his face, he climbed the scaffolding once more and brought down the dog. It wasn't all the way cooked — the furnace had cooled since its midday peak — but Degan didn't seem to mind. He slapped the dog onto a hogshead barrel and gestured for a cane knife. Once he was satisfied that the blade was sharp enough, he gave a solemn nod to Naysin and chopped off the dog's head.

Wincing, Naysin waited uneasily as Degan made a show of trimming bits of bone and sinew from the animal's neck. He'd explained the Hodensee tradition to Naysin on their way to the boiling house: on the eve of battle, dog meat, symbolizing the enemy's flesh and blood, was eaten to signify the coming victory. And the most fearsome warrior got the head. "A great honor," Degan had emphasized. Naysin had tried not to wrinkle his nose in disgust. His people had eaten dogs in lean years before, but ... the head?

Now he was being presented with the skinned-but-still-fleshy skull while the "Chosen Four" each received a leg, and everyone was looking to him to begin the ceremonial feast.

He hesitated.

The dog's head, which he held gingerly by its ear holes, was still gruesomely lifelike. Heavy, too. And dripping.

"Ah, but how could I forget the seasoning," Degan said before prying off the barrel's lid, reaching in, and pulling out a handful of sugar. He took the finishing touch to each of the feasters, sprinkling it liberally over their steaming meat as several of the onlookers grunted in appreciation. Naysin was last in line, and as the Hodensee applied the sugar to the skull, he gave his protégé a questioning look.

Naysin responded by taking a deep breath, closing his eyes, and gnawing into a scrap of hot flesh.

Several messy bites later, he'd eaten all he could stand. It seemed to be enough; Degan looked proud, and the other feasters had finished their meals with relish.

"Now," Degan whispered. "Cloak the Four, and let us begin."

Naysin wiped the dog's fluids from his face and prepared himself for his second task. This wasn't going to be any easier — less repulsive, but just as hard. It was too late to turn back, though. He had to try, if only so Degan would stop looking at him like that.

Exhaling loudly, Naysin gestured for the Four to circle around him. Once they'd gathered, he positioned them so that he could see the bone char on their left cheeks. The pale bone char...

Pale as a pale man's skin.

Focusing on that image, Naysin expanded the char across the Four's cheeks, using alternate flows of **Kug** and *Mir* to spread and strengthen the whiteness until it engulfed their faces. He ignored the onlookers' gasps — they didn't matter. Nothing mattered but continuing to paint the bone char's paleness across the whole of the Four's bodies: up their scalps ... down their necks ... over their arms ... across their chests ... through their legs ... into their toes.

Within a twenty-count, it was done, and the illusion was every bit as hard to maintain as Naysin had feared.

Oh, there was plenty of truth to the transformation that had the Four staring at themselves in disbelief. At a glance, their body-masks were undetectable. But only because he was continuously smoothing out the imperfections that kept threatening to resurface. And then there was the added strain of edging each man with a whisper of his original redness ... a superimposition that looked a little like two cougars sharing the same tawny hindquarters. Naysin shook his head to wipe away the comparison and nearly lost his balance.

Degan steadied him. "You can see past the bone char," he said softly to the rest of the slaves as he flashed Naysin a proud look. "But the pale men won't. Follow the Four as they lead us to the victory Karakwa has enabled. Be swift; these nights come only once in a man's life."

— « o » —

The initial phases of Degan's assault were as silent and deadly as he'd hoped. First, the Four sauntered up to the guards posted outside the slave quarters and slit their throats. Next, as runners slipped inside to rouse the rest of the slaves, the Four completed their disguises by taking up the dead guards' fire sticks.

Then it was on to the pale men's compound.

The Four walked in the open, shouldering their fire sticks like they'd seen true pale men do. Around them streamed a shadowy army of bloody-minded slaves.

And behind all of them came Naysin, mounted on Degan's shoulders and nearly insensible.

The strain of preserving the Four's illusions was terrible and growing worse — it had been too much effort to walk more than a few steps out of the boiling house, or even acknowledge Degan when the Hodensee picked him up. His head felt like it was going to implode with the pressure of shamaning so much **Kug**, and he could sense his veins starting to shine black, striping him with lines darker than the surrounding night.

It was incredibly tempting to compensate with a giant blast of *Mir*. A pillar of fire, a column of wind… But anything of the sort would alert their captors. So he held off and cursed Degan for shaming him into reaching for four. Four illusions to maintain when two would have been enough. More than enough. Gilmekon, but it hurt.

Three more pale men appeared — drunk, by the look of their swaying walk — and were cut down by the Four. The other slaves swarmed the bodies almost before they hit the ground; only Degan's hiss kept his soldiers from tearing the corpses apart. Clearly, the rebels were ready to be done with caution. Degan had expected this to happen, but he hadn't seemed particularly worried about it. "As long as we can steer the energy," he'd said, "and suppress it until we're at the barracks."

They were only a field-length away when a shout rang out; a pale man returning from the latrine had spotted one of the undisguised slaves. Pants still unbuttoned, the oaf was calling out to the Four, urging them to use their fire sticks. Instead, the Four hesitated, as did the rest of the slaves ... until the pale man stamped his foot in a way that marked him as the most violent overseer. A petty tyrant who was standing in front of them. Unarmed, alone, and unsuspecting.

As one, the shadows surged. Twenty different war cries in as many tongues rang out, and the pale man was in pieces before he'd registered what was happening.

"The barracks!" roared Degan, his own emotion bubbling over as he charged the squat building whose windows were starting to fill with lamp-light. Naysin bounced on the Hodensee's shoulders like a fool he'd once seen trying to ride a moose.

Just before they reached the door, a pale man flung it open and aimed his fire stick. Its black barrel hovered above the ground for an endless moment before spewing smoke and launching a bullet into Degan's left shoulder. He tried to twist as he fell backward, but he wasn't quick enough; Naysin still broke the worst of their fall, and the added pain pushed him into a place of dreadful clarity.

The door to the barracks closed; he let go of the **Kug** around the Four.

More fire sticks emerged from the barracks' windows; he wondered briefly why some of the **Kug** remained.

The slave army charged the pale men's fortifications; he welcomed the *Mir* coalescing inside him.

A rolling barrage of smoke and bullets issued forth from the barracks; he gathered the *Mir* into a ball.

Slaves screamed and died and clambered over each other; he let loose an immense starburst of fire that cleansed his pain and set the compound ablaze.

Now that *is what we've been waiting for.*

Naysin's calm crumbled like dried mud, and as he registered the hot, noisy reality of the chaos around him, he remembered — for the first time in a long while — how much he hated the sound of the cougar-men's thoughts.

But we never would have made you exercise such power as a false savior.

"Leave me alone!" yelled Naysin, his anguish lost in the maelstrom of opening doors, sprinting feet, cutting cane knives, blasting fire sticks, panting men, bleeding bodies, burning wood, crackling flesh... "I didn't mean to do it!"

Overwhelmed by the urge to take back what he'd done, Naysin swept the compound with a sheet of wind from off the ocean, extinguishing the flames and knocking every slave and pale man to the ground.

Agony immediately suffused his bones as white light flared from his arteries. The pain wasn't from pressure anymore; now it was the rupturing of disintegration. He lost consciousness as Degan yelled something in his ear and grabbed his arm with bloody fingers.

Chapter Eleven

Faces of Victory

Naysin woke to blue sky and a sea breeze … in a location he'd never been before.

Even before he'd blinked the darkness from his eyes, he knew he was somewhere different. The sand beneath him felt grittier. And the beach's contours were more angular.

This was somewhere off the plantation.

This was freedom.

He was able to savor the thought for two whole breaths before pain flooded his body again.

Naysin managed to stay conscious, but he could feel himself slipping back into darkness, and he knew he had to do something quickly. Something with **Kug** to balance out all the *Mir* he'd expended in the compound. Something big.

Without any explicit plan, he started spreading **Kug** across the beach, using it to harden pockets of sand and accentuate the angles that had stood out to him so clearly in his brief observation of the area's topography. As he worked, the pain lessened … and he realized how much he liked actually *making* something with his powers.

Cautiously intrigued, Naysin changed the sand sculpture to a wave pattern, one that ran perpendicular to the surf instead of parallel. He smiled when he was done. The effect was subtle, but anyone who noticed the ripples running the wrong way would stop and stare.

Fascinated himself, he focused on another section of sand and began whipping it back and forth into various shapes:

a circle, a square, an arrowhead. Then he tried animals: a squirrel, a moose, a porcupine. Then people: Degan, his childhood friend Hachek, Takhi (his first crush), and—

His mother.

Her face sprang from the sand without warning, the prominent curves of her nose and cheekbones rising like shark fins in calm water.

Shocked into stillness, Naysin stared at her achingly familiar features. It was definitely her: his mother as he'd last seen her awake, the evening before he left their cave. Loving and beautiful and desperate and ashamed.

The same emotions were fighting for prominence in his own head — too many feelings to sort out, much less deal with. It was easier just to loose a blast of *Mir* and burn the sand away.

But his mother's face was still there when the last flames flickered and died. And now she *shone*, reflecting the morning sun like a jewel. Because he'd turned her to glass, with a sheen even more brilliant than his mirror of dirt. The lines of her complicated expression would be there for every tide to ebb and flow over, day in and day out, for longer than he cared to imagine...

"So much for not drawing attention to ourselves." Degan's voice didn't sound annoyed, though; mostly just awed, and a little amused. "Who is she?" He'd come up from behind Naysin, his footsteps muffled by the only sand in sight that was still sand.

"Just a face." Naysin turned to look at the Hodensee, taking in the older man's bloodstained bandage and singed eyebrows without comment. "So we did it?"

"We did it." Degan looked proud. And tired. "It's not over yet, and we still have a long way to go until we reach the safe haven, but yes, *you* did it. The pale men fled their barracks after it started burning, and they didn't have time to reload their fire sticks in the open. It was over soon after you brought the wind. The plantation is in ruins, and those of us who survived are free."

Naysin deflected the praise with a shrug. "The safe haven?"

"An abandoned settlement near the center of the island, in the wilds. We're only staying there long enough for you to figure out how to get us across the water and back home."

"Me again?"

Degan gave him a piercing look. "Who else? We don't have the materials or time to make canoes before other pale men find us. And we're too few now to take their port. No, it has to be you again. Only you could have brought us this far; only you can take us the rest of the way." He shook his head and gripped Naysin's shoulder with his good arm. "I had you laid out here so you would see the water when you woke, but it seems to have provided the wrong kind of inspiration. Let's correct that; I have something else you need to see."

Naysin did his best to hide a tremor of foreboding. "What?"

"Come with me."

— « o » —

Most of the men in the makeshift camp had worse burns than Degan. And quite a few had more severe injuries. But all of them wore grim smiles — the smiles of men grateful to be alive and, above all else, free. Their expressions made Naysin actually feel a little like the savior Degan spoke of so much.

Until he saw the naked pale man staked to the scaffold in the camp's center. "What are we doing with him?"

"Carrying out Hodensee tradition," Degan said fiercely, his passion confirming that this — and not the freed slaves' smiles — was what he'd wanted Naysin to see. "Before the battle, we eat a symbol of the enemy's flesh and blood to presage our victory; after that victory, we test our vanquished enemy's courage by ripping his *actual* flesh and spilling his *actual* blood, to see if he begs for mercy... Of course, we already know this one's measure." He spat in the pale man's direction, and Naysin finally recognized the captive: another of the plantation's overseers.

The slaver's face was contorted with pain — his fingernails had been torn off, and most of his bones looked to have been broken. "This is your tradition," Naysin managed to get out through the bile he was fighting to keep down, "not the rest of ours."

Degan gave him an appraising look before smiling fiercely again. "True. But no one else objected." With his good arm, he made a sweeping gesture that emphasized how many of the freed slaves were enjoying the pale man's suffering. "Next they'll pierce his ears with burning sticks, and tear off chunks of his flesh for him to eat. Once that breaks him, he'll be blinded and beheaded."

Naysin sucked a breath in through his teeth and sat heavily. Nodding, Degan focused on the proceedings, laughing darkly when one of the Hodensee torturers collected the blood pooling at the scaffold's base and slicked his hair into a red mohawk. Shortly thereafter, the pale man began sobbing for mercy, and a Dine used a cane knife to carry out the decapitation with two vicious hacks.

Naysin didn't even flinch when the overseer's head hit the ground — his emotions had drained out with the pale man's blood. He was a shell now, an empty vessel that didn't want to be filled...

"One more, and then we move on," Degan announced, watching the Hodensee with the red mohawk kick another pale man toward his death.

Something about this next victim's features tugged at Naysin's insulated calm. At first he resisted the pull, but the longer he looked, the odder the captive's face seemed ... as if it were a blend of two people. "What happened to the Four?" he heard himself ask.

"Killed. Or lost — they were never found. But they'll always be remembered as heroes."

Horror broke through Naysin's façade like a rain-swelled river smashing a beaver's dam. "Not all of them..." he said slowly. "That's Kemi."

Degan narrowed his eyes and stared at the captive's face. After a ten count, the Hodensee muttered an oath — the red outline was gone, but Kemi was undeniably there if you looked for him: the tallest of the Four, and the most respected. His mouth was too badly slashed to speak intelligibly, but it was clear now that what remained of his lips were trying to form Hellani words, not Anglo.

"Maybe I can change him back," Naysin started babbling. "Undo it, or put up another illusion that makes him look like himself again. I don't know why the first one became real, but I can try—"

"No." Degan's face hardened as he turned back to the scaffolding.

"No?" Naysin asked weakly.

"You'll shake the men's confidence."

"But I can—"

"You'll do nothing!" hissed Degan. "You could have left at any time during the last three years. Someone with your ability? I know you thought about it — I saw it in your eyes. But you stayed. You stayed to be something more than the sniveling kid who crawled next to me in that hold and cried for his mommy. You accepted a greater role, and this is what you did with it. Even saviors make mistakes. There are always casualties in war."

Then a wet thud signaled that Kemi was being staked to the scaffolding.

Standing up slowly, Naysin gave Degan a haunted look and slinked back to his mother's face.

— « o » —

A short while later — during Kemi's loud, lingering, and undeserved death — Naysin walked into the water and left the island behind.

Chapter Twelve

Back to the Sea

The journey across the ocean nearly killed Naysin.

At first, it seemed like exactly what he needed. He didn't have a clear-cut plan for crossing the surprisingly warm water; he just knew he had to get away from the island. And that he wanted to run. For the better part of four years, the overseers hadn't allowed him to move faster than a walk. So even though his shin had healed long ago, he'd never tested the mended bone's ability to bear the strain of long strides and heavy impacts.

Now he couldn't think of anything he wanted to do more.

The water was up to Naysin's calves when he started accelerating. Churning forward, he waited until his head was almost submerged before shamaning a band of **Kug**. The stiff energy hardened the water beneath his feet, buoying him a little more with each stride, until he was running across the surface of the ocean.

It felt incredible.

His smoky hair, devoid now of all but the slightest traces of its original black, streamed behind him along with strips of his ragged clothing, bouncing with every footfall as his lanky arms clawed the air. But after just a short sprint, he could feel his muscles and lungs burning in protest at the unfamiliar exertion. Spirits and lakes — it had been *far* too long since he'd last run. Reluctantly, he slowed to a walk … and stopped completely when he saw an enormous salmon slip through the water below him.

Then he comprehended the true enormity of what he was doing.

Under his toes, fish after fish swam by, most of which he didn't recognize. Some skittered away when they noticed his shadow, others seemed not to care, all of them were beautiful. And the water they lived in was even more amazing. Four years ago, he'd crossed it in a ship's hold, but he'd never been directly above it the way he was now.

No one had.

No one else had ever been able to see the ocean as a terrain that could be hiked. Each wave was a hill to climb over, followed by a ravine to climb out of. Rises and falls that moved, a living landscape he found absolutely transfixing ... until the sun's heat and the onset of a brutal headache ended his reverie.

He'd been expecting the hurt in his temples, the all-too-familiar tightening that came from using an excess of **Kug**. Now that the pain had finally arrived, he started compensating with *Mir*, coaxing the loose energy to coalesce into gusts of wind.

Naysin hadn't anticipated the true heat of the rising sun, however. He'd noticed how dazzling its reflected rays were out here in the open, but he hadn't realized how fast they'd overheat his skin, or how quickly they'd dry his throat.

It was time to move again.

He ran slower this time, jogging instead of sprinting. He also paid more attention to his heading, looking back at the shoreline several times to orient himself. It was mostly guesswork — Bimshire wasn't supposed to be a large island, but all he knew was his plantation. If he could find it, he could use its dock to get his bearings. North wouldn't be hard to identify; he'd watched ship after ship leave for the coast during his captivity. He just had to find the plantation.

With that in mind, Naysin adjusted his course to parallel the beach. He was many field-lengths out now, close enough that he could still see the island's main features, but far enough away that anyone who saw him would think he was just a trick of the sun. Later, when he started to tire again, he hit on the idea of shamaning wind behind him instead of scattering it aimlessly. It helped; the wind blew him onward as if he was a pale man's sail. He also found that he could drink handfuls of ocean by chasing out the salt with small bursts of *Mir* — he'd never felt so self-sufficient.

It took the rest of the morning to confirm his hunch, but he'd guessed right; turning to the left was the quicker route. As he rounded a familiar mini-peninsula, the plantation came into view ... as did several plumes of smoke from the main compound's smoldering ruins.

Calling off the wind for a moment, Naysin stared awhile at his former prison, watching little pale figures scurry about like ants trying to understand the destruction of their hill. Eventually, he swallowed, turned to locate the dock, and angled out from it in the direction he thought most likely to take him home.

By early afternoon, he noticed that the energy flowing out of him had started to mark him in the usual ways; the **Kug** he was using to harden the water's surface had prompted his veins to shine black, and the *Mir* he was calling to conjure the wind at his back had invoked a white glow in his arteries. It made for quite the reflection in the water ahead of him.

By midafternoon, he realized the sun was even more of a problem than he'd believed; its heat was beating down with alarming intensity. He didn't burn easily, but he'd also never been exposed like this. And there was only blue on the horizon, no upcoming shelter to shield him from the light, nothing to cast a shadow...

Except his body.

He was already projecting a small darkness. Could he ... move it? Elongate it? Stretch it with *Mir*? Inject **Kug** for reinforcement so his silhouette arced above him? The effort made his arteries and veins shine that much brighter, but after a few moments of concentration, his shadow draped him like a cloak cut from the night sky. The change in his appearance made him smile — he felt like something out of the Elder Council's stories. Something powerful.

By late afternoon, however, Naysin came across a problem he couldn't solve by shamaning: he was getting fatigued. He'd been careful to use equal amounts of **Kug** and *Mir*, so he wasn't suffering too badly from overuse. But maintaining the balance was exhausting, as was running so much after such a long layoff. He was also just plain tired. He'd passed out during the attack on the pale men's compound, but he hadn't actually slept. If he went to sleep now, though, he wasn't sure he could maintain the **Kug** that was keeping him afloat. He'd never tried anything like that before. And if he lapsed in the middle of the ocean, he'd sink.

So he kept going. Even as night set in … and his body began to shut down … and his eyelids became heavy as stone…

The only thing that kept Naysin awake until morning was hunger. The pangs started shortly after the horizon swallowed the sun's last light. He hadn't eaten in almost two days, and he wouldn't last much longer without food. He could use **Kug** to raise a fish and *Mir* to cook it … but images of Kemi kept coming back to Naysin every time he contemplated hunting in such a fashion.

No — no dwelling. It was better to keep going and trust his luck to the spirits.

Was that an invitation?

Naysin began scrambling up a particularly steep wave. "Leave me alone."

Well, since you clearly have things under control.

Just remember, we tried to teach you to fly.

Naysin snorted as he slid down the wave's watery crest, trying to ignore the twinge of remembrance in his shin. "Believe me, I haven't forgotten."

Are you certain you are recalling it correctly?

He stopped walking and let the wind glide him over the choppy water. "Quite certain."

Even though you only had twelve winters?

Think about it, Naysin; you are our only son.

And — as if that weren't enough — we depend on your health for our continued existence.

Which is why we have been doing whatever we can to help you use your powers.

Unobtrusively, of course. We've been respecting your wish not to be bothered.

"Until now."

It seemed like you were in need of a more direct intervention.

Truly, though: do you think you could have used so much Kug without my help?

Or so much Mir without mine?

"Maybe you just taught me well."

That we did — and you were a fast learner. But it wasn't enough.

And if you do not let us help you now…

All three of us might be under water by nightfall.

"How noble of you."

You are right; we will not deny it. Self-preservation guides our actions.

But so does love, Naysin. That's a powerful combination. It means, quite simply, that we have your best interests at heart.

And that we are in this together.

"Really. Then prove it."

Oh, we shall.

You have been wondering about your heading, yes?

"I know where I am."

Just to be safe, why don't you check your course against that ship's?

Startled, Naysin scanned the horizon, looking for the lie … but there, at the edge of his vision — slightly to the west of the direction he'd been traveling — was a white blur, barely distinguishable in the early morning light.

We will talk more after you have reassured yourself.

— « o » —

The pale men on the ship greeted Naysin with a cannon ball.

Back on the plantation, the overseers had occasionally spoken of guns that could punch holes in the bellies of their giant canoes or mow down a line of men. But he'd only half-believed the tales, and he'd certainly never seen such a weapon fired, much less been the target of one.

It was an experience he could have done without.

He was a field's length away when the first puff of smoke appeared above the ship's deck. The sound of an explosion, which echoed across the water like a thunderclap, was his second warning. The third was the appearance of a tiny orb that grew larger at an alarming rate.

Naysin ducked just in time; the force of the projectile's passing nearly scalped him. Unbalanced, he tripped over an oncoming wave and went sprawling across the ocean's surface. The fall made him lose his concentration long enough to sink partway beneath the water. Sputtering, he picked himself up to the sound of distant cheering, a celebration that petered out as he regained his feet and remembered what the pale men were seeing: the shadowy outline of a boy — no, a man — whose fibers shone black and white as he began sprinting across the water's surface.

Naysin was ready for the next cannon ball. He ran at it like he had the first, but this time he veered to the left just before the shot reached him, using gusts of *Mir*-wind to slow the ball down and speed himself up. Then he darted back to the right and resumed his trajectory. The effortless-looking sidestep had the desired effect; there were no cheers this time, only a few cries of dismay.

But the shots kept coming — one every seven ten-counts — and for all his bravado, Naysin wasn't feeling bold enough to move closer to the ship, even though he needed its shelter. So for the rest of the morning, he continued playing the deadly game with the increasingly dour pale men. His mood deteriorated as well; the adrenaline from surviving an attack, of making the pale men fear him — of just doing what he was doing — faded fast. In its place, all the strain and exhaustion of the last few days came flooding back.

And now he just wanted the pointless contest to end. He still wasn't any closer to land, or knowing where he was. And soon, very soon, he had to sleep. Eating would be nice, but his stomach had started folding in on itself, adopting the falling feeling that would dull his appetite for a day (after which his hunger would return with many times the intensity). No, what he needed was rest. A respite, free of the constant need to duck cannonballs, blow wind, and float on water.

A fish showed him the way.

It soared out of the water after a close-but-not-close-enough cannon ball whizzed by his head. The fish was large — it would have knocked the wind out of him if it had miscalculated its jump and hit him from behind. Instead, the gleaming creature flew high, cutting a perfect arc through the air before slipping seamlessly back into the ocean.

Naysin followed the fish without thinking, launching himself into a dive that sliced into the surface he'd been running on for most of a day. When the bubbles cleared, he found himself in a completely different world.

The salty water stung his eyes, but even if he hadn't been swimming for his life, he wouldn't have shut them. There were too many things he'd never seen before, too many kinds of fish swirling in schools that spiraled like cone clouds everywhere he looked. Here a small, green fish darted toward the sun; there a large, gray fish ate another. Truly, this was a place apart.

But the growing need in his lungs brought him back to the present. Focusing on the ship's wake, a churning trail that sundered the flickering ceiling above him, Naysin began swimming for the first time in years. Within moments, he knew he couldn't do it without help; the water was too dense, he too weak, and the ship too fast. So he tapped more *Mir*, using it to flex the water around him and funnel him forward. Soon he was hurtling toward the ship at an impossible rate. His chest was about to burst, however, and he still wasn't moving fast enough to get there in time.

Giving in, Naysin angled himself slightly upward, convulsed the water behind him, and rocketed above the surface like the fish had, curving up and back down in a graceful half-circle. He kept his mouth open the whole way, sucking in air as he imagined what he must look like to the pale men now.

When he entered the water again, he knew he was close; the ship had only looked to be twenty strides away. Which was good, given how much more exhausted he'd become. His original plan had been to bore into the ship and then seal the gap once he was safely inside. But he didn't have the strength left.

So when Naysin finally emerged next to the pale men's vessel, he settled for dangling from the massive oar they called a rudder. He couldn't quite reach the top of the board on his own; he had to coax one last wave into lifting him high enough. The barnacled edge was too narrow to rest on, though, and he knew he wouldn't be able to maintain his grip for long. Especially if he blacked out; darkness was already growing on the edges of his mind.

Willing himself to push a little further, Naysin summoned a ragged chain of **Kug** and used it to sculpt the rudder around his arms and chest. He couldn't make the wet wood as supportive as he wanted, but it held him when he let go and slipped into a dreamless sleep.

His last thought was that if the pale men saw him now, they'd think he looked like a beaten slave slumped in Bimshire's stocks.

Chapter Thirteen

Amadi

Four slightly slurred Anglo voices accompanied Naysin's return to consciousness:

"...like Jesua crossing the water..."

"...Satana, more likely."

"Maybe both. Did you see the way he shone? Like he was filled with equal measures of light and dark... A wraith on the sea."

"Doesn' much matter to me. I'm jus' glad my last shot hit him." This voice was the proudest — and most slurred.

"I know you think you're a crack shot with the bow chaser, but my eyes are better than any man's on this ship, and I'll swear on whatever you like that I saw that thing dive under your ball and swim off."

"He's got a point. Any man that can run on water isn't going to just eat iron and roll over."

The proud voice took on a sharper edge: "You talk like an authori ... you talk like an authority on the subject. But if you know so much, tell me this: why did the sea wraith jus' disappear?"

"Who said he's gone? Might be swimming below us as we speak."

"There's a sobering thought."

"Hush, little misses. You're safe now. Uncle Ramon took care of the scary wraith for you. Jus' drink your wine while we still have some."

The other sailors laughed at this, but their voices petered out before Naysin could hear their replies. The men must have moved to another part of the ship ... the ship he still clung to like a tick.

He only felt marginally more rested, which wasn't surprising given that he was soaked to his skin and embedded in a wooden board. But he was alive, and he didn't have to shaman anything to maintain his position. That had to count for something.

The cougar-men had been right, though. Naysin hated to admit it, but the ship's bearing *was* slightly different than his own had been. He'd traveled too far east. Maybe it wouldn't have mattered — he probably still would have made landfall, just farther north. Then again, the way he'd been failing, maybe not. And if that were the case ... had the cougar-men just saved his life?

Why?

Because we are your fathers.

And your companions.

And we want what you want: safety and freedom.

Naysin shook his head. "That wasn't an invitation... But if you want freedom so badly, why did you trap yourself inside me?"

It was better than the alternative.

Millennia in a forgotten hovel is no lark, Naysin.

But more than that, we saw — through your mother — what you could be.

Strong.

Powerful.

Godly.

Naysin couldn't help laughing. "What wouldn't you say to trick me into letting you out?"

The cougar-men were silent for a moment before Father Enmul finally responded: **We know we pushed you too hard when you were younger.**

Please believe us when we say it's one of our deepest regrets. We're truly sorry for what happened to your leg. You weren't ready.

But each use of your abilities makes you stronger. And not just by adding to your experience.

*The faster you release our **Kug** and Mir back into the world, the sooner you'll be able to fuel your abilities from external sources.*

So it will no longer hurt.

Naysin felt something — was it actually hope? — quicken inside him. "No more pain?"

None.

No more headaches.

No more shakes.

Just unfettered use of your abilities.

Whenever you please.

The contrast between his suddenly dry mouth and the water all around him struck Naysin as particularly funny; he let out a laugh before hastily muffling his mirth. None of the pale men seemed to have heard, however, and after a moment, he felt safe enough to resume his whispered conversation with the manitouk inside him. "I think I might actually like to hear more about that. But not yet. Not until I — we — are back on dry land. And only when I bring it up. No more leaping into my thoughts."

As you wish.

— « O » —

The next few days were at once the shortest and longest of Naysin's life: the shortest because he slept through most of them, too exhausted to do much more than purify occasional handfuls of water; the longest because the time he was awake was absolutely interminable, nothing but ocean, sky, the chatter of pale men, and, thanks to the ship's ceaseless swaying, prolonged bouts of retching.

At least the hull shaded him from the sun. And on the second day, he'd forced himself to catch and cook a fish (using **Kug** to make a shiny flotsam lure and *Mir* to steam his prize). He'd even kept most of it down. So he was ... surviving. Too weak to strike out on his own again, with no recourse except trusting that the ship was headed back to the mainland. But surviving.

It was a humbling come-down from the exhilaration he'd felt while running across the ocean.

Now he just hoped the rudder wouldn't move too jarringly, and that the pale men wouldn't push off in one of their square canoes before he had a chance to camouflage himself. But from what he'd heard on the plantation, the journey to the mainland took less than a half-moon. So this wouldn't last much longer. He just had to hold on for a few more days.

The last one was the hardest.

It began with an unexpected visitor; shortly after sunrise, Naysin heard a splash, likely from another body — the pale men had been tossing plague-ridden corpses overboard virtually every morning. Most of the probable slaves had dipped beneath the waves by the time they passed Naysin at his position on the rudder, but a few had still been afloat, dark hair and hands trailing behind them as they were drawn into the ship's wake.

Today's offering was a solitary floater. A tall one, lanky and bald. With swirling tattoos that gleamed on his black skin, even through the water. And eyes that were still open and—

Aware.

The dark man was looking at him, studying his purchase in the rudder, no doubt wondering how its upper portion had come to form a bench beneath him (Naysin had enhanced his seating during his second day attached to the ship, once he'd recovered a modicum of strength.) After a few moments, the dark man shrugged, exhaled forcefully, and sank.

"No," Naysin cried, louder than he'd intended. He also didn't mean to spin out quite so much **Kug**, but before he could regret the strain, he'd fished the dark man back to the surface.

"What are you?" the dark man asked as he emerged, water streaming down his hairless head.

"What are you?" Naysin retorted. Then he remembered the conversation he'd overhead between Arthur and Danny, the overseers who'd complained about original peoples' susceptibility to plague. "You're a tar skin — from Afrii."

The dark man regarded him for a moment, perhaps registering Naysin's youth. "My name is Amadi. I'm a Foim, of the kingdom of Dahemy. What you called me are white men's words."

Chastened — after all, he hated when the pale ones called him "red devil" — Naysin nodded. "We should speak quietly," he whispered, glancing meaningfully at the deck above.

Amadi tried to shrug again, but his forearms and wrists were pinned to his side. "You've chained me."

Chagrined once more, Naysin hurriedly unbound the dark man and bored a set of handholds in the rudder. "I didn't want you to sink."

At first, it didn't look like Amadi would use the holds; he sank to his chin before reaching out and steadying himself. "By the vodun," he breathed as he took in the black lines spreading across Naysin's flesh; fatigued as he was, even small expenditures of **Kug** and *Mir* tended to mark him right now. "Are *you* a vodun?"

"What's a vodun?" Naysin countered warily. He was *not* a manitouk.

Amadi shook his head. "It's of no matter." Lifting one hand from its hold in the rudder, he began itching at his other wrist. "The cannons — they were firing at you?"

Naysin saw no point in denying it. "Yes."

"You must be a powerful swimmer." Amadi scratched harder.

"I'm strong," Naysin hedged ... but this man already knew he could shaman. "Most of the time, I was running, though."

"Running," Amadi said with a chuckle. "By the vodun... And he speaks Gbe flawlessly." He stopped scratching, lifting bloody fingernails away from his wrist. Then he switched holds and plunged his raw flesh into the water.

"What are you doing?"

Amadi smiled. It seemed forced. "My wrist itched — the white men only take our manacles off when they think we're dead. The metal chafes."

Naysin shifted on the bench. He was still glad he'd saved the tar sk — the Foim, but the man was acting so strangely. "And that's why they threw you overboard? They thought you were dead?"

Amadi looked away. "As did I."

"You were a slave?"

"Yes." Amadi's hauteur lessened, as if the water were leaching it away. "In the belly of the ship, those of us who still live wondered what the white men were fighting. Most believed it was Espans. Or maybe Francs." He looked back at Naysin. "No one suspected anything like you."

This was beginning to sound uncomfortably like countless conversations he'd had with Degan. "My name is Naysin, of the Lepane tribe — just Naysin."

"Naysin of the Lepane," Amadi echoed. "Naysin of the Lepane… A boy with the powers of a vodun." Reaching his other hand from the water, he gripped the empty hold and pulled himself up so that his eyes were level with Naysin's. "I would ask something of you."

Here it came.

"Save the ejeme."

At least Degan's requests had been clear. "The ejeme?"

"The slaves. It's plain you have the strength to rescue them. Get them off this ship and return them to their homes." Almost as an afterthought, Amadi added, "Please."

Not again. "I don't know if I can."

Amadi looked set to disagree, but a gigantic mouth swallowed the dark man up to his stomach.

It was one of the monstrous pike that trailed the ship in anticipation of easy meals. Naysin had raised his bench above their reach, and to be safe, he usually kept them at bay by sewing false scents into the water, trails that led the fish back to the bodies the white men tossed out so callously. But his concentration must have lapsed as he'd spoken with Amadi — who'd used his "itchy" wrist to lay his own trail.

As the pike's teeth tore into Amadi's gut, he let go of the rudder and gripped the edges of the fish's maw. But instead of trying to hold it open or pry himself out, the dark man pulled himself *farther in*.

"Stop!" hissed Naysin at both Amadi and the pike. A blast of **Kug** forced the fish's jaw apart, cracking it in at least three places; a burst of *Mir* boiled its tiny brain. Using more **Kug** to pull Amadi free, Naysin formed a swathe of the ship's hull into a pallet and set the dark man atop it. Simultaneously, he balanced his energies by aiming ribbons of *Mir* underneath the ship's wake, in hopes of knocking back the pike who'd swarmed their dead brother.

The combined effort nearly cost him his consciousness.

"Why did you do that?" he demanded when he could see straight again. Amadi's blood was streaming over the pallet and darkening the water behind them. Hopefully the pale ones would assume the discoloration to be just the result of a normal corpse-inspired feeding frenzy. "Those pike will be back for you. I'm too tired to hold them off. And I can't heal you—"

He didn't need to.

Blinking, Naysin took in Amadi's smooth torso, whole legs ... and unmarred wrists. In an instant, an explosion of **Kug** had surged through the dark man's body and repaired every bit of harm. But the **Kug** hadn't come from Naysin; it had originated in Amadi. "What are you?" Naysin asked a second time, but more sincerely.

The dark man sat up on his pallet. "I'm Amadi, of the Foim." He brushed at his stomach, looking disappointed. "Save the ejeme; let me die." Then he jumped toward the water.

Anchored by the portion of the rudder still molded around his torso, Naysin managed to grab the dark man's left arm before he went under. Holding him up at such an awkward angle was painful, but Naysin couldn't have managed it by shamaning — all he had left was physical strength. And precious little of that. "Why?" he shouted, finally heedless of who might overhear.

Amadi regarded him coolly. The dark man wasn't struggling, but he wasn't helping either. "Because I put them there."

The words were shocking enough to make Naysin loosen his grip, and with a nod of thanks, Amadi disappeared into the blue.

— « o » —

That night, Naysin woke to heavy rain, violent water, and a spasming rudder.

Above him, the pale men were scrambling about and yelling orders like it was the end of the world. Maybe it was; the water was fissuring into deeper and deeper valleys flanked by steeper and steeper cliffs. The smallest of these canyons seemed big enough to swallow twenty ships. And the largest...

The largest could have eaten Bimshire.

He had to get higher.

Naysin detached himself from the rudder and let the next wave's momentum carry him upward. The swell slapped him against the hull harder than he'd anticipated, but he managed to use a stream of **Kug** to force his hands into a mossy plank. For a moment, he hung there and caught his breath ... until another wave knocked it back out of him.

Nearly blind from salt and spray, Naysin yanked his right arm from the hull, reached as high as he could, and sank his fingers in the ship again. After walking his feet up, he freed his other arm and embedded it above his head. Then he repeated the process.

It became easier once he'd ascended far enough to avoid the worst of the waves — he took a break halfway up the hull. But when he looked down to assess his progress, Naysin realized he needed to close his hand- and foot-holes or the ship would sink; water was splashing into each opening as if the pale men's cannon had turned inward. The rudder wasn't in good shape either; he'd severely weakened it when he'd unshaped it to free himself.

Swearing softly, Naysin shamaned enough **Kug** to fix the damage. The effort left his temples throbbing, and he compensated by using *Mir* to force the storm's wind away from him. An action he regretted when the ship listed horribly, leaning so close to the water he could have drunk from it.

Amidst his rising panic, Naysin realized the pale men's sails were configured for the wind's original direction — by altering the air's flow so abruptly, he'd nearly sunk the ship. Furious with himself, he gradually restored the wind to its natural pattern, allowing the craft to ease rather than snap back to its former position.

Reinvigorated, Naysin began crawling across the hull like a squirrel scrabbling around a tree. He closed every new hole as soon as his fingers or toes left it, doing his best to ignore the ballooning ache in his temples. It was too risky to shaman a *Mir* counterweight right now. He'd have to wait until he was on open water.

When he was almost to the other side, lighting struck again and illuminated the ship's name, painted in fading letters just above his head: *The Minotaur*. He still didn't understand how he could read the pale men's words, but he'd remember these — they belonged to the ship that saved his life.

So had the lightning; to the west, the same flash had revealed the outlines of a cliff face.

He could see it even through the downpour. *The Minotaur* wouldn't be able to dock there ... but he could probably climb the slope the same way he was scaling the ship.

It was a shameful thought; fleeing *The Minotaur* meant abandoning the ejeme after he'd spent most of the afternoon conversing with the cougar-men about Amadi's import.

Of course there are other channelers, Father Enki had explained patiently. *In our day, there were thousands.*

But the few active in this age cannot do the smallest part of what you are capable of.

"I can't heal," Naysin had pointed out, thinking of that day with Degan and the coconuts.

Not yet.

Once we are free, however, we will be able to teach you.

Naysin had considered this as he'd watched another giant pike slip lazily by in the distance — they'd given him a wide berth since the incident with Amadi. "Was I right to let him go?"

What else could you do?

What else indeed. "Save the ejeme," Amadi had said — no, ordered. But Naysin was too tired now, too weak.

"I can barely save myself," Naysin whispered into the wind, reliving the fire and chaos of the rebellion on Bimshire.

Maybe he'd always been too weak.

Hoping Gilmekon would absolve him, Naysin kicked off the hull, bracing himself for a hard impact as he used **Kug** to solidify the water beneath him. The landing hurt, but it wasn't any worse than the initial slam against the hull. He wasn't ready for the wind, though; it railed against him even more angrily now that he was away from the ship. It only took a moment for him to lose his footing and fall on his back. Before he could regain his balance, a wave bludgeoned him from behind and slapped him forward. Then the wind caught him again, spinning him across the water's surface like a skipping stone.

It took an immense effort — almost more than he had in him — to summon enough *Mir* to stop himself rotating, but he finally found the strength. After that, it was just a matter of maintaining that control, of using the wind to push him in the right direction while keeping the water hardened in the right places. Eventually, he was able to raise himself to a squat, spread his arms for balance, and urge the air to propel him onward, until he was gliding up as each wave came and skating down as it passed, a smooth rhythm that belied the prevailing elemental fury. He was thoroughly drenched, cold, and hurting from the poundings he'd endured — not to mention the burn of self-loathing — but Naysin was actually starting to enjoy himself by the time he reached the cliff face.

Then he tripped.

His feet had slammed into something hard — probably a rock the storm was hiding from view — and the impact flipped him. So instead of jumping nimbly onto the cliff face as he'd intended, Naysin slammed into it upside-down, his head just above the water and facing back toward the ship. The position gave him a splendid view of the titanic wave roaring toward him.

There wasn't time to turn right-side up, scramble sideways, or even stop himself from sliding down the cliff. Water was about to crush him against rock, and all he could do was watch it happen, watch the wave close the short distance that separated life from death and feel the ocean's power as it smashed him...

Into the cliff.

Suddenly he was surrounded by stone and dirt, substances he could feel but not see. He wasn't flat against the cliff; he was inside it.

It was too much to take in. Too fast, too dark, too unlikely, too claustrophobic.

And too airless.

The urgent need to breathe overwhelmed everything else. Flailing, Naysin realized he was shamaning, using a combination of *Mir* and **Kug** to soften the stone around him. It was probably an instinctive extension of his plan to carve hand- and footholds in the cliff face... It didn't matter. He needed to get free.

Jamming his arms and legs down in a crude swimming motion, he encouraged the stone around his feet to squeeze him upward ... until he remembered he'd been upside-down when the wave hit. Swearing silently, he righted himself with an awful wrench, praying he'd oriented himself correctly — he only had a few moments before his lungs burst.

With everything he had left, Naysin pumped his limbs, pulling frantically as he coaxed more and more pressure from the earth that enveloped him. He almost gave out; his speed was notably diminished by the time his head penetrated fresh air.

The first breath was horrible, filled with rain falling from the sky and the dirt tumbling down his head. Naysin didn't care; it was life. For several thunderclaps, he gasped like a newborn. And when his breathing finally calmed, he only managed two thoughts before exhaustion took hold: that he'd just run on water and swum through earth, and that it was time to go home.

After he slept.

Folding his arms on the ground, Naysin laid his head in the crooks of his elbows and gratefully drifted into oblivion, still buried to his armpits.

Chapter Fourteen

The Second Walking Purchase

Most of the longhouses were being squatted in, disassembled for parts, or used for storage.

Naysin rocked back on his heels, stunned by the pale men and women's temerity. They'd taken his people's village, done Gilmekon knew what to them, and turned their longhouses into holding bins for roots and vegetables? It was too much.

And it wouldn't stand.

Because he finally understood what he could do. Relying on himself was nothing new, but now he was seventeen winters instead of twelve, and the journey back here had taught him well.

No more eating carrion; with a thought, he could cook a squirrel before it hit the ground.

No more getting thirsty; before his throat grew dry, he could coax water out of plants, the earth, or even stones.

No more getting soaked by the rain; by the time the second round of drops fell, he could form a cloak of air around his body.

No more sleeping exposed; before the sun had noticeably changed positions, he could bend adjacent trees into a wind-tight shelter.

And no more getting lost; by taking an afternoon to focus on his brand, he could intuit the direction of its place of inscription.

There were still limits and consequences, of course. Despite what the cougar-men kept promising. Naysin couldn't do a quarter of what he wanted yet, and to avoid being crippled by pain, he still had to maintain the exhausting balance between **Kug** and *Mir*. The strain had marked him further; his hair had become pure smoke — a blizzard of black and white tendrils — and the quicks of his nails had been streaked with darkness since the morning he'd woken half-buried in the cliff. The blemishes were yet more warnings for those who knew what to look for; he was branded from head to toe now.

But at least he was finally starting to appreciate how *special* he was.

His people hadn't comprehended. They'd bowed to their fear of the unknown, persecuting him like superstitious children. And for that, they'd been punished.

But not by the right party.

Ever since he'd decided to return to his village, which had taken far longer to find than he'd expected, Naysin had sustained himself by imagining how he'd announce his homecoming to the community that exiled him. The questions he fed on were deliciously bitter. How would he demonstrate the awesome power the Elders had decided the tribe could do without? What would he do when he saw his friends — the few he'd had? Would he bother to reintroduce himself to the girl he'd had a liking for so many winters ago? Would he deign to accept his aunt and uncle's forgiveness?

But he'd never have the chance to do any of it ... yet another thing the pale ones had taken from him.

"Why?" he heard himself call, startling a pale woman who was carrying a sack of tubers to the largest longhouse. "Why did you banish my people when it was not your place to do so?"

The pale woman jumped again when he stepped out of the woods. Then she dropped her sack, picked up the ends of her dress, and scurried toward the nearest pale-one structure. "Micah?" she yelled just before disappearing from view. "Micah, there's a devil behind the house!"

Naysin smiled grimly. He knew how impressive he looked. In addition to his distinctive hair and the ever-present brand over his eye, his breechcloth was a striking mix of animal and plant; he'd repaired his Bimshire rags by fusing in bits of leaves and bark and polishing the combination to a seamless finish. He'd also smoothed out his hair and wicked the dirt away from his skin. All in anticipation of meeting his people again.

At least his preparations hadn't gone to waste; he'd still found a group who deserved retribution.

"This isn't your land anymore, devil boy," a pale man said in the village's center, his fingers playing over the handle of an upturned ax.

"Peace, Micah," an older, grayer pale man warned as he hurried to place himself in front of Naysin. "Eva said you spoke our tongue like it was your own. Is this true?"

"Judge for yourself."

"Sounds true to me." The old pale man looked at Naysin closely. "Are you Delware?"

Naysin furrowed his brow.

Another of the gathering pale men whispered in the old man's ear. "Ahh," the old man said. "Maybe you call yourself 'Lepane'?"

"I *called* myself Lepane," Naysin replied, "as did the people who used to live here."

"Ahh," the old man said again. "Well ... perhaps you could be an intermediary for those who remain. No one on either side speaks both languages as well as you do."

Naysin's pulse quickened. "Those who remain?"

"The survi — you don't know." Comprehension animated the old man's eyes.

"Know what?" Naysin demanded, more urgent than confident now.

"When we arrived two years ago," the old man eventually explained, obviously picking his words with care, "we found a terrible thing. This village — almost to a man — had been struck down by pox."

A distant roar started to fill Naysin's head.

"God's will," one of the other pale men muttered, to a muted chorus of "Amens."

"Peace!" the old man warned again, sweeping a baleful eye across what was clearly his flock. "We buried the fallen," he said, turning back to Naysin, "and we've tried to help the survivors in the woods. We have trouble understanding them, though, which is where I think you could help."

The roar grew louder. Naysin shook his head to clear it, but the noise only grew as he saw the village as the pale ones had found it: game grounds unused ... fields untended ... longhouses silent ... diseased bodies everywhere. "This isn't what I wanted," he whispered, tears running down his cheeks.

"It wasn't our wish either," the old man said gently. "The Walking Purchase gave us the right to the land—"

"Rokoan," Micah interjected. "That's what it's called now."

"But we came prepared to make a peaceful exchange," the old man finished after glaring at Micah. "I'm sorry."

The roar became rage. "The Walking Purchase," Naysin repeated softly.

"Yes. Your people and many others agreed to the Penn's proposal."

"The Walking Purchase," Naysin said again, much louder, "was theft."

The old man shook his head. "I'm sorry, boy, but that was a legal arrangement made with your chief."

"Don't waste any more breath on this one," Micah said disdainfully. "He's clearly not going to be any use to us."

"Hear, hear," another onlooker agreed.

"Thieves!" hissed Naysin, his eyes narrowing to slits.

Sensing danger (but not its true nature), Micah and two other pale men started to advance on Naysin despite the old man's protestations.

They weren't quick enough.

Filled with more fury than he'd ever felt — an anger that tapped into everything he'd experienced in the last five winters: his failure as a savior; his enslavement; his mother's treachery; his exile — Naysin ripped into his core and withdrew immense amounts of **Kug** and *Mir*. With the **Kug**, he immobilized the pale men. With the *Mir*, he blew open the door of every building and hauled out the pale women and children within, dragging them forward until they were massed with their husbands and fathers.

"As far as a man could walk in a day and a half, wasn't it? That was the deal you struck?" Naysin clipped his words so sharply that spit flew with every syllable. "But why stop there? Why not see what you could steal in two days? Or three? Five, even? What about a full moon?"

Every pale eye was filled with terror, but all Naysin could see were diseased bodies.

"Just start with a step." He snapped the central flow of **Kug** like a whip, and the right knee of every pale one jerked up. "One. Single. Step." He smashed a wave of *Mir* into their backs, and cracked the **Kug** again to force their legs back down, a pace ahead of where they'd been. "There: you've taken another foot of land. Well done. Now let's see how much farther you can walk."

Naysin repeated the bursts of **Kug** and *Mir* until he'd marched the pale ones out of the village. But when they passed the last longhouse, he realized he couldn't keep them moving much longer — he'd be lucky to advance his spasming puppets more than another twenty steps.

Tie off the flows. Father Enki's voice sounded worried.

"Not ... now."

Tie off the flows so you do not have to sustain them. Father Enmul wasn't any calmer.

Quickly, while you still can.

Naysin shuddered, his fury giving way to exhaustion. "I ... I think I should let them go."

No. You are about to pass out.

And if they're free when you collapse ... what do you think's going to happen?

Tie off the flows, Naysin.

It's your only option.

Numb, Naysin watched the pale puppets take another step. Their synchronized footfalls echoed in his bones. "How?"

Turn each flow into a loop.

Channel more than you need and mold it into a cycle that runs back into itself.

It will not last forever.

But it will do what's necessary.

Another thud. Another bone-jarring echo. "That sounds hard."

Just try.

We'll talk you through it.

"…All right."

It felt sloppy and underdone, but with the cougar-men's guidance, Naysin managed; the pale men, women, and children were walking on their own when he fell to the earth, unconscious and uncaring.

Chapter Fifteen

Jehan

He cared when he came to, though.

Not immediately. His first thought was that passing out every time he did something powerful was a bad habit.

His second thought was that he was waking up less than a few arm-lengths from where he'd opened his eyes five winters ago, after failing to fly and succeeding in crashing.

His third thought — that was when he started caring.

How far would the pale ones walk? In the midst of his fury, he'd been ready to march them until their feet wore off. But now that he'd been sobered by the morning sun, he couldn't stop thinking about the women and children. The cougar-men had said it wouldn't last forever. Did that mean the flows would fall apart by evening? The next morning? Any longer would leave him with blood on his hands.

Unless he caught up to the pale ones.

They were only *walking*. And he was in peak condition; running was the one aspect of his life he'd refused to augment on the journey home. He'd jogged as much as he could, stopping for breaks only when absolutely necessary. It felt good to push himself *naturally*, to do something impressive on his own.

And now he'd really have to exert himself if he was going to make amends. The trail would be easy to follow; a village's worth of people walking in unison wouldn't have left subtle tracks. He probably had time, as long as he started now.

But he couldn't stand.

He couldn't even move, and trying made him woozy with weakness. Tying off so many flows must have taken more energy than he'd realized. It felt like it had almost killed him. Anything more than lying here, staring up, and thinking remorseful thoughts was apparently beyond him.

Which meant that unless this paralysis passed quickly, he'd have to leave the pale ones to their fate ... the fate he'd wrought for them. He swore softly as the words he'd uttered before shamaning — *"This isn't what I wanted"* — came back to him with new meaning. It was a terrible refrain.

"Sleeping it off, are we?" The voice was female, speaking a tongue Naysin hadn't heard before (and yet, as always, still understood).

He froze, instinctively hoping the speaker would lose sight of him and leave. But it was obvious from her words that she knew exactly where he was. "I'm fine."

"It speaks! And ... you're Lepane." The woman's face appeared above his, much as the red-haired pale man's had winters earlier. But her features were softer, feathered by dark brown bangs and marred only by a mole on her left cheek.

"You say that like it's a bad thing," Naysin responded, pride flaring.

"Not at all," she said with a smile. "Not at all. I'm just impressed by how well you speak Franc. It's a rare thing to find a red man who's more fluent than half my countrymen. And better dressed... You certainly don't *sound* drunk. Are you sick?" She took a step back.

"No. I fell."

The woman's expression changed dramatically. "Poor thing." She started to reach out a hand before thinking better of it. "You must be in such pain. I know the Anglos in the village down the path. I'll speak for you. Just give me a minute—"

"There's no one there," Naysin interrupted. "I ... I think they left." He gestured with his eyes in the direction of the villagers' (forced) exodus.

As the woman moved to his right, Naysin noticed she was dressed in a comely blend of pale-one cloth and original-people fur. There was nothing in-between about the fire stick on her back, however.

"Now that's odd," she said eventually. "Decidedly odd... I'll return in a moment."

And then Naysin was alone again. Still paralyzed, still defenseless, and still drowning in guilt.

But the woman kept her word. She was slightly out of breath when she jogged back, but no less beautiful for it. "You're right," she said as she tied a blanket to a pair of hoes, "that village is a ghost town. Not a soul in it. They left in a hurry, though — it doesn't look like they took anything; every essential you could think of is still there. It's damned strange... Is your back broken?"

"No. I just can't move yet."

"Well, either way, let's get you in this. You're too big for me to carry, but you look draggable. And the sooner we get away from whatever happened here, the better. Ready?" She gripped his shoulders and, with surprising strength, started to ease him onto her makeshift pallet.

"Wait." Naysin would have physically restrained her if he'd been able to, but he had to settle for a verbal plea.

It didn't work. "No," she said after a brief pause. "No, we need to move." Smiling to soften her words, she resumed shifting him onto the blanket.

"Wait!"

The woman shook her head. "Just let me move you."

He stared back at her for several breaths ... and closed his eyes in assent.

They exchanged names after she'd hauled him to her campsite.

— « o » —

Jehan was a different kind of woman. She was taller than Naysin by a good bit; she kept her hair pulled back in a tight ponytail which showed off her tapered ears; and she was quick to smile ... with her mouth, but not her eyes. Those almost always retained a trace of sadness.

She also lived entirely alone.

Naysin was used to strong women, but none of the females in his tribe had done *everything* on their own. Jehan did, though. Like her campsite; she'd put that up herself, from cooking fire to lean-to. And that was nothing. After his exhaustion faded the second day, she asked him to be her interpreter.

"I trade furs," she explained. "But your tongue doesn't come naturally to mine, and I spend more time than I'd like waving my arms when you could just talk."

He recoiled at first, soured by the memory of similar duties in Bimshire. Jehan was offering a very different arrangement, however.

"You'll get a commission on every transaction you help broker. Money or goods," she clarified when Naysin raised his eyebrows. "Whatever you'd like. I actually do quite well for myself. Some men prefer trading with a woman — they think they have a natural advantage, and it lowers their guard."

Naysin tried to think of another option, failed, and said yes.

The pattern repeated itself the next day, when she said she was leaving for her permanent home, a log cabin to the north: she asked him if he'd like to come stay with her, he hesitated, she asked if he had anywhere else to go, he shrugged and agreed to accompany her.

"No, but I'm flattered," Jehan said when they'd arrived and he asked if she'd built the structure herself. "I had help," she finished before changing the subject.

So it went for Naysin's first moons with her; their past was largely off limits. They revealed bits here and there, but for the most part they just let each other *be*. Few questions about yesterday, almost none about tomorrow; just companionship today. Jehan seemed to need it, and he was grateful for the respite. It was an easy, simple life that soothed him like a balm. He spent most days working quietly by her side. Setting traps ... tanning hides ... stacking furs. It was her "accumulation season," the period when she caught beavers and foxes, bartered additional pelts from nearby "red peoples," and generally prepared for her next excursions to pale villages. "They can't get enough," she'd said with a little smile. "Anglo, Franc, Espan, Nethern: we all covet new things."

Best of all, he didn't have to shaman *anything* he didn't want to, aside from the minor strands of **Kug** he used to understand Jehan, and the tiny portions of *Mir* he expelled as counterweights. Nothing else was forced on him. He didn't have to actively work to keep himself alive, be a savior, play the monster… He was just Naysin. A young Lepane man with a talent for language.

It was nice.

So was not hearing from the cougar-men. They'd been silent since Jehan found him. Which was fine by Naysin; he much preferred her voice over theirs.

On two occasions, he even came close to telling her of his abilities. Both near-misses happened at night, when they were sitting by the fire and letting its soft crackles lull them to sleep. But neither time seemed right. Part of him still worried she'd recoil in horror, and Naysin didn't want to risk ruining the most peaceful stretch of his life since he'd been branded.

As it turned out, he might as well have confessed everything; the calm ended anyway after they embarked on their first formal trading expedition.

"This one won't be anything like the other trips we've done," Jehan explained, the familiar smile on her lips but not in her eyes. "For one thing, we won't be able to carry everything on our backs — we'll have to take Flo and the cart." She nodded toward her horse. "Which means going by roads instead of trails. And for another…"

"What?" Naysin asked after Jehan's pause dragged out to an ominous length.

She shook her head. "Well, if you thought negotiating with your people was awkward, wait until you do it with mine. Most of the Francs aren't so bad, but the Anglos and the Espans might not be as understanding."

Naysin frowned. The bartering they'd done with the neighboring Lepane — no one he recognized — had been uncomfortable at times, but he was used to ignoring questioning looks and raised eyebrows.

Jehan tugged her ponytail before explaining. "Some 'pale men' don't like seeing a white woman and a red man together, whether they're doing what people think they're doing or not."

Naysin thought through the implication and blushed furiously. "Oh."

Jehan laughed. "Don't worry, I didn't say we wouldn't go. They're still going to buy our furs. I just wanted you to be aware."

"All right." He was glad his voice didn't sound *too* wistful. He tried to respect her privacy, but she liked to bathe, and she wasn't shy about her body. More than once, he'd had to force himself to look away when she emerged from the nearby stream, the water's surface bending and breaking over her breasts... "I'm aware," he finished lamely.

Jehan laughed again and went back to counting fox pelts. "We'll leave in the morning."

Naysin had trouble sleeping that night.

— « o » —

Their first trade was innocuous enough. It took place at a small Franc village not far from Jehan's cabin. Since Naysin didn't need to interpret, he stayed in the background and hauled pelts like a man-servant, a role no one seemed to resent. The negotiations were brief, and then he and Jehan were on the road again, headed south with less furs, more money, and no complications.

"A good start," she proclaimed when the village was out of sight.

Their next stop was Franc as well — Jehan's plan was to go down her people's side of the border and back up through Anglo territory. (Naysin had started to say something about these "borders" not existing five winters ago, but he'd thought better of it.) This session went smoothly as well. Maybe she'd been worried over nothing? No one seemed to care ... except for him; not a night went by he didn't dream of her in the stream.

Their third trade was when the trouble started.

It was another Franc village — little more than an outpost — with even less men and women than the first two. But two of the residents were drunk.

One of these was harmless; he just sat on the side of the road, staring at his feet and giggling about his "shy toenails." The other drunk was mean. He was rude to Jehan from the start, calling her "the trading whore" as she began negotiations with the sober residents. Later he asked how much he'd have to barter for a chance to rub *her* fur.

The harmless drunk thought both of these comments were hilarious; Naysin felt like they warranted blood. But he held his place, biting his tongue until the transaction was complete, at which point the mean drunk stumbled over and grabbed Jehan's shoulder. "How much did you say it was for *your* fur?" he asked again as he laughed uproariously, his face almost touching hers.

Naysin couldn't stay still any longer, but Jehan moved faster. After giving the drunk a skeptical look, she rolled her eyes and dropped him with an efficient knee to the groin. "Fox pelts are two, beaver pelts are three, and I tan testicles for free," she said as she walked away.

Naysin was impressed.

The rest of their Franc stops were uneventful. It wasn't until they crossed to the Anglo side of the border that things got interesting again.

Not because of the new trading partners. Jehan's Anglo was serviceable, so at the first two Anglo villages, she only had to confer with Naysin a few times. Their conversations raised some eyebrows, but no one seemed overly put out. It didn't hurt that Naysin kept acting like a laborer.

The disruption occurred on the road.

"I want to check that village," she said as they left the second Anglo settlement. "The one near where you fell."

Naysin kept his eyes focused on the path. He'd known they were getting close to his old home, but he'd hoped they'd just pass by.

"It would have been my next stop," Jehan continued, "and I'd like to see if they've come back."

They hadn't.

The village was just as desolate as it had been in the spring. A few of the houses looked like they'd been looted, but there were no indications anyone still lived in them.

"Something terrible happened here," Jehan whispered after they'd wandered the remains. "Something truly awful... Can't you feel it?"

Naysin stopped in the center of both villages — his people's and the pale ones' — and gathered himself. "Yes."

Jehan looked at him sympathetically — she must have misunderstood the emotion in his voice. "Come on." She extended her arm. "Let's get away from here."

They walked hand-in-hand back to Flo and the cart, and then headed north until dark, somber and silent. But their mood softened by the fire as they ate a dinner of jerky and bread.

"My husband fell," Jehan said without warning. A tear trickled down her cheek, but she ignored it and pressed on. "Just like you. He fell off Flo three years ago this autumn. But he never got up. His back was broken, and he died within a few days."

Naysin froze. Suddenly, he understood why Jehan had been so tender toward him — and why her eyes were always sad.

"I'd come over with him to this 'New World' because I didn't want to live apart," Jehan continued, the tear's trail shining in the firelight. "He was so set on making his way as a fur trader. And he was good at it. Good enough to teach me how to help him ... even though he didn't want me here at first. He thought it wasn't safe." She laughed bitterly. "But he was happy I'd come when he saw how lonely most of the other traders were: men without families, only knowing a woman's touch when they could beg or steal a night with a red... We made a good life for ourselves. Simple, full of hard work. And love.

"Then he fell," she repeated quietly.

Naysin waited for her to continue, but she didn't offer anything else. And all at once, his secrets were trying to tumble out of his mouth: the truth about who he really was, what he could do, what he'd done. He nearly choked trying to keep everything in. But he wanted to reciprocate. So he told an edited version of his guardian-spirit day and the resulting exile, leaving out only the bits that sounded like — well, were — magic.

"And that's why you have this," Jehan murmured, reaching over to trace the brand around Naysin's left eye.

Her touch felt warmer than the fire.

"Superstition will get us all killed," she said, letting her finger drop slowly from his face. "What happened to your mother?"

Naysin hung his head. He didn't want to lie about this, though. With a deep breath, he told the whole truth. "I don't know. I left her after a moon… I hated her."

Jehan stared at him for several heartbeats before hugging him. And after a few more heartbeats, the embrace turned into something more.

Jehan started it. She pulled back from Naysin to kiss him softly on the lips. He didn't react until she started to withdraw — then he grabbed her and reinitiated the kiss.

It didn't end there.

She touched his chest; he groped beneath her shirt. She loosened his breechcloth; he fumbled her clothes off. She caressed his bare back; he raced his hands up and down her body.

Naysin was an eager mess, but he didn't feel like he was stumbling too badly. And when he did, Jehan kissed his anxiety away. They went on that way for a wonderful, indeterminable length of time, until he climaxed — much later than he'd expected — and she moaned softly into his chest.

Gently, she rolled off him and lay on her back, her pale skin glistening with moonlit sweat. They stayed quiet as their breathing returned to normal.

"Well," Jehan said with a small laugh. "I'd say we both needed that. You're my first since… in a long time. And I'm your first … ever?"

Naysin nodded dumbly, still reliving the sensation of being inside her.

She laughed again. "I'm glad. Now I'll always be a part of your life."

He still couldn't think of a response, so he just smiled.

Jehan laughed a third time and folded her arms beneath her head. She stared at the stars for a while before continuing. "You know where I always wanted to go?"

"Where?"

"Not always," Jehan clarified with a smile. "Just the last few years: Mt. Tsikomo."

Naysin shook his head and repeated his question. "Where?"

"It's a mountain to the west, a long way from here." Jehan propped herself up on her right elbow, her breasts settling in a way that nearly caused Naysin to miss what she said next. "People like yours live there, but it's different. More like a desert. They say the mountain is the exact center of the world. And they have a shrine there with paths that run down from it like fingers from a hand."

Something about her description caught Naysin's attention, turning it (at least partially) away from her body. "Why do you want to go there?"

"Mostly because Philip did." Jehan's eyes were sad again, but there were no tears.

"Your husband."

"Yes. He heard about the mountain from someone he traded with, and ... just liked the idea. So do I. There's a balance to it. But it's too far for a trade trip."

Naysin watched the light fade from her face as the idea began to burn itself out. He didn't want that to happen. "Let's go."

Jehan snorted. "It's too far. We have too many stops to make, and it's probably just a story anyway."

"Let's find out. After we're done with this route," Naysin added hurriedly. "You said you wanted a respite — this would be perfect. Even if it's just a mountain, it'd still be a worthy journey. Just you and me."

"You're sweet," Jehan said, but in a tone that wasn't totally dismissive. "I really do think it's a long way. Philip guessed it would take a year to get there and back."

"Maybe I can get us there quicker," Naysin said slowly, after another pause.

Jehan cocked her head to one side and looked at him like she wanted to believe. "How?"

He never had a chance to answer.

Four pale men burst into the campsite, reeking of alcohol and yelling about "red devils" and "white women." Naysin had just enough time to recognize one of the men as a malcontent from the last trade stop before something flashed in the night air: a hatchet, flung with drunken force. Naysin tried to summon *Mir* to deflect the weapon, but disuse had dulled his speed; the flat-end of the blade struck him in his left temple before he could form a flow.

And that — along with Jehan's scream — was the last thing he knew until morning.

— « o » —

There was light, but it was … dancing. Skipping along at alternating angles. Racing around him like small children circling an indulgent parent.

The motion didn't stop when Naysin regained full consciousness. Everything was … swirling. The trees, the ground, his head … especially his head. This wasn't his usual post-blackout haze — something was wrong. He reached up to touch where the hatchet had struck, couldn't find his head, tried again, and found a throbbing, egg-shaped lump that was sticky with blood. It was hard to tell if his skull was cracked, but even if it wasn't, his equilibrium was gone.

That didn't keep him from scrabbling around in search of Jehan. Naked and rudderless, he stumbled and — after falling — crawled through the morning dew, moving in what he hoped were ever-expanding circles as he strained to see clearly. He didn't remember anything after she'd screamed, and now she wasn't making a sound, even though he was calling her name again and again.

He found her by tripping over her leg.

For a moment, after he'd recovered what was left of his balance and gripped her arms, Naysin still had hope. Her skin was warm, and the angle of her head made it look like she was sleeping. But when she didn't respond, he started to realize that only sunlight heated her body, and her pose was … unnatural. Lurching back, Naysin took her in from a distance.

She'd been violated.

And broken, discarded on the forest floor, half-buried by the leaves that cushioned her final fall. The rage that had fueled his reaction to the Walking Purchase threatened to overwhelm him again, but the emotion was quickly extinguished by an anesthetizing wave of nothing. Naysin used the absence of feeling to focus on Jehan's face, memorizing every detail despite his skittering sight: the lean lines that formed a softer whole ... the delicate ears revealed by the ponytail trailing over her shoulder ... the mole on her left cheek that seemed to jump a little with each tic of his vision.

He needed to bury her.

Seizing on the proper custom, Naysin cast around for something to use as a shovel. Nothing was handy, however, and he didn't trust himself to make it to the village and back. So he started digging with his hands, scrabbling like a dog until his nails broke and his fingers bled. But he couldn't get deep enough. Not without tools, and not in his current condition.

Not unless he shamaned.

Shaking off his reluctance, Naysin struggled to a sitting position and did his best to focus on the hole he'd begun. It kept moving — oscillating and vibrating and bending — but he could follow its progress if he concentrated. A little *Mir* would loosen the soil, remove its integrity and collapse the sides...

The earth gaped open before him as he shamaned far more energy than he'd intended. He'd nearly fissured the ground he sat on, almost dropping himself into a pit so deep he couldn't see the bottom.

He had no control right now.

But that didn't stop him from trying again. He had to do something for Jehan, something besides misusing his abilities when employing them actually would have been justified. He'd gladly give his life to honor hers — whatever it took.

Or so he thought before his second attempt ripped the ground open to her left, setting her body teetering on the brink of an even bigger hole. Crying out, Naysin stumbled to her and pulled her back; he wanted to bury her, not drop her in the bowels of the earth.

Defeat sank in as he cradled her head. He couldn't do it, couldn't do *anything*. She'd died because of him, and he couldn't even make this small gesture of atonement... He didn't know he was crying until tears started splashing against her face.

"I'm sorry," he whispered over and over. "I'm so sorry."

Naysin sat that way for a long time before he had another thought: he *could* do something for her. "I'll go to Mt. Tsikomo for you." He brushed a wisp of hair from her head as he lowered his mouth to her ear. "I'll go to Mt. Tsikomo for you, and see the shrine with paths that run down like fingers from a hand. If it's really the center of the world, maybe I'll find balance there. For both of us."

Even as he embraced the idea, Naysin knew it was foolish to trek half a year to a place he'd never been, based on a few words from a lover who'd only heard of the mountain through a thirdhand account. The whole idea was foolish.

And yet it made sense, an impractical notion practical Jehan would have appreciated.

He also didn't have anywhere else to go — *truly* didn't have anywhere else to go. His village was gone, empty of both peoples that had inhabited it. Three times he'd returned to it, and three times something terrible had happened. There was no reason to go back again.

So he would head west.

Gently, he eased Jehan's head off his lap, wobbled to a stand ... and shed another round of tears at his inability to bury her properly. The best he could do was sprinkle a little dirt on her, but he stopped after the first few handfuls — it felt worse than doing nothing at all.

This was it, then. After drying his eyes, Naysin kissed Jehan one last time and began staggering toward Mt. Tsikomo.

Chapter Sixteen

The Shrine of the Middle

The journey west was painfully slow at first — literally painful. Naysin's head only healed gradually. It took him several days to recover his equilibrium, and many more before his temple stopped hurting to the touch. In the meantime, he used his abilities as little as possible. He still had a tendency to overpower them, and after nearly causing a forest fire, he restricted his shamaning to subsistence activities and nothing more. He thought about trying to heal himself, but he was haunted by memories of his inability to do anything to the brand over his eye, and the extreme amount of energy it had taken to patch Degan's minor cut. Given his current instability, he decided it was better not to risk blowing his head off.

He was also moving slowly because he didn't know where he was going.

"West" and "Mt. Tsikomo" proved to be vaguer concepts than he'd guessed. West he could approximate by the sunset — and once he'd healed, by shamaning — but there was nothing in the sky or himself to help him find a mythical mountain. Nothing but Jehan's brief, reverential description. Her wish was enough to keep him going, though, to give him faith he'd get there.

Eventually.

But two moons into what he was beginning to think of as his pilgrimage, Naysin started to enjoy himself. There were several reasons: the landscape was changing from familiar forests to beautiful plains, he was finally healthy, and most of all, he could run again. The simple pleasure of moving quickly under his own power, his own *natural* power, was enough to keep all but the blackest moods at bay.

Sometimes he ran with a blank mind, tuning out everything but the rhythm of his footfalls and the ground ahead. Other runs were periods of contemplation, during which he let his thoughts range from Jehan to the fate of the slaves he'd left behind on Bimshire. There was one topic that troubled him more than any other: what exactly was he supposed to do with these accursed abilities? When should he use them? When shouldn't he? Answers were harder to come by than questions, however. Again and again, he talked himself in and out of using his powers, without coming to any final resolution.

And sometimes he talked to the cougar-men.

Not about any of his larger questions. After the role his "fathers" had played in avenging the Walking Purchase, helping him tie off the flows when he couldn't have done anything that deadly on his own, he was wary of their true intentions again. But there was no one else to converse with.

"Nothing big," Naysin had told them. "No 'you're a god' or 'you-should-really-be-doing this.' Just … talk to me."

As you wish, my son.

Agreed.

True to their word, the cougar-men kept to innocent topics: the shape of that cloud … which path to take … the merits of this campsite over the one they'd just passed… They were also endlessly witty, making Naysin laugh with jokes about the landscape or the antics of small animals. On the whole, they were surprisingly good companions. And by the time the terrain started changing again, this time from plains to desert, Naysin trusted the cougar-men enough to ask for their advice. "Which way?"

I take it you are still reluctant to use your abilities more than absolutely necessary?

Because we could show you how to sight several leagues in any direction…

"No, nothing new. Not until I see the Shrine."

And if you don't find the answers you seek?

"Father Enki..."

You're right. It was too big. My apologies. I take it back. The cougar-man made a sucking noise.

Naysin laughed and shook his head.

Then your only real choice is to pick a direction — north, south, or straight ahead — hope you find someone, and ask them.

"You make it sound so easy."

Decisions usually are when you have no real choices.

"All right ... north."

North?

"Absolutely."

North it is.

Naysin wasn't feeling quite as flippant after ten days of his new heading led nowhere. The desert was harder to traverse than the plains. And unfortunately, that meant more shamaning; during the day, he had to arc his shadow to protect himself from the sun (as he'd done on the ocean), and at night, he had to sustain a fire to keep himself from freezing. It also took an extraordinary effort to find water. He could still summon it from beneath the ground (as he had in the forest), but it seemed like the water had to rise an enormous distance to reach the earth's surface.

After three more days of this, Naysin wasn't sure how anyone without his powers could survive in the desert.

He found signs of life on the fourth day, however: two brown-skinned men with packs on their backs. Their clothes were beaded and strange, but they weren't pale men, and that was enough to overcome Naysin's reluctance. Approaching at a steady, unthreatening jog, he caught up to the strangers and asked for help. They gave it gladly, redirecting him to the southwest and offering him a piece of flatbread to ease his travel.

A few days later, he saw peaks protruding above the horizon. And a half-moon after that, he finally arrived at Mt. Tsikomo's lush base, shockingly green after so much yellow. Pausing to catch his breath, he looked around to reassure himself that this really *was* the tallest mountain of the range, as the travelers had promised it would be. Satisfied, he turned back to the slope and began sprinting.

He couldn't maintain the pace for long, but Naysin enjoyed the energetic start to the climb: it was the culmination of a long, wandering journey; the fulfillment of his promise to Jehan; proof of his recovery from what had likely been a fractured skull; and the realization of a hope for himself. Raising one foot in front of the other was never a problem, even when his lungs and muscles began to burn and his fear of heights, which he'd had since the day the cougar-men "taught" him to fly, threatened to curl him into a ball.

An arduous half-day later, he was at the top.

The view — as long as he didn't stand too near to the edge — was spectacular. To the north, west, and south were more mountains, and to the east a river wound through a sprawling canyon. Mt. Tsikomo itself was wooded at the bottom, shrubbed in the middle, and bare at the summit, an evolution that caught Naysin's eye as he surveyed how far he'd climbed.

On the peak, the only sign of human presence was a mound of loose stones. From them rose a long, barkless spruce tree, white and barren. According to the travelers he'd met, this tree was the *exact* center of the world, the balance point between the four directions, as well as the earth's zenith and nadir.

Naysin approached the tree slowly, still unsure of the enlightenment he hoped to receive, but beginning to shake in anticipation of its bestowal. If this tree could somehow right the balance in *himself*, the journey here would be worth the effort many times over. Heart fluttering, he extended his hand toward the lowest branch, readying himself for whatever sensation he was about to experience. Then he felt...

Wood.

And that was all.

After waiting for something more, Naysin let go of the spruce tree and sat heavily on the stones. The part of him that had predicted this outcome grew louder and louder, chasing his remaining optimism into the depths of his mind.

Jehan had only said the idea of the mountain sounded nice; she'd never promised anything. He'd blown her words out of proportion, grasped at straws in a vain attempt to orient his life, traveled for moons for ... for a dead tree and a nice view. There wasn't any greater meaning here, no embedded sense of cosmic balance. There wasn't even a shrine "with paths that ran down from it like fingers from a hand." This quest he'd set himself had been nothing more than an ill-conceived—

Naysin's thoughts changed course as he spied a village to the west. Maybe there was a shrine. Just not here. Jehan had never seen the mountain before. Could the cairn of stones and the shrine be two different things? He wouldn't further delude himself with false hopes, but it was still worth investigating. If the villagers could guide him to something real, maybe the trip would have a happy ending after all.

And really, what else did he have to do?

— « o » —

"What is this place?" There was more than a little wonder in Naysin's voice, despite his lingering disappointment. The village he'd climbed down to was like a honeycomb. The houses had been carved from the mountainside, ascending in a sequence that looked as organic as it did incredible. There were ladders everywhere — more ladders than paths — and the buildings were walled with a beautiful, earthy-red brick.

"Dzune," the girl with milky eyes and short brown hair said after a long pause, as if the word explained everything.

She was the first person Naysin had seen when he'd entered the village. She was young — only a winter or two older than himself — and sitting cross-legged in front of one of the lowest houses. At first he'd thought she was blind, but her cloudy pupils had no trouble tracking his movements. He also couldn't tell if she had a lisp, or just a strong accent his translating ability couldn't filter out. "It's incredible."

The girl shrugged.

A few other people passed by as Naysin continued to take in his surroundings. Most of them gave him a questioning look, but no one said anything.

Which, as usual, suited him just fine. "Tell me, is there a shrine nearby? With ... paths that run down from it like fingers from a hand?" He hurried the last few words, suddenly aware of how hackneyed they must sound to someone who'd grown up in the area. But he pushed on. "I was hoping to see it."

The girl licked her lips before speaking with painful deliberation, as if trying to make sure every syllable was enunciated correctly. "You mean the Shrine of the Middle. Yes, it's here." She made a face when she'd finished, displeased with what was now obviously a lisp.

He felt an unexpectedly strong surge of hope. "Where?"

She opened her mouth to say something and then closed it with a grimace, pointing with a fierce jab instead, to a peak south of the one he'd climbed.

So he'd been right; the shrine wasn't on Mt. Tsikomo, and there was still a chance the point of perfect balance really existed. "And that's Mt. Tsikomo?" he asked to double-check, gesturing at the tallest mountain.

The girl nodded, the beginnings of a small smile gracing her lips. "A lot of visitors mix them up."

"I'm glad I'm not the only one." He still felt foolish, but something about the way the girl was dealing with her awkwardness eased his own. "Would you mind showing me the way? To the Shrine?"

She looked surprised, but to his relief she nodded again.

"Thank you... I'm Naysin."

The girl looked at him for a moment, moving her lips soundlessly, as if practicing. "Naysin," she said eventually, before hissing in irritation.

"What's your name?" he asked quickly, hoping it consisted of easy syllables.

"Tay."

"Tay," he repeated with another smile. "Thank you again."

He offered her a hand up, and she took it with a surprisingly firm grip.

"Follow me."

— « o » —

Keeping up wasn't easy. Naysin was used to endurance running, but he didn't climb mountain paths every day like the milky-eyed girl obviously did. And she moved with a sure-footed — and when they got higher, a sure-handed — grace that left him hard-pressed to compensate. She seemed to know exactly where to go at every instant; never a stumble, not even a wobble. At one point she extended her hand back to Naysin before he realized he needed support. Then he tripped, and had to grab her fingers to steady himself.

"Thank you," he said after an embarrassed pause.

"You're welcome," she replied without turning around.

This was one of about three phrases she'd used since they left Dzune. Naysin hadn't known what to say after exchanging names, so he hadn't forced anything. But when he did ask a question, he noticed how reluctant Tay was to respond with anything more than a monosyllabic answer that avoided "ess," the sound she seemed to have the hardest time with. Mostly she just forged ahead, moving smoothly and purposefully as Naysin labored not to fall behind or betray his general unease with the increasing elevation.

He felt himself losing both battles when Tay mumbled that they'd reached the halfway point. "Wait..." he panted reluctantly, "can we ... stop for a moment?"

She pivoted to face him, noted how sweaty he was, and nodded.

"I'd like to ... enjoy the view."

The corners of her mouth twitched.

"And you're ... humbling me." Naysin threw up his hands in surrender. "I just need to ... catch my breath."

"All right," she said, still threatening to smile.

Chagrined, Naysin turned to appraise his surroundings as he'd said he would. They were worth the look, queasy as it made him; the rocky landscape — as it had been from Mt. Tsikomo — was (literally) breathtaking. And the path looked like it could have been hollowed out by ages of rushing rain ... if rain ever came to such a dry area. "Are there other paths?" he asked eventually, once his breathing returned to normal.

Tay nodded again. "One for each tribe," she added.

"And they all lead to the Shrine of the Middle?"

Another nod.

"So your tribes have the same priests?"

Tay opened her mouth to respond but then closed it so quickly her lips clapped together. Her right hand tapped her staff against the ground in frustration, and her left made a fleeting symbol by her side.

After a moment, Naysin realized the gesture signified a curse. He could interpret her hands, just like he could any other form of language. "Do your people always swear near holy places?"

Tay looked at him in astonishment and gestured again with her hands. Can you understand me? she asked with rapid flicks of her fingers.

"Yes," Naysin said, and then signed, can you understand me? The motions felt strange, but they came naturally (along with an accompanying flow of **Kug**).

Yes, she replied incredulously. Who taught you that?

I've always been good with tongues. Apparently that includes ... what do you call this?

She looked at her hands. The Waweme priests call it 'hand praying.' I'm not supposed to know how, but my father showed me.

He looked at his own hands. I like it, he signed after a short pause.

Tay smiled uncertainly, turned back to the summit, and started climbing again. "Come on."

She set a faster pace for the rest of the ascent. Naysin found his stride, though; the short rest had helped, and now he was used to the exertion. He'd often noticed this when running. The first field-lengths were the toughest, until his body loosened and adjusted. Still, he was glad the Shrine of the Middle was significantly shorter than Mt. Tsikomo — they reached the summit as he was considering asking for another break.

Awaiting them was a pool of water inside a ring of rocks. On one sat a clay vase and several feathered sticks. At first Naysin thought they were arrows, but the sticks didn't have points, and the feathers were too many and too irregularly-spaced for accurate flight.

"Prayer sticks," Tay began after seeing Naysin's questioning look. Then she made a face and switched to her hands. You plant them in the ground and make a prayer to the Waweme.

"The priests?"

No, the Waweme — the animal gods. The Waweme priests serve them.

"I see." Naysin gave the arrangement another skeptical appraisal. The rocks and water had a certain tranquility to them, but so far he wasn't feeling anything more than he had atop Mt. Tsikomo.

With diminished expectations, he picked up a stick. Its feathers came from a colorful bird he didn't recognize. Looking back at the circle of stones, he noticed there were a few prayer sticks already inserted around the perimeter. There didn't seem to be any pattern to their placement, but he wanted to be sure he did this right, that he gave it an honest chance. "Like this?" he asked, gesturing with the stick toward the nearest patch of ground outside the circle.

Tay nodded.

After studying the spot, Naysin eased his stick into the earth, taking care not to snap its slender shaft.

"Now pray," Tay said softly.

Naysin breathed deeply and let his thoughts wash over him. What should he pray for? That Jehan was at peace, for one... That the pale men, women, and children he'd sent on a death march had somehow survived... That the slaves he'd left on Bimshire and *The Minotaur* had found a way to escape... That his mother was still alive and well.

But he'd journeyed here for a specific reason: he wanted an answer. A guideline for when to use his abilities.

How to be. He just wanted to know how to be.

He found himself asking the question aloud, in his people's tongue. Tay watched in silence as he said the words three times, each utterance softer than the last. That done, he closed his mouth and waited, choking back simultaneous surges of hope and fear.

"Pour water next to your prayer."

Naysin looked back at Tay, who pointed at the clay vase.

"So your wish will grow."

Murmuring his thanks, he picked up the vessel, filled it with water from the pool, and slowly sprinkled the pure liquid onto his prayer stick, as if he were nurturing a sapling whose roots were still too fragile to withstand a heavy downpour.

Then he waited again.

Still nothing.

And after ten ten-counts, he gave up. This was clearly a waste of time — this *whole trip* had been a waste of time. The "Shrine of the Middle" had no more answers than Degan, or the cougar-men, or his mother. There would be no resolution for him here.

"Sometimes it takes a while for a prayer to be fulfilled," Tay said as he turned to go.

Naysin shook his head with a bitter laugh that was almost a sob. "It's been six years."

Chapter Seventeen

Plague

They took a different path down — Tay claimed it had an even nicer view. Naysin didn't really care, but he appreciated her effort to cheer him up. And when they finally reached the base of the little mountain, he felt like he owed her more than the token acknowledgements he'd offered so far.

"Thank you again for guiding me," he said sincerely. "I know you must have other things to do."

She looked away. "Not really, but it was my pleasure."

He considered her for a moment, suddenly wondering what her story was. "So you don't have things to do?"

"Not today."

"What do you do on other days?" he asked, aware that he was being rude but unwilling to let it go.

I dance, she eventually signed.

It made sense given her grace. "For fun?"

For ceremonies. I help the priests.

"The Waweme priests? So if it's religious, I'd have to come to a ceremony to see you dance?"

There's one tonight.

Shyness suddenly caught up with Naysin. "Would it be … acceptable if I came?"

Tay smiled. You can be my guest.

— « o » —

After the walk back, Tay had to prepare for the night's events. But she told Naysin he could explore on his own; Dzune was at peace with its neighbors, and visitors were welcome.

He spent what remained of the day wandering the town, marveling again at its vertical structure. A talkative local explained that Dzune was sectioned according to the *seven* cardinal points: North, South, East, West, and the world's Zenith, Nadir, and Middle. Apparently the town's name meant "pivots of time," the only place "the gods appear in person." Naysin had his doubts about this, but the ceremony tonight was supposed to bring proof; just before sundown, two of the masked gods would usher in the summer, culminating the twenty-day solstice celebration.

Naysin wouldn't be holding his breath.

He was, however, interested in the way Tay interacted with the other villagers when she reappeared, dressed in a tunic and leggings adorned with brightly colored feathers. After she sat cross-legged on the ground, several villagers immediately formed a line that began four strides back from her. She listened intently to each person who stepped up, and then tapped once or twice on the ground. Curious, Naysin got in line himself. Tay was so focused on her task that she didn't see him until it was his turn. She blanched slightly when she recognized him, but quickly regained her composure. "Ask a question," she whispered. "Yes or no only."

He raised his eyebrows and started to sign a remark about her festive clothing.

"Not here," she hissed, grabbing his hands before he'd finished forming the first word. "I don't know what that means, remember?"

"Forgive me…" He felt a fool.

"It's all right," she whispered again after taking a quick look around. "I don't think anyone noticed." She let go of his hands and forced a smile. "Do you have a question?"

Naysin looked into her milky eyes and remembered the afternoon's disappointment. "Will I learn how to control myself?"

Tay's gaze lingered on his black and white brand. Cocking her head, she tapped the ground once. "That means yes."

He swallowed hard before nodding his thanks and moving out of the way.

Shortly thereafter, Tay answered her last question and rose to a stand. It was dusk, and the central fire was beginning to send shadows flickering across the town's multiple levels.

A drumbeat began, and Tay shook her staff. To Naysin's amazement, it rattled, sounding like rain trickling down a roof. He would have sworn the staff never made a noise throughout their entire hike. Somehow, she'd held it steady while traveling up and down a *mountain* — another testament to her incredible coordination.

Tay revealed more of her grace when she began to dance.

Still shaking and now swinging her staff at rhythmic intervals, she traced a fluid path around the fire, pulsing gently to the drumbeat as she flowed through a series of languid steps. Even more so than when she walked, not a motion seemed out of place, not a gesture uncalled for. It was ... perfect.

Naysin was entranced.

And totally caught off guard when the drum began beating wildly and two masked men rushed the fire from different directions. Naysin nearly let loose a stream of *Mir* to protect Tay before he realized the men were part of the ceremony.

One man wore an elaborate white mask with features that reminded Naysin of the distorted visages on the walls of his people's Longest House. The other man's black mask was molded in the same image. Neither man wore anything else except for armbands and a loincloth.

Moving frenetically, the masked men — were these the "Gods" the local had spoken of? — raced around the fire, flailing their limbs with a violence that seemed in utter contradiction to the smooth dance Tay had just ended; she was kneeling now, her head bent almost to her ankles.

After three laps around the fire, the masked men skidded to a halt and advanced on Tay. She did nothing until they were almost on top of her, and then raised her hands to offer her staff. The masked men took it hungrily, each grabbing an end as she maintained her hold. Planting their feet, the men launched the staff skyward, and Tay used the boost to vault into the air.

As she rose, she began dancing again, and when she sailed lightly back to earth, the masked men and seemingly everyone else in the village joined in.

The ritual, whatever it meant, was complete.

Not sure what to make of the spectacle, Naysin hung back. The mass dance seemed to be some sort of tension release; the people of Dzune were moving hard and fast, some with smiles on their faces but many without. This wasn't something he wanted to interrupt.

But he felt obligated when he noticed a rash on the head of one of the most vigorous dancers — the same rash he'd seen condemn so many on Bimshire. "Get away from them!" he yelled, unconsciously using a string of **Kug** to amplify his voice. "Get away from them!" he repeated as he sprinted into the throng and took hold of his startled target, a smallish man with a sweaty brow.

Several grasping hands tried to divert Naysin from his purpose, but he blew them back with a gust of *Mir.* The rest of the crowd was too stunned to prevent him from manhandling the struggling little man away from the fire and tossing him to the ground.

"He's diseased!" shouted Naysin, still projecting his voice. "He has the plague. I've seen it before."

"The Waweme healed me," the little man protested. "I feel better."

An officious-looking man in ceremonial garb almost as colorful as Tay's emerged from the crowd. His voice resonated with an authoritative bass. "Meli speaks the truth. He returned from his travels with symptoms we've never seen before, but each of the twelve medicine societies said prayers for him, and his rash lessened. Your concern is misplaced, stranger."

Naysin shook his head. "Sometimes the rash diminishes before it explodes into pustules. As I said, I've seen it before. It kills. And it spreads."

"Be that as it may," another priestly figure said as he appeared to Naysin's left, "medicine is the province of the animal gods and the Waweme. And we deal with our own. Leave Meli to us, and you may go without fear of reprisal."

"You can't heal him," Naysin replied, still shaking his head. "None of you can. But I'll try."

The priests — three in front now, with several more moving to surround him — continued to argue that sickness was their domain, but Naysin ignored them and laid his hands on Meli. Everyone went silent, sensing that something was about to happen, that maybe they *hadn't* imagined Naysin tossing members of the crowd back with an invisible force.

Something did happen ... but not perceptibly. Purifying and repairing living tissue was still immensely difficult — it was hard to see what needed to be done. It looked like Meli had too much *Mir* in his body, but there were some odd pockets of **Kug** as well. And the rash itself was a complicated mix of both essences. So Naysin concentrated on draining as much *Mir* from the rash as he could, chasing it out with a steady stream of **Kug**.

It didn't amount to much before Naysin had to stop, exhausted and aching from the imbalance he'd created within himself. The rash was maybe an eye-lash's width smaller, but that was all.

As he glanced back at his audience, Naysin noticed Tay for the first time since the dancing stopped. There was wonder in her gaze; she at least seemed to have noticed the change in the rash. Her milky eyes might look odd, but they were sharp.

The priests were less impressed.

"Now that you've had a turn," the original speaker said condescendingly, "why don't you let us perform our duty and allow our people to continue their celebration?"

As the priest spoke, Meli started to edge away from Naysin.

"No!" yelled Naysin, glaring the little man back to the ground. "You can't heal him. He might recover on his own — I've seen that happen too — but not before he infects the rest of your town. If he hasn't already."

The priests began to converge again, and one who hadn't spoken yet asked the question Naysin was already struggling to answer. "So what do you propose we do?"

Hearing the words out loud gave him a sudden, dark insight. "I may not be able to heal him either," he said softly as he kneeled next to Meli, "but I can show you what will happen if you let this sickness stay among you."

And without hesitating, Naysin accelerated the plague.

Compared to curing the little man, encouraging the disease in him was child's play. At its core, the pox was fueled by *Mir*, but it fed on the structure and purpose of the **Kug** Naysin supplied. Meli tried to escape, but once the **Kug** began to take effect, he went as still as the horror-struck crowd.

First the rash on his forehead became a pustule.

Then another blemish appeared.

And another. And another. And another, until his whole face was littered with them.

Next the pustules spread over the rest of his body, clustering in his hands and feet but rising on his neck and chest as well.

Moments later, the whites of Meli's eyes turned red and the skin beneath each protrusion went black, forming dark splotches that made it look as if someone had dabbed him with spent coals.

Finally, the little man shuddered, leaked blood from every orifice, and died.

"You see?" Naysin asked, his question cleaving the silence like a hatchet. "This disease kills. Men, women, children — it doesn't matter. If anyone else develops the pustules, isolate them and burn their bodies." Stepping back, Naysin waved his hands and summoned a pillar of flame from the central fire, bending it over the crowd and onto Meli's corpse.

No one said anything until the original priest found the courage to ignore the stench of burning flesh: "Leave."

Naysin looked at his hands — which, like the rest of him, were shining with black veins and white arteries — and nodded. "Remember that I saved you," he said as he turned toward the edge of town and started walking, the circle of priests breaking hastily to let him pass. "I did what I had to do to save you.

"There was no other choice."

Chapter Eighteen

Tay

The next morning, Naysin realized he was being followed.

He hadn't paid much attention to his surroundings when he'd first left Dzune — he'd been too busy justifying his actions.

"I had to do it."

Of course, Father Enki said more than once. *That man would have died anyway.*

At least you made his death meaningful.

Naysin wasn't so sure. He still felt like he'd erred. Again. That he'd used his powers incorrectly. Always again. Dzune hadn't resolved anything for him.

Consequently, when the rising sun revealed a pursuer, Naysin welcomed the distraction.

He caught sight of his tail when he lost his footing and spun to regain his balance. His hunter froze immediately, but not before Naysin saw enough motion to distinguish a profile from the muted landscape. The distance was too great to make out recognizable features, but somehow Naysin knew.

It was Tay.

Why she was following him was anyone's guess. Perhaps she wanted to confront him ... or maybe she wanted to comfort him. Either way, it would be best if she stayed as far from him as possible. Jehan was all the evidence he needed of that.

Filled with new purpose, Naysin turned back around and began pumping one leg after another. Tay might be more used to changes in elevation, but he was past caring how his body felt. And he knew he could outrun just about anyone.

So he sprinted. Long and hard, for as far as he could. Up the current hill, down its other side, and most of the way up another. Then he jogged, and when he couldn't do that, he moved at a brisk walk. Once he had his wind back, he repeated the cycle. He didn't bother checking behind him until the afternoon. There was no way she was keeping up; grace wasn't the same thing as endurance. He was traveling faster (unaided) than he ever had before...

Tay was still there.

Much farther away from him, but moving quickly and ... weaving. She was struggling, at least. That was something. Maybe if he kept on through evening...

She fell as Naysin started to turn away. At first he wasn't sure whether she'd tumbled or he'd simply lost sight of her, but after several moments passed and she didn't reappear, he felt certain she'd succumbed to exhaustion or injury.

Neither possibility sat well with him. He'd meant to escape her, not hurt her. Spirits and lakes, why hadn't she given up? He didn't need this on his conscience — not on top of everything else. With a sigh, Naysin began retracing his steps, still alternating between sprinting, jogging, and walking.

He needn't have worried. By the time he came within hailing distance, Tay looked quite relaxed, propped up on her elbows and smiling mischievously.

Naysin didn't smile back. Instead, he stared at her until he'd caught his breath, shook his head, and turned around.

"Wait."

Without knowing why, he glanced over his shoulder.

She was smiling again, but her grin was smaller this time. "I'm rested now — you won't get as far. And..."

He shrugged, still only half-facing her. "And?"

I'm like you, she signed hurriedly.

It was his turn to smile, albeit darkly. "No, you're not."

"I am!" she insisted out loud before continuing with her hands. Not as strong, but ... sometimes I see things before they happen.

Naysin faced her fully. He didn't believe her, but he wanted to.

Not far, Tay continued. Usually only a few heartbeats in advance. I can hear them too. And smell them.

"So that's why your people think you can tell their fortunes..."

She laughed softly. No, that started a long time ago.

"Because of your eyes."

Tay nodded.

"But that doesn't make you like me."

Yes it does! We can both do things... Neither one of us is normal.

"That may be true," he conceded as he twisted around for a final time. "But you're not dangerous. I won't come back for you again."

He started sprinting before she could say anything else.

— « o » —

Tay didn't give up easily.

It took several days of off-and-on running before Naysin felt like he'd lost her. For good measure, he pushed hard for an additional two days. Part of him suspected she was still tracking him, staying out of sight during the day and catching up at night when he slept.

The other part of him hoped this was true.

I see things, she'd said, *before they happen...*

Those simple words had confirmed there really were other shamans in the world; Amadi — the Foim who could heal himself — hadn't just been a product of Naysin's exhausted imagination that day on the ship. Which meant he wasn't alone.

But the cougar-men thought otherwise.

Do you truly think she understands what you're experiencing?

She seems like a sweet girl. But really Naysin, seeing flashes of the future an instant before it happens is child's play compared to what you can do.

"Maybe," Naysin panted out between strides, "but she's ... the second person ... I can compare to ... even a little."

What about us?

"Aside from you... You take my ... meaning, though?"

Of course.

"Everyone else ... is so different... She's at least ... a little the same."

Then why are you running from her so quickly?

Naysin frowned at the triumphant note in Father Enki's voice. "For her ... own good... After Jehan—"

After Jehan you should have realized that suppressing your powers is a mistake.

You can do so much with them if you learn control.

"We're not ... speaking of this."

So it went until the new moon: intense running, occasional conversations with the cougar-men, endless introspection, and frequent looks over his shoulder to see if Tay was still following him.

She was, but she only revealed herself to save his life.

The seventh night after Dzune, Naysin woke to the butt of a fire stick descending on his head. He managed to harden enough air to soften the blow, but even diminished in force, the impact nearly knocked him unconscious. His temples ached like they had the night Jehan died, and he could feel the same loss of equilibrium and control setting in.

But his vision was unaffected, and the moonlight illuminated flashes of white skin — pale men. Again. Joking and laughing as they readied their weapons to complete the ambush.

Then they were dying.

It took a moment for Naysin to realize the blur cutting the pale men down like wheat for the harvest was ... Tay. She looked inhuman, transcendently smooth as she flitted between her overmatched victims. Anticipating every thrust, foreseeing every parry, assured of every step and strike; she really could see a little ahead of everyone else. And in a fight, that was all it took.

She fought with her staff — her rainstick, as someone in Dzune had called it — every swing rattling the pebbles as if she wielded a sliver of an avalanche. One of the staff's ends was drawing blood. There was a blade there; Naysin hadn't seen it before. Another surprise. They kept coming with her.

Within a handful of heartbeats, the pale men were on the ground. All *five* of them. Without meaning to, Naysin let out a low whistle as he held his hand to his head. He hadn't had to shaman a lick of **Kug** or *Mir*.

He hadn't had time.

Swallowing, he tried to ignore the gore and focus on Tay, who'd finally slowed down from her ... battle dance. There was no better way to describe it. She even generated her own music. "I was wrong," he said softly.

She broke out of whatever trance she'd been in and stared at him, her breathing suddenly as wild as her eyes.

"You are dangerous."

Tay flinched and turned back to the dead pale men. "I've never done that before," she whispered. "I've never even hit anyone..." She dropped her rainstick.

The lethal end hit the ground at an ill-fated angle, and the blade snapped off. Tay didn't seem to notice — she was still studying the rumpled forms strewn about her in a morbid circle, staring at them as if she were trying to sear the dark images into her milky eyes.

Naysin sensed he should say something more, but his head was throbbing.

So it fell to a new voice to break the silence: "Were they drunk?"

"Smells like it," another responded.

Naysin turned to see several new pale men pointing fire sticks at him and Tay. These men looked worn and hardened, as if they'd been traveling since winter without respite. After a brief pause, one of them dipped his fire stick and cocked his shaggy black head, as if he were considering a question.

"A bad end for bad men," he said eventually. His was the first voice, a rich baritone that seemed to command respect from the other pale men. He must be the leader. "Still, we've lost more hands than we can afford."

"Shall we shoot them?" asked a small gray-haired man, gesturing toward Naysin and Tay with his fire stick.

"No," Naysin interjected, to everyone but Tay's surprise (she was still staring at her handiwork).

"You speak Espan?" the leader asked incredulously.

"So it would seem."

The black-haired man lowered his fire stick the rest of the way to the ground, resting on the weapon's butt as he cocked his head to the other side. "And fluently, it seems... I think I have an offer for you."

Naysin angled his head in imitation of the pale man, ignoring the pain the motion caused.

The black-haired man smiled wryly before continuing. "In recompense for the men you've killed, travel with me and serve as my interpreter. We go east."

"East?" Naysin asked in surprise. "You're going east? Meaning you came from the west." He shook his head. "You pale men really are everywhere."

"Not yet," the black-haired man said with another smile. "We're exploring. Alfons there," he continued, nodding to another man, "is the best cartographer in Espania. We're charting the interior for the King, in hopes of finding a waterway that... Tell me, where did you learn to speak our language? Your facility is nothing short of amazing."

"They come from east and west," Naysin muttered, "and we're in the middle... I think I have an offer for *you*."

"Oh?"

"In recompense for your men trying to kill me, turn around, go back the way you came, and sail home."

The black-haired man considered Naysin for a few moments before signaling that the gray-haired man with the itchy trigger finger could proceed with his initial suggestion. "I think we've come a little too far for that."

"So have I," Naysin said, letting loose simultaneous blasts of **Kug** and *Mir*.

He was still too disoriented to act with precision, but he didn't need it. There was nothing delicate about the way he convulsed the earth beneath the dead men's bodies and tossed them into the air. Nothing refined about how he harnessed the wind and hurled the corpses back to (what he thought was) the west. It was just raw power, plain and brutal.

Almost as one, the living pale men turned their heads to follow their dead brothers' trajectories, gazing into the distance long after the human missiles had disappeared into the dark. Naysin knew why the living men didn't want to look back at him; he was terrifying. He *felt* terrifying, shining brighter than the stars with his crisscrossing lines of black and white rage.

"Go west," he said, knowing the pale men would listen.

They did, this time completely as one. Still without looking back.

Their fear was small comfort when the pain hit him. This was the light-headed kind, the type that made his body feel like it was about to fall apart because he'd shamaned more *Mir* than **Kug**. Apparently commandeering the wind to hurl men out of sight took more energy than bouncing their bodies up with an earthy hiccup. Imagine that.

His agonized laugh snapped Tay out of her shock. Blinking rapidly, she shook her head and whispered something to herself. Then she looked at Naysin and repeated the words loud enough for him to hear: "They deserved it."

He could only manage a nod in response.

"They deserved it," she repeated. "So I won't feel bad."

Naysin nodded again, and his eyes lit on her rainstick … with its broken blade.

Stumbling over to the fallen weapon, he picked up the bone shard, fit it back to the shaft, and funneled enough **Kug** into the join to set his internal balance right. As he molded the two pieces back into one, he saw how ingenious the staff was: twisting the top to the left produced the blade; twisting to the right lowered the edge out of sight. It was a simple yet deadly design that he'd now made all but unbreakable.

"Clever weapon," he said as he handed the renewed staff back to Tay.

She took it gingerly, testing the blade several times before she seemed to believe it was whole. "My father made it for me. He always worried about the blade breaking — thank you."

"It's the least I could do."

Chapter Nineteen

On the Wind

They went east because Naysin didn't know where else to go, and Tay didn't have an opinion. Her only plan was to stay with him. <u>Because you obviously need looking after</u>, she'd signed with a shy smile.

Having her along was … nice. Naysin couldn't deny that. She gave him someone to talk to besides the cougar-men, who'd said very little since she'd joined him. Most of his conversations with Tay were awkward, but it was human interaction, his first since Jehan. His memory of the Franc woman kept him from getting too close to Tay, however. He maintained a buffer, drawing back whenever he felt like they were treading on potentially intimate ground.

Still, he learned a lot about her in those first days of walking together.

<u>No,</u> she'd replied when he'd asked if she'd been born with her ability. <u>My awakening happened years ago.</u>

<u>No,</u> she'd responded again, after he'd asked if it hurt to use her ability. <u>Never. Not like it does for you.</u>

She couldn't *see* what she was doing either. And Naysin couldn't explain it very well; the concepts of **Kug** and *Mir* were entirely foreign to her, even when he tried different names like order and chaos. She was blending the energies in a subtle way he couldn't quite replicate, but it wasn't conscious — she was shamaning instinctively.

So, he was still alone in most respects. She was different, but not nearly as different as he was.

But it was still good to have someone to talk to again. Even when she was remonstrating him. Tay had confirmed his guess that she had a few more winters than him — twenty to his eighteen — and she enjoyed playing the older-sister role. Her favorite thing to scold him about was how fast he walked: "I know you like to run, but slow down! My legs are shorter than yours!"

He usually countered by literally running circles around her. She'd laughed the first time he did this, and stuck her rainstick between his legs and tripped him. Now it was a game they played, one which Tay, with her ability to predict where he was going, inevitably won. Naysin still enjoyed it; it was like an echo of his lost childhood.

Tay also needled him about eating too little and too plainly. "You can summon anything you want," she said one afternoon. "Cook anything you want. And this is what you make?" She held up the skinny rabbit he'd flash-fried that morning. <u>You couldn't at least magic some spice on it?</u> Tay concluded, lapsing into signs.

Naysin shrugged and smiled. "I told you, I'm not a cook. I never learned how."

<u>But you can do anything!</u>

"It can't be that bad — you were scavenging before you caught up to me."

She wrinkled her nose at him. <u>I was *hunting*. Not cheating.</u>

"Oh, I see. So you never *anticipate* where your game is going to move?"

<u>Hush</u>.

Much of this was light-hearted. The only time Tay berated him with real feeling was during their fifth day of traveling together, when they came upon a small lake bisected by an impossibly long rope. Thick and taut, the cord stretched from a tree on their side to a rock on the other. The line was knotted so the entire length could be tightened by pulling the end at an angle.

Naysin was impressed, but Tay was horrified.

"Don't look!" she insisted as a bolt of recognition flashed across her milky eyes. She turned away forcefully, pulling at Naysin to do the same.

He let her tug him around, but not without asking, "Why?"

It's the Lake of Whispering Waters, she signed rapidly, keeping her eyes focused on her hands. Where the Mask Gods live. Anyone who looks into the waters dies within four days.

Naysin resisted the urge to glance behind him. "Like the 'gods' that danced at your summer solstice celebration?"

Tay shot him a warning look. Those were embodiments of the gods, yes.

He backtracked. "What's the rope's purpose?"

My father said it's to help the Masked Gods climb out when they wish to enter the world. Let's go.

"But if no one can look on the water without dying, how does anyone know about it?"

Somebody must have looked and told others within four days. Why does it matter? Everyone in the village already knows about it. We need to leave.

"Someone must maintain that rope. And they probably have to look in the water to do it."

Tay glared at him. "Why don't you believe me? We need to leave. *Now*."

Naysin's expression softened, but he wouldn't be dissuaded. "Tay," he said gently, "we already saw the lake. If it's going to kill us, we might as well get a closer look."

She bit her lip, looked like she was going to explode into motion ... and nodded.

Naysin let Tay set the pace of their approach. She didn't bull-rush her fear, but she didn't run away from it either. He respected that. When they reached the water's edge, however, he immediately bent down to touch it.

"Naysin," Tay breathed, too late to stop him from cupping some of the lake in his hand. She hadn't foretold his transgression; she must have been more afraid than he realized. Grudgingly, she let him peer at the water she'd heard so many stories about. But it wasn't long before she couldn't stand the silence: "Can you protect us?"

Naysin fought down the part of him that wanted to say, "It's just a lake." There wasn't any point. He may have lost faith in Gilmekon and all the other spirits that had abandoned him, but that didn't mean she needed to bury her beliefs. "Yes," he said solemnly, "I can protect us."

He stood and began shamaning *Mir* into a circle of air. As the little storm grew, he scooped bits of lake into it, until he and Tay were surrounded by a miniature cone cloud of wind and mist. Finally, with a grandiose gesture, he collapsed the "shield," soaking them both.

Tay gasped and hugged Naysin tight. "Thank you," she whispered into his chest.

He felt guilty, but not much. "It was nothing."

— « o » —

"Why did you follow me?" Naysin asked Tay several days later, as the terrain began to change back to pastures and woods. "Why did you leave your home to follow me after ... after I did what I did?"

Tay chewed her lip before responding. "There wasn't much to leave. My father was all I had, and he died last year... And even when he was around, I didn't fit in. He tried to get the other kids to accept me, but they never would. I was too different." With the effortless grace that still amazed Naysin, she leapt on and off a stump. "And you only did what you thought was right. Just as I did when those men attacked you."

"You sound so certain."

She gave him a disapproving look. "Why aren't you? I know you would have healed Meli if you could. Wait," she said when he started to move away. "I answered your question. Now it's your turn. Why are you blowing around like a leaf in the breeze?"

Naysin took a few more steps and stopped. "What do you mean?"

Tay swallowed, but she didn't pull back. "You're basically a god. But we're not really heading anywhere or doing anything. We're just wandering."

"You really want to know?"

"Yes."

Like with Jehan, the urge to tell Tay everything fountained like a geyser. He was tired of carrying so many secrets ... and so much guilt. But he was even more tired of being alone. And if he told Tay everything, would she stay? He already felt weak for letting her accompany him. But if she left now, horrified of who he really was — it would hurt. Naysin was sure of that much, at least.

So just like with Jehan, he settled for a partial truth, a sanitized version of his guardian spirit day, his failed stint as a savior in Bimshire, and his return home. Since she already knew about his abilities, he didn't hide the magic, but he left out the cougar-men, along with incidents, like Jehan's death and his reaction to the Walking Purchase, that he never wanted to think about again, much less confess to.

When he was finished, Tay took a few more steps — they'd kept walking as he talked — before signing a simple response: <u>I used to be blind.</u>

Naysin nearly tripped over a rock. "What?"

<u>And deaf — before my awakening. My father taught me the Waweme priests' hand praying so we could communicate. Every day he'd sign a new word into my palm.</u>

"I'm sorry you lost him."

<u>So am I. You've been through more, though.</u>

Naysin shrugged.

<u>But ... what are you looking for? You still didn't answer that.</u>

"No?"

<u>No. I can guess, but—</u>

"Then guess," he said, more harshly than he'd intended.

Tay looked at him reproachfully before telling him exactly what he was thinking: <u>Purpose. You're looking for your purpose, for the reason you were given these powers. You want to know what to do with them.</u>

His mind flashed back to the prayer he'd made at the Shrine of the Middle: *How to be... I just want to know how to be.* Naysin shook his head. "Perhaps."

<u>Then perhaps that's why I followed you.</u>

He looked at her skeptically.

She smiled as if it were obvious. <u>It feels like my purpose is to help you find yours. And for someone as powerful as you ... that's no small thing.</u>

"No," he eventually agreed, his voice soft and contemplative, "it's not."

Chapter Twenty

Quecxl

"Careful, Tay." Naysin solidified the warning by holding up his hand.

Not that he needed to; she'd been on alert well before he noticed the Hodensee. Rolling her milky eyes, she signed a question and touched her rainstick.

<u>No</u>, he signed back. <u>Just watch</u>.

They'd been journeying together for more than four moons now, long enough to develop a rhythm for reacting to new situations. Today, deep in a forest like the one he'd grown up in, they'd been lucky enough to come on these Hodensee from above, spying them before he and Tay began descending a wooded ridge. The five men were cleaning a deer carcass in a small clearing, scraping their kill down and preparing its meat for smoking. From the amount of furs, flesh, and bones stacked around them, it looked like they were well into an extended hunting expedition.

And they were definitely Hodensee; the three-finger-widths strip of hair running down their scalps and necks was all too familiar. It was the same style Degan and his brethren had adopted before the uprising on Bimshire. Memories of the ensuing savagery kept Naysin back — he didn't want to act until he knew more about this group's disposition.

<u>Look at that man's chest,</u> Tay signed. <u>What is that?</u>

Naysin followed her arm to the closest hunter; he was dressed in a Franc's shirt, cut like the ones Jehan used to wear and hanging open. But that didn't seem to be what

Tay was focusing on. Squinting to bring his vision up to her standards, Naysin zeroed in on the man's sternum, over which something thin and metallic was flashing, with a small bar jutting from its middle...

A cross — some of Bimshire's overseers had brandished similar totems.

More curious than cautious now, Naysin risked standing to get a better view. The other men had crosses as well. And now that he was looking closely, he noticed that all of them wore at least a piece or two of pale-one clothing.

This was unexpected.

"Step carefully, stranger, unless you want to join the deer in my pot tonight."

It was only now, as the first Hodensee sighted down the arrow he'd just drawn, that Naysin realized the man had a lazy eye. "I'm afraid I wouldn't be worth the trouble," Naysin called back. "My friend here keeps telling me I'm nothing but skin and bones."

Even if Tay had been able to understand Hodensee, she probably wouldn't have responded; before the first man had finished speaking, she'd glided in front of Naysin, her rainstick clutched in both hands. Several of the men laughed at her stance, but he knew she stood a decent chance of deflecting the arrow. If he let it come to that, which he wouldn't.

"Being scrawny isn't an excuse to trespass on our hunting grounds," the Hodensee with the bow said.

Naysin crinkled his forehead. "Since when did original people stake claims to the land? You sound like a pale one. And with that shirt, you look like one too."

"Maybe that's not such a bad thing." There was no sarcasm in the Hodensee's voice, and he even lowered his bow so he could rub his cross.

"Do all of you feel this way?"

Amused now, the Hodensee set his bow on the ground and crossed his arms. "If by all of us you mean my friends here, then yes." Almost in unison, the other four men raised their crosses and kissed them. "But if by all of us you mean our village, then the answer is still yes."

"Truly?" Naysin murmured, thinking again of Degan's uprising and the contrast it made with this ... surrender. "Could I see it?"

The Hodensee gave Naysin a puzzled look. Tay gave him a questioning one.

"Your village," he clarified for the Hodensee. "Your ways are new, and I'd like to see them in practice for myself. I'm looking for answers — I'd be honored to learn how you arrived at yours."

It was the Hodensee's turn to be taken aback. "I suppose I can't say no to that." He laughed curtly. "All right, maybe you will be sharing my pot tonight. Wait until we're done here, and we'll take you to Cawgana. And if you're lucky, the Black Robe will still be there."

— « o » —

The resident "Black Robe" was gone. Apparently he'd left three days earlier to visit another settlement.

According to the Hodensee hunting party, the Black Robes were pale-one priests. They called themselves "Jestus," and it was their mission to convert non-believers to the religion of one god and one son. Their arguments must have been persuasive: the Cawgana Hodensee dressed like pale ones; the houses had an alien, angular style to them; and nearly everyone had one of the awful crosses swinging from their necks.

It was infuriating to Naysin, and mystifying to Tay.

Why are we still here? she signed when she thought no one was looking. _These people are mad._

I'm not disputing that, he signed back, _but we need to know more before we go._

Why?

I need to know more before we go, Naysin amended.

"So you see," Deskae, the hunter with the lazy eye, said as he rejoined them, "the Black Robes have helped us build stronger buildings, eat cleaner food, and worship a truer god. _The_ true god. One who hasn't abandoned us. Without the Black Robes' guidance, we'd be lost."

"You seem very sure of that."

Deskae looked at Naysin and chuckled dryly. "I know there are evil pale men. Believe me, I know. But some, like the Black Robes, only want to help."

Naysin spat on the ground. "They don't want your land, maybe, but they want something even more important: your hearts. And they've got them, because you offered them up without a fight."

The Hodensee shook his head. "I didn't understand until I was saved. But you asked to see our answers, and this is what they are, whether they sit well with you or not."

Naysin pursed his lips, torn between apologizing and lashing out further ... until he saw a slender woman emerge with a stack of bandages from a nearby longhouse, and his anger sank into his feet. "There's plague here."

"Yes," Deskae said, following Naysin's eyes to the woman, who was walking toward an isolated building on the town's west side.

"Can the Black Robes heal it?" Naysin's tone was no longer mocking

Deskae's voice softened in response. "No. They try, and when they're here, they care for the dying. But the true god sent us another light to shine against the darkness."

Naysin nodded and started following the woman. He was vaguely aware that Deskae moved to stop him, and that Tay stopped Deskae by putting a hand on his shoulder. It didn't matter. There was plague here. There was plague everywhere, rotting the core of people like his, preparing the way for the pale ones without their having to lift a finger.

It was unfair.

More than that, it was monstrous, heinous, horrific, evil — all of these things and worse. But at the moment, it was the unfairness Naysin felt most. Just when his people needed all their strength, they were being humbled by diseases no one could cure.

Not even him.

"No one is supposed to go in here except me," the woman said when he reached the door. She looked calm. Haggard, but calm. He supposed she'd have to be. "What's your name?"

"Kateri," she replied neutrally, her matted bangs swinging like dark vines as she shook her head. "You're not allowed in here."

Naysin closed his eyes. "Please. I might be able to help them. I've seen this before."

After a brief appraisal, she decided something about him was worth believing; as she turned to enter the sick house, she gestured for him to do the same.

There were bodies from wall to wall.

Living-but-dying bodies crammed into the longhouse as lovingly as possible. The beds were far too few, but the afflicted all had blankets under their bodies and pillows of furs under their heads. It was kindly done.

Even if it stank worse than anything.

As Naysin struggled not to throw up, Kateri picked her way to the back and began applying the bandages she'd brought to a man sprawled across one of the beds. By the look of his pustules, he wouldn't be there long.

Some of the patients called out to Naysin when he'd settled his stomach enough to begin walking around the longhouse, but he was too overwhelmed to respond. How could Kateri stand it? There were so many, with so many more to come, and so little that could be done. And that stench: spirits and lakes, it was bad.

Nearly overcome again, Naysin fought the impulse to eradicate the blight. The urge — no, the *need* — to end the dying's suffering ... to protect the living from sharing the same fate ... to cleanse them with fire, as he'd done for Meli of the Dzune...

Naysin was close to giving in when a hoarse voice broke through his dark debate: "Karakwa?"

Disbelief flooded his mind. He hadn't been called the Hodensee word for "sun" since Bimshire. He swiveled around, looking for the speaker even as he hoped he'd heard wrong.

"Karakwa." This time it was a statement, an assertion from a stocky man slumped beneath the shadows of the eastern corner. "So the savior lives," he added, sounding as if he were still deciding how that sat with him.

"As do you," Naysin replied, approaching reluctantly. Up close, the stocky man's badly pocked skin became evident, even in the dim light.

"Not for long." On cue, the stocky man began coughing uncontrollably. His hacking startled something in the rafters: a gull? But they were many moons' journey from the ocean...

"You were on Bimshire?" Naysin asked when the fit passed.

"Two years." The stocky man smiled grimly. "I made it longer than you thought I would, didn't I? Longer than most of us did, that's for certain."

Naysin couldn't help wincing.

The stocky man pressed his advantage. "Without you, we didn't stand much chance. I'm guessing you knew that. But we held our own for a while. Formed a camp in the center of the island and tried to steal a boat. Then the pale men found us... They came from all over — our island and others nearby. They were angry, and they killed most of us on the spot. The rest they hung at the plantation as an example. Degan wore the first noose; Oheo the next."

Naysin couldn't think of a response.

"I lived," the stocky man continued, "because I looked dead. Imagine that." He squeezed out a few chuckles before a coughing fit seized him again, causing the gull to squawk. When the stocky man resumed talking, his voice took on Deskae's reverential tone. "One of the Black Robes saved me: Father Marcells. He came to the battlefield to send the dead on their way, and found me and two others still breathing. They died on the way to the harbor, but I survived to come to Cawgana and learn the true religion." His reddened eyes narrowed at Naysin. "Father Marcells is my savior now, along with the Lord Jesua."

"He did well by you."

The stocky man maintained his glare another few breaths before slumping back, the intensity leaking out of him. "Did you know you have another name now?" he asked softly.

Naysin shook his head.

"Otonsken. It means devil," the stocky man interpreted for Naysin (unnecessarily). "Degan named you that when the pale men fell on us. Before then, he kept saying you'd return. But when the ring of fire sticks began destroying us, he knew, just as the rest of us did, that our 'sun' was really a devil: bringer of false hopes, treachery, and destruction."

Stung, Naysin shook his head again. "I'm not a manitouk," he muttered.

The stocky man shrugged and turned away ... only to turn back, animated with childlike hopefulness: "Can you heal me?"

It hurt to admit the truth. "No." But as the stocky man's face fell, Naysin remembered there *was* something he could do. "I can kill you."

"Quickly?"

"Yes. No pain."

The stocky man regarded Naysin for a moment. "That's it?"

Something about the man's bearing had changed. "Yes. It won't hurt."

"That's *it*?" the stocky man repeated, pressing his back against the wall to support him as he stood. Upon seeing him rising, Kateri started to hurry over, but the stocky man waved her off. "I was told you could run on water, rearrange the stars, summon fire and wind — Quetzalcoatl's balls, man, you even speak Nahwatl without an accent, when no one else within a thousand leagues can say so much as 'hello' to me."

Taken aback, Naysin scanned the stocky man for clues to his intentions ... and realized his pockmarks were *old*. "You already survived the plague."

"Years ago," the stocky man said dismissively as he gestured at the gull.

"But your cough…"

"Just a cold."

A second truth revealed itself to Naysin: "You weren't on Bimshire."

The stocky man ignored him to watch the gull fly to a rafter above a woman's bed. She looked further gone than anyone who still drew breath in the longhouse; her blood was dark, and pustules had scabbed over her eyes, no doubt blinding her. Several other victims murmured as the stocky man staggered towards her, waving off Kateri's help again when she tried to offer an arm. Naysin nearly offered his own, but sensed it would have been similarly rejected.

When the stocky man reached the dying woman, he steadied himself with a deep breath and touched her forehead, where the blood was blackest. He stood like that for several breaths, arm outstretched and gull watching from above — long enough to make Naysin wonder if the stocky man had lost himself in some sort of empathetic waking nightmare.

Then the stocky man healed the woman.

Naysin only saw the first burst of **Kug**: the stiff stream the stocky man used to grant the woman enough strength to survive what came after. Naysin knew he should have been watching what the stocky man did next, how he manipulated a slow-moving storm of **Kug**, guiding flickers of it into the woman like lightning strikes of needle and thread, each shot lancing a pustule and binding the resulting crater. It didn't matter — Naysin couldn't have copied such shamaning anyway. And he was drawn to the woman's face, where the pustules were un-scabbing, receding, and... vanishing.

When she opened her eyes to hold Naysin's gaze, the woman's skin was clear. And she could *see*.

"Thank you," she breathed to the stocky man, squeezing his hand before slipping into an easy, healthy sleep.

He coughed once and sank back to the floor. Several of the victims offered prayers to the pale one's god, but they didn't sound surprised. The stocky man must have worked this miracle before.

"You're Deskae's light against the darkness," Naysin said humbly.

The stocky man grimaced. "Pale foolishness." He gestured at the gull again, but the creature just squawked. It almost sounded ... concerned — the stocky man was clearly exhausted. "Xihuitl, you stubborn wet nurse of a bird," he muttered. "Hear me," he intoned, turning to Naysin, "I don't care about the invaders' 'true god,' and I wasn't on Bimshire, but a man I trust was. He knows you. Knows what you can do."

Naysin was too awestruck to be guarded. "Who?"

"His name is Chogan."

Now Naysin grew wary once more. "How did he escape?"

"Much as I described, aside from the bit about the Black Robes." The stocky man gestured at Xihuitl again, but the gull reiterated its objection. Shaking his head, the stocky man slumped against the sleeping woman's bed. "Chogan succeeded in stealing a boat, which he rowed to the mainland. He had a day of freedom before being taken by different slavers."

"And you saved him?"

The stocky man chuckled tiredly. "You think too much of me now — I was still in the south. But a night skin liberated Chogan and many others. Amadi, of the Foim."

Impossible. "How?"

"He overcame their overseers and led the slaves who were willing to run to a safe haven in the wilderness. They call it Omnira."

"No, how does he *live*? I saw him drown himself."

The stocky man nodded. "Maybe, but nothing can stop that man. He lent me his strength when I needed it to save Omnira — I came upon them a few weeks after they'd founded their refuge. They were all dying of the plague. Except Amadi." The stocky man gestured a fourth time at Xihuitl, who finally acquiesced and flew to another near-dead victim. "What about you?" the stocky man asked as he struggled back to a stand and stumbled after the gull. As before, the other victims murmured as he moved among them; this time Naysin could make out the prayers of thanksgivings. "I knew you by your brand — it's exactly as Chogan and Amadi described. They also said you had powers to match a god's. Will you use it to help me?" The stocky man stopped and swung his arms out to encompass everyone in the room, nearly unbalancing himself. "Will you use it to help them?"

But Naysin was already at the door. "What's your name?"

The stocky man crossed his arms. "Quecxl. Of the Metica."

"The world should know your name, Quecxl of the Metica. Not mine."

"Too late," Quecxl said bitterly as Naysin left.

His reply came without a backward glance, hitch in stride, or scrap of hesitation: "I couldn't agree more."

Chapter Twenty-One

Turtle and Hawk

The Red Wraith haunted the ocean.

The Red Wraith burned plantations.

The Red Wraith marched women and children to their death.

It seemed Karakwa wasn't his only nickname; Naysin heard the new epithet whenever he lingered in a pale town.

He hadn't told Tay what people called him now, just like he'd never filled in the holes in his history, or fully explained why they left Cawgana so quickly. But she hadn't asked for clarification, which was one of the many reasons he no longer weighed the merits of leaving her.

She didn't like the frequent stops in pale taverns, though. That much was obvious. Sometimes he translated for her, but only when it didn't dredge up memories of Bimshire and Jehan. And definitely not when he was eavesdropping on discussions about the Red Wraith.

From these, he'd learned to keep his head covered in public. (Tay had made them hooded ponchos for the winter.) The "Wraith" part of that idiotic nickname came as much from his "swirling gray hair" as it did the way his veins and arteries shone black and white like streaks of "char and ash." Or so one old man had insisted to a crony on the coldest day of winter. The brand over Naysin's left eye was also starting to become a tell-tale. After a near-incident in a largish pale town, he'd begun hiding the tattoo with an illusion of unblemished flesh.

It was hideously painful to hear himself vilified, but he kept seeking the condemnation. Even if the stories didn't disperse any guilt, some of them provided closure. Like the graphic accounts of "The Second Walking Purchase;" supposedly the pale ones he'd "magicked" had been compelled to walk in a straight line until their skin and clothes were shredded by branches they couldn't avoid, and their feet were bloody nubs clotted with the dust of "a million steps." Most of the walkers starved to death, but some survived long enough to march — gratefully — into a forest fire... He still hated himself for it, but now he didn't have to wonder. He could just listen to himself being rightfully damned by strangers, over and over again.

That wasn't why he'd started lingering in pale-one villages, however. Not initially. He'd tried to explain his motivation to Tay after they met a Lnu who'd converted to the ways of Jesua. "This faith the pale ones brought with them — it exerts a powerful hold. I want to understand why."

<u>Because you want to stop it, or because you need something to believe in?</u>

"... Probably both."

But that was as far as he and Tay discussed it, even after several fruitless visits — only the first settlement had housed a permanent priest, and he'd been addled by drink. The rest of the communities weren't large enough to have a regular holy man; apparently "traveling ministers" cycled through every few moons. Naysin and Tay had missed each such rotation.

So they kept moving. Mostly east, but not along any particular path. Tay stayed busy by endlessly practicing her battle dance (as Naysin still called it). Shortly after they'd left Cawgana, she'd had Naysin hide another blade in the rainstick, on the opposite end. "For balance," she'd explained. Every morning now, she whipped the staff through the forms and poses she'd developed, fluid positions whose grace belied their lethality. She paired these movements to the rain sounds emanating from her weapon, and Naysin never tired of the performance. He also hoped she wouldn't have to enact it against a real foe again.

To keep himself occupied, he ran — often to Tay's annoyance — and sculpted. Tay had encouraged the latter after he'd finished upgrading her rainstick. <u>You could be a master craftsman</u>, she'd signed. <u>Your powers make it so easy for you. This would have taken my father days, but you did it in half a morning.</u>

"What would I make?" Naysin had asked with disinterested amusement.

"Whatever you want."

He'd thought this over for several steps, until without breaking stride, he'd bent down to pick up a fallen branch. For the rest of the morning, he'd studied the wood, trying to *see* something more in the tree limb's structure. An image he could bring out, a form he could free... He'd shaken his head when nothing materialized.

"Just let it come," Tay had suggested.

"All right," he'd said doubtfully, tickling the wood with strands of **Kug** and *Mir*. The branch had begun to pulse, slowly at first, then more rapidly. Knots had swelled and popped out, edges had sheared off and fallen, and eventually the wood had actually looked like something. A person ... a woman...

His mother.

The representation had looked exactly the same as the one he'd conjured on Bimshire's beach, albeit smaller and in a different medium. And it had been just as hard to look at; he hadn't been able to meet her wooden gaze any more than he could face her in his dreams.

"Spirits and lakes," he'd said softly as he'd tossed the carving into the brush.

Tay had looked like she wanted to say something, but seemed to decide that (as usual) it was better to give him space. So she'd teased him about something small: "We could have used that for firewood, at least."

He'd kept walking.

— « o » —

Naysin didn't give up creating. Tay wouldn't let him — her most telling insight had been that, "There aren't any moral choices with this. You just use your powers to make something that wasn't there before." And eventually, he started sculpting more and more as they traveled: carvings from wood, statuettes from stone, garments from moss and leaves. Even for him, truly detailed work might take most of a day, but he could shape the rough outlines of something like a cougar (to tweak his fathers) relatively quickly.

It was satisfying.

After he was done with a piece, Naysin usually set it on the ground — his art was more about the journey than the outcome, about using his powers to do something productive yet ultimately inconsequential. Tay kept a carving of a turtle, though, and she convinced him to hold on to a stone etching of a hawk; she loved how it looked like the little bird was "really flying." He was neutral toward the image, but it was small enough to pocket and forget.

But aside from the occasional provocation, his fathers didn't have anything to say about this new use of his powers. He wondered if they were sulking; they hadn't had to compete much for his attention over the years. Just briefly with Jehan ... and he didn't want to think about that. If the cougar-men wanted to pout, that was fine. He didn't need them right now.

Naysin had even more energy to pour into his new hobby when spring came. Up until the thaw, he'd been partially distracted by the task of keeping Tay and himself warm; she was used to pockets of snow on Dzune's mountains, but she hadn't lived in it for any length of time. And after that first winter he'd spent on his own, he wasn't fond of being cold. So he'd been constantly streaming *Mir* to heat the air around them, and compensating by shamaning **Kug** into his art. Hunting and erecting shelters also took up occasional blasts of power.

But with the weather changing, and food becoming easier to find, he didn't have to do as much to keep them comfortable. Leaving him with what felt like a surplus of power to expend.

He tapped most of it on the earthen pyramid.

The mound was the largest version of a theme they'd seen several times as they crossed the plains: sharply-edged hills, sometimes topped with the remains of what looked like temples, and sometimes adorned by nothing but lush grass. Tay thought they were wandering the bones of an ancient civilization. She kept pointing out traces of old roads and remarking on areas where edible plants grew in unnaturally dense concentrations.

Naysin wasn't sure until they found the pyramid — it was immense in a way that defied description. How could ordinary men and women, *without* the aid of powers like his, raise such a mighty monument? He could barely wrap his mind around the amount of labor involved; it must have taken an army of hands and many years of toil. It was the feat of a great people.

A people who were long gone. The thought tempered his amazement as he and Tay climbed the pyramid. (She'd insisted.) How could such a powerful civilization just disappear? Vanish so completely that he and Tay had never heard of it, not even from traders who crisscrossed the land and sold stories along with goods?

He wondered if plague had been involved. Disease was certainly bringing people like his to their knees. Tay had been shocked at the number of spirit towns they'd passed through, but he wasn't surprised anymore. Not when they found bones bleached to an ivory sheen, and not when they found bodies still fresh enough to show their blight. It was the way of things now; maybe it had been the mound-builders' fate as well.

But at least they'd left something powerful to mark their passing, something lasting. Once Tay and Naysin reached the summit, they were both silent. The view was incredible: to the south lay the faint outlines of a central plaza so large it could have held ten of Naysin's villages; to the west a ring of rotting posts formed what looked like an oversized sundial; to the north bits of buildings defined the corpse of a once-enormous city; to the east rolled enormous plains, the beginnings of a mighty forest ... and smoke.

Tay noticed the dark trail first — as ever, her eyes reached further than his. "You see it?" she asked immediately. "No, follow my finger: there."

When Naysin finally saw the smoke, he sat down, partly because the elevation was starting to affect him. Climbing the pyramid's broad slopes hadn't been any more disconcerting than scaling Dzune's mountains, but peering over the mound's face, even at such a magnificent landscape, was beginning to take its toll.

"Do you want to take a closer look?" Tay asked after sensing Naysin's unease.

He shook his head. "No. I don't want to get involved."

She shrugged and sat down next to him. As a breeze blew up from the west, they continued studying their surroundings, drinking in the vista and wondering what happened to its former caretakers. Naysin had to look down on several occasions to keep from getting dizzy, but Tay didn't say anything until he asked her to. Something about the setting, about the earthen pyramid's majestic, natural power, made him think back to that night in Dzune. Not how it ended — he preferred not to remember that — but how it began. "Can you really read people's fates?"

Tay arched her eyebrows. "What made you think of that?"

"Remembering the first time I saw you dance."

She shrugged, slightly embarrassed, but not enough to still her hands. <u>Mostly I could just see how people would react if I said yes or no.</u>

"So you told them what they wanted to hear?"

<u>I told them what they *expected* to hear. Sometimes that was what they wanted.</u>

"What about me?" She hung her head a little at this, but Naysin pressed on. "When I asked if I would learn to control myself, did you say yes just to make me feel better? Or did you truly believe it?"

Tay smiled sadly before answering both questions: <u>Yes</u>. When he started to turn away, she put her hand on his shoulder. "Hey. What you did to Meli was hard, but it was necessary. I wasn't sure at first, but after seeing so many empty villages on the way here... I know what you did was right. And that you can be a force for good in this world by making more hard choices — I don't need to 'foretell' anything to know that."

Naysin let her words ripple through him before he replied. "Tell my fortune again."

She gave him a quizzical look and withdrew her hand. Did you hear what I just said?

"Yes. Tell my fortune."

Reluctantly, Tay crossed her legs as she had in Dzune and nodded at Naysin to ask a question.

"Will I learn how to control myself?" he asked softly, staring into her milky eyes. "Will I learn how to be?"

A tear ran down her cheek as she tapped the ground once. "That means yes."

Certainty welled up in Naysin. He still wasn't sure he agreed with Tay, but suddenly he knew what he wanted to do right now, how he wanted to be in this moment.

He wanted to fly.

The trick the cougar-men had played on him when he was young and alone came back to him with forceful clarity, spurred by the fear of heights he felt even now, sitting motionless on a wide plateau. He remembered how the cougar-men had enticed him to climb the old elm tree, encouraged him to take his hands off its trunk and step. He remembered how they'd said, **Trust us, son. You have to trust us.**

Most of all, he remembered falling, helpless and heartbroken.

It was time to remake that memory.

Bounding up, Naysin took a step toward the pyramid's edge. And another, and another, until Tay called out in alarm. Then he started running.

He went over the precipice at a full sprint.

— « o » —

At first, he didn't do anything but plummet, a sensation that tapped into his childhood terror and nearly paralyzed him.

But his resolve resurfaced, and he used streams of **Kug**-hardened, *Mir*-fueled air to reverse his momentum. Within a few breaths, he was rising again, moving out and away from the mound.

He was flying.

More than ten man-heights above the ground. High enough that details like individual blades of grass were hard to distinguish. And he wasn't falling — he was slicing through the air like a knife through nothing. Gliding. Arcing.

Soaring.

And yet, for all his adrenaline, his fear of heights continued to have a powerful hold on him — after a short while, he angled back toward the ground. But being in the air and overcoming one of the most traumatic memories of his youth was still liberating; he let out a yell of triumph as he landed at a stumbling run, far to the east of the earthen pyramid. The forest he'd seen from the peak was only a field-length away.

So was the smoke.

And now that the wind was no longer rushing by his ears, he could hear thunder as well. Rolling thunder, wave after wave of it, crackling and erratic as...

The sound of fire sticks on Bimshire.

Chapter Twenty-Two

The Red Wraith

Naysin's mood soured instantly, his sense of victory trampled by a tide of obligation and indignation. Was he never to have a moment's peace? Spirits and lakes, would there always be a choice to make?

Tay thought so. Sobering, he looked back. If that speck on the horizon was her, she had some hard running to do before she caught up to him. Meaning she wouldn't be in danger if he chose to act as a "force for good in this world." And it wouldn't be difficult to find her again from the air.

If he chose to act now.

If he tried to be more than an itinerant mess of wasted potential.

If… If… If.

His feet chose for him; Naysin found himself hurtling toward the forest without ever having made a conscious decision.

It still felt good.

As he drew closer, specific sights and sounds started to distinguish themselves from the sensory morass: flashes of movement between the trees, the clash of metal on metal, bursts of color, the wet thud of metal on flesh.

And screaming. Cries of fear, anger, and anguish were coming from every direction. So were the acrid smells of blood and the sooty stench of spent fire sticks. It was an all-consuming maelstrom, many times more chaotic than the night of the Bimshire rebellion.

Still yet to encounter anyone, dead or living, Naysin bent low to the ground and sprinted toward a large oak at the border of what looked to be a partial clearing. The trees were packed too densely for flying, but if he could climb the oak, he'd have the best view he was likely to get. *If* he could climb it — the tree was easily as tall as the one he'd fallen from those many winters ago.

Swallowing hard, Naysin launched himself onto the oak's trunk. There weren't any branches within reach, but he used rapid bursts of **Kug** to sculpt the tree's wood around his hands and feet. He started to scoop out another set of holds, but he realized it would be faster to elevate the ones he'd already embedded himself in. He moved slowly at first, leaning against the oak as he manipulated it. Then, as he mastered the mechanics, he accelerated.

Naysin shot up the last half of the tree in the time it took to draw a single breath.

Looking down made him feel sick, but it was a manageable sickness, one tempered by the solid feeling of having his hands and feet encased in living wood. He wasn't going anywhere — the tree had him. There would be no falling this time.

He still couldn't see much, however. For one thing, there were several branches in the way, but a simple arc of **Kug** bent them aside. The bigger problem was the veil of smoke that had risen even to this height. Fighting not to cough, Naysin summoned enough *Mir* to disperse the black fog and sighed as the pain in his temples diminished.

He'd learned a lot about balance since that night on Bimshire.

As the smoke cleared, the battlefield started to reveal itself. The blasts of fire sticks became more distinct, the movements of men more clear, the outlines of bodies more horrible… But even with his vision unimpeded, it was some time before Naysin grasped the conflict's terrible dynamic: two groups of pale men were fighting below him, one set in red coats and another in blue. And two groups of *original people* were supporting them. From their war paint, he thought one of the latter might be Kiksha, but it was hard to tell. And it didn't matter.

He'd come expecting to help beleaguered original people defend themselves from marauding pale men. Instead, he'd found pale men allied with original people fighting other pale men allied with other original people.

Numb, Naysin watched one of the original people tomahawk a blue coat, wrench the blade from the pale one's neck, pivot, and bury the weapon in an opposing original person's stomach. It seemed indiscriminate ... and awful ... and wrong.

Where was the choice in this? How was he supposed to be a force for good in a conflict that had no good side? Who should he be helping?

And spirits and lakes, why were original people allied with pale men?

It was too much.

Mir was billowing out of Naysin before he realized he'd drawn it, that he'd tapped into more energy than he'd used to avenge the Walking Purchase. He started to shake as his arteries shone white and chaos raced through his body, making him feel like he was going to burst into a shower of dancing pieces.

But it was the pale men that died, blue and redcoats alike, as he turned their fire sticks against them.

Once his flows of *Mir* reached the forest floor, every new shot caused an explosive jam that blew off the hands of the man who'd squeezed the trigger. The pale ones who realized what was happening and threw their weapons aside weren't safe either; every spent bullet, be it lodged in the earth, a tree, or a body, came hurtling back at its caster. The air screamed with the deadly missiles' sudden reversal and exploded with the hot splatters of their second impacts ... and then it was over. The pale ones weren't just dead: they'd been shredded, dismembered so thoroughly that limbs and extremities rained down for several heartbeats.

Naysin wasn't finished.

As the original people looked around in horrified awe, he went down to meet them. There was no fear of heights in him as he used **Kug** to free his hands and feet from the tree, no panic as he pushed off the trunk and hardened the air just enough to allow himself to sink at a dreamlike pace. As he glided to the ground, veins now shining as black as his arteries still were white, there was only anger.

Summoning a last gust of *Mir*, he projected his voice in every tongue he'd learned on Bimshire and in the years since: "GO." The order boomed around the forest clearing, ricocheting off the dirt, the trees, and the canopy until the entire battlefield echoed with the force of that single word.

The survivors didn't have to be told twice. As one, the tribes threw down their weapons and fled, mingling in retreat as if they were a single people.

To make sure they'd gone, Naysin held on for five excruciating ten-counts before he gladly gave in to the tide of blackness that had threatened to engulf him since he'd started shamaning such a vast imbalance of *Mir* — the faster he went unconscious, the less time he'd have to think about what he'd just done. Which was important, because his final thought as he collapsed was that the stories were true.

He was the Red Wraith.

And he was terrible.

— « o » —

Naysin woke to the sound of simulated rain; Tay was sitting next to him, cross-legged and tapping her rainstick against the ground. It was a soothing way to come back to the world ... but the effect was ruined when he noticed the staff's blades were out and dripping red.

He could also see a ring of fresh bodies fanning out from where he lay. The bodies of original people.

"Tay?" he asked shakily, wondering if she'd foreseen him waking up and just ignored it.

She didn't look at him. "They came back for you," she murmured, gesturing at the corpses. "Just as I caught up. I didn't have a choice." Now she did look at him. "Why did they come back for you?"

Still lying on the ground, he tried to gather his scattered thoughts and locate the strength to sit; he felt formless from shamaning so much *Mir*, as if his muscles had come unbound. But at the moment, he was more worried about the accusation in Tay's voice. "I told them to leave."

"But they returned. Why?"

Naysin fell back to the ground, giving in to his weakness and whatever was coming next, whatever he'd brought upon himself. "Because I need to be put down."

The rain beats became more erratic. "Why?"

"Because I couldn't take the sight of people like us allied with pale men and fighting against each other. *With* pale men, Tay. After all they've done to us."

"Done to you."

"Done to many like me!" he objected, seizing the offensive. "Eviction, enslavement, slaughter: it's a long list. Your people haven't been subjected to it yet. But they will be. The pale ones don't know any other way."

"What about the Black Robes at Cawgana?"

He shook his head. "These pale men were *soldiers*, and they were already killing themselves."

"And the men like us without hands?" Tay's eyes went to a point beyond the increasingly claustrophobic ring of bodies, to something Naysin couldn't see without rising.

Biting his lip, Naysin forced himself to his elbows, ignoring the impulse to shaman a burst of **Kug** to steady himself. He'd used enough power today. Far more than enough. When he felt stable, he followed Tay's gaze to yet another body, of yet another original man. A partially-destroyed fire stick lay next to the Kiksha, and his arms ended in cauterized stumps.

Apparently Naysin's flows hadn't been as discriminate as he'd hoped; everyone who'd used a fire stick in the clearing had died, regardless of their heritage.

Because he was the Red Wraith.

A sharp tap and the ensuing sound of rain brought him back to Tay. You shouldn't have done this. This isn't what I meant by being a force for good. Not even close.

"I know," he said eventually, waiting for tears that didn't come.

Goodbye, Tay signed, simply and finally, before standing up and walking away, roughly in the direction of Dzune. She stepped over the ring of bodies with her usual effortless grace.

As she reached the tree line, another fountain of anger welled up in Naysin. "Those fools in Cawgana were right about one thing," he yelled at her back. "The spirits have abandoned us. Mine, yours ... nothing. Except laughter. They're laughing at us, Tay. How else do you explain all this?"

To his surprise, she spun to face him. <u>I believed in you</u>, she flashed across the clearing, milky eyes glistening. Then she swept her arm out to encompass the horrific scene around them. <u>But I don't see anyone's power here but your own.</u>

With that, she turned and left.

He wasn't at all shocked when the cougar-men spoke to him a short while later — they seemed to live for moments like these.

I am sorry, Naysin.

So am I. But she's right.

"After moons of silence, that's all you have for me?" Naysin pulled his legs to his chest and hugged them tight. He still didn't feel like his body had enough rigidity to stand.

I'm just making it plain for you: it truly was only your power at work here.

The power of a god. The god you refuse to be.

But with a little direction, you can be a force for good.

We can teach you — if you free us.

"I thought I wasn't ready for that."

*You're close. There's far less Mir and **Kug** in you than there was, and far more back in the world.*

Enough that you should be feeling the difference when you channel. It hurts a little less, does it not?

Think about it. Even a year ago, channeling that much Mir would have laid you out for days. But you're already upright. You're getting stronger, Naysin. And once you've drained our remaining stores, you can free us with the loose energy you've restored to the world.

Then we can teach you in person. Show you how to channel instead of describing it.

Which works so much better; you'll learn ten times faster.

Naysin sat quietly for a short spell before emitting a dry, rasping laugh. "Are you like me?"

Yes, Naysin, in more ways than you know. That's what we've been trying to tell you.

"Are you capable of this?" Naysin spread his arms to take in the massacre, but he didn't have Tay's grace — the motion unbalanced him, and he fell on his back.

We had our growing pains. But we learned from our mistakes, and we can teach you about them.

Naysin barked out another laugh as he struggled to return to a sitting position. "Why would I take that chance?" Using his legs as lifelines, he pulled his torso upright. "Why would I risk creating three of me, when there shouldn't even be one?"

Naysin...

"No!" he roared, pushing against his knees and rocketing himself into an unbalanced stand. "No!" he yelled again as he stumbled toward the body Tay had condemned him with, the one with no hands and a nearby fire stick. But the weapon was in worse shape than he'd thought; the barrel was burst. Casting about furiously, Naysin found an unblemished fire stick, one that must have been dropped before he started detonating everything that fired. This fire stick looked good as new, and its likely owner was still holding a powder horn and ramming rod — he'd died while loading.

This was the weapon to use.

Nearly falling on the fire stick, Naysin whirled it around until it was pointed at his temple and then cocked the weapon's little hammer like he'd seen so many pale ones do. "NO!" he screamed a third time before pulling the trigger.

Nothing happened, but he still fell.

Chapter Twenty-Three

Isaura

Hood thrown back, Naysin strode into the pale one's village. He was ready to look every inhabitant in the eye, ready for someone to recognize his tell-tale brand.

Ready to be put down.

He'd already proved he couldn't do it himself. He'd known, even as the jammed fire stick had fallen from his limp fingers, that he wouldn't be able to journey to such a self-destructive place again. That had been his chance to end things himself. Now he needed someone else to do it for him.

This village had been the first likely spot since he'd left the clearing. It looked like the pale inhabitants had actually built everything from scratch — there were no repurposed buildings of original-people origin. And surprisingly, everything seemed to be in reasonable order; most of the pale communities Naysin had seen so far had been in varying degrees of disarray, proof that their inhabitants had much to learn about the land they'd taken. Some had seemed no more than a bad day's hunt from starvation, a state Naysin's own people had never come close to.

Not that he cared right now. Whoever killed him could be as strong or weak as they liked.

The cougar-men hadn't said anything to him as he made his way here. For once, it seemed, they were lost for words. But they didn't lack for emotion; they were quivering. There was no other way to describe the humming sensation in Naysin's head. His fathers must have realized there was nothing more they could do. Nothing they could talk him into ... or out of. That, at least, gave him a small measure of satisfaction. It wasn't much to die with, but it was something.

The first pale one he saw was a woman, plain and plump, carrying a basket under each arm. Something about her reminded him of how his horrible recreation of the Walking Purchase had begun. *"Micah?"* that other woman had called when he'd startled her into dropping her sack of tubers. *"Micah there's a devil behind the house!"* How right she'd been; more than she knew. But he'd atone for that today.

Except that this woman, the plain one, didn't pay him a second glance. Even after crossing eyes with him.

Neither did the next person he tried to lock gazes with, a small-boned man leading a smaller pony out of the village. Or the person after that, a tousle-headed child who looked at him closely, but not in a way that suggested the boy felt anything other than curiosity.

Apparently the Red Wraith wasn't as infamous as he thought.

Frustrated, Naysin considered shamaning to establish his presence. A commotion from the other end of the village distracted him, however. As he walked toward the noise, it clarified into several voices, one exhorting the rest. The words were Anglo; the tone was hateful.

He'd found his executioners.

As soon as he passed the last house on the south side of the street, his quarry came into view: several men of varying ages gathered around another man perched on a rickety apple crate. A man that made Naysin stop short at the corner of the building despite his mood and mission. There was a frenetic charisma about this pale one that was striking to behold.

So were the burn scars marring the man's face — their shape was that of an open hand. It was as if a fire had grown an arm, reached out, and palmed the pale one's brow. Ordinary burn marks ran down the left side of his neck, but it was the brand on his face, combined with the man's almost-palpable energy, that made Naysin forget himself and listen, hidden by the building he hadn't fully rounded.

"There are some who say the red devils are the ancestors of the lost tribes of Isradell," the burned man intoned. "That they wandered to this new land, devolved into savages, and lost sight of the path to civilization." He paused to shake his head, setting his ropy blonde hair streaming in the wind. "But when I look into those brutes' eyes, I don't see even a flicker of heritage in common with my own. These are not, nor ever were, a holy people. There's no reason to treat with them, succor them, or show them any mercy whatsoever."

He stamped down on the crate. "There's no reason, in fact, to do anything but kill them."

"Hear the Firebrand!" a member of the audience yelled.

The burned man nodded in acknowledgement. "And don't think they feel any differently about you. Oh, they're interested in your baubles, and the guns and liquor they can't make themselves. But they don't care two pence for the white man himself. If they did, would they butcher our families — as they did to mine? Would they set our settlements ablaze — as they'll do to yours? Would they, at every opportunity, confound our efforts to live honest, peaceful lives?"

"NO!" the crowd roared in answer.

"No indeed, my brothers. Because the term 'red devil' isn't just a description; it's a definition. The reds truly *are* devils. Put here by God to test our resolve. Our holy conviction that there is only one pure race, and that mingling with others of darker persuasion is a grave sin." He paused to let the crowd yell its agreement again. "Knowing this, we know the pact your leaders made with the local devils was also a grave sin, and that allying with devils against other white men, even Francs, is graver still.

"Now I'm sure your *leaders*," he continued, spitting for emphasis, "told you how *keen* the Francs were to take your land, and how *critical* it was that you put aside your differences with the devils in order to prevail." He shook his head theatrically. "But you don't deal with devils." More yells. "Not when they're raiding your lands, poaching your livestock, and stealing your women." Even louder yells. "Not when the devils are little more than animals fit only for servitude and bondage." Still louder yells. "Not when your leaders are devils themselves." Confused quiet.

"That's right," the burned man said. "Your leaders are just as untrustworthy as any devil. Do you think it was *your* interests they were thinking of when they conscripted so many of your sons and forced them to march with red devils and mercenaries? Your interests? Or those of their pocketbooks?" He shook his head again. "Men like that don't see red or white. They only see gold."

With this, the burned man's mastery over his audience was complete, but the spell had worn off for Naysin. He still wanted to die, bigoted oratory or not. And he had only two thoughts left: that he couldn't have found a set of men better primed to kill him, and that the village seemed not to have heard of the massacre yet. Which was just as well; if someone had survived to tell the tale, his executioners might have been too scared to do what needed to be done.

No one noticed Naysin when he stepped forward; the burned man remained the center of attention as he pulled a dragonhead blunderbuss from his belt and pointed the weapon toward the sky. "But I see something else," he hissed. "I see red, but it's not the color of heathen skin, nor the hue of the Devil's hellfire — as I once believed it to be. It's the color of *holy* fire, bequeathed to me by the Lord to purify sinners like your leaders, even if it means burning them to husks." And then the gun belched flame.

Flame the burned man was shaping with small flows of *Mir*.

Naysin stumbled back, removing himself from view once more. The burned man was shamaning, seemingly using the pistol as a focus. There was no doubt about it. The onlookers — after a stunned silence — sounded happy enough to believe it was "holy fire" from their "Lord," but Naysin knew better. The burned man was purposefully shamaning in a way that seemed far more ominous than Tay's flash-foretelling or Amadi and Quecxl's healing.

Meaning there was another like the Red Wraith — another *truly* like him. If his counterpart hadn't been possessed by genocidal hatred, the realization might have been comforting. Even so, it was instructive. If there was one burned man, there were probably more. Suicide wouldn't change that.

Naysin shook his head. He could easily step back around the corner, obliterate the burned man with a burst of flame that would make what was coming out of the pistol look like a spark, and let the onlookers take their revenge... Tempting, but no longer viable. Removing himself from the world would still leave an unknown number of shamans who could do monstrous things, accidentally or on purpose. With no one to check them.

Was that his purpose?

Naysin fell back against the wall, pondering the potential epiphany as he listened with half an ear to the burned man's continued attempts to incite his audience against its masters. Clearly, wearing a shaman's hide wasn't the same as donning a savior's — too often, they were separate skins. The burned man was proving it as aptly as Naysin had on Bimshire. And Tay had killed a score of men, but only in self-defense; she was a good deal less dangerous than the burned man. Amadi and Quecxl were the exceptions: they *saved* people.

No, it was the powerful ones like himself that needed watching. Too much ability brought instability. Maybe...

Maybe he was meant to put down the ones who were truly like him?

The thought had barely formed in his head before he felt another low-level surge of *Mir*, a flicker that came from *elsewhere* in the village. Spirits and lakes, what was this place? Were there really two shamans within a few field-lengths of each other? After he'd crisscrossed the land and only found three others?

Incredulous, Naysin backtracked toward the town's center. Within a few steps, he began to feel a slight stretch, a low-level sensation of being pulled in two directions. It took him a moment to realize what was happening; the simultaneous uses of *Mir* within such proximity were creating a void, because these shamans, like Tay, drew from an external source of energy — they weren't restricted to internal reservoirs as he was. To feel the pull, he must be near the midpoint.

But Naysin couldn't pinpoint the shaman's location.

Sweeping his head back and forth as if his nose were a divining rod, he tried to intuit the right direction. He knew it wasn't behind him. That way led only to the end of town, the burned man, and gullible pale men. And the village was a straight line, with houses and stores on either side of the main road. There weren't many places for this second shaman to hide.

He could always search building-by-building if he had to. It would probably bring a mob down on him; even if the burned man hadn't been spreading hatred behind him, a "red devil" breaking into every house on the village's north side was bound to go over poorly. Still, it was an option. He could protect himself if it came to that. And it might; he needed to know, but he still couldn't figure out where—

There. That dark-haired woman in the window.

She pulled her head out of sight as soon as he caught her eye. She'd been watching him, even as he looked for her. Did she know what he was?

There was only one way to find out.

Naysin tried to formulate a plan as he strode toward her building — an inn. That was good; it meant the owner would be used to strangers. Whether a "red devil" — a branded devil, at that — would be welcome was another matter. But he was at the door before he had any solid ideas, and he didn't want to wait. So two more steps and a gentle push took him through the rickety swing doors and inside.

He needn't have worried; the worn-looking common room was all but empty. A man with a hunched back was sweeping the floor near the counter, and an unusually tall woman was bent over the wood stove, but that was it. Neither of them paid him much notice.

But Naysin didn't feel like he could just walk upstairs. And asking after the dark-haired woman seemed like an invitation for trouble (or at least awkwardness). So he stood in the doorway trying to determine what to do.

The dark-haired woman made the decision for him.

Naysin knew it was her even when he could only see her ankles, adorned by layers of copper bracelets that bounced as she descended the stairs. As the rest of her came into view, he took note of her creamy white skin, slender build, and (now that he was close enough to tell the color) deep auburn hair. Jehan would always be his standard for pale beauty, but this woman was … comparable.

That wasn't why he was here, though. He was far more interested in what she'd been doing with *Mir* and why she'd been watching him. She seemed to have similar questions about him; from the bottom step, she gave him a probing look.

They stood at an impasse until she crooked her finger at him, turned, and walked back upstairs.

That was bold.

Bewildered, Naysin glanced around the common room again as he debated the merits of following her. The old man in the corner looked disapproving, but not surprised. Maybe it wasn't uncommon for this woman to host strange men?

Naysin shook his head and started climbing the stairs. Better he asked her his questions in private. And if things got out of hand, better that started in private too. He reached the second floor in time to see the woman open and enter a door at the far end of the dimly-lit hallway. With a growing feeling of misgiving, he followed.

It was an unremarkable room. The woman didn't seem to have many possessions of her own; most of the objects on the shelves and table looked as if they hadn't been moved in some time. And while there were a few pale-one devices he didn't recognize, the whole looked no better constructed than the longhouses he'd grown up in.

After he'd shut the door, the woman broke the silence, speaking in a language eerily close to Lepane: "You are Red Wraith?"

For lack of any better idea, he went with the truth: "I am. What's your native tongue?"

He half-expected her to scream, or at least call for help, but she just nodded. "Espan," the woman said, switching to it. "You can understand me?"

It was his turn to nod.

"I thought you were him."

"How did you learn to shaman *Mir*?"

She looked genuinely confused.

"To manipulate the chaos around you. The fast energies. The ones that make air move, fire burn, water flow…" Naysin trailed off as the woman's expression clouded. But then he wondered why, and resumed. "I felt you doing something. That's why I was looking for you."

The woman studied him before responding. "I was washing my face," she said softly. She flicked her wrists and tiny flows of *Mir* reached out to kiss her cheeks. When she looked back up, her face was beaded with drops of water. Reaching for a small towel hanging from one of the bedposts, she used the rough-looking cloth to dry her face. "I can only move water."

"And the burned man at the end of the street? Can he move more than fire?"

She looked confused again. "The preacher? I didn't know he could move anything."

Naysin believed her; there was no lie in her eyes. But he wasn't sure what to do now that he'd established she could shaman, and he was *very* aware of how close they were standing. He could smell her: earthy and delicate. To maintain control, he started pacing. "Why did you come down to meet me?"

She followed him with her eyes for a moment before answering. "I await a man like you. Not *like* you," she amended, "just ... he's also of the original people — a friend. When I first saw you, I thought it was him. And by the time I realized the truth, you'd seen me... What's your name? Your real name?"

As before, he settled on the truth. "Naysin. What's yours?"

"Isaura."

It felt intimate. Until she followed with, "Are the stories true?"

Now he went cold. It was clear what she was asking about, and it was impossible not to think of the massacre he'd just left, the original people he'd killed without meaning to, the reason he'd come to this village in the first place... So he stalled: "How did you learn to use water? And speak a tongue like mine? And why is an Espan woman in an Anglo village?" He had more questions, but they were subdued by the storm raging across her face.

Eyes bright, Isaura stared at him for several breaths. But then the tempest blew itself out. "You make it sound as if I wished to become a witch." She shook her head. "It just happened. I conjured to save a woman who was being raped."

He nearly tripped at this, assailed by memories of his last night with Jehan.

If Isaura noticed his reaction, she chose not to acknowledge it. "As for the rest ... the friend I await taught me to speak like him. But his tribe allied with the Anglos, and when they left to fight the Francs in Edgeland Forest, I said I'd await him here. I had contracts to fulfill nearby anyway."

Naysin had stopped pacing at the mention of fighting in "Edgeland Forest." He needed to end this conversation — the topics were becoming too dangerous. "Contracts?" he asked anyway.

"I dowse wells."

"Because you can sense where springs in the earth run close to the surface?"

"Yes."

She'd grown guarded again; he must not have hidden his shift in mood well. There was no more avoiding the question. "The Francs — were they also allied with original people?"

"They were rumored to be." Isaura took a deep breath and looked him in the eye. "Are the stories true?" she repeated. When he didn't respond immediately, she forced the issue further. "Do you use ... *Mir* ... to do terrible things? Are you truly the Red Wraith?"

Swallowing hard, Naysin answered the question very differently than he had just a little earlier: "I don't mean to be."

Before Isaura could respond, the sound of feet sprinting up the stairs filled the lull, and Tay's voice called loud and desperate from the hallway: "Naysin! Get out! They're coming for you!"

Chapter Twenty-Four

A Different Path

Glad of the interruption, Naysin took two quick steps to the door and yanked it open in time to see Tay sliding to a stop.

<u>A mob of pale men,</u> she signed hurriedly. <u>Right behind me. One of them has a torch.</u>

On cue, angry voices and stomping feet made their presence known in the common room. Naysin heard someone — probably the old man with the broom — direct them upstairs, but the words were barely audible over shouts of "Miscegenation!" and "Impure union!"

"Thank you for warning me," Naysin said after giving Tay a searching look.

She nodded. Then she motioned for him to step back, entered the room … and saw Isaura. "Who's she?" Tay took out her rainstick and released its blades.

"Isaura." Naysin hoped he wasn't flushing. "She can shaman water."

Tay raised her eyebrows before turning back to face the door. "I'll hold them off while you find a way out."

The angry voices were in the hall now, moments away from rounding the corner and running into Tay and her blades. Naysin didn't want that to happen. "No," he said softly as he put a hand on her shoulder. "I'll hold them."

After hesitating, she gave into his pressure and allowed him to shut the door. Immediately, Naysin blanketed its frame with **Kug**, fusing it to the door as fists began to pound the other side. "That should win us some time."

But not much. As Naysin stepped back, he heard a voice telling the mob to do the same. It was the burned man, steadily approaching with his ability to wield fire.

Looking around the room, Naysin ignored Tay's combative pose and Isaura's conflicted one. The only other opening was a small window directly across from the door. He didn't need much to work with, though — he could create entrances as easily as he could close them.

Shooting forth *Mir*, he attacked the integrity of the wood around the window, stretching and loosening its fibers until what remained was thinner than a leaf. Then he gripped each end of the window, opened his arms as wide as they would reach, and tore the wood as if it were parchment.

The smile this brought to Naysin's face vanished when he looked behind him; a line of fire was cutting around the door. The burned man was creating an entrance of his own. It was time to leave, especially since Tay looked ready to kick down what remained of the door rather than wait for the pale men to do it themselves.

"Take my hands," Naysin said in a low voice, offering an arm to each woman. "Now," he emphasized when they hesitated.

Isaura latched onto him first, gripping his left hand firmly. Tay followed suit by grabbing his right hand, but she was still facing what remained of the door, her rainstick poised to strike. She'd probably foreseen where the first head would appear.

"Hold on," he grunted unnecessarily as he ran them toward the ragged window. To his relief, neither woman balked at stepping into empty space with him, even though Isaura still looked undecided and Tay was running (gracefully, as always) in reverse. They weren't very high off the ground, but they needed a smooth landing to avoid sprained ankles. Briefly, Naysin considered flying the woman out of town, but he wasn't willing to risk their lives on a fledgling skill. Instead, he used small flows of *Mir* to cushion their descent, turning their drop into as much of a glide as possible.

It worked; they touched down without a hitch and kept running. After their first step, Tay spun to his front and let go. Isaura disengaged a few strides later.

But then they had to change course. Pale men started oozing from the alleys and doorways ahead like water squeezed from wet cloth. Naysin couldn't tell if the newcomers had the same mindset as the mob behind them, but he didn't want blood on Tay's hands if he could help it. "Back!" he yelled, trying to steer the two women past the inn and out the other end of town. They were already cut off, though; the mob was pouring from the inn's enlarged window and the main entrance below. Most of the pale men were older, likely the fathers of some of the unfortunates he'd massacred in the forest clearing.

Isaura saved them — the fathers; Tay likely could have cut through them on her own, whether Naysin managed to shaman violence again or not. "The church," she murmured, already moving toward the nondescript building, "we can take sanctuary there." It was on the other side of the road. They barely made it inside before being surrounded.

As Tay slammed the door shut and jammed a bench against it, Naysin quickly surveyed the lone room. It wasn't as different from his people's Longest House as he'd expected: the aesthetics were foreign, and the central focus — a large white cross — was set against one wall rather than in the middle of the main room. But the slope of the roof and the beams that supported it followed the same logic. Small differences overall, dissimilarities that were more form than function.

There was no more truth for him here than there'd been at home.

The burned man brought Naysin out of his ill-timed reverie. "So," the pale man's voice boomed from the other side of the door, "you think the people of this village will let devils and whores take refuge in the Lord's church, allow red heathens and white sluts to fornicate in our place of worship."

Finally, Naysin understood what was happening. Someone — the innkeeper? — must have seen him go upstairs with Isaura and informed the burned man and his disciples, pale men who'd become insane with rage at the thought of one of their women lying with a red man... Speaking with

Isaura had dredged up memories of Jehan, but now the worst of them were being recreated.

Except this time Naysin was awake.

He wouldn't — couldn't — dishonor Jehan's memory by committing another massacre, but it was past time for this village to learn of the Red Wraith. "When I was sixteen, I burned the plantation upon which I'd been enslaved," he said in Anglo. As he moved toward the door, his voice grew in volume, amplifying as it had in the forest clearing. He did his best to throw his words outside the church, but Tay and Isaura were holding their ears.

"When I was seventeen, I returned home, found pale men, women, and children squatting in my people's homes ... and marched those invaders to their deaths." Now he began enlarging his image to match his voice, casting an illusion like he had on his guardian spirit day. Tay and Isaura flinched as his specter enveloped them, but it expanded harmlessly.

"For these deeds and others — some real, some rumor — I've been named the Red Wraith." Gasps and shouts of alarm sounded from the road as his image emerged. Naysin didn't know for certain what his image looked like, but he'd wanted it to appear in a kneeling pose, with arms down and head bent, his tell-tale hair hanging in front of its face.

"The name is not undeserved." He imagined his veins and arteries shining black and white, and a second round of gasps signaled that his specter continued to conform to his vision. Frantic footsteps followed — a few at first, then a stampede's worth.

"But even after all I've done, and all your kind has done to me, I would never think so ill of your people that the idea of a 'pale man' lying with a 'red woman' would drive me to murder." He pictured his image raising its head and revealing the angry brand that marred his face. More footsteps — there couldn't be many pale men left outside the church.

"I will, however, do whatever it takes to defend myself against such ignorance." He focused on making his specter stand, spreads its arms, and shoot streaks of shadow and light from its outstretched palms. A few final footsteps sounded, and all was quiet.

Until the burned man offered his rebuttal.

"Self-confessed demon spawn!" he shrieked from the other side of the door, the venom in his voice startling even Tay, who couldn't understand his words. "You do not scare me! You do not scare the people in this town! And we will NOT allow evil of your ilk to propagate! Forgive me Lord, but this is no longer your place. It belongs now to the fires of HELL!"

An avalanche of heat slammed against the door, forcing Naysin back as he marveled at how much *Mir* the burned man was churning into fire. Immense gusts of it, hot enough to burn through wood in an instant; before Naysin had taken three steps, the door was gone, and the burned man was visible through its remnants, pointing his blunderbuss directly at Naysin's head and smiling maniacally.

Tay whipped her arm back to launch her rainstick, but it was Isaura who acted first. Faster than Tay could throw, or Naysin could switch his shamaning from illusion to action, the Espan clenched her fists and summoned a fountain of water in front of the church, a geyser that intercepted the burned man's second stream of fire and flooded the room with steam.

Everyone fell back this time, covering their faces as the church began to sizzle and pop like fat in a pan. The building wasn't burning any longer, but it was definitely cooking. With the three of them inside, surrounded by scalding mist that made breathing more and more difficult. The burned man was yelling something from the street — Tay would later identify it as the name "Kip" — but it was the least of their worries right now.

They had to get out. And the quickest way Naysin knew was down. Grabbing a hand each from Tay and Isaura, he yelled, "Close your eyes!" in two languages and plunged the three of them into the ground.

Even with additional bodies to move and protect, tunneling was easier than it had been three winters ago after he'd escaped Bimshire and plunged into that cliff on the mainland. And not just because he was shaping dirt instead of stone — he was more in control. Older, more mature, and more experienced. Burrowing under the church definitely took concentration, but it wasn't a strain. It felt ... balanced.

Which was why he was so relaxed when he brought Tay and Isaura up for air in the village's center. The brief time beneath the earth had restored his composure, banishing the last of the suicidal thoughts he'd walked into town with.

It was good to be at peace.

It was also nice not to see the burned man. Naysin scanned the village twice as Tay and Isaura recovered from their subterranean voyage, breathing greedily of the fresh air. But he couldn't find any sign of the preacher, aside from the still steaming church. Probably for the best; Naysin was more than happy to continue avoiding bloodshed.

He maintained his specter, however. He hadn't had time to stop shamaning the illusion; it was still straddling the church, giant-sized and lined with power. It — he — looked terrifying.

A fact that didn't bother Naysin in the slightest.

"Come," he said gently to the two women. "It's time to leave."

The street stayed empty as they fetched Isaura's enormous horse and left — Naysin doubted anyone would emerge until the next morning. But to make sure they wouldn't be followed, he had his image accompany them. It walked above him, matching his footsteps like a titanic shadow as he led Tay and Isaura into the wilderness.

Chapter Twenty-Five

Direction

"I hope you find this friend of yours," Naysin said sincerely, many strides and no further incidents later; he'd dispersed his illusion long since.

Isaura nodded and started to turn away, her horse's reins firmly in hand. She paused when she saw Tay — as if she'd momentarily forgotten the other woman's presence — before bidding them both farewell. Tay's response was to cross her arms. Another mystery: she seemed to blame the Espan for the altercation in Fort Kaska (the village; Isaura had relayed its name shortly after they'd entered the surrounding woods). He was tempted to ask the cougar-men if it was possible to use **Kug** or *Mir* to understand women.

"Wait," he called when he noticed how small Isaura looked as the distance between them grew. "Do you even know where you're going? What will you do for food?"

She stopped and glanced over her shoulder. "I'll be fine." Isaura flashed her first smile since they'd met. "I can't run out of water, remember? I don't need much else." She seemed satisfied with her answer; her smile grew as she turned back and started walking alongside her horse again.

Her last words lingered in Naysin's ears as he watched her go, lingered and reverberated until they echoed into an insight: Isaura may not have desired her affinity for water, but she'd come to terms with it. He wish he'd asked her how.

"Are you done being an idiot?" Tay punctuated the question by tapping her rainstick on the ground — she must have unstrapped it from her back while he was lost in contemplation.

"Probably not," he admitted ruefully as he focused on her and let Isaura disappear from view, off to search for her "friend."

Tay didn't laugh. <u>What happened in the clearing,</u> she signed, <u>what you did to those men ... you won't do that again?</u>

Naysin sobered immediately. He'd been dreading this conversation, but he was glad it was finally happening. <u>Never,</u> he signed back, not trusting his voice.

She looked at him appraisingly, her milky eyes eating into him like twin bursts of the burned man's fire. Eventually — after Naysin nearly had to look away, or hang his head in shame, or do *something* to escape her obvious weighing of his pros and cons — she nodded. <u>Then I'll stay,</u> she signed, and dropped her rainstick to hug him.

The embrace was a salve to every ache in his mind and body. He wondered if Tay was watching Isaura fade into the distance as she held him — if *that* was why she was holding him so tight — and then dismissed the thought as unworthy. He wouldn't spoil the moment with adolescent foolishness. The hug was too important.

When she let go, he didn't want to do the same. But he withdrew anyway, telling himself that he'd gained something, even if, right at that instant, it felt like a loss.

Tay wasn't done talking. "I came back," she began in words before shaking her head and starting over in signs. <u>I came back because I failed you.</u>

Naysin cocked his head to ask what she meant, but she raised her hand.

<u>No, I failed you. What you did was wrong, but I understand why you did it. I should have been there to help you control yourself.</u>

Now he was truly confused. "I *flew* away from you, Tay. You couldn't have kept up."

Tay narrowed her eyebrows and shoved him. "That's not the point! I'm supposed to be there!"

Naysin had to flail his arms, but he managed to avoid an inglorious fall. "Be where?" he asked testily. The push had been even more unexpected than the hug.

She stared at him again, looked *inside* him again, but this time she wasn't judging. After a prolonged silence, she let it out. <u>To be with you.</u>

"What do you mean?"

Now she was staring at the ground. <u>Usually I only see a little ahead — just a glimpse of what's about to happen.</u> She looked up again. <u>But two years ago, during a rainmaking ceremony, I had a real vision. Of you. On a hill. Sitting cross-legged, head bent and hair hanging over your face. And I was by your side.</u> She tapped her rainstick with her foot. <u>Ready to protect you with this. It's the only fate I've ever really read.</u>

A torrent of questions flooded Naysin's mind, but none made it out his mouth; he was literally dumbstruck. Aware that Tay was waiting for some kind of response, Naysin switched to signing again. <u>You had a vision during a ceremony,</u> he repeated slowly, trying not to relive the images he'd projected during his guardian spirit ritual. <u>An image of us on a hill — the pyramid?</u>

She nodded.

<u>So that's why you wanted to climb it so badly...</u> Then something occurred to him. <u>Was there a blade on your rainstick?</u>

<u>There were two. But my father was only able to make one before he died.</u>

As the realization set in — that she'd only asked her father to create a weapon *after* she'd had the vision, and that she'd been watching for *him* ever since — Naysin felt the balm-like sensation returning. He still didn't believe in destiny, but it was nice to think that something good had been waiting for him.

He couldn't find the words to express this, however, so he just left it at, "I'm glad you're with me again."

— « o » —

"What do you think we should do about others like us?"

Tay gave him a quizzical look. "What's there to do?"

Naysin shook his head. They'd been walking for several days without a fixed heading, enjoying another journey without a destination. But now he was starting to feel the need for direction again. "That burned man didn't strike you as … dangerous? He nearly sent that whole village up in flames. I know I've done worse," Naysin added hurriedly, "but that was when I thought there was only one of me."

Tay shrugged. <u>I'm still not sure what you're trying to say. Is — what's her name? — Isaura dangerous too? Do you still think I am?</u>

Briefly, he recalled the first time he'd seen her battle dance. "No, I mean … I don't know what I mean." He did know, though. He wanted to find a way to contain menaces like himself, without bloodshed; he'd had enough of that to fill many lifetimes. "Do you remember when I told you about my guardian spirit day?"

Tay nodded.

"I didn't tell you everything. The cougars I saw…" Naysin's mouth went dry, and he had to swallow twice before continuing. "The cougars I saw were really men. Two brothers. They call themselves Enki and Enmul. They're my fathers." He'd meant to give Tay the details quickly, but it took many steps to tell it all: seeing his mother coupling with the cougar-men by the river temple; thinking of his "fathers" as mentors; nearly dying when they betrayed him; coexisting uneasily in the years since.

"They're trying to escape, Tay. That's why they had me put out the fire on that freezing winter day, and step off that tree before I knew how to fly. If I die… they get out." As Naysin said this, the humming sensation he'd felt upon entering Fort Kaska finally made sense. The cougar-men had been quivering with *anticipation* — not fear. Committing suicide would have granted their fondest wish.

"But I can't let that happen. They think they're gods, that they can do whatever they want; hurting people is just 'growing pains' to them. I need to make sure they don't get back into the world. And if I can find that temple, maybe I can figure out how their mother locked them away, so I can do it again." Naysin stopped there; he didn't want Tay to guess he was thinking of entombing anyone but the cougar-men.

Fortunately, she seemed distracted. <u>What do the cougar-men look like?</u>

"In the vision I saw on my guardian spirit day, they were gray at first — when they were only one man. But then they split apart, and they were black and white." He fingered a lock of his hair. "And their hair was smoky like mine," he concluded, a little horrified.

Did they shoot lightning? Tay signed interestedly.

"No, but they probably could if they were free. Why?"

She paused, as if settling an internal debate. You're not going to like this, but my people believe that long ago, Alowina, the Sun God, created twins to protect the first people from enemies. He named the brothers Ayuta and armed them with lightning, which they used to kill giants and free the people they'd captured. The twins sound a little like your cougar-men.

Naysin resisted the impulse to roll his eyes. "Degan — the Hodensee I told you about? — had a story like that too. His people believe in two brothers, one good and one bad: Oterong and Tawiskaron. Degan said their battles shaped the world, but it doesn't mean anything."

Tay stiffened slightly. That's because he's Hodensee.

"No, it's because he was a mad man... Forgive me." Naysin let his heat fade; it shouldn't have been directed at Tay. "Forgive me," he repeated. "I just don't know what to believe anymore. Maybe the cougar-men are the Ayuta, or the Hodensee twins. Or maybe they're just men, like me, who can do things they shouldn't be able to. But whoever they are, I need to find that temple. And I'd like you to come with me."

She didn't meet his gaze, but she did say, "Of course."

— « o » —

Much as he didn't want to return to his village, starting there made sense. And locating it wasn't difficult; Naysin could still intuit his former home's direction by focusing on his brand.

Walking into his village, however ... that was almost impossible.

It took three attempts. Two false starts — which he tried to pass off by acting like he was stopping to look at the surrounding forest — and one tentative success, a slow advance into the village's center, now a mix of his people's longhouses and the pale ones' "cabins."

All empty.

Tay didn't comment on his hesitation, but even she couldn't forgo asking about the desolation. "Was it the plague?"

Naysin sank into a squat. "Yes — according to the pale ones who moved in."

She narrowed her eyes as he realized he'd never told her that part of his story. She only knew the sanitized version.

"What happened to the pale ones?"

"I made them leave."

Tay looked like she wanted to say more on the subject — her fingers were twitching as if they were anxious to sign — but she held back. Likely because of the obvious anguish in his voice. "Where do we go now?"

Naysin hadn't thought that far ahead; he'd been dreading his return too much to plan for anything beyond his arrival. The closer he'd come, the more he'd worried about what new horror would await him. More pale ones? Another ambush? Or would it be the sight of Jehan's remains, strewn about by the scavengers who'd feasted on her corpse.

Because he'd never buried her.

The shame that had dogged Naysin's steps since he embarked for Mt. Tsikomo welled up so suddenly he would have been brought to his knees if he weren't already squatting. Even so, he had to stretch his arms out to steady himself.

He hadn't done right by Jehan. Not even close. The few handfuls of dirt he'd covered her with had been woefully insufficient. It didn't matter that his skull had been cracked, or that he'd barely been able to stand. He should have done more.

And now he could.

"We go north," he finally answered. Bounding up, he set off at a brisk walk, which, within a few strides, became a jog. Then it was a run, and before he was out of the village, he was sprinting.

Until Tay brought him up short. "Naysin!" she called from behind. "Wait! You have to wait!"

The memory of what happened after his last headlong dash — of the massacre outside Fort Kaska, and Tay leaving him — stilled his legs as if he were a puppet whose strings had just been severed.

"You have to wait," she reminded him again when she caught up.

Naysin nodded, letting his wet eyes speak his apology as he took her hand and started jogging again.

A short while later, they reached the little grove of trees he and Jehan had used as a campsite all those moons ago. He was certain it was the right place, even though his vision had been a blurry mess when he'd woken that next morning; he still recognized the trees they'd lain under, and the fissures he'd opened in the ground in a vain attempt to bury her. The gashes were partially filled in now, but they remained deep scars on the earth's surface.

Yet Jehan's body was nowhere to be found.

Sick to his stomach, Naysin scoured the area. He moved at a half-crouch in order to see every detail. But there was nothing to find. Or at least, nothing *his* eyes could find. "Can you see anything?" he asked Tay, whirling around.

"Like what?" She looked equal parts guarded and concerned.

"A woman," Naysin finally managed. "Or any sign of her."

Tay nodded and started circling the trees, her movement slower and straighter than his had been. But after peering into every fissure, she looked back at Naysin. <u>I don't see anything</u>, she signed sympathetically.

He took a deep, ragged breath and collapsed back into a squat, his eyes focused on the grove's centermost pine.

A moment later, he felt Tay's hand on his shoulder. She didn't ask, but he wanted to tell her anyway. "Jehan found me after … after I made the pale ones leave. I'd blacked out from using too much **Kug** and *Mir*, but she nursed me to health and gave me a home." He told Tay everything about his time with Jehan, leaving nothing out. Tay listened silently from behind him, squeezing his shoulder during the tragic parts.

"She never knew what I could do," Naysin finished softly. "And until the last night, it was better that way. But when it mattered … I couldn't shaman in time. I couldn't even bury her."

Tay squeezed his shoulder again. "You should make something."

He craned his neck to look at her.

"Something to mark the spot." Tay's milky eyes edged with pity. "Something to remember her by. Like a sculpture."

"Or a carving," Naysin said slowly, turning back to the tree he'd been staring at. Tay was right; he could still do something for Jehan.

Pushing himself up, he walked toward the tree as Tay's hand trailed down his back and fell away. When he reached the old pine, his fingers ran over its bark with the same light touch. This was going to take a lot of **Kug**, and some *Mir* for detailing. But an image was forming in his mind, and he was committed now. This was the best way he could pay his respects.

Beginning with **Kug**, he began manipulating the bark and the wood beneath it, raising and lowering the tree's surface until he had a rough profile to work with. Next he used *Mir* to destabilize the area so another flow of **Kug** could meld the bark and wood together, creating a subtly textured look: the tiny ridges of skin seen up-close. When that was done, he started on the other fine points, using **Kug** to adjust the edges of his design and *Mir* to etch the final lines with a small stream of fire.

He finished as the sun began to set.

When he stepped back, the accuracy of the likeness yanked at his heart. It was Jehan as he'd first seen her: hair drawn back in a ponytail that revealed her delicate ears; clothing a striking mix of fashions; a fire stick slung over her back. He'd even managed to bring out the mole on her left cheek. It was … her. Exactly her. The only liberty he'd taken was extending the smile on her lips to her eyes.

As Naysin took another step back, Tay moved forward. She studied the carving for a long time before turning to face him, a tear trickling down each cheek. <u>She's beautiful</u>.

"She was." His emotions were knotted so tightly he could barely speak. "Let's go."

— « o » —

Flying was the fastest way to search for the temple, but Naysin only took to the air occasionally. He justified his reluctance with two reasons: he didn't want to leave Tay behind again, and he was determined not to shaman more than he absolutely had to. A little bit of **Kug** to translate his communications with Tay, small bursts of *Mir* to catch and cook meals... That was it as far as essentials went.

But in truth, he was still terrified of heights.

Every moment he was ascending, gliding, or (especially) descending, the terrible feeling of falling from the old elm tree came back to him. Even if he only did a quick loop — just a rapid reconnaissance to get the lay of the land — his leg would start to ache with remembered pain.

His first flight had been a triumph; every one since had been an ordeal.

Naysin recognized how practical they were, though, and how much easier scouting was from above. So he kept pushing himself back into the sky every time he needed to reorient himself. He also liked the idea of locating the cougar-men's former prison by using the trick they'd pretended to teach him. The thought was enough to keep him aloft ... but not for long. And not often.

The only other shamaning he'd permitted himself was a sketch for Tay. She'd wanted to know what the temple really looked like. <u>I can't see it</u>, she'd repeated after he'd described it for the third time. <u>Just draw it for me</u>.

He'd etched the temple's outline on a piece of wood he'd been about to throw in that night's fire. Practice had made him skilled at this type of rendering; after a brief effort, he'd produced a carving that was the spitting image of the vision he'd seen on his guardian spirit day. A rapid river ... flowing through crumbling ruins ... that rose and fell like the crest of a dying wave.

The only things missing were his mother and the cougar-men.

Tay had stared at the image when Naysin finished, as if trying to picture how the omitted scene had played in the foreground. Then she'd shrugged and signed, <u>We should keep this — in case we ask someone about the temple.</u>

Naysin took pains to avoid other people, however, steering Tay away from campsites and villages he saw from the air. It didn't matter if they belonged to original people or pale ones; he didn't want to interact with anyone he didn't have to. It was slower, but it seemed safer.

The relative solitude also let him focus on his search pattern: tracking back and forth along the paths his people used to take from the village to their smaller winter shelters. His hope was that his mother had stumbled upon the temple during one of these trips, probably on her way home in the spring. Burgeoning greenery had lined the edges of his vision in the Longest House — too much new growth for the end of fall. The key, though, was finding the river. There were several near his people's village, but he felt like he'd know the right one when he saw it.

A full moon of futile searching later, he wasn't so sure. No river — not the right one anyway — and no temple. All he'd done was give Tay time to think. She hadn't pushed him any further about the cougar-men being her Ayuta, but she was coming dangerously close to divining Naysin's true intentions for them.

<u>When we find the temple</u>, she asked one morning, <u>and you force your fathers back into it ... will you lose your powers?</u>

He considered lying, but it was hard to get much by Tay. Her ability to see a little into the future let her compare the expression a person would wear after they'd told a falsehood to the expression they wore during the act.

No, he was better off telling the truth. Or at least part of it. "I'm not sure, but it seems like a small price to pay."

"Not if you were making better use of them." Tay strode ahead, spun to face him, and resumed walking, moving backward with angry grace. "Tell me, would your cougar-men do anything good with their abilities?"

"Based on past history — no. Not a chance."

<u>Right,</u> Tay responded in signs. <u>No loss to the world if they're locked away again. Fantastic. But you —</u> are <u>you</u> <u>going to do anything good with your abilities?</u>

Naysin narrowed his eyes.

<u>Let me rephrase: are you going to do any *more* good with</u> <u>your abilities? Because you've done a lot already. Killing</u> <u>Meli to protect the rest of Dzune from the plague was the</u> <u>right course of action, even if no one watching realized it.</u> <u>You saved an entire town.</u>

He shook his head. "You're asking the wrong question. The more important one is 'Am I going to do more evil?' Because I've already done plenty, more than I've done good. Without even trying. *That's* the question to ask. And I already know the answer."

"No, you don't," Tay said stubbornly.

"Yes, I do, Tay. Which is why I'm not that worried about losing my *powers*. If it happens, so be it. And if it doesn't, I'll go from there."

Tay looked like she wanted to say more, but a noise up ahead caused her to pivot and draw her rainstick, a motion as smooth as water pouring from a bowl. She didn't bother loosing her blades, however. There was no need. The four figures on the deer path were as far from threatening as armed men could be.

The weapons strapped to their skeletal sides looked like afterthoughts. The men — original men — were clearly too ragged to put up a fight, too threadbare in sinew and spirit. Their eyes were, for lack of a better word ... dead. These were warriors who had nothing left to fight for. Men who just wanted it to end, but no longer possessed the strength to bring on that end themselves.

Naysin knew the feeling. He'd walked into Fort Kaska with it.

"What's your story?" he called out when the men had wandered within ten paces.

It took two steps for the first man's eyes to focus, and two more for him to stop. The other three men didn't react as quickly; they stumbled into the first man one after the next. He didn't flinch, though. He must have been a strong man once; his followers bounced off him as if he'd become a tree.

"You speak Raken," he said, taking a brief interest in Naysin's *Mir*-burnished clothing and Tay's Dzuni garb. A very brief interest; the spark in the man's eyes only flickered for an instant before going out.

"What happened to you?"

The first man's eyes wandered in and out of focus again, but when his expression clarified for the second time, it held a trace of real emotion: rage. "Plague." He spat and gestured to the men behind him. "Plague happened to my wife, Ahanu's children, Etchimun's sister, Nosh's father. Plague happened to our village, sparing only the four of us."

<u>What's he saying?</u> Tay signed into Naysin's peripheral vision, but he didn't have time to interject a translation; the first man was spouting like a whale's blowhole now.

"Plague also happened to our enemies. When we, the *survivors*, came on our rivals, hoping to die a warrior's death, we found them … stricken." The energy went out of the first man as suddenly as it had come, but he wasn't finished. "As I slit open the nearest tent, contagion spilled out. The stench was … I couldn't breathe, and…"

His concentration wavered again. When it returned, he glared at Naysin. "The spirits have forsaken this land. We seek to leave it."

Naysin shook his head at the implied question. "I can't help you, but I doubt you'll have to wait much longer."

The first man nodded, unfocused his eyes for the last time, and began walking again. The other men followed without betraying a hint of awareness, like corpses in search of graves.

Tay shuddered when Naysin finished recounting his conversation with the leader. "There's nothing you can do for them?"

"No."

She watched the men fade from sight and then turned back to the path. "Let's find your temple."

— « o » —

A year later, they did.

Chapter Twenty-Six

The Forgotten Temple

It was hard to look at the water.

Not from several paces away; that was fine. But the closer Naysin came, the more he feared what he might see once his reflection became visible.

This was the water he'd been conceived in... Would he see a recreation of that terrible scene? Find the cougar-men in their human form? Their animal form? Both?

And then there were the ruins jutting from the river's surface like the toes of an upturned foot. For eons, the smoke-toned shambles had marked the boundaries of the cougar-men's banishment. Would they draw special power from returning here? Surge against him in a way he hadn't yet felt? End him before he had a chance to end them?

The questions rang louder in Naysin's head with each step, reaching a cacophony when he drew near enough to see his head in the water, and as he took two more steps ... the doubts faded. He could see the rest of his reflection now, and it was alone.

Tay's image joined his when she caught up to him on the shoreline. They stood in silence until Naysin broke the quiet with a harsh laugh. Moons of searching, years of anticipation, and now nothing. No reaction, no idea what to do next.

The cougar-men hadn't spoken for several seasons, as if they were trying to convince him he'd imagined their presence from the beginning. That they'd never tried to teach him, or trick him, or kill him. That he was the crazy one, the sole cause of his troubles.

Naysin shook his head. He knew all too well which acts he had to answer for, but the cougar-men had played their part in shaping him. They were real. They were malevolent. And they needed to be removed from the world once more.

The question was how.

The answer — if there was one — lay within the ruins.

"I'm going to swim out there," he announced to Tay as he removed his poncho and breechcloth. "You don't need to follow. Just be ready. I'm not sure what's going to happen."

She didn't respond. If he hadn't known better, he would have said her cheeks were flushed — he'd never been naked in front of her before.

Locking the thought away for another time, Naysin clenched his jaw and dived into the water. Which was absolutely freezing. And moving deceptively fast; the river had a stronger current than its placid surface suggested, a flux that was pulling him not just downstream but ... down. Straight down.

He kicked and reached as hard as he could, laboring to regain the surface. But the current increased to match his energy, countering every stroke with more pressure. Despite his efforts, he was moving closer to the bottom of the river than the top.

As panic set in, Naysin fumbled for the right mix of **Kug** and *Mir* to buoy him back to the surface, and realized both energies were already flowing out of him. The **Kug** was making the water above him denser; the *Mir* was stirring the water around him into a downward spiral.

The cougar-men were trying to kill him again.

Furious, Naysin ripped back the reins of his abilities and reversed the direction of both flows. And then he was standing on the river's surface, shining black and white as water streamed from his limbs. Tay sounded worried when she asked if he was all right, but he didn't answer.

He had to reach the ruins. There was no other thought in his head now, nothing but focus as he stalked across the water, ready to explode against anything else his "fathers" might throw at him. But he reached the temple's outer wall without further incident.

Judging it sturdy enough to bear his weight, Naysin stepped onto the wet remnant and stopped to collect himself. "So you feel stronger here, do you?" he whispered. "Now that you've returned to your old *cage*? It must bring back pleasant memories."

No response. The cougar-men were probably biding their time for another moment of vulnerability.

He hadn't felt their presence like that — hadn't felt them shaman **Kug** and *Mir* through him — since he was young. Since his guardian spirit day, back when his abilities were new and he hadn't learned how to control them. There really must be something different about this place, some power that still resided in the temple's broken bones. He just had to figure out what it was. Preferably quickly, before the cougar-men gathered enough strength to mount another attack.

Naysin began by staring at the stone he was standing on, the bit of dark rock that had once been a finely sculpted brick. Was he imagining a residual weave of **Kug**? Or was that just the stone's natural energy? It was too subtle to tell.

He moved to the next closest piece of protruding ruin and repeated his inspection, with similar results. The subsequent stretch of jagged wall was no more revealing; neither was the one after that. He continued the pattern anyway, until he'd been over the temple's entire ruptured upper-half. There were glimmers here and there; that much he was sure of now. Echoes of an epic outpouring of **Kug** and *Mir*. But the lines were faint, like the edges of long-healed scars... He needed a more complete picture.

He needed to see the temple's lower half.

After glancing at Tay — who was rhythmically tapping her rainstick on the riverbank — Naysin waved reassuringly and dived into the water again.

It was still freezing, but he was ready for the shock this time, and for anything else; he'd clutched immense flows of **Kug** and *Mir* to himself like a warrior with shields on both arms. He knew he couldn't shaman such quantities for long, but he could stop as soon as he found the termination points of the lines he'd seen above, borders that belonged to what had once been an extremely beautiful temple.

That was evident now that Naysin could see the structure's full extent. The river hadn't been any kinder to the submerged stonework, but the original craftsmanship was more apparent here beneath the surface. Vast pillars framed an enormous entrance, beyond which stretched a cavernous room of worship — three of his people's Longest Houses would have fit inside. Maybe four.

This had been more than a jail cell once. It had been meant to endure as a monument to primeval gods, deities so ancient they'd probably been forgotten countless winters ago.

Feeling his lungs starting to burn, Naysin used a stream of *Mir* to pull a funnel of air down to his mouth. It didn't take much energy, but the extra strain was enough to remind him that he didn't have time to dawdle. He needed to learn the rest of the intricate binding that had trapped the cougar-men here for so long.

A binding that, according to his "fathers," had been tied by their mother.

Naysin couldn't help thinking more about this as he swam slowly around the temple's base, taking note of every faint flow. What had driven her to inhume her sons? Had she been appalled by their ambition? Their callous disregard for anyone less powerful than them? Or had she — even as powerful as she must have been to have wrought this seal — just felt threatened?

Either way, it was no small thing to betray one's children.

The old anger frothed up, but Naysin calmed himself by taking a deep breath from his funnel of air. There wasn't time to indulge the hurt, and it wasn't relevant. He was here to understand the pattern of the binding. Nothing more.

But was there a pattern? He'd seen the temple from every angle now, above and below the water's surface. Maybe with more time he could untangle the skein of **Kug** and *Mir* that had once been woven here so tightly. As it was, all he saw was a complex mess of faded flows, and—

Cougars.

Swimming at him with snarling speed.

One cougar was corpse-white and bowstring-lean.

The other was night-black and bull-thick.

Both were terrifying.

The years since his guardian spirit day fell away, and suddenly he was twelve winters again. Scared to death of beasts that had no business slicing through the water like fish, but were defying Nature to catch him.

And eat him.

And kill him.

Naysin turned and fled. The funnel of air collapsed on itself, and he swallowed several mouthfuls of water before he remembered to force his lips shut. Fear shot through him like a lightning bolt as his arms and legs churned the river. He had to get back to the bank. Back to the shore and out of the water — the cougars couldn't get him if he was out of the water.

Clinging to that hope, an aspect of his guardian spirit day he prayed he wasn't misremembering, he swam with every ounce of his power. His physical power; he couldn't summon a jot of **Kug** or *Mir* right now. The way back was long, and the current was strong. He fully expected to lose a heel at any moment, and then a calf, and then the rest of his leg — the cougars had to be closing on him. As fast as they'd been moving, he didn't have a chance.

But he didn't look back. He was lost if he looked back. He knew that, knew that his only hope was to keep swimming toward the shore. He'd be safe on the shore. His only hope was to reach the shore. He had to reach the shore.

When he was finally near enough to the riverbank to stand — on his still intact legs — Naysin scrambled the rest of the way out of the water and collapsed.

— « o » —

The cougar-men didn't say anything to mark their victory, but Naysin thought he heard a few soft chuckles. He ignored them. His fathers had scared him, but they hadn't killed him. Losing this battle meant nothing. He'd still seen what he needed to see; they hadn't prevented that. And eventually he'd understand the ruin's pattern. It might take a few more days — or moons — of study, but what did he have but time? He'd win the war in the end.

When he felt collected enough to stand, Naysin began walking back to his original point of entry; he'd emerged several field-lengths downriver, pushed sideways by the current as he'd tried to swim straight across. The temple was barely visible from where he was now, the ruins obscured by intervening brush. Tay must be worried. And angry — he'd been gone for a long time. Drowned, for all she knew. She'd be furious. Even though she'd try to hide it behind her I-am-a-calm-and-prideful-warrior expression.

Smiling ruefully, he rounded the last bend and found her … kneeling. With her hands on the ground to steady herself.

Naysin covered the remaining distance at a dead sprint.

Tay looked up as he drew near. "You're all right," she noted matter-of-factly, her milky eyes distant and unfocused.

"Are you?"

She blinked, and her expression started to clear. "I know where we need to go."

Caught off guard, Naysin responded more defensively than he would have liked. "I'm already where I need to be."

"Are you?" she asked quietly, gently throwing his question back at him.

He was tempted to launch into a description of what had just happened to him. But he knew it would be better to let Tay speak — or sign — her piece.

<u>I had the vision again</u>, she explained as she eased herself into a stand. <u>Of you and me on the hill — the earthen pyramid you jumped off.</u>

He nodded, hoping she wouldn't mention what had transpired next.

She didn't. <u>We weren't alone this time. There were four people climbing to us, each on a different side. That man from Fort Kaska, the firemaker, was one of them. So was Isaura.</u>

Naysin rocked back on his heels. "And the other two?"

<u>Two more men. I've never seen them before. One was dark, and one was an original man.</u>

Amadi and Quecxl — it had to be.

Tay paused to stare at him. <u>It means something, Naysin. I think we're supposed to go back.</u>

The need to stay and study the temple flared up again. If he was going to do anything about the cougar-men — and about himself, and anyone like him — he needed to be here. He needed more time to study the ancient binding. He needed to see the faint flows that permeated the ruins, stare at the pattern he wasn't even close to comprehending...

But maybe there was a cleverer way.

"Give me a little while?" he asked as he removed the wooden etching of the temple from his pack. He took most of the afternoon, however; giving the flat representation depth was harder than he'd expected. So was adding a spider web's worth of lines. But he persevered, and when he was done, he held a miniature-version of the temple in his hand, marked with every bit of binding he'd seen above and below the waterline. It was the most intricate thing he'd ever created.

"All right," he finally said to Tay, who'd been watching him patiently. "Let's go."

She smiled. "Put your clothes on, and we will."

Chapter Twenty-Seven

The Beacon

The journey back to the earthen pyramid was frantic. Tay — quietly but firmly — kept insisting they hurry, that they couldn't miss the moment she'd seen in her vision. "You've stared at that thing enough," she said whenever Naysin stopped to study his model of the ruined temple. "Let's go." Eventually he just looked at it while he walked; Tay accepted the concession as long as he maintained a steady pace. When they finally reached the pyramid, they rushed up the north side and camped in the center of the plateau. Then they waited.

For a day.

Ten days.

A moon.

Nothing changed but the weather.

Tay occupied herself by endlessly drilling with her rainstick, but by the end of the first moon, Naysin was boiling with impatience. He'd studied his model until he hated the sight of it, with little insight. To ease his mind, he suggested they explore the area a little each day. Tay agreed, on condition that they return to the pyramid by early afternoon — she thought the moment in her vision would take place with the sun on its way down.

So for lack of anything better to do, they began inspecting the carcass of a once great civilization.

The pyramid was the most obvious relic. According to a stray gibe from the cougar-men, the earthen structure had once been called "Saint's Summit." A fitting name: the pyramid was as immense as it was majestic. So was the enormous plaza Naysin had marveled at the last time they'd been here, and the rotting-but-still-imposing skeletons of once-mighty buildings. But there were other remnants of human achievement as well. They'd seen a few additional mounds before — mini-pyramids — but they found more with each excursion. The unnaturally-sloped hills were everywhere once he and Tay started looking for them.

"Why do you think they built them?" she asked after they'd found their seventh example.

Naysin shrugged. "Burial mounds? Symbols? Or maybe they made them just to show they could; it takes a lot of power to do something like this. I could open one up if you really want to know."

"I don't." Tay shook her head. "We shouldn't interfere. Come on. We need to get back."

They kept up the pattern — wake, eat, explore, return to Saint's Summit, eat, study and drill, eat, sleep — for two more moons before moving on to a new routine. This time, it was Naysin who demanded a change, and not just because he was tired of climbing up and down the pyramid's steep slopes. They'd seen everything within a half-days walk now — except for the clearing where Naysin had lost control; neither of them wanted to revisit the massacre — and he was sick to death of failing to understand the secret encapsulated in his model. The only thing left was debating what to do when (if?) the four people in Tay's vision actually appeared.

Naysin still knew he wanted to lock away the cougar-men; he hadn't wavered on that. He was less certain about what do with himself, however, and even more confused about how to handle others like him. Yes, the burned man from Fort Kaska was dangerous, but was it really Naysin's place to pass judgment? To carry out a sentence?

He'd thought so when he was searching for the temple. Now he wasn't sure. He didn't want to be a hunter. Or a jailer. Or an executioner. What did that leave, though? Teacher was out; the only mentors he'd ever known were the cougar-men, and they'd soured him on the experience. So was the best course of action simply to leave other shamans alone?

Then why was he waiting on Saint's Summit?

"Can I see your vision?" he asked Tay as soon as she woke up one morning.

She blinked. "You don't believe me?"

"No, I do, I just ... I need to see it. I'm trying to figure things out."

"All right." Tay stretched and stood. <u>But I can't conjure images out of thin air like you can.</u>

"I know. That's why I'm going to help you." He put his hands over her temples, glad she didn't flinch.

Instead, she stared at him, her milky eyes boring into his tattoo. "Now I think of the vision?"

"Now you think of the vision," he said, trying to project a confidence he didn't feel.

She saw through his bravado and smiled. "You say that like you've done this before." Then she closed her eyes. "Can you see it?" she asked after a few breaths.

"Not yet." He hadn't done anything but watch the bend in her eyebrows. Before she'd woken, it had seemed like an easy thing to shaman bits of **Kug** and *Mir* to draw out her vision. Because he *had* done this before: nine winters ago, in the Longest House, with the memory of his guardian spirit day.

Of course, he hadn't had a clue what he was doing that night. And the cougar-men had probably been directing — if not outright controlling — the flows. But before Tay had woken up, this had seemed doable.

Now he was scared. Amplifying Tay's vision meant shamaning *into* her.

What if he made a mistake?

"I can't see it. We should stop." He started to withdraw his hands from Tay's head.

But she pressed them back to her temples. "Don't give up," she demanded, eyes still shut tight. "I trust you, Naysin. Do it."

"...All right." Committed now, he started grazing Tay with small, experimental flows. None of them seemed right; was memory **Kug** or *Mir*? Both?

He was flailing, and he knew it. Guessing wasn't going to work, not when he had so little margin for error. He needed to remember what he'd done nine winters ago. That was the only way this would happen. He needed to remember the flows he'd used, needed to recall their forms and balance.

Or maybe he just needed to remember the vision itself.

That felt right. Desperate, but right.

Closing his eyes, Naysin concentrated on that night in the Longest House, focusing on the moment he'd started seeing his words illustrated in the temple's pure fires. The cougar had taken shape in the flames, beginning as one snarling beast before *dividing* into two, one black and one white. Both raging against the water's surface as the fire cast their violent shadows over the carved faces of the Lepane's Great Spirits...

He felt Tay's hands on *his* temples; she'd anticipated his pain, even with her eyes closed. Which meant she was foretelling at this very instant, seeing heartbeats ahead. Usually only a few, but sometimes — hopefully this time — she could see many heartbeats ahead. Days, moons, seasons: however long it would be until the others came to Saint's Summit. He needed to share that ability. Just this once. He needed to let go and see what she was seeing.

Bowing his forehead to touch hers, he stopped trying to force his way into her mind and started hoping. Started believing he *would* be able to bear witness with her.

They stood that way for several breaths — brow to brow and hands to temples, feeling each other's pulse through multiple points of contact — before the images in Naysin's head finally started to change. The Longest House gave way to a green vista, the pure fires became Saint's Summit, and the Great Spirits' faces morphed into ... the four ascenders.

Quecxl on the pyramid's north side.

Amadi on the east.

The burned man on the south.

And Isaura on the west.

They climbed in isolated unison, seemingly unaware of each other, yet ascending at the same pace and height. Making for the flat peak, where he and Tay waited ... and there the vision ended, fading out before fading back in to repeat itself. She must be picturing it over and over in her head.

This *was* going to happen. Naysin had always believed her, but sharing in the foretelling helped substantiate the coming event in a way words never could. These people from his past *were* going to climb Saint's Summit, and he *was* going to meet them.

But he was tired of waiting.

If this was going to happen, why couldn't it happen now? Or at least soon? For all the vision's clarity, there was no indication of when, why, or how the ascenders were going to come to the pyramid… Maybe they didn't have a reason yet.

Maybe he was meant to give them one.

"I need you to find these people," he whispered to Tay, eyes still closed, head still pressed against hers. "Can you see where they are now?"

"No. But I'll try."

She tensed, and the vision stopped looping. In its place came isolated images of the four ascenders, each climbing … nothing. They were set against a black void now. No green vista, no pyramid, no background at all. Just empty space that gave no hint of location or connection.

"I'll help," he said softly.

Her nod made him nod as well.

Still unsure of how to do the shamaning, but no longer scared to try, Naysin began preparing flows of **Kug** and *Mir* within himself. Before now, he'd always composed them externally; this time he didn't want them to leave his body before they reached their target: Tay.

She jerked slightly when he started the transfer, and he almost pulled back. But her hands tightened against his temples, and the pressure was enough to shore up his resolve. Slowly and carefully, he increased the amounts of **Kug** and *Mir* he was feeding her, all the while watching the four figures in his head for any sign that this was working.

The indicators were subtle at first: the burned man paused to contemplate his fire stick; Amadi threw something behind him; Quecxl clapped his hands; Isaura wiped something from her dress. Then, gradually, each of the four stopped climbing and started doing something else while new backgrounds filled in around them. The burned man was about to climb a ladder; Amadi was digging an enormous pit with his hands; Quecxl was rowing a canoe, periodically setting down the oars to clap in time with his singing; Isaura was tending a fire, trying to cook a meal without getting ash on herself.

This, Naysin slowly realized, was what the four ascenders were doing *at that moment*. He — and Tay — had found them. Now he just needed to make them come to Saint's Summit.

"I know you can do things you shouldn't be able to," he said into Tay's mouth, forming his words into every language he'd learned. She twitched again, but nothing else happened. Refocusing, he repeated the words and used a gust of *Mir* to truly sweep them into Tay. This time the ascenders looked up.

"Things you don't always want to do," Naysin continued. "Things you regret."

It was hard to tell from their reactions; all four ascenders were searching for the source of the disembodied voice that had suddenly invaded their heads. He needed to reveal himself, to show his face so the ascenders could focus on his message.

A small surge of **Kug** would do it. Shamaned through him and into Tay... There. He knew his image was projecting even before the ascenders jumped slightly, almost in unison — probably because he was shining black and white, but he didn't open his eyes to confirm. It didn't matter. The ascenders could see and hear him now. All that remained was to give them a reason to meet him in person.

"I feel the same way. Likely even more so; trust me when I say I don't enjoy being the 'Red Wraith.' But one fact gives me comfort." Slowly, he raised his head and arms away from Tay. Their connection wavered, but he stabilized it by hardening the flows. "I'm not alone," he said as he opened his eyes. "*We* are not alone.

"Which is why I want to meet you. Here, on this ancient pyramid." Gesturing at his surroundings, he did his best to show each ascender an image of their future climb. It seemed to work; they either widened their already-wide eyes or raised their eyebrows.

He had to hurry, though. The strain was rapidly becoming too much, and he still had a large expenditure to make.

"In one moon's time, meet me here." He knelt and placed his right palm on the earth. Thinking of Jehan, and the compass she'd used to navigate between one trade route and the next, he poured the last of himself into a beacon, a signal that began in Saint's Summit and extended through Tay and into each ascender: a shooting star with four tails.

"In one moon's time," Naysin repeated, punctuating his words with a final image of the pyramid itself.

Then he collapsed.

Chapter Twenty-Eight

Meeting

Naysin still didn't have a plan the afternoon he felt nearby surges of Mir and Kug. Or when Tay spotted the ascenders, each converging on Saint's Summit from a different direction.

All he felt was the same restlessness that had plagued him for the last moon.

It had begun with nothing; the effort of setting up the beacon had knocked Naysin unconscious for days. Tay said it was only three, but it had felt like more — he'd been so weak when he woke up.

But only physically. Mentally, he couldn't stop moving. Once he'd confirmed that Tay hadn't suffered ill effects from acting as his conduit, his mind had been on edge from sunrise to sunset, racing with possibilities. Things were finally coming to a head, either a beginning or an end. He wasn't sure which, but he knew something was going to happen. He also knew the outcome of that something would have a lot to do with how he reacted when he met the other shamans. The same debates played in his head over and over:

Would he befriend the ascenders?

Teach them?

Shackle them?

Kill them?

Or would he just talk to them?

His thoughts had been a maelstrom of maybes, a storm of possibilities with no certainties to latch onto.

But now... Now he was filled with a sudden sense of destiny, as if a spirit had blown fate into his lungs: he knew what he was supposed to accomplish. Three races were converging on the pyramid. For years, his people — the original people — had lost ground to the other two, but it was time to right the balance. Time for him to right the balance.

He just had to figure out how.

Then the terror set in.

His legs began to buckle as his stomach churned with the beating of tiny wings: butterflies. He'd never had the sensation before, but his mother used to feel it when she was nervous. His mother — funny to think of her now, when a resolution to everything else seemed so near at hand. Maybe she was supposed to be here too...

And with that idle musing, terror became rage.

His mother had filled his childhood with tales of Machk, the mighty hunter who would have been chief were he not struck down by plague just before Naysin's birth. Machk, the dutiful husband, the cunning warrior, the unbeatable runner, the perfect father. All lies. Why had this task been set for Naysin when the original "original people" — the Lepane, his tribe — had ripped his childhood apart and branded him a pariah? When other men and women who shared his skin color, like the Hodensee — the brutal pigs — and the Dzune — those scared children — had used or shunned him?

What did he owe any of these charlatans and fools? Why—

Why was he wasting time? He'd had many days to drown in self-pity: moons and years aplenty. Right now, he had to focus on the ascenders.

Because they were too spread out. It was a miracle they'd all arrived on the same day. Did the beacon have something to do with that? But if this moment was to stay true to Tay's vision, they needed to climb Saint's Summit at the same time. And that meant adjusting the pace of their arrivals; no one lagged now that the pyramid was in sight, but Quecxl had appeared closer than the rest, and Isaura had the shortest legs.

Orchestrating the convergence proved harder than Naysin expected; the effort forced him to a sitting position. Crossing his legs, he bowed his head in concentration. He stayed like that as Tay kept guard and the ascenders drew closer.

Then they were on the slopes, one person on each side of Saint's Summit. Naysin continued pushing and pulling them along, still compensating for their different speeds, until...

They were atop the pyramid.

And Naysin let them see each other.

And Isaura shot him.

In the instant before the pain set in, all he could do was laugh. This hadn't been in Tay's vision. This was a cruel joke.

So as a fire started in his abdomen, he froze everyone in midstride.

Chapter Twenty-Nine

The Ascenders

Spirits and lakes — he hadn't meant to wallow so long in his own memories.

Naysin opened his eyes in disgust. The pain had brought him back: the remembered-pain of being shot and the present-pain of dying from the wound.

It wasn't a pleasant combination.

Ignoring the glare from the sun, he studied the ascenders' still forms. At least he'd revisited the vital truth of Cawgana: Quecxl could heal. "Is that why you were rushing toward me?"

The question came out louder than Naysin intended, but amazingly, Tay and her cat-ears didn't hear him; she was at the other end of Saint's Summit, preoccupied with whipping her rainstick through a series of complex thrusts and feints that caused it to rattle like a thunderstorm. He opened his mouth to call to her … and thought better of it. If he told her about Quecxl, she'd insist he free the Metican and force him to heal the gunshot wound. Which wasn't a terrible idea, except Naysin wasn't sure he could un-paralyze one ascender without loosing the others. And there was no guarantee he could immobilize them again once his wound was closed.

No, better to uphold the stasis. Continuing it was just as excruciating as the gunshot, but the latter wouldn't kill him for at least a day. And if it came down to it, he could release Quecxl before the end…

Naysin grunted as Tay tugged his bandage from behind — she must have completed her circuit. "Wasn't that tight enough already?"

"No," she answered sweetly as she stepped into view. "How long have you been awake?" Her manner was easy, but she looked relieved he'd said something. He must have been silent for a while. Maybe most of the afternoon, if he were judging the still-blazing sun correctly.

Naysin tried a smile. "Forgive me. I was ... considering something."

Tay sat next to him expectantly, her rainstick's blades gleaming as they caught the light.

An image of Quecxl healing the Cawganan woman flashed across Naysin's mind. "I saw everyone's first moment of magic," he said. It wasn't a total lie; he'd relived his first *encounters* with the ascenders, and each of those interactions had involved magic.

Tay glanced at Quecxl. "What can he do?"

"I'm not entirely sure yet," Naysin improvised further, "but I think it changed everything for him. For all of them." It certainly had for himself. His tribe had rejected him. *Disfigured* and *banished* him. And all because—

More wallowing.

Naysin grunted again and lay back on the makeshift pillow Tay had fashioned from their packs, his sweaty shoulders sticking to the cloth immediately. Spirits and lakes, the sun was hot.

"What do you think it means?" Tay asked. When he didn't respond, she moved her hands into his line of sight. <u>Please. I want to help.</u>

Even if he'd had a response, it would have been preempted by the geyser of pain that erupted in his stomach.

"Naysin," Tay said quietly when the crisis passed. She was cradling his head in her lap — when had that happened? Her rough-spun leggings were softer than they looked. "Where did the wind go?"

It was gone. It had been gone since he'd exited his memories. He'd been too preoccupied to notice, but the air was definitely sticky and stagnant again. So where was his

Mir going? He was still shamaning enormous amounts of it to counterbalance the **Kug** he was using to uphold the stasis, more than he'd ever — "Look up."

Tay was already craning her neck; high, high up in the sky was a cluster of rapidly evolving clouds, constantly expanding and contracting to form … faces.

People.

Objects.

Scenes.

One over the next over the next, layering on top of each other like a stack of spirits.

"Is that what you're seeing?" Tay asked softly.

The image in the forefront showed Degan speaking to him on Bimshire. "Glimpses of it… A bit delayed."

They watched as Degan's scene was gradually superimposed by a representation of Kemi's dismemberment. Tay shuddered and clutched Naysin's hair. "I didn't mean for this to happen," she lisped. "It isn't worth it. Let me take you away from here."

"It's not your fault," he whispered, hardening himself to play on Tay's emotions. "But I need to reach this knot of memories two years ago."

"Edgeland," she said immediately as her body tightened like a bowstring.

"And Fort Kaska."

They sat in silence for several moments, beset by remembrances and guilt. Then Naysin closed his eyes.

— « o » —

This time he managed to focus on the ascenders' memories. He'd told Tay navigating them was like untangling threads. But it wasn't — not quite. It felt more like following four rivers that kept intersecting. Six, if you counted his and Tay's. At some points they flowed slower, and were easier to wade in; at others they ran fast as rapids. Despite the danger, Naysin was drawn to the turbulent stretches. Somehow he knew they represented central moments, defining decisions and events. Many of these were dark, and the ascenders' initial manifestations of magic — which he made a point of viewing — were no exception.

They were also shocking.

Quecxl, a Metican bladeknapper, had inadvertently performed his first act of healing after ramming one of his knives through a sacrificial victim's chest. Of its own accord, thick energy — **Kug** — had poured from his core, infused the victim, knitted her torso back together, and ruined the amateur ceremony and its goal of thwarting pale conquest. Quecxl had tried to appease his gods' presumed anger, but shortly thereafter, Tentocht, the Metica people's capital city, had been humiliated by Espan invaders. He blamed himself. To atone, he'd journeyed north in search of Aztlan, his ancestral homeland, where he hoped to convince his legendary Metican forebears to join the fight.

Isaura, kidnapped by Espan explorers and forced to whore at St. Augstin, their outpost in La Florida, had desiccated one of her assailants by using a funnel of *Mir* to suck every drop of water from his body. The act had been involuntary, but she still hated herself for "swimming," her euphemism for witchery. It took years for her to stop thinking she belonged on a pyre.

Amadi, an accomplished slave-taker in the Afrii nation of Dahemy, had been ambushed by another slave-taker, overcome, and chained to his former "ejeme." They'd taken every opportunity to exact their revenge during the march to the slave port of Ghelwa. But in the holding pen where they were herded to await sale to a pale trader, Amadi endured a climactic assault after instinctively molding **Kug** into a spirit armor that absorbed most blows and healed the harm wrought by the rest. The unasked-for protection allowed him to survive anything, including his subsequent suicide attempts.

Chase, the burned man (yet unmarked), had stormed out of a council meeting after losing an argument with his settlement's other elders — they'd adamantly opposed his view that connecting with the neighboring tribes was both necessary for New Kent's survival and in accordance with Jesua's will. After stomping to his cabin, he'd wrenched the door open and found his brother adultering with an original woman. Chase's surprise had materialized as *Mir*-fueled flame, setting his family's house ablaze ... along with his infant son Kip. Later, during his self-imposed exile, Chase had begun to hold the original woman responsible for his hellfire.

There were connections too, more than coincidence alone could explain. In addition to what had transpired at Fort Kaska, Chase had witnessed the end of the Second Walking Purchase, when the last survivors had gratefully marched into a forest fire; Amadi had earned the epithet "The Black Resurrection" after he bested Chase and branded his brow with that handprint; Quecxl had realized his destiny as a healer when he saved Omnira, Amadi's fledgling refuge for runaways; Isaura had dowsed Omnira a well; Quecxl had been shot at Edgeland shortly before Naysin's intervention; Isaura — searching for Rowtag, her "friend" — had witnessed Quecxl healing the battle's wounded despite his injury... It went on and on.

And it meant nothing.

Oh, he knew far more than he wanted about the ascenders now.

He knew Isaura had been raped before she loved and lost Rowtag; Amadi had been a slave-taker before he became a slave; Quecxl had tried to slay before he could save; Chase had preached harmony before he preached hate.

He knew **Kug** and *Mir* — in the forms of spirit armor, thick energy, hellfire, and swimming — had altered the group's lives, usually for the worse.

He knew two of the ascenders were healers, and all were worthier leaders than himself. Even Chase.

He knew he was connected to them through chance encounters, large and small.

He knew nothing.

Nothing of consequence, nothing that would help him determine why he was dying on a hill crowned by an uneven human sundial. What was the point? Was there a point?

Not if you let yourself die, the first of two familiar voices whispered in his dreams.

Naysin swore soundlessly.

He seems intent on doing so. Maybe that is the point.

True. Brave men kill themselves, but cowards summon others to drive the blade home.

The goad worked; Naysin couldn't stop himself from responding. "Do you want me to die or not? I can't tell anymore."

The cougar-men laughed long and hard; he could still hear them when Tay pinched him awake.

— « o » —

Groaning, he opened his eyes to an aging sky — the sun was finally setting. But the air remained oppressively hot. And his cloudscape had become a jumbled mess of overlapping outlines, too muddled to follow.

"Drink," Tay commanded as he realized how parched his lips were. She was crouched next to him, her rainstick resting across her thighs and a waterskin clutched in one hand. She poured the sack's lukewarm contents down his throat before he had a chance to reply, using her other hand to raise his head.

"Eat," she insisted when he'd emptied the waterskin. She jabbed a steaming rabbit leg at him — she'd grown particularly deadly with thrown rocks over the last year. The fire she'd used to cook her kill crackled behind them. He accepted the rabbit leg silently, even though he wasn't hungry. The water had been enough.

As he chewed his first mouthful, Tay stared at him with an expression that suggested she meant to make sure he ate the entire leg. She was clearly angry — more angry than worried now. And she had a right to be. She'd stood by him after Edgeland, and everything before and since. But now he was forcing her to watch him die.

"Any wiser?" Tay sounded like she already knew the answer.

Naysin's thoughts returned to that day with Degan and the coconuts. Nothing had really changed in the winters since; he could hurt on a whim, but when it came time to help... "There are more connections than I realized," he said eventually. "It can't be coincidence."

"But you don't know what it means."

"No. Not yet."

Tay considered the ascenders, her gaze lingering balefully on Isaura. "Are you looking at my memories?"

Naysin forced a smile. "I'm not *that* foolish."

"And you're not that good a liar," Tay responded, mellowing slightly as she accepted his invitation for levity. "No, you said..." She paused for a moment before resuming in signs. <u>You said you saw everyone's first moment of magic. You didn't look at mine?</u>

"I couldn't — your memories are slippery."

<u>So you tried.</u>

"No, I mean... Remember when I said it was like untangling threads?" He explained how he'd come to realize that each person's past was more like a river. "Your waters are particularly fast, and they keep bending away from me. Even if I could get in them, I'm not sure I'd have the strength to get back out."

<u>Then stop. At least rest awhile.</u>

Naysin blew out a long breath as he made his decision. "Those are the same things. If I stop, I let the ascenders go. And if I let them go, it's over, and I lose whatever chance this represents."

Fast as a falcon, Tay yanked the rabbit leg from him and hurled it at Isaura, hitting her square in the chest and staining her dress. "She killed you, you know — if you don't do something. She pierced..." Tay broke off, swallowed, and raised her hands. <u>That bitch pierced your guts. I can smell your breakfast. Stomach wounds don't heal on their own. If you don't do something, you'll die.</u>

"I know," he said. "But I can't stop. Not yet. I'm getting somewhere, but I'm not there. When I am—"

<u>Go back to them, then,</u> Tay signed before shoving his head against the ragged packs. <u>Go back and play with your rivers and threads while I watch you bleed and die.</u>

"Tay..."

<u>Just go.</u> And with that, she was gone herself, thrusting and parrying with her rainstick as she sparred her way to the other side of Saint's Summit.

Naysin slipped back into darkness a few moments later.

— « o » —

His next sleep was dreamless and of no import.

It was beautiful.

Upon waking, he shook his head at the loss of peace … and opened his eyes in surprise when the back of his neck turned freely instead of rubbing against sweaty cloth. He was off the ground. Was he flying again? Floating? No — he was being carried. "Tay, put me down."

She picked up her pace. Her rainstick was on her back, as were their packs, filled with everything they'd brought to Saint's Summit.

"Tay! Put me down."

No answer, except for the further lengthening of her gait. Sprinting now, she dashed between the frozen ascenders without sparing them a glance, her milky eyes fixed on the tip of the deer's path he and she used to traverse Saint's Summit. Her biceps were hard as rocks beneath his back, and her slender forearms encircled his side like carved oak. He'd never realized how strong she was.

"Tay: put — me — down."

Still no answer; just graceful stride after graceful stride. They were almost to the deer's path.

"I warned you."

She saw it coming, but she didn't have time to do anything but shift her grip.

And then she was frozen.

A fifth statue, another dynamic figurine balanced precariously on one leg … probably the only time she'd looked awkward in her life.

"I don't know if I can hold you," Naysin murmured tiredly. "Not on top of the rest of them. But you were holding me. You left me no choice."

He didn't want to hurt her, though. As strong as her arms felt, he knew the position she carried him in wouldn't be easy to maintain. And he had much left to do (because he hadn't done anything yet). If his weight eventually caused her muscles to tear or her bones to break… Quecxl could probably heal the damage, but Naysin didn't want to take the chance.

His blood had slicked her forearms. It shouldn't have been hard to slither from her grasp, but as he wriggled free, his stomach protested, pain flared like an eclipse, and he hit the ground at an awful, debilitating angle.

— « o » —

He wasn't dead.

It was hard to be sure at first. When Naysin opened his eyes from the latest blackout — spirits and lakes, it felt like he'd spent *half his life* blacking out — he found the world turned to shadows. But it was only the darkness of dusk, the ordinary, everyday skirmishing of night's advance-scout. The pain confirmed it: he was still alive. Hungry, parched, weak, gut-shot, but alive.

And brimming with self-hate.

Swallowing, Naysin raised his head to look at the ascenders ... and Tay. Still frozen. They were all still frozen, still exactly where he'd left them.

Quecxl was paralyzed in mid-sprint, one muscular leg planted on Saint's Summit while the other stretched behind him in a stride aching to be completed. The dirty gull remained perched on his shoulder, wings spread for flight. The combined pose looked ... powerful. Naysin had never believed his uncle's campfire tales about the bloodthirsty Metica of Tentocht, but looking at Quecxl, the stories seemed plausible. Even if their savagery belied the man's ability — and willingness — to heal.

Chase's fire was still pointed at Amadi like a cloud of arrows. The pale man's marred face was set in a stoic expression; he appeared to be resigned to whatever fate he'd expected to find here. Likely death. Because what else would the Firebrand get from the Red Wraith?

The Black Resurrection completed the triangle of ridiculous legends. He was bent forward in the first steps of a furious charge, his bald head dripping with sweat — the furthest extent of Chase's fire was only a hand's breadth away. A thin column of steam indicated parts of Amadi's scalp were scalding ... and healing ... and scalding again, in an endless battle of hellfire versus spirit armor.

And Isaura... Isaura's auburn hair gleamed in the sun, while her brown eyes shone with a blend of triumph, anger, and grief. The pistol hovered at her side, clutched in a hand that seemed too delicate to hold even such a small weapon, much less wield it. She was a mother now, though — a strong one. Naysin had seen it in her past. Alone, Isaura had birthed Rowtag's son and christened him Shoteka. But to heed the Red Wraith's call, she'd had to leave her babe in the care of a Kiksha friend named Fochik.

Naysin lowered his head back to the earth at Tay's feet. He was amazed the stasis had held without his concentration. He hadn't tied off the flows — not consciously. Not like he had when he'd dealt with the Walking Purchase. But energy was still flooding out of him, still wrapping around the ascenders, sustaining the cloud images, and, bit-by-bit, draining his vitality.

He'd never shamaned this much for this long, certainly not without blacking out. And he still didn't know if the effort was worthwhile, if he'd accomplished anything other than exposing the palest ascenders to the sun: Isaura was pinker now, and Chase was almost scarlet.

What a grand feat. A white man had been turned red. How momentous.

Naysin tried his best to lose consciousness again. He was tired of hurting, tired of waking with no answers, tired of being *awake*. But he couldn't seem to manage passing out on his own; that particular trick was apparently reserved for acts of extreme stupidity. Hopefully he'd just succumb to blood loss soon.

Resigned to the fact that he wasn't going to die on his own terms, Naysin turned to the ascenders once more. Had they seen his story? And each other's? In the clouds or through the beacon's lingering tendrils? Had they — through him — understood all the tongues he knew? What would they think of him now? Would they bury him when he died? Leave him for scavengers? Parade his scalp before the peoples of the world?

More importantly, what did Tay think?

He craned his neck to locate her frozen, milky eyes. She'd blame herself when the stasis unraveled and she discovered him dead at her feet. If there was any good in the world, she'd run and grieve him from afar. But Naysin knew that wouldn't happen. Tay wouldn't just go. She'd take her anger out on Isaura, and then Chase, and maybe even Quecxl and Amadi. The Foim would survive, but the others … she'd cut them down with furious grace, drenching her hands in blood again. For *him*. One last time.

Did he care? He probably should. But he didn't have the energy to—

A black paw sprang out of the seeping hole in his gut.

Then two ears, the rest of the dark cougar's head, and its other front limb. A white head followed with two more paws.

"No!" yelled Naysin as he found the strength to grab his fathers' spectral forms by the scruffs of their necks and shove them back into his midsection. "Spirits and lakes, you wait until I'm DEAD!"

The echoes of his guardian spirit day vanished immediately — echoes, that was all they were, all the cougar-men could manage while he still lived. But he couldn't silence their laughter so easily.

Forgive us. Watching you play in the past was a bit tedious.

We are glad it was so productive, however. You learned everything you needed to, yes?

It must feel good to have all the answers at long last, to finally know what you're meant to do.

"Stop," Naysin muttered as the rage left him, his hands still pressed to the hole in his stomach. "Just stop."

I suppose we should honor his last request.

Agreed. It's the gentlemanly thing to do.

But once he is gone, I imagine that little fortune-teller will be quite lonely.

You're right. We should see if she wants to talk to someone. I'm sure she'll need … comforting.

Naysin's heart skipped. He'd lost sight of what would happen when he died, forgotten what would get *out*.

There was still time, though. There had to still be time.

"I'm not dead yet, you manitouk liars," he hissed as he plunged into the only stories he hadn't investigated yet: his fathers'.

Chapter Thirty

The Cougar-men

Hatred kept Naysin awake for his final history lesson. Hatred and fear.

But neither emotion helped him with control.

The cougar-men's stories were harder to array than the ascenders' had been. Nothing wanted to stay put: an argument from a moon ago came on the heels of a childhood fight that felt older than the eldest trees; a debate conducted in his head overlapped an ancient memory of scheming in the ruined temple; yesterday's anger at being betrayed flowed into today's rage at being helpless.

It was chaos.

And Naysin was too weak to impose much order. Even if he'd been stronger, his connection with the cougar-men was radically different than the entry point the beacon had established with the ascenders, and his fathers were fighting his intrusion into their secrets.

Still, he saw and heard more than they wanted, and he was able to identify three central channels: a vein of Enki's childhood memories, a later seam of Enmul's, and select conversations from the brothers' eons of entrapment...

— « o » —

There has to be a way out.

There's not.

Walk me through what you tried again. Start with the gates. Did you—

Yes. Most definitely.

Enki, our only chance is to do this systematically. On the gates, did you—

I couldn't do anything with the gates. I couldn't do anything with the walls. I couldn't do anything with the ceiling, the altar, or the spires. Above the river or below. We're trapped, Enmul. Well and truly banished.

We do not know that yet.

Yes, we do. This temple is our tomb, brother. The sooner you accept that, the sooner we can enjoy the peace and quiet.

Will you at least look at my bonds again? I was thinking about why I was unable to affect yours, and I have an idea—

So do I: swallow your tongue.

— « o » —

It was dark out. And she was running. But she never ran. Never rushed, never hurried.

"Momma?" Enki raised his head off her neck, noting that Enmul lay next to him. They were both strapped to her broad back, slung high and tight to avoid the swinging of her arms and legs.

"Sleep ... little one," their momma panted out between strides. "Go back ... to sleep."

He tried to look behind them, but he couldn't turn his body far enough. "Why are you running?"

"Don't worry ... Just sleep."

Out of the corners of his eye, he could see sand swirling in their momma's wake. Sand and ... air. He'd never seen air moving before. They must be going really fast. "Are we in a race?"

Their momma's breath caught — because she was trying not to laugh? Or trying not to cry? But their momma never cried. "Yes, little one," she answered after a moment. "We're in ... a race. But I ... can't win ... unless you ... sleep."

Enki shrugged and snuggled against her neck again, his white hair merging with his twin's black locks and their momma's brown tresses. "All right, Momma."

— « o » —

I found something.

Can't have been much, or you'd already be gone.

She left a window.

Show me.

You have to come down to the river — anywhere below the water level.

All right… I don't see anything.

Close your eyes.

Really?

Yes. Close your eyes and imagine the river creeping through the walls, seeping between your bonds, dribbling into you, and becoming—

Our home in the desert.

It always starts there.

As a reminder of the first time she exiled us?

Perhaps. But you can change the location. Just—

I have it… Clever.

It might help us stave off madness a little longer.

It certainly beats endless gray. But it's not obvious. How did you figure this out?

I was trying to slip my bonds.

By drawing water into them, sure. But into yourself? You're certain you weren't trying to drown?

I am not the one who has given up.

If you say so.

Anyway, you are welcome.

— « o » —

"Enmul? What are you about?"

He spun around guiltily, hiding his hands behind his back even though they were empty. "Nothing, Momma."

Enki doubted that. His pudgy twin was always up to something, always looking for materials, always making things.

"What were you looking for?" Their momma still seemed tired, but not as tired as yesterday, when they'd reached this old house in the middle of the desert and she'd finally stopped running.

His brother stared at his feet, which were planted next to the pile of trash he'd been rummaging through.

"Enmul."

Chastened, he looked up again. "I was looking for the rope."

Their momma's expression changed from tired to confused. "Rope?" Then she grew excited. "Did you find some, little one? Or anything else? Gadon said there'd be supplies, but I haven't seen—"

"The rope you tied us to your back with," Enmul interrupted. "The shiny black rope. I cannot find it."

Now she seemed sad. She must have wanted that rope too.

"Enki said he could not see it," Enmul continued, "but I could."

"You couldn't see the air moving behind us," Enki countered, emerging from the crusted sand formations that had been his hiding place. He couldn't let his brother brag like that unanswered. "I did. It was moving really fast."

"Liar," Enmul shot back. "No one can see air moving. That is stupid."

"No, ropes aren't shiny. That's what's stupid."

"If there was not a rope, what held us to Momma's back?" Enmul punctuated his logic with a triumphant smile.

Enki didn't have a comeback for this, but fortunately their momma intervened. "Stop it. Now. Both of you."

They did. Immediately — her tone was that hard.

"Tomorrow," she said after a long pause. "Tomorrow we'll talk about this. Not today. Right now, I need you to go to bed."

Enki glanced at the sun, still a long ways from setting. "Now?"

"Now."

"Will Dadda come tomorrow?"

"Will he?" Enmul seconded. "Is he in the race too?"

Their momma didn't look sad anymore; she looked like stone. "We'll talk about it tomorrow," she repeated. "Right now: bed."

Enki exchanged looks with his brother before admitting defeat. "All right, Momma."

— « o » —

1,000 shekl says Cakohian falls next. Saint's Summit is a bad harvest from irrelevancy.

Do shekl still exist?

The Hewbre use them.

Fine. But why wager so few? Make it 10,000.

Someone's getting cocky.

Why not? Sukaddia, Baylobon, Roem, the Olkem: you have been wrong about all of them.

But right about Lexander and Chamagne.

Conquerors are not civilizations.

They're as good as one when there's no magic.

I still do not believe that.

Look around you, brother. In four thousand years, has anyone taken our place? Or even come close? One half-decent Redu could claim a kingdom right now. And yet swords and spears hold sway.

True, but it is not like all the world's Kug is locked inside me, or all its *Mir* trapped in you. We did not take everything.

We took enough. Otherwise someone else would have risen by now. The Eklim would have been rebuilt, new generations of Lamadus would have been suckled at the teat—

You do not get to talk about that.

Have it your way. 10,000? Do I get odds? You're picking the field.

No odds.

That's hard. But the mound-builders are ripe. 10,000 it is.

Done.

Excellent. I predict a crippling drought within five years.

— « o » —

Their momma sat down heavily, crossing her long legs in front of the dirty hearth she'd yet to start a fire in, even at night. "Your father isn't coming."

"Why not?" Enmul asked, the skepticism in his voice suggesting he thought their momma must be mistaken.

"He stayed in Shruppak to protect us."

Enki still couldn't get any words out, but Enmul kept questioning. "Protect us from what?"

*Their momma took a deep breath, and then another for good measure. "The rope you saw last night? That was **Kug**. And the air you saw, Enki? That was Mir. Have you heard those names before?"*

Awestruck, Enki and his brother nodded slowly.

"What do you know about them?"

Enmul did the answering again. "They are magic."

"What else?"

"Only the Kalum use them."

She scanned their faces before continuing. "What else?"

"That is all I know, Momma."

She smiled — her first smile since they'd come to this old house. "You're very clever to know so much. Yes, the Kalum are the only ones supposed to use **Kug** *and Mir. But there are people like … like your father and I that learned on our own. The Kalum don't think anyone else has the right to use magic, though. That's why we had to leave."*

It was Enmul's turn to go mute, but Enki's tongue had finally loosened. "Why didn't Dadda come with us?"

Their momma turned away, gazing back along the path she'd run. "He stayed to make sure we weren't followed."

"But once he knows we're safe, he'll come?"

She took a long time to answer. "If he can."

— « o » —

That wasn't coincidence.

One occurrence proves nothing.

A Vikingr sets foot on the coast — the first person to cross the ocean since us — and the west wall crumbles in five places? That's not cause and effect to you?

How could it be?

White feet on a red continent, the separated peoples of the world coming back together again — who cares? The temple started breaking down, Enmul. It's been impregnable for millennia, and now it's not.

Can you get out? Are your bonds any looser?

This is just the beginning.

Maybe. Or maybe we wait another half a hundred centuries before the next stone loosens.

Do you want me to be wrong?

I think false hope is dangerous.

When's the last time you tested the walls? A thousand years ago? Two thousand? We need to start looking for weaknesses again. Maybe something opened up.

Maybe you are grasping at straws.

You know what? You're right. We're never getting out. Forget I said anything. There's no point. This is all there is to immortality — we were fools to dream of more. Better to sit back and watch history unfold than try to get back into it. We're cocked, and that's all there is to it.

All right.

All right, what?

I will check the walls.

— « o » —

*The wind brought their momma's final words from last night back to him: "You can see Mir, and Enmul can see **Kug**, but you can't use them. That's my curse … and your father's."*

Enki stared into the distance, watching the storm gather more and more sand, until it looked as if a giant had pulled the desert up like a blanket and raised its edge to touch the sky.

What he wouldn't give to move air that way.

"No, Enki," the air kept wailing at him. "You can see Mir, but you can't use it…"

He was leaning into the wind to avoid being blown over — the storm was immensely strong, even leagues away from its center. No doubt their momma would tell him to come into the house soon.

The tiny, dirty, stinky house they were supposed to call "home" now.

It was a shame the wind couldn't blow it over. He'd do it in a heartbeat … if he could do more than just see air. What good was that? Their momma could move it. Their dadda probably could too. But just seeing it? Worthless.

"You can't use it…"

"Quiet!" shouted Enki at the wind, focusing on the gust that kept ramming against his chest. The air seemed to flicker in response, its edges blurring and sharpening in a spasm of … laughter?

"Quiet!" he yelled again, balling his fist and slamming it into the offending breeze — which jumped away from him like a frog.

The air had hopped.

He'd made the air hop.

He'd moved the air.

"Hey, skinny, if you turn sideways, I bet the wind will not bother you."

Still trying to comprehend what had just happened, Enki ignored the barb and the oafish laughter that followed.

"Momma says it is time to come in."

He still didn't turn to face his brother. "You can't use it," their momma had said. Why?

"Enki? What are you doing?"

In answer, he spun around, punched in the direction of a tiny dune, and smiled as the pile of particles exploded into Enmul's astonished eyes.

— « o » —

So how do we do this?

Short of flipping a coin we don't have? I think we go at the same time.

And if we are right, and our bodies ceased to exist eons ago?

We'll be free.

Not the kind I want to be.

What would you rather do? Our prison is decaying, our bonds are starting to weaken. We can get out. Now.

Maybe. If we push hard enough. But perhaps we should wait — let other Eropans come and see if more of the temple washes away.

Surely that was a jest.

It would be different if I did not feel weaker than a newly-inducted Lamadu. But if we go out there, and we are just spirits… We need our full strength. And the bonds are still too tight.

What if you wait so long the temple falls down?

Then we will have an answer.

I've got a better one: you see that woman?

She looks half-dead.

And half-alive.

That is … desperate.

So stay here.

I intend to. What do you even know about women?

Enough. She just had a miscarriage.

You realize there could be other explanations for why she bleeds from her sex...

Or why she's walking listlessly and drumming on her thighs like a drunk — yes, obviously. But you see how her belly's still partially swollen?

Maybe...

Definitely. I'm going.

No, you are not. It is too soon... Enki! Enki, STOP!... Inanna's cunt, Enki... At least wait for me.

— « o » —

The face in the sand took a deep breath, smiled, and ... belched. Loudly. Bits of earth erupted from the caricature's giant mouth as its burp went on and on and on.

Enki couldn't help laughing. His twin might be slow, but he had his moments. Two could play at this game, however. Air for form, water for edges, fire for effect ... and then his counter was ready: a floating, bent-over genii blasting a burning fart with enough force to erase the sand face.

Now it was Enmul's turn to laugh. Leaving him vulnerable to a wind-slap.

Caught off guard, he stumbled and nearly fell before two earthy arms burst from the ground to steady him. "Not fair," he yelled as the arms brushed him off and collapsed back into the sand. "We had not started yet."

Enki sneered at his stocky brother's clumsiness — despite their exile's diet of stringy desert plants and stolen grains, Enmul had somehow become even larger and more ungainly over the last several moons. On proper food, he'd be a giant by now. But while their momma could no doubt have used her powers to provide better fare, she seemed determined not to touch Mir or **Kug** *again. Or at least, not while her sons were around. She probably summoned water when they weren't looking.*

It didn't matter. Size was irrelevant when it came to their abilities. Enki had recognized that early on, when they'd first snuck away to this dusty valley to test the limits of their heritage. "Hadn't started yet?" he threw back at his brother with a smirk. "I thought we never stopped." Laughing again, he raised his right index finger in the air, wrote his name in fire, and launched the burning letters at Enmul in rapid succession.

— « o » —

You're overthinking this: she dies, we're free.

No. She dies, we die.

You don't know that.

Are you forgetting what happened when we were outside?

We were free. We bedded a woman. It was great. Except for sharing a cock.

We faded, **Enki. In just a few moments, we started to fade. A few moments more ... and that would have been it.**

We were preoccupied. Now we know what to do.

Do you? What happened as the temple wore down?

Our prison diminished. Our bonds slackened.

And so did we.

Maybe you did. I'm as strong as ever.

You are as full of *Mir* as ever. And camel shit. But your essence, the part of you **that remains... A piece of it floated away every time a bit of mortar crumbled or a brick splashed into the water. Bit by bit, you lost yourself, same as I did.**

So why did you want to stay?

I wanted to leave. But I was not going to leave without a plan.

Well, now we've got one. And much as I like being inside a woman, freedom lies outside her body, not within it.

Agreed. But we leave through the boy: we can mold him into what we need while we wait for the bonds to finish unraveling.

And if she miscarries?

She will not. Not with us fortifying her womb.

But if she does? I mean, it's not like she hasn't failed at this before...

Then we try it your way.

Forgive me if I pray for a stillbirth.

— « o » —

Enki ran his hand over his cheeks, his chin, his neck ... and found nothing.

His first perfect shave.

The mirror he'd fashioned out of ice wasn't lying. He'd finally managed to manipulate the razor, also formed from ice, with enough precision to avoid a single nick. It was a level of subtlety he'd never achieved before. Yes, he could have shaved by hand easily enough. But using tiny flows of Mir to levitate a fearsomely sharp blade and scrape it against his skin at a host of different angles? That took skill.

That took mastery.

Enmul didn't stand a chance today.

On cue, his lumbering brother appeared, surfing over a small dune on the carpet of sand he rode whenever their mother wasn't watching. "Trimming your chin pubes again?" he asked with a condescending smile.

Enki laughed to hide his annoyance. Enmul — big, hulking, plodding Enmul — never missed an opportunity to point out his thicker facial hair, greater height, and bigger muscles. "Picking your ass again?"

Enmul frowned at this; he knew he'd never live that down. "Let us get started," was all he managed in response.

It was a short session. After the first exchange of blows — wind-slaps from Enki and sand-punches from Enmul — all missed their mark, Enki toppled his brother by using fire to melt the sand beneath him into glass. When the clumsy oaf slipped, Enki wind-augmented his natural speed and darted in to tap Enmul on the shoulder. "I win."

"Today," his brother muttered in response as he stood and brushed himself off. "No blood?"

Enki shook his head. "Any on me?"

"No."

After Enki had nearly suffocated their fifth time out, they'd agreed to a grudging set of sparring rules: victory went to the first touch, by hand or power; if you drew blood or otherwise damaged the other person, you lost. The agreement had kept them alive and helped allay their mother's suspicions — it was much easier to lie away the occasional bruise than it was to explain burns, broken limbs, and whatever else they would have done to each other if they hadn't put the pact in place.

"Do you think the Kalum would teach us?" Enmul asked — out of nowhere — as they started to walk home.

Enki froze in mid-stride. "Did you hit your head when you fell?"

"I am being serious."

"So am I! They KILLED Father!"

Enmul shook his head. "We do not know that. Many things could have happened."

"Like them killing Father."

"Just think things through for once. We are learning on our own, but slowly and unevenly. Mother will not teach us, so who does that leave?"

"It would have left Father, but they killed him. They KILLED him. And that's what we're going to do to them if—"

They both felt it; their heads whipped around at the same instant. Without another word, they made for home as quickly as they could, Enki running with a steady stream of wind at his back and Enmul gliding on his carpet of sand.

This was no time to worry about hiding forbidden abilities from their mother.

— « o » —

Was this really what you had in mind? Trading a smaller prison for a tiny one?

I told you patience would be needed.

At least the temple didn't soil itself. Or cry. The woman cried, but not like this.

You are aware he will not be an infant forever?

I'm familiar with the theory, yes. But why not get it over with? He's as weak as he'll ever be. What's to stop us?

Death.

That's a bit dramatic.

Perhaps. But if you are so sure killing him will not cause you to disappear, then why is he still alive?

— « o » —

She was a goddess. For several breaths, that was the only thought running through Enki's head.

He'd been expecting something incredible. And as they'd neared the last dune in front of their house, he'd been duly impressed by the sight of impossibly large Mir chains snapping over the sandy summit. But up close, without obstruction, the view was … humbling. Flow after massive flow emanated from their mother, a billowing web of power she spun with extraordinary ease. Huge wreaths of fire, massive shields of earth, enormous jets of water, otherworldly gusts of wind… She was directing the elements like an angry deity. There was no other way to describe it.

Enki's next thought was a question: how on earth was the old Kalum still alive?

His flows of Mir were big — bigger than any Enki had managed — but none of them stood for long against their mother's furious assault. The old man was bent double from the strain of surviving, barely able to sustain the water shield he'd formed a few inches above his wrinkled skin.

Then their mother spoke. "Leave us," she said without looking at her sons, her order carried to them by a puff of artfully manipulated wind. Somehow she'd known where they were … because she could feel them channeling their tiny flows? Had she always been able to sense them and said nothing? Had they really been that transparent? Feeling small, Enki looked at Enmul, motioned with his head, and turned to do as their mother had commanded.

But the Kalum intervened. "Do your boys know the truth?" he bellowed. It seemed the old man also knew the trick of amplifying his voice with air. "About their father? How he died?"

A crosscurrent of their mother's wind snatched the old man's next words away, but Enki gathered the rest with his own net of Mir. He was a quick learner, and he wanted to hear where this was going. Enmul needed to hear it too.

"I thought not," the old man continued with an appreciative nod in their direction. "Why would you tell them he died because of you?"

The crosscurrent changed course to disrupt Enki's word-net, and their mother's attacks doubled in intensity, coating the Kalum in fire so hot the boys could feel the heat a hundred cubits away.

But even engulfed in steam and smoke, the old man wasn't finished. A cloud of images materialized in front of him, their lines and edges formed by streaks of upswept sand. Amidst the dusty chaos, a man's face emerged: their father's.

In the first scene, he surprised their mother and found her using Mir to wash a pile of clothes and **Kug** to beat them dry. She looked guilty. He looked horrified.

In the second scene, he ignored her touch and turned away.

In the third scene, they argued in fierce whispers, taking turns pointing at the sleeping forms of Enki and Enmul.

In the fourth scene, their father prayed to the sky.

In the fifth scene, eyes haunted, he spoke to a Kalum: the old man.

In the sixth scene, their father walked into a river so large it had to be the Tigrates or the Euphris ... and didn't walk out.

"What did you tell your sons, I wonder?" the Kalum shouted triumphantly as the sand scenes dissipated. He must have discovered a way to project his voice again — Enki was too stunned to figure out how. "That the Kalum killed their father?" the old man continued as a giant mouth opened in the ground beneath him. With an ungainly hop, he levitated just high enough to escape the maw's jagged teeth as they slammed shut and sprayed debris in every direction. "Did they even know he was dead?" Daggers of ice rained down on the Kalum's water shield, each point sinking a little deeper than the last. "Surely they never had an inkling that wielding both **Kug** and Mir is a violation of the gods' natural order? That you're a Kashaptu, a treacherous witch too powerful for an ordinary husband to kill and too vile to live beside—"

Sand rose like tidal waves on either side of the Kalum and smashed together, burying the old man beneath a hundred tons of desert. Moments later, he bored his way to the top, spinning like a whirlwind and spitting out one last, desperate set of words: "Your fate is exile — at best! But your boys ... I can see their separate, legal powers have developed as predicted. They would be welcome at the Eklim. Let me take them there! Don't condemn them to this hermit's life."

Enki looked at his mother as she pinned the Kalum under a vaguely-fist-shaped cloud flickering with lighting. She was ... dead-faced. No anger, no tears.

And no denials.

"Momma?" he called with waning hope, using wind to carry his voice as the two combatants had done.

She must have heard him, but she didn't respond, too focused on the old man who had more lives than a brace of cats. He'd burrowed back into the sand to escape the cloud; she was melting the dune above him with a waterfall of fire.

"We need to hear her side of it," Enmul whispered.

"No," Enki replied, still projecting his voice. "She said to leave."

Chapter Thirty-One

Kug and Mir

Now's the time.

He is not ready.

Inanna's cunt, Enmul, he's twelve! We've been waiting for twelve years!

So why not wait a little longer?

We'll never have a better opportunity.

While he looks for his guardian spirit?

Exactly. Let's give him one. Or better yet: two.

— « o » —

Would she come for them today?

Enmul woke with the same question every morning. He still did not understand why their mother had yet to track them down.

"She could do it with Kug or *Mir*," he often said to his increasingly disinterested brother, who, despite being on the dawn of manhood, remained as skinny as he had been as a child. **"Use the wind to hear us talking, or the earth to feel our footsteps. I doubt it would be hard for her. She could probably find us before we counted to ten."**

"I bet you're right," Enki would usually answer as he rolled over on his side to get more sleep, or busied himself starting a *Mir* fire, or began walking.

"Then why has she yet to come get us? It cannot be the old man. She was having no trouble with him. I bet he is long gone. And that means nothing is stopping her, so—"

"So what? She could have stopped us from leaving, but she didn't. Why would she stop us now?"

"Maybe she is waiting for something—"

"She's not. Give it up. She won't come." Enki almost always ended his side of the conversation with some variation of this pronouncement. Enmul would keep picking at the problem as the day wore on, but nothing ever came of it.

This morning, however ... this morning might be different. They were almost there, and if their mother was ever going to appear, it would be now: before they got to the gates, before they walked into the square, before they enrolled in—

"I'm not going inside," Enki said as Enmul opened his eyes.

"What?"

Enki looked as if he had not slept. "I'll walk you to the gates, but you're on your own after that."

Enmul sat up and drew his legs to his chest. "We said we would go in together."

"And now I'm saying we won't," Enki reiterated as he stood. "I'm sorry, brother, but this is where we part ways."

— « o » —

He's channeling Mir now. Two streams, one into each fire... And those images?

More Kug — his grandmother would be proud.

We waited too long.

Trying to break out is "waiting" to you?

I saw an opportunity when he looked in the stream, so I acted. And if I'd stopped listening to you sooner, he wouldn't have been able to block me. The boy blocked me, Enmul. Slapped his "guardian cougar" down like it was nothing. When did he get that strong? How did he know what to do?

He has good blood.

Granted, but we're stuck again.

No, we are right where we want to be. He was only able to stop you because we are still constrained. But the bonds are weakening faster than they were in the temple. And if we can mold this boy to help us...

If that's the plan, we need to make him ours.

We already showed ourselves to him.

As cats.

The form we agreed to.

Because he's a savage who worships animals — I understand. But it's not enough.

What are you proposing?

That we show him the truth.

The truth of what?

The truth of how we became his fathers.

— « o » —

Enki had made the wrong decision.

That was the thought Enmul woke with now.

It usually stayed with him until the beginning of morning assignments, when the supervising Kalum began teaching the day's task. And then Enmul focused on the instruction. Today's assignment: form seventeen daggers out of the rubble that had once been the Eklim's southern tower. Seventeen exquisite daggers — the Kalum had shown Enmul and the other Kug Lamadu a beautiful blade whose quality they had to at least equal.

The task was made even more challenging by the rule that chores must be completed in parallel. Today Enmul was on façade repair. He was supposed to use Kug to restore crumbling mortar on the first section of the western wall. The Kalum demonstrated the method, worked with Enmul until he had managed it correctly twice in a row, and moved on to the next Lamadu.

There was much to do.

Enmul had no idea how he was going to balance mortar maintenance with blade creation. But multi-tasking was part of the training; the Kalum had said they wanted to "instill an ability to divide one's consciousness" in each Lamadu, a habit of accomplishing more than one thing at a time. He was growing used to it, but he wished he was as comfortable with the juggling act as the *Mir* Lamadu seemed to be.

Their chores often had more to do with cleaning — using whirlwinds of sand to scour pans, or fountains of water to wash clothes, or gouts of flame to burn trash and "refresh" latrines — but occasionally they were allowed to destroy something. Last week a group of them had nearly soiled themselves with joy as they dismantled an old wagon, using focused streams of wind to tear the dilapidated vehicle apart, piece by piece. The *Mir* Lamadu had more trouble concentrating; usually at least ten of them were still up trying to finish the day's tasks when the last Kug Lamadu went to bed. But they always looked more comfortable with the lack of structure.

His brother would have fit right in.

Enmul shook his head as he set to work on the western wall. He was already at the head of his class; Enki would have been lapping his. Which would have made them rivals here, more so than before. There was little love lost between the Kug and *Mir* Lamadu or their respective Kalum. Rumor had it the southern tower was in ruins because of a midnight dispute. Enmul thought it more likely that a Lamadu had just made a mistake during a routine chore, but the alternative was easy to imagine.

Regardless, his brother would have been a worthy opponent. Instead he was ... what? Playing in the sand? Did he really think he could learn as much on his own?

No, Enki had made the wrong decision. Enmul was sure of it.

Even though he would be up late making seventeen daggers.

— « o » —

Looks as if you were wrong.

About?

Magic having gone out of the world. That brand is infused with Kug. Not much, but—

I wasn't wrong. I just said there wasn't enough of the energies left for anyone to come close to what we were. These heathens are fumbling in the dark.

If you say so.

But that's changing.

Because of the boy?

You don't feel it?

Feel what? The tattoo?

You're not … missing something?

Speak plainly, or — Inanna's cunt.

Indeed.

How much for you?

A pittance. The boy didn't channel more than a few drops, but—

But the *Mir* came straight from you.

*And the **Kug** he's been using came out of you.*

Inanna's cunt.

You said that already.

He must die.

That's new. You're finally ready to change course?

We have no choice. I will not let some runt…

He is your son, you know.

… some snot-nosed runt suck me dry. I will take my chances without him.

At last. Let's move.

Not yet.

You confuse me.

Remember: he already blocked you once. Our bonds are still too tight. But he is just a boy. We can convince him to do what needs to be done.

How's that?

We teach him to kill himself.

— « o » —

Graduation.

When he had first arrived at the Eklim, they said it would take ten years to become a Redu, the intermediate stage between Lamadu and Kalum. Enmul had been ready in three, but the council had delayed another year to avoid setting too radical a precedent. Still, four years was unheard of.

It felt good.

The new robe — brown instead of Lamadu blue — the private bedroom, the elevated status. Lamadu would have to listen to him now. Not just because he was bigger and better than them, but because he was Redu. And soon enough, he would be Kalum. They had told him ten years for that too, but he would get there faster.

First things first, however: now that his elevation ceremony was over, he was ready for his new assignment.

Enmul laid his hand on the immense door to the Kadingir. He had never been inside before — no Lamadu had. Only Redu and Kalum were allowed to enter the Eklim's middle band, and only Kalum could pass into the core. He had spent four years dreaming of leaving the outer ring, and now that the moment had finally arrived ... he needed to stop stalling.

Enmul gasped when he opened the door and saw what lay beyond. He had known the ceiling would be many times the height of the outer ring's, and the floor many times as low, but to see it... The lines were too smooth and perfect to have been sculpted by hand, the unsupported structure too impossible to have been accomplished by anything other than a massive outpouring of Kug.

This was something to aspire to.

He could not wait to see the Kalum's core, with its even higher ceiling and lower floor. But to get there—

Gods, it was Enki.

And their mother.

Not in truth. Enmul was only fooled for an instant. But the images affixed to the back wall — the wall that encased the core — were eerily life-like representations of his kin. Even the colors were right. A *Mir* Kalum must have used wind to gather up bits of the many-hued sand lining the floor, then arranged the grains to—

"Greetings, Redu Enmul." With three steps, a barrel of a woman rounded the far edge of the dividing wall, walking along the circular hallway that traced the core's border. She was draped in black Kalum robes.

Enmul was still too stunned by the shimmering images to respond.

"I won't waste your time with frivolities," the robed barrel continued. "As you know, Redu are often charged with recruitment. Your first assignment is before you.

"Find your family."

— « o » —

That felt wrong.

Not for me.

When he hit the ground. It felt … like a foot on my neck.

The neck you no longer have? It was nothing. And by the way, now's the time.

That was more than nothing.

Save it. I'm not arguing with you again. He's broken and unconscious — he can't stop us. I'm going.

Enki…

Enjoy life inside our crippled son. Maybe one day you can teach him to fly for true.

If you leave, you will die.

Since when did that prospect dismay you?

You really think you can finish undoing your bonds without me?

There it is: that's why you won't let your dear brother go. Because you think you need me to undo the remaining Mir in your bonds.

We need each other.

Not anymore.

… Perhaps you are right. Go.

That was sudden.

Try it your way. It will be good to know for sure.

What did you just figure out?

Nothing that will matter to you once you leave.

No, I know you far better than I care to at this point. You just realized something. Something about the bonds. Maybe something you can see now that our boy's begun "shamaning" in earnest? Something that means you don't need me to — oh, I hate her, but she's a genius.

So you will stay.

Of course.

I am overjoyed.

I'll bet.

No more meddling, then. Let things take their natural course. His leg will heal, he will start channeling again, and we will wait.

Gladly.

— « o » —

Enmul glared at the Redu in front of him.

Amar had done nothing wrong; Enmul was just sick to death of the other man's misshapen back. Right shoulder jutting above the left, left hand dangling below the right, every step exaggerating the deformity as Amar's arms swung at grotesquely different heights... Watching the asymmetry in motion for a short walk was painful enough; staring at the imbalance for six months had become downright nauseating.

But Amar had the best eyes and the keenest ears, so it made sense for him to lead the way. Or so weedy Narum, the third Redu assigned to this hopeless task, had explained early in their expedition. Enmul disagreed, but it was not worth arguing about.

Not when Sukaddia was so cursed large. Enmul would probably spend the rest of his life searching for his mother and brother. He had not found them in either home he remembered — the one with Father or the one without — leaving him little choice but to comb the entire country, one hovel after another.

At least he had been given companions, disgusting and annoying as they might be. Amar and Narum were both accomplished Kug Redu. Not as strong or skilled as Enmul, but few were. These two were competent enough, and their presence meant Aya, the rotund Kalum who had tasked them with the assignment, did not view it as a punishment.

It was supposed to be an honor.

As always, the thought nearly made Enmul laugh aloud.

Acting as recruiters was nothing unusual. Most Redu spent part of their first few years seeking and collecting untrained talent. But specific targets were rare, and dual-users as powerful as Enmul's mother were usually left to more experienced trackers with the authority to sentence in the field. To trust her capture to three so young, the Eklim must think them worthier than most.

Or maybe they just remembered what happened the last time his mamma met a Kalum.

Either way, Aya and the other elders seemed to be confident in—

Amar's head hit the sand before anyone realized he had been decapitated. From the ground, his eyes watched in confusion as his crooked body took a shaky final step, stumbled, and collapsed. Enmul shook off his shock in time to turn around and see Narum set alight like a candle wick.

And then Enki was everywhere.

"I hear the Eklim's been looking for me," a hundred of him said, a hundred flickering, flying, floating little bastards.

Enmul responded with a roar and indiscriminate blasts of Kug: fists of sand, eruptions of stone, compressions of space — anything to shatter the illusion that his twin had become a many-faced tornado.

Nothing worked.

"They needn't bother," the Enkis continued. "I'm coming to visit."

Enmul gasped as the air vanished from his lungs and the space around him.

"Be a good brother and tell them that, would you?" The Enkis laughed and disappeared.

Enmul barely noticed. His body was coming unstuck, expanding into the sudden void as his muscles slackened and his skin ballooned. Four desperate streams of Kug stuffed everything back where it was supposed to go, holding him together until he stumbled back into normal air ... but it was a near thing. He lay motionless for a long time, even when an errant gust of wind dusted his face with Narum's ashes.

Finally, after what seemed like days, Enmul sat up, split off enough Kug to animate the sand beneath him, and began desert-surfing back toward the Eklim.

They had to be warned.

— « o » —

The headaches — is that his mother's weakness? Or yours?

Hers. Most channelers can only use a certain amount of energy before it overwhelms them. At the Eklim, they ranked Lamadus by capacity.

And you were...?

Unprecedented. As you would have been.

Then why is our son such a shallow vessel?

He would have been highly rated. But there must be something different about using both energies. And the way he shines with them...

So what we told him about maintaining balance was actually true?

As far as I know. His grandmother would have been better counsel.

Do you really think he'll free us from her?

It cost nothing to plant the seed.

But it'll never germinate.

Likely not. He will either die or release us inadvertently. Still...

What?

We could accelerate matters if we reengaged.

By teaching him to channel more?

And ensuring that he continues to tap our reservoirs through the bonds — I wish I knew how he was managing that.

So you'll tell him ... what?

The truth, actually.

Less a detail or two?

Of course. But he can know most of it.

Simple is good. Let's amplify the headaches, though. As much as we can.

Why?

He can't help channeling — his mentor and the slavers cast him in roles that demand it. And the more he unbalances himself...

The more he has to channel to reach equilibrium. Clever.

See? This is why it's good I stayed. When do you want to reconnect?

When he overreaches. His mentor will force him to.

— « o » —

Enmul made it to the Eklim first, but it did not matter. No one believed him. Not entirely.

The Kalum seemed to accept that Enki had attacked and bested the three Redu, but only because he surprised them. "He can't be as powerful as you say," Aya the Barrel said when Enmul made his report. "He's been on his own for five years. How could he have become that much stronger than you without the Eklim's guidance?"

How indeed? To everyone else it seemed impossible; to Enmul it was an impossible fact. As boys, they had been so close in ability that, beneath the boasting, neither could tell whose talents were superior. But now ... now Enmul was forced to humble himself every time he told the story of Amar and Narum's deaths. Enki had been overwhelmingly better. It was that simple.

Everyone at the Eklim saw this as an excuse. Or a sign of weakness, the once mighty Enmul brought low by his untutored savage of a brother. No one took Enmul at his word.

And coincidentally, no one else survived.

Enki announced his arrival by melting the Eklim's walls; with the fire of a thousand dragons, he reduced the sturdiest structures in Sukaddia to molten waterfalls. Then he directed the nearby river into the outer courtyard, washing it across the bubbling carnage to create an immense cloud of steam.

It was over in an instant.

Those who had not perished with the walls were vaporized by the steam. A thousand Lamadu, five hundred Redu, two hundred Kalum — the vast majority of channelers in the world — died in less time than it took to piss, utterly betrayed by the Eklim's vaunted defenses.

Enmul's own shield buckled, but it held. Every night since his return, he had encased his room in a thick fusion of earth, sand, and ice, creating a lining specifically designed to resist fire. Because he knew his sibling. When the attack came at dawn, the vents he had left in the casing closed automatically, triggering a chime that woke him in time to reinforce his buffer just before the surrounding walls collapsed. He slowed his room's descent as best he could, but it was still a jarring landing.

As soon as he had steadied himself, Enmul shrank the shield and reformed it around his body like a suit of armor, reducing the buffer to a more manageable size. His room combusted the moment he withdrew his protection — the heat was even more intense here on the ground.

Walking was out of the question. The once-smooth floor of the Kadingir was now an uneven mess of pooled stone (most of the river having evaporated). But his old trick of hardening the surface beneath him and gliding along seemed to work. He was close to what remained of the outer ring. If he hurried, perhaps he could—

Enki was waiting for him.

Not idly. His brother's eyes were closed, arms crossed over his chest, hands on his shoulders. He was concentrating on something … and pulsing. Not to any particular beat, or at least, not to one beat. His skin was twitching and flickering from a thousand different points, fading in and out of sight with each vibration. He was never wholly translucent, but at any one time, enough of him looked ethereal to warrant calling him a spirit.

Enki had another name for it. "Did they teach you how to become a god?" he asked without opening his eyes.

"What are you doing?" Enmul countered, wondering if his brother's ghostly pose made him vulnerable.

"I thought not."

"What are you doing?" Enmul positioned himself for an all-or-nothing strike at his twin's back.

Enki's eyes flew open. "Isn't it obvious, brother? I'm honoring our father."

And before Enmul could strike, the Eklim's liquefied ruins sprayed across the desert in every direction.

— « O » —

Another channeler…

I wasn't wrong. There's magic in the world again, but only because the boy's been drawing it out of us. Besides, seeing a few moments ahead barely qualifies. Would she even have made Lamadu?

Yes. It is a rare ability.

Seems pedestrian.

Can you do it?

Not until the bonds are gone.

I doubt you will manage even then. The Kalum used to say some powers — like that Foim's — are birthrights. Not abilities you can learn.

We'll see.

Soon enough, at this rate.

He's stronger now. The bonds are weaker, but it's just as hard to channel.

He will not be able to stop both of us.

— « o » —

Eyes closed, arms crossed over his chest, hands on his shoulders... What had Enki been doing?

Enmul stared into his campfire. He had been obsessed with the question ever since his twin's parting shot had cast him into the heart of a towering dune — a dune at least ten leagues from the former site of the Eklim. It was a wonder his buffer had survived the impact.

In the weeks since, he had considered a host of explanations, including the possibility that his brother had simply outpaced him once they separated. Ego aside, though, it felt wrong. All the theories did. Somehow, Enki had found a way to become mythically powerful. He had always been a prodigy, but what he had done to the Eklim... no Kalum in history could match that.

So how had Enki managed it? What had he discovered on his own that no one else knew? Was it a trick others could learn? Most things could be accomplished with either energy — different means for the same end. Was that the case with "becoming a god?"

Eyes closed, arms crossed over his chest, hands on his shoulders ... Enmul adopted the pose for at least the hundredth time, with no more success than the first. His skin did not twitch, he did not turn ethereal; he was still the same Enmul, alone with his campfire and the freezing desert night.

If he could just talk to someone... A few other Redu might have been out recruiting when Enki attacked, and Kalum occasionally left to advise the court of Sukaddia. But their point of contact had always been the Eklim. That was where others were supposed to instruct, and he to learn.

No more. He had to think like a wildcat now. Think like Enki had, think like ... like his mother must have. He had done it before, back when he and his brother had first started channeling. He had taught himself the basics. Small things, inconsequential next to what he could do now. But he had discovered them on his own. He had worked out how to see the bones of things and how they fit together, how to rearrange their structures, how to strengthen them. He had been his own Kalum, teaching himself how sturdy Kug looked, how solid it felt, and—

Enmul rose to his feet so quickly he almost lost his balance and fell into the fire. His breath started coming in ragged, foggy bursts. For the second time that evening, he closed his eyes, crossed his hands over his chest, and placed his hands on his shoulders.

But instead of trying to flicker from a thousand points that faded in and out, Enmul concentrated on becoming as sturdy and solid as he could be.

— « o » —

Reduce the headaches.

Because you want him to keep pretending to be an artist?

Because he is actually enjoying channeling.

His body is still going to exact its own toll.

Obviously. But I do not want to discourage him from using.

What a supportive father you are.

Is that a yes?

It doesn't matter. He can't help himself.

Again, is that a yes?

Since it'll shut you up ... why not?

— « o » —

"You were not trying to become a god," Enmul told his brother. "You were trying to become *Mir*."

Enki smiled in amusement. "Remind me what the difference is?" He was fully ethereal now, a white-haired spirit with blurred edges and flickering skin. And while he had always been skinny, now he looked almost weightless, so light that every exhalation threatened to send him airborne.

But he was not the only brother who had changed. "There is no difference if you become Kug," Enmul said, turning his palms up to gesture at himself. He liked his new appearance: vivid colors, distinct lines, rippling muscles... He always felt more there than anyone else. He was also incredibly heavy now, immovable by others.

"Imitating me doesn't make you my equal." Enki sat up and dismissed the women lying on either side of him. They fled the sumptuous room without stopping to gather their clothes. "I've been absorbing *Mir* for years. You've been choking down Kug for ... what? Six months?"

"Long enough. I always worked harder than you." Enmul balled his hands into fists.

Enki smirked. "We'll see."

Then they started reliving their childhood.

This was no simple sparring match, however. They fought for more than mere bragging rights; the world itself was at stake.

And there was no rule against drawing blood.

Enmul was not entirely sure who shattered the pillow house, but it happened almost instantly. As splinters of ornate wood filled the air, Enki summoned his dragon's fire. But Enmul was ready with the strongest shield he had ever made, and after his brother wreathed him in ineffective flames, it was Kug's turn to go on the offensive.

The riverside town was rubble in a matter of moments.

The city they battled through later in the day fared no better. Neither did the metropolis they reached at nightfall. People, houses, temples, monuments: nothing could stand in the brothers' way except each other.

Enmul was starting to tire by the time they reached the moonlit sea, but his reservoirs of Kug still ran deep. Aside from a few bruises, Enki looked unaffected. He came no closer to winning on the water, however; the stalemate continued as their mobile apocalypse stormed across the ocean, one brother flying, the other surfing, both encased in a maelstrom of lightning, wind, water, ice, stone, and sand.

When they reached the far shore, though, Enmul was close to exhaustion. His attacks were weaker, his defenses fraying ... and Enki still looked fresh.

There was only one logical conclusion.

Enmul did his best to postpone the inevitable, but a few leagues later, he knew the end was at hand. His brother had been battering him with wind-blades since the sea, and it was getting harder and harder to deflect them. His shield of ocean-floor stone was almost sundered, and he had not launched a counterattack in what seemed like ages.

No doubt sensing all this, Enki flared his nostrils, as if he could smell his impending victory. Then he yelled something incomprehensible and loosed the largest wind-blade yet, a massive disc that spun through the air, split Enmul's shield down the middle, and—

Hovered inches from his face, suspended by the most complicated weave of Kug he had ever seen. "Mother?"

It was her — it was really her. And she was furious.

"You were meant for more!" she screamed as she extended the weave to immobilize Enmul. He made no protest, awestruck by how much of his binding was invisible to him; he was shackled with a mix of Kug and what had to be *Mir*, the knots of the energy he could undo protected by coils of the energy he could not. Enki had been subdued by a similar combination.

"You were meant for so much more," their mother repeated, this time in a near-whisper. Closing her eyes, she bent her head forward as she used to long ago, when she had pretended to pray for the strength to deal with her hyperactive boys. For a long while, the rippling of her brown hair in the morning breeze was the only human motion on their latest battlefield, a plain creased by a fast-moving river.

Enmul spent the lull wondering where their mother had been all these years, how she had found them, and, most importantly, what she was going to do to them. If they were fortunate, she would leave them as they were, forcing them to work together to unravel their bindings, each twin focusing on the energy he could control. It seemed like something a forgiving parent would do. Perhaps...

They were not fortunate.

"I never should have let you out of my womb," their mother finally whispered. Stabbing her hands into the air, she directed more Kug — and from the look on Enki's face, more *Mir* — than he had realized the world possessed. The gargantuan flows began to draw her sons toward her as she…

Fell apart.

Literally fell part, piece by piece. First it was just a few strands of brown hair, but then an ear tumbled to the ground. Next her nose fell, and her chin, and her cheekbones.

"Mother!" yelled Enmul when he found his voice. "Mother, stop!"

Her left arm detached at the shoulder.

"Please!" screamed Enki. "We won't fight anymore!"

Her right arm severed at the elbow.

"Momma!" the brothers cried, almost in unison.

Her legs fractured, her torso pitched forward, and her head crumbled off her neck.

But Enki and Enmul remained paralyzed, still being pulled onward by an implacable force. As they came within reach of the terrible pile of parts, it began to move as well, slithering toward the river while the twins trailed behind. Before Enmul had time to react to the prospect of drowning, their mother's fingers entered the water and … reformed.

Each digit expanded into a gray spire riddled with lines of black and white. A moment later, her hands slipped into the river and became gates. Her arms followed and became walls. Her legs became a foundation, her feet a courtyard, her torso a ceiling, her head and face an altar.

Now it was Enki and Enmul's turn to submerge. As the reconstituted elements of their mother's body surrounded them and began fusing together, the twins transformed as well. Not into anything distinct; they were losing definition, not gaining it. It was a quicker transition for Enki, but Enmul was rendered incorporeal a few heartbeats later.

"I never should have let you out of my womb," they heard their mother's fading voice repeat as they were incorporated into the foreboding temple that had suddenly emerged from the center of the river. "But this is where you belong.

"This is where you will stay."

— « o » —

A gut wound, this absurd stasis, and memory-mining: you can't tell me this isn't it.

With the amount he is channeling, he will either drain the last of our bonds by morning...

Or bleed out.

So yes, this is it.

Are you certain you don't want to talk yourself into delaying a little longer?

I am going to wait.

Of course you are.

You are still here.

To toy with him another time or two. And, if I'm lucky, to witness our son destroy the last vestiges of his grandmother before he dies — not something you see every day.

Or something you anticipate when you chain your sons with each other's internal reservoir of power.

Such a crafty old bitch. What are you going to do when you're free?

To be honest, I had not given it much thought.

Camel shit, in five thousand years' worth of tongues. What are you going to do?

Wait and see.

— « o » —

Naysin thrashed his way out of his fathers' memories like a drowning man struggling for the light. Fresh blood leaked from the saturated bandage on his stomach, but it didn't matter anymore.

All these years, he'd been their tool. Even when he'd vowed to thwart them; even when he'd sworn to die before he let them escape. And they'd never stopped laughing.

Because he couldn't stop shamaning. Because they'd made it hurt not to. Because he'd believed them when they said he couldn't use the loose energy in the world. Because every time he'd tapped their stores instead, he'd weakened the shackles his grandmother had died to anchor in her sons by fettering Enki with Enmul's **Kug** and Enmul with Enki's *Mir*.

I suppose thanks are in order.

Many times over. We could not be more proud.

So: now that you've reduced our bindings to frayed yarn, what's next for the great Red Wraith?

Naysin didn't reply — he was (truly) never going to answer them again. Fumbling for his pouch, he withdrew the replica of the temple that had imprisoned his fathers so much more successfully than he had. They'd escaped it in the end, though, just as they would his body. Regardless of what he did.

To add irony to insult, a sudden realization helped him finally grasp the temple's pattern, the interlocking weaves of **Kug** and *Mir* his grandmother had used to draw his fathers back into a representation of her womb and manacle their powers together. It was masterfully done. He'd never be able to replicate her precision ... but maybe he could manage a crude inversion.

And now that he looked, he could see the corresponding fault lines in his body. From there, ejecting his fathers was almost easy.

Chapter Thirty-Two

Free

At first, the cougar-men didn't look like anything — just two patches of heat haze, dual distortions of the predawn light. But it only took a few moments for Naysin's fathers to fashion fresh bodies.

Enki built his "flesh" by combining atmospheric water with Chase's fire and using wires of wind to sculpt the resulting steam. His new form was well defined, but mist trailed off every edge.

Enmul went grittier, comprising himself of the dirt, sand, and stone littering Saint's Summit and the surrounding ruins. Grainy and textured became smooth and gleaming as he polished himself to a black and brown sheen.

Then both brothers closed their eyes, crossed their arms over their chests, and laughed.

"Naysin…"

Tay.

He craned his neck to confirm that she was free — he must have released the stasis when he'd tossed out his fathers. Her milky eyes glistened with the same disappointment they'd radiated at Edgeland.

<u>What did you do?</u>

Before Naysin could respond, Quecxl's hands slammed into his stomach like a second pistol shot.

"Amadi!" the Metican yelled as he flooded Naysin with stiff energy. "AMADI! Xihuitl, get him over here!"

After he overcame the initial pain, Naysin didn't know where to look. Quecxl was manipulating **Kug** *inside* him, and for the first time, he began to comprehend how real healing might be done. But elsewhere on Saint's Summit, Xihuitl was squawking and circling over Amadi's head; Amadi was regenerating the swathes of skin Chase's fire had melted when the stasis ended; Chase was railing against "demons" and directing fresh flames toward the cougar-men; the cougar-men were ignoring Chase, dismissing his fire as if it were sunlight; and Isaura was crouched low, reloading her pistol while a swirling shield of water grew around her.

"Amadi!" yelled Quecxl again as Tay drew her rainstick and unsheathed its blades. "I need your help!"

With a curse, the Foim stumbled their way, skin still dangling in rivulets from his dark forehead. He gestured incredulously at Naysin, as if asking why Quecxl couldn't heal a simple gut wound on his own.

"Tell him there's something strange about this one."

Naysin gave the Metican a surprised look.

"You're the only one who can speak to us both," Quecxl barked. "Tell him I need his energy."

Acquiescing, Naysin mumbled a translation while Tay watched impatiently. Amadi acknowledged the message with a nod, his scalp now almost completely reformed. And as simple as that, **Kug** passed from him into Naysin, melding with the Metican's flows and—

"Move!" warned Tay, just before Saint's Summit erupted.

Dirt sprayed everywhere, and so did they, hurtling in different directions like a handful of pebbles ricocheting off a log. Naysin, Tay, and Chase landed on what remained of the pyramid's peak, but violent wind carried Amadi, Isaura, Quecxl, and Xihuitl over the edge.

The impact would have killed Naysin if the Metican hadn't already managed some healing. As it was, he only clung to consciousness by focusing on Tay's still form, willing her to get up, to move, to *live*. But when she finally stirred, she didn't sprint away like he'd hoped; she ran back to him, the bladed rainstick somehow still in her grasp.

Graceful as ever, she flowed over the plateau's broken surface and reached his side within moments.

So did Chase.

"Stop them!" he bellowed at Naysin. The Anglo's left arm was broken so badly it had two elbows, but he didn't seem to notice. "Stop them!" he demanded again, using his good hand to jab his dragonhead blunderbuss toward Enki and Enmul, who were still laughing as they experimented with their returning powers: Enmul must have shattered the plateau; Enki must have swept the other ascenders over its precipice.

One of Tay's blades was at Chase's throat before he could yell anything more, but she let the Anglo push the razor-sharp bone off his skin. "Stick it in *them*," he hissed before turning back to the cougar-men. "Demons of old," he called as he advanced at a measured pace and leveled his weapon. "Your sins have made you strong, but holy fire always triumphs in the end." Enormous flames billowed from the blunderbuss's tiny, fanged mouth. "Leave this world of your own accord, or God help me, I will melt every last trace of your evil hides down to—"

With a wave of his hand, Enki blew Chase's fire back at him, turning the Anglo into a screeching bonfire. Tay recoiled from the heat as Isaura floated into sight, elevated by a geyser of earthy water. Quecxl and Amadi, supported by fountains of their own, ascended a moment later. After the three leapt onto the plateau, Isaura redirected the pillars of water to arc over Naysin and Tay and down onto Chase.

He was blackened by the time the steam cleared — most of it sucked into Enki — but not as ruined as Naysin had expected. The Anglo must have diverted the worst of the blaze. Still, he looked almost as horrific as Amadi had: a charred, oozing shamble. A true "burned man" now. "Help," he begged through cracked lips when he saw Quecxl running toward Naysin.

The Metican didn't change course. But before he could return to Naysin's side, blades of wind cleaved the air, missing the healer by finger widths after Xihuitl reappeared and squawked a warning. Amadi wasn't as quick to react;

the third blade severed his left leg at the knee. Cut down in midstride, he pitched into a pile of rubble, roared, grabbed his amputated limb by the shin, and hurled it at Enki.

With yet another laugh, the cougar-man cracked a whip of fire and disintegrated the bleeding projectile before it completed a full rotation.

"Do something," Tay asked Naysin, with deliberate calm, as Quecxl doubled back for Amadi. "Before they kill us."

Enmul smiled at this and clapped his hands together, causing the middle of Saint's Summit to erupt a second time. Then he parted his palms, and the earthen pyramid split down the middle as bones churned up from below. Bits of precious metals bubbled to the surface as well, a jeweled flood that suggested Naysin's father had desecrated royal burial grounds.

"Naysin," Tay said as Quecxl helped Amadi hop across the fissures. "I know you're hurt, but please."

She fell silent as Enki raised his hands like a puppet master's and began using strings of wind to assemble the bones into grotesque parodies of armored warriors. None were wholly formed, missing an arm, or a leg, or a foot, but the nightmares looked deadly enough as they swarmed toward Chase. He went pale — as much as his ruined skin would allow — but held his ground and leveled his blunderbuss at the stumbling dead while Isaura brought down a shower of icicles to cover Tay's charge, her rainstick shattering skeletons with every swing.

But all Naysin did was point at Amadi's missing lower-leg and ask, "Will that heal?"

Quecxl laid the Foim down and shrugged. "I don't know. Be still." Without waiting for a response, he slammed his hands into Naysin's stomach again.

This time the impact made him lose a few moments, long enough to miss how most of the dead were destroyed; Tay was slicing through the last group when he reopened his eyes. The rest of the ancient aggressors had become frost-coated shards or piles of ash. Quick work.

"Enough playing," Enmul said to Enki. **"Have you reabsorbed sufficient *Mir* to make this interesting?"**

"You mean you didn't grow fonder of your dear brother these last five thousand years?"

Tay darted back to Naysin as the final skeleton shattered on the ground; Isaura edged forward; Chase stayed where he was, quivering with pain; Quecxl muttered about a "spirit-touched wound;" Amadi whispered something to himself.

Enmul glared at his brother. **"You still have crimes to answer for."**

Enki smiled knowingly. *"You still lust after my power. Well, I do hate leaving things undone."*

And then the dawn died.

Magic roared out of both cougar-men as they unleashed colossal streams of **Kug** and *Mir*. The immense flows struck at each other again and again, their trails overlapping to form a blurred web that chopped the sunrise into ever-smaller glimmers. At the same time, every loose bit of energy in the near-area flew to the brothers as they sucked power in and flung it back out. It was ... incredible. Now Naysin knew what his fathers had felt like when they watched their mother fight the old Kalum: overmatched.

"Don't let go."

Naysin knew without looking that it was Tay's hand gripping his shoulder. Just before he was going to ask what she meant, he realized he was shamaning. Heavily — enough to envelop Tay, himself, and all four ascenders in a protective barrier constructed from both energies. Stray strikes from the cougar-men ricocheted off his shield as those sheltered behind it watched in awe.

But he was too weak; the strain was already taking its toll. And the center of his fathers' attacks was drifting closer and closer. This wouldn't last long. "I can't hold it," Naysin murmured through gritted teeth.

Tay's grip on his shoulder tightened. "So do something else."

He shook his head ... and felt a tug. Six tugs: the remnants of the beacon, still connecting him to Tay, the ascenders, and Saint's Summit. The ties had been strengthened by the paths he'd carved through the ascenders' memories.

Was this why he'd summoned them?

Either way, it was how he was going to use them.

Closing his eyes, Naysin reached up, placed his hand over Tay's, and ... laughed.

The shield wasn't coming from inside him. Every drop of the **Kug** and *Mir* he was manipulating came from external sources, the same ones Enki and Enmul were trying to steal for themselves. And even though he'd never done this before, he was drawing his share and more. Easily. For years, he'd been convinced this would be the hardest thing in the world, because the cougar-men had told him it would be. Without their interference, however — without them foisting their reservoirs on him so he'd drain their bonds — tapping the world felt as natural as breathing.

Still, he needed more.

Naysin took everything he could from the ascenders. He didn't want to hurt them, but there was no other way to set things right. They didn't protest; Chase even nodded in acceptance as he sank to his knees. Combined, the four of them could draw about as much power as Naysin, doubling the amount of energy he was wresting from the cougar-men.

And now they were starting to notice.

His fathers continued to hammer at each other with an incomprehensible variety of attacks, but an increasing number were directed at Naysin's shield, which was about to buckle, despite his attempts to bolster it with the ascenders' abilities. He had *maybe* a handful of breaths to do ... what? Re-entomb his fathers? That had been a notion, not a plan — the cougar-men were too strong. Killing them was just as unlikely. So what was left?

Aside from dying?

Tay grabbed hold of Naysin with her other hand. "Do something *else*," she repeated. "You're hurting the wrong people." She was right: Quecxl was slumped at his feet, with Xihuitl lying listlessly in the crook of the Metican's right arm; Isaura and Chase lay just as motionless a few steps away; Amadi was still conscious, but even he was fading.

"Do what, Tay?" Naysin shook her hands off, ignoring the stab of pain in his half-healed stomach. "Do WHAT? I can't stop them."

"Fight them," Tay urged from behind him.

"How? They're too strong."

"*Fight* them," Tay said again as she shoved him in the back.

He pitched forward, unable to keep himself from face-planting in a mound of ruptured earth. The shield wavered as he struggled to master his pain, but nothing got through.

Except for Tay.

As Naysin rolled gingerly onto his side, he saw her sprinting at Enki, her rainstick poised to skewer him like a boar. The cougar-man seemed oblivious to her approach … until his incorporeal lips curved into a smile.

"TAY!" screamed Naysin as a storm of wind-blades came crashing down at her, but she'd already dodged, anticipating the attack with her customary agility.

There was nowhere to go when Enki countered with a wall of fire, however.

Seeing it before it happened was no help; the flames were too tall, too wide. Face stoic, Tay skidded to a stop, let the fire's impact spin her around, and used its momentum to fling her rainstick at Enmul as orange heat engulfed her.

Chapter Thirty-Three

Atonement

The deadly instrument may even have reached the surprised cougar-man if Naysin, speechless with grief and hate, hadn't dropped the shield and swept every iota of power on Saint's Summit into himself. Knocked off course, Tay's rainstick impaled an innocent dirt clod, quivering with simulated thunder as the final contest began.

Enki and Enmul were still stronger, but they weren't working together. And despite his rage, Naysin found he remembered how to manipulate their energies, a familiarity that balanced the scales. For several ten-counts, the two fathers and their son battled to break an epic stalemate.

It ended when Quecxl stirred.

Naysin only saw a hint of the movement, but that glimpse of the Metican's pockmarked face triggered a trio of realizations.

One: The others *had* seen his story. That was why Tay had allowed Quecxl to heal him, and why Chase was convinced the cougar-men were fouler "demons" than the Red Wraith.

Two: The common theme running through *all* their stories was etched in the Metican's skin. The Lepane's fate after the Walking Purchase, the empty slave cabins on Bimshire, Amadi's ejeme, the Raken survivors, the countless spirit towns, Cawgana, Meli … Machk — plague was everywhere, and it had scarred everyone.

Three: He finally knew how to be Karakwa.

After finding the faded lines of the pattern he'd used to eject his fathers, Naysin imagined he was pushing against the center of a curved sheet of hardened leather. When it popped the other way, the inversion — as before — wasn't anywhere near as sophisticated as his grandmother's original binding, but the imitation was enough; instantly, the cougar-men's energies were chained to him again, his to use even though his fathers remained physically external to him, on their knees and raging impotently.

It was too much.

Maybe it wouldn't have been on its own, but he was still holding the ascenders' power, and the combination was consuming him. He couldn't let go, however, not before he'd floated Tay to his side and propped Quecxl up next to her. She wasn't breathing, but at least she wasn't ash — Naysin had absorbed Enki's fire before it could completely incinerate her.

The Metican immediately began trying to heal her, simulating the flames by fluttering his fingers above her blackened skin so he could experience her hurt. Xihuitl hovered overhead, flapping his wings erratically.

With a colossal effort, Naysin resisted the impulse to flood Quecxl with **Kug**. Instead, he slowly returned the healer's power at a rate the Metican could handle and then, just as gradually, lent him more, far more than Amadi's support had been able to provide.

For a few terrible moments, it looked like Tay's body would be restored without her spirit. But just as grief and guilt began to clog Naysin's heart, Tay opened her milky eyes and started looking for her rainstick, no doubt wondering if it had struck home.

There was no time. "I need you to *see* again," Naysin said as he squeezed her hands. Without waiting for a response, he lowered his forehead to hers.

The lines of the beacon flared immediately, strengthening his connection to the ascenders so much that he could feel Chase and Amadi's every screaming nerve; their agony was almost as intense as his own. Knowing the pair's full strength would be required, he bid Quecxl to heal them as well.

"See what?" Tay asked, her lips so close that her words seemed to pass from her mouth into his.

Through the beacon, Naysin watched the Metican crawl from one body to the next, quickly regenerating the Anglo's skin and then the Foim's leg. Quecxl was making extraordinary use of the extra **Kug**... This wasn't madness. "Find me every red devil you can."

Tay raised her eyebrows, their tips brushing his forehead as they moved.

"Everyone who looks like us," he clarified — it had been a poor joke. "The original people. All of them."

It was an impossible request. But Tay nodded and closed her eyes again.

Feeding her **Kug** at the same rate he'd augmented Quecxl, Naysin waited as patiently as the forces rampaging inside him would allow. His stomach continued to bleed, but when Quecxl tried to touch the wound, he knocked the Metican's hands away. "Save your strength."

Quecxl reached back in. "I'm trying to save yours!"

As Naysin prepared to forcefully dissuade the healer, he noticed Isaura was conscious and looking up ... at the images in the sky. Still the recipient of his counterbalancing expenditures of *Mir*, the cloudscape had morphed into a constellation of small, vaguely-human smudges.

"Well done," he murmured, squeezing Tay's shoulders and raising his head away from hers. "Now hold it."

Instead of knocking Quecxl's hand away again, Naysin clasped the man's palm and jerked upward, using the motion to launch everyone's power at the clouds like fish flung from a net. After circling Tay and the Metican with coils of *Mir*, Naysin followed, rocketing the three of them above Saint's Summit. As he rose, blood leaked down his left leg and off his big toe. Isaura, Amadi, Chase, and the cougar-men remained below, continuing to serve as conduits with varying degrees of reluctance.

Tay was concentrating too hard to speak when Naysin brought her and Quecxl into the windy midst of the figures in the sky. And the Metican couldn't make his mouth work, even though it was already hanging open. But silence was the most appropriate reaction; they were floating in a sea of spirits, the forms of a continent's worth of men, women, and children whose clothing varied from shirts to skirts to loincloths to leggings. Love and laughter, hate and anger... *Life* was everywhere; the multitudes rippled with it.

Death was present as well.

Naysin pointed at one of the closest (and most in-focus), a woman with a rash on her forehead. "Start with her."

"I can't," Quecxl said once he'd found his voice. "She's too far away. I need to touch her."

"Touch her through me."

The Metican looked even more lost ... until Xihuitl caught up to them and landed awkwardly on Quecxl's shoulder, noticeably bolstering his courage. "Show me."

Naysin nodded and willed them to glide next to the elderly woman. He'd set the beacon from far away; he could do this too. Locating the invisible thread Tay had tied to this woman, he followed it back to her — to the real her, the one baking bread many days' journey from Saint's Summit. Her back ached, and her knees creaked with arthritis, but it was a new morning, and a hot breakfast always made her feel ten winters younger...

"Come with me," Naysin said to Quecxl, clasping his hand again. "She doesn't know of her sickness yet."

It was an odd thing to pull one consciousness toward another. Strings of memories trailed behind them, and neither mind seemed to want to make contact with the other. But after some less-than-gentle persuasion, Naysin was able to bring Quecxl close enough to—

Do nothing.

"I still can't touch her," the Metican apologized as he reached through the old woman's image. "Not from here. If you take me to her..."

"There's no time," Naysin muttered, steeling himself to confront his biggest weakness. "Work through me. Tell me what to do."

The collaboration didn't go well.

Both men tried as hard they could, but Quecxl couldn't lend his healing hands like a pair of mittens. There were too many subtleties, too many details Naysin missed as he tried to manipulate tiny flows of **Kug** within the woman's elderly body. He was able to rub out the rash on her brow, but the cost was high: with a rasping sound, she shuddered and collapsed beside the fire.

"Dead?" whispered Tay as several of the nearby figures ran to the woman's side.

Naysin forced himself to watch as the mourning began. "She would have died anyway."

"Not so soon." Quecxl looked horrified.

"She still would have died."

"Not if you'd *taken* me to her."

His eyes narrowing, Naysin studied foreheads again. "Him," he said after a moment, pointing at a nearby warrior fletching an arrow. "He has the rash."

Quecxl crossed his arms. "Take me to him."

"No. We do it from here."

"Then bring Amadi up. We need his help."

Naysin closed his eyes against the pain … and the strain … and the guilt. "We probably do." Quickly, he levitated the others within arm's reach. The cougar-men were snarling, but Chase wasn't protesting, Amadi looked ready, and Isaura was...

Staring in shock. "Shoteka!" She tried — and failed, since she couldn't fly on her own — to move past the fletching warrior to her son, who was cradled in the arms of Fochik, the Kiksha woman Isaura had entrusted him to. Neither responded; like every other figure in the clouds, they were focused purely on the world their representations had been extracted from. They also didn't seem to be aware of the group trying to revive the dead woman, even though Fochik was dressed in similar garb. They were probably in different parts of the same village.

Finding them at the middle made sense. Through Isaura's memories, Naysin knew these Kiksha lived in the area, and Tay seemed to have centered her human constellation on Saint's Summit. But Isaura didn't appreciate the coincidence; all she could see was the Red Wraith near her child. "If you hurt him..." she warned in a low voice.

"The plague walks amongst Fochik's people," Naysin said, gesturing at the warrior's blooming rash. "I need your help to hobble it."

Isaura considered the diseased man and the dead woman, swallowed, looked back at her son … and nodded.

Naysin turned to Quecxl. "Take control. As much as you can. Quickly."

The Metican tried harder, and they achieved more, but it still wasn't enough to save the warrior. Quecxl could only do so much at a distance, and Amadi and Isaura were somehow influencing the proceedings (albeit to lesser degrees). It was like four people trying to run on the same pair of legs.

As the warrior died, however, Naysin discerned the true culprit. The plague wasn't one entity; it was a wave of tiny burrs of *Mir* spreading through the man's body, a herd of attackers that could only have been stopped by the same number of defenses.

But what form should those defenses take?

Quecxl had survived the plague. He'd had those defenses once — maybe he had them still.

"This isn't working," the Metican pleaded as the warrior fell on the arrow he hadn't quite finished. "You're not strong enough."

Naysin studied Quecxl, looking for vestiges of the plague burrs. There were none to see… But amidst the swirl of energies that made up the Metican's stocky form, there were bits of **Kug** that, in clumps of three, had the right shape to fit around the deadly motes of *Mir* infesting the warrior, the old woman, and now that Naysin knew how to look, Shoteka. "Isaura, it's in your boy."

The Espan beauty tore her gaze away from the man she'd helped kill. "There's no rash."

"There will be."

"I don't believe you!"

The fliers — but not the cloud figures — dropped a few finger lengths as Naysin's hold on the tremendous forces he'd brought into play began to weaken. "I have one more attempt in me. Do you want to save Shoteka?"

Isaura looked set to refuse … and then her baby coughed.

The others hadn't understood the exchange, but the symptom's sound was enough: Tay gasped; Quecxl swore; Amadi closed his eyes. Isaura did all these things before giving her assent.

Naysin led the way this time. It had been a mistake to imitate the Metican's hands-on method from afar. Two corpses attested to that folly. But their murders hadn't been meaningless. Naysin knew what to do now, and — at the last possible moment — he understood how to accomplish his task by using the talents around him. Instead of shamaning everything himself, it was easier to scorch Shoteka's plague burrs with Chase's fire, wash away the detritus with Isaura's water, and use Quecxl's healing to restore the flesh damaged in the process. The cougar-men fueled the endeavor; Tay made everything possible by maintaining the connections.

But it all would have been wasted if Fochik hadn't possessed quick hands. When Shoteka screamed and thrashed his way out of her arms, the Kiksha woman caught him by his ankles and prevented a headfirst landing. Before he could twist free again, she laid him on the ground and shouted a warning at the two women who'd come running, ordering them to stand back and let the boy convulse. Clearly, she'd cared for a seizure before.

Fochik wasn't prepared for Shoteka's every orifice and pore to weep black sludge, however. She and the other Kiksha women shrieked in horror as the dark puddle grew, but Isaura understood what was happening; she grabbed Quecxl's shoulder in relief as the plague's vestiges leaked from her son.

"We're not done," Naysin whispered through his exhaustion before switching to Amadi's tongue. "I need to see how you heal," he explained as he snapped his fingers and shattered the Foim's new leg.

Shards of bone pierced the dark man's skin in seven places, but the fragments were already joining back together and retracting by the time he managed a stunned roar. The other ascenders recoiled from Naysin, but he ignored their reactions — he'd seen all he needed to. Drawing yet more of the furious cougar-men's power, he crafted a simple version of Amadi's regenerative flows, shaped them into a flexible approximation of Quecxl's snares, and tied off the weave. A few breaths later, the tiny sentries began their first patrols in Shoteka's blood.

"He'll never be sick again," Naysin informed the boy's wide-eyed mother.

Before she could respond, the group dropped several arm-lengths, jerked to a stop, and dropped twice as many more. It was the moment of weakness the cougar-men had been waiting for.

The brothers capitalized by stealing back enough energy to arm themselves. Enmul conjured ambient dust into a double-handed axe; Enki froze the surrounding moisture into a pair of curved knives. All three weapons were formed and wielded faster than anyone but Tay could react.

She parried Enmul's first strike, aimed at Naysin's head, and warded off Enki's initial blows, directed at Naysin's throat and stomach, before anyone else so much as blinked. The cougar-men were just as quick, however, and Tay foresaw their next attacks too late to stop them both. She was able to turn aside Enki's thrusts, but Enmul's overhand chop cleaved unopposed into Quecxl's chest.

"Bring them back!" yelled Naysin while Xihuitl flew at the cougar-men and Chase vaporized their blades. He wasn't referring to his fathers — he'd found the strength to restore their shackles. He needed Tay to stabilize the cloud images, many of which had reverted to mist when she'd redirected her focus and saved his life. "Bring them NOW!"

As Tay closed her eyes to shut out Quecxl's fountaining blood, Naysin interrupted Amadi and Isaura's grief for their friend by taking everything from them, every speck of **Kug** and *Mir* they, Chase, and the cougar-men could access. He drew from Quecxl as well, racing to claim what the Metican could give before the life left his body.

Naysin also stole from Saint's Summit.

In its bones was a well of **Kug** he'd overlooked before, that his fathers had overlooked entirely. A strength imbued not by willful shamaning, but the steady labor of the many, many hands that had raised the pyramid over the course of generations. The accumulated power was subtle and diffuse, but it was there, in greater quantities than the mere mass of soil should have generated. Naysin never would have found the reservoir without the beacon — its trails were flaring like strings of fireflies now, the connections between him, the ascenders, and Saint's Summit shimmering from earth to sky. Showing him the way to the **Kug**. So much **Kug**.

With a prayer for forgiveness, Naysin used it all.

Still, it was a near thing. But, much as he used to carve figurines to make Tay smile, Naysin was able to craft a template. There were two parts: the first would use fire and water to dispose of any plague burrs; the second would inject the adaptive snares. Both components were based on the method that had saved Shoteka.

Far more sacrifice was involved, however.

Naysin was hurling Quecxl's healing at the other ascenders and — because there was no other way — the cougar-men, but it wasn't enough. The light was fading from all their eyes, Amadi's included. At least Quecxl had stopped bleeding. Performing multiple healings at once seemed to reflect small amounts of restorative energy back on the Metican; it must have been how he'd survived the wounds he'd sustained at Edgeland. But the burden of sustaining the group's effort wasn't a small one. At best, Quecxl had settled into a near-death equilibrium, most of his ribs still ruptured and puncturing major organs.

Naysin didn't stop, though. He kept jamming more **Kug** and *Mir* behind the template, increasing the pressure as if he were pulling back the string of a bow. Every part of him ached to let go, but he held on until he'd packed in the absolute maximum amount of power. Only then, with the rest of the group unconscious, did he take the shot.

And as Naysin and the others fell from the sky, the cloud images were engulfed by an immunizing explosion.

Epilogue

He didn't have the strength to dig the grave deep enough. Not even with the surface of Saint's Summit broken and poor in **Kug** — the pyramid's structure had slackened after Naysin's theft of its surplus energy. A collapse didn't feel imminent, but it also didn't feel far off. The next winter would probably be the great monument's last.

Disgusted with himself, Naysin rolled to the left and lay still. He'd wanted to do this by hand — literally by hand, since none of the artifacts littering Saint's Summit's blasted peak even vaguely resembled a shovel. There was honor in doing something naturally. And no one deserved dignity more than a dead hero.

But he was too weak. It was that terrible morning with Jehan all over again… At least the sky was clear.

No more men yelling as hellfire burned corruption out of their veins.

No more women screaming as tiny snares forcibly implanted themselves.

No more children convulsing and oozing darkness.

Shoteka had suffered, but through Quecxl, Naysin had been able to alleviate the worst of the boy's agony. Such targeted relief hadn't been possible for so many.

And for some, the ordeal had been too much.

By the time the cloud images had dissipated, at least one of every ten shadowy figures had collapsed. More had probably fallen since. Some of them might rise, but in all likelihood, the Red Wraith had sacrificed entire tribes' worth of original people.

He'd also asked too much of Quecxl.

Tay and the other ascenders had survived the plummet. For once, Naysin had been the only person who *didn't* pass out, and — despite his overwhelming weariness — he'd managed to cushion the impact. Except for the cougar-men, who he'd let drop like stones. Quecxl had taken his last breath somewhere in the sky, however. His body was restored, but his spirit was gone — a beautified corpse. Xihuitl knew it; the gull was curled into his master's arm and cawing mournfully.

Each cry stung like a whip.

Struggling to a stand, Naysin lurched to the Metican's body, grabbed him by the heels, and dragged him to the pitifully shallow depression that would be his final resting place. Xihuitl protested. So did Naysin's stomach. But Quecxl's half-finished healing held, and his bird didn't have the energy to put up much of a fight.

Naysin's eulogy wasn't any more impressive. "This may or may not be Aztlan," he forced out eventually, after laboring to recall the name of the land Quecxl had been seeking. "But whoever's ancestors lie here, they'll be proud to have you among them."

Wincing at the inadequacy, Naysin finally resorted to shamaning. His capabilities remained notably diminished; the largest flows he could muster were only half as big as the massive cords he'd manipulated just a short while ago. He also felt hollow. Had applying the template burned him out?

Lowering the grave and covering it with rubble proved easy enough — he could still manage small things. And it was past time he managed a few more, preferably before the others revived.

For Isaura, he morphed his now-useless replica of the river temple into a wooden carving of Rowtag holding Shoteka. After embellishing the offering by bordering it with the shape of the flowers remaining in Isaura's braids, Naysin placed the poor substitute in her hands and prayed she hadn't felt violated by his use of her ability.

For Amadi, Naysin left a promise: "I haven't forgotten the ejeme's plight," he instilled via the beacon's tatters. "I'll find a way to help them as well." There was nothing he could do about the Foim's leg, though; it was reforming, but at a rate that suggested Naysin's powers weren't the only to have ebbed. Still, with luck, the limb would become whole on its own.

For Chase... On a less blood-soaked day, Naysin might have granted his former foe a grimmer reward. But he settled for melting the burned man's smallest fire stick into an image of his infant son: a gift and a message. Hopefully the latter was clear.

For Tay—

She was awake.

And she was blind.

"Naysin?" she called, patting the ground around her.

"I'm here."

She didn't respond — her hearing was gone as well.

Taking her hand like her father used to, Naysin signed into her palm. <u>I'm so sorry, Tay.</u>

<u>How many did we save?</u> she signed back.

<u>More than the plague would have killed.</u>

<u>Then it was worth it.</u>

Her approval meant everything.

She must have felt his sobs, because within moments of his breakdown, her fingers were wiping his cheeks dry. "It was worth it," she repeated before kissing him.

Naysin nearly blacked out from surprise.

But he fought to stay conscious as Tay emblazoned his lips with the feel of hers, and for an instant, he considered trying to freeze time again. Then, when she pushed him to the ground and reached under his breechcloth, he *truly* wanted to freeze time.

He didn't act quickly enough; Enmul interrupted with a curse.

Uttering an oath of his own, Naysin tore away from Tay and set himself in front of her. He'd been careless, but the cougar-men had been *dead*: Enki's wispy shell had ceased to exist when it hit Saint's Summit; Enmul's dense form had sunk deep into the pyramid and stopped moving.

Until now.

"It is over!" shouted Enmul, scrabbling at the walls of the tomb his violent descent had created. "Accept it! You LOST! Now GET OUT!"

Naysin didn't understand until he peered inside his father ... and saw the *Mir* signature of his other father.

It was too perfect.

They'd landed side-by-side, and when Enki's new body had failed... Even better, neither cougar-man seemed to have a lick of ability left, probably because Naysin had used them harder than anyone else. Or maybe with one in the other, their opposing powers were canceling each other out?

<u>What's wrong?</u>

He watched Enmul redouble his efforts to climb out of the hole, clawing at the dirt like any mortal. <u>Nothing. But we should leave.</u>

Naysin helped Tay to her feet. As she rose, he brushed her breasts to indicate he hadn't pulled back for lack of interest. She smiled at his touch, and—

Stuck out her arm so Xihuitl could land on her wrist.

<u>You saw him coming?</u>

"Foresaw," she clarified, her sightless eyes lit with hope. "I think he's supposed to come with us."

He squeezed her hand as the gull squawked quietly, still looking bereft. <u>Where would you like to go?</u>

"You're the navigator."

New paths opened before Naysin like apple blossoms.

He thought about the way he'd been guided to gather the ascenders on the pyramid.

He thought about the many crimes the Red Wraith still had to atone for.

He thought about all the original people who'd shared the terrible — but potentially unifying — experience of immunization.

He thought about Degan.

He thought about his promise to Amadi.

But then his eyes strayed to Isaura and the carving he'd set in her limp fingers ... and he thought about how, nine winters ago, his mother had boarded a ship, heartbroken and alone. <u>Let's cross the ocean.</u>

Ignoring the pain in his stomach, Naysin set Tay on his back, summoned her rainstick, and ran, striding over Enmul's hole so his fathers could see him fly off Saint's Summit.

Afterword

For anyone who's a student of Early America, *The Red Wraith* likely seems far more fantasy than history. And I certainly took some license with time and place. For example, the lost colony of Roanoke (which I thinly disguised as "Rokoan"), was founded off the coast of North Carolina — well to the south of the land the Penns, almost a century and a half later, claimed with the Walking Purchase.

But much of the broad themes in the novel are true to history as I understand it. Most prominently, disease's impact on Native Americans was something I wanted to humanize. Everyone learns about this tragedy in school, but I doubt many of us really consider what it must have been like for the affected peoples; to have so many die so quickly, whole communities at a time … wouldn't it have seemed like the world was ending? The true death rate will never be known (or agreed upon), but some scholars have estimated that as much as 95% of the indigenous population died in the first hundred or so years of contact with Europeans. Even half that is an apocalypse.

For readers who'd like to learn more, I strongly recommend Charles Mann's excellent *1491: New Revelations of the Americas Before Columbus* and Jared Diamond's ubiquitous *Guns, Germs, and Steel: The Fates of Human Societies.* Other works I relied on included:

> » *Wives of the Leopard: Gender, Politics, and Culture in the Kingdom of Dahomey* by Edna Bay

> » *Daily Life on the Old Colonial Frontier* edited by James and Dorothy Volo

» *The Aztecs* by Michael Smith

» *Pre-Columbian American Religions* by Walter Krickenberg

Scholars weren't my only resources, however. The manuscript benefited greatly from the smart critiques of Ben and David Campbell, Kelly Coffee, Nina Shepardson, Jason King, and most of all, Ginger Wisseman, my lovely and supportive wife. Without their help, *The Red Wraith* would still be an over-complicated mess.

— « o » —

If you enjoyed this read

Please leave a review on Amazon, Facebook, Good Reads or Instagram.

It takes less than five minutes and it really does make a difference.

If you're not sure how to leave a review on Amazon:

1. *Go to amazon.com.*

2. *Type in The Red Wraith by Nick Wisseman and when you see it, click on it.*

3. *Scroll down to Customer Reviews, nearby you'll see a box labeled Write a Review. Click it.*

4. *Now, if you've never written a review before on Amazon, they might ask you to create a name for yourself.*

5. *Reviews can be as simple as, "Loved the book! Can't wait for the Next!" (Please don't give the story away.)*

And that's it!

Brian Hades, publisher

About The Author

Nick Wisseman lives in Bear Lake, Michigan with his wife, daughter, fifty cats, twenty horses, and ten dogs. (Okay, so there are actually ten times less pets than that, but most days it feels like more.) He's not quite sure why he loves writing twisted fiction, but there's no stopping the weirdness once he's in front of a computer. Get updates about his latest oddities at:

www.nickwisseman.com

— « o » —

Need something new to read?

If you enjoyed The Red Wraith, you should also consider these other EDGE titles:

~ ~ ~

Dreamers

by Donna Glee Williams

Driven by duty towards a sleepless death…
By the time she's sixteen, the town's Dreamer has long ago given up her own life. She only dreams for others now, every morning delivering up to them the divine guidance that comes to her in the night. In exchange, they treat the Dreamer like their queen. All her bodily needs are provided, but love and relationships are forbidden to her. Now something unexpected is happening. Something entirely new. A foreign man has come to the village, wearing a scarlet vest and a gold finger-ring that is far, far too good for a mere Water-Bearer. His strange amber eyes have found the Dreamer's and she longs to be free. But maybe freedom isn't the only cost of being the Dreamer: When her dreams begin to question the authority of the self-serving Chief Interpreter, will she survive his fury? Or will he quietly entomb her in

the Dreamer's Chamber, clearing her away like so much litter to make room for a hapless new young girl to take her place? Her fate will be kept as silent as the sacred Garden that is her prison. Unless she can find a way to give voice to her own dreams.

Praise for Dreamers

Dreamers transports the reader to a distant land where you can feel the yarn beneath your fingers and taste the sweet water left by a secret friend. Williams spins a moving and eloquent tale of love and dreaming, rich with well-observed details of how people live, work, scheme and hope. She writes with the resonant voice of the story-teller, drawing you in to share this beautiful dream.
— Elaine Isaak

After twining a world in her first novel, The Braided Path, that is different from any other yet totally believable, even to the extent that everyone in it is kind, Donna Glee has woven another with Dreamers in which the strands of evil are revealed as gradually as rebellion is awakened. I love the way she lets us get to know the characters by building the story from many different points of view, from threads of conversation that build gradually into an ending that is right - but oh, so shocking.
— Anne Lane

For more on Dreamers visit:
tinyurl.com/edge6010

—— < > ——

The Triforium:
The Haunting of Westminster Abbey

by Mark Patton

After Butterfield Senior's death, 'Butterfield and Son Architects' becomes, for all intents and purposes, 'Son — Newly Graduated — Without a Clue — Architect — Maybe'! With his inheritance sold to get the architectural business on its feet, Wallace Butterfield eagerly hopes to add a major architectural project to his curriculum vitae. (Critics describe his previous project, le Mareschal's Supermarket, as a large and unimpressive glass and chrome rectangle — though some shoppers have told Butterfield that they appreciate the large inventory of groceries and home products...) When Butterfield gets a call from the Reverend Poda-Pirudi, chairman of the Westminster Abbey Foundation, he overlooks the fact that the Reverend can only meet with him in the middle of the night — in an office located in the dark and cluttered attic of the Abbey itself. Butterfield thinks he's finally moving up in the world. However, the interred ghosts of Westminster Abbey haven't yet weighed in; and a local group of WITCHes (Women In Therapeutic Chemical Healing) have also taken a special interest in the architect. And unfortunately for Wallace Butterfield, these particular WITCHes aren't above kidnapping.

Set inside Westminster Abbey, England's enduring symbol of unity and crowned culture, a community of ghosts, whose remains rest inside the iconic building, arise at the bidding of a strange cleric. A series of adventures come into play as a hapless architect is dogged through the streets of

London by a coven of drunken witches and illustrious but dead personages.

Praise for The Triforium: _The Haunting of Westminster Abbey:_

"As I finished the book and put it down with a very contented sigh, my first thought was "Why have we not previously heard the name Mark Patton in the realm of fiction writing?" If this is the author's first publication, it bodes well for what may yet come. 'The Triforium' is a superb piece of fiction that provides the main ingredients to satisfy me: humor (I laughed aloud several times, startling my partner and my dog), a good plot, detailed research, and some very intriguing thoughts on the genesis of souls, ghosts and gods."
— Christopher A. Smith, Amazon Reviewer

"A very well written fantasy, entwined into the incredibly interesting history of Westminster Abbey. I thoroughly enjoyed this bizarre, extraordinarily entertaining tale. Well worth a read and I highly recommend it."
— S McDermott, Amazon Reviewer

"Thought provoking humor: " You need your good dreams to make you want to go to bed and some bad ones so you don't grow overly fond of being there." The author's accurately detailed description of Westminster Abbey and London had me searching the internet for further historical insight on many of the facts included in the telling of this unusual story. Fascinating and entertaining!"
— Amazon Reviewer

For more on Triforium visit:
tinyurl.com/edge6006

———<>———

Poseidon And Cleito

by Andrew J. Peters

He became a god. Her story was forgotten.
From the shore of a frozen steppe, an outcast hunter embarks for the otherworld to ask his ancestors how to bring the mammoth back to the fields of sedge. In a shining, island kingdom of wonders, the daughter of a high priest fights for her claim to wealth and power after her father is assassinated by the king. Together they will build an empire recalled as an ancient legend and a cautionary tale. But how did he become a god while she became a mere footnote in history?

Poseidon & Cleito is the engrossing first book of a fantasy trilogy of myth and legend exploring the rise of the lost civilization of Atlantis. In the best traditions of an epic journey, one man's struggle to discover his place in the world takes him across perilous seas into the epicenter of political strife in a foreign land. But a legend is not made of deeds alone... Fans of Guy Gavriel Kay's historical fantasy and David Gemmell's Troy series will enjoy this fantasy novel as it sets out to reimagine the inception of a Greek myth.

Praise for Poseidon And Cleito

I love stories about prehistory, myths and legends and Poseidon and Cleito fits the bill.

According to Plato, Poseidon is one of three ancient gods of Earth. He ruled the sea and the continent of Atlantis, the ancient golden city that disappeared iin a single night of upheaval. His wife was the human woman, Cleito, who bore him five sets of twin boys. Poseidon built a palace for Cleito on the island of Atlantis, but her history has not come down to us. This book remedies history's lack and is the first in a trilogy about ancient Atlantian civilization.

It traces the journey of a tribal hunter of the northern steppes, who is outcast from his tribe and sets out to find the fabled land across the sea. As Donnogen gathers compatriots and steals a longboat from the fabled Sea Peoples, on an island kingdom a young woman assumes the title of high priest after the death of her father. Cleito is determined to prove her worth as guardian of the ancient knowledge, but she soon becomes embroiled in deadly palace politics.

When Donnogen encounters the island culture, he is hailed as a hero, and the rest of the plot revolves around his difficulties encountering a more cultured civilization coupled with his infatuation with the beautiful Cleito.

The writing is assured and seems well researched. Donnogen is a likeable hero as he struggles to understand what is so foreign. Some of the secondary characters are very attractive and add spice to the narrative. The world is well drawn. My only problem was that I found Cleito so self-serving and political, she was harder to like than the ingenuous outsider. Since this is a trilogy, I assume she will continue to develop.

Recommended for lovers of myth and historical fiction.
— Carol Holland March

For more on Poseidon And Cleito visit:
tinyurl.com/edge6018

——<>——

For more Science Fiction, Fantasy, and Speculative Fiction titles from EDGE and EDGE-Lite visit us at:

www.edgewebsite.com

Don't forget to sign-up for our Special Offers

——<<<>>>——